CHALLENGES OF THE DEEPS

CHALLENGES OF THE DEEPS

RYK E. SPOOR

BAEN

A Baen Books Original

Baen Publishing Enterprises
P.O. Box 1403
Riverdale, NY 10471
www.baen.com

ISBN: 978-1-4767-8208-9

Cover art by Alan Pollack

First Baen printing, March 2017

Distributed by Simon & Schuster
1230 Avenue of the Americas
New York, NY 10020

Printed in the United States of America

10 9 8 7 6 5 4 3 2 1

Acknowledgements

To Toni and Tony,
for opening the doors to the Arenaverse once more

To my Beta Readers, for feedback that kept me
from making some really stupid mistakes

To Morineko-zion, for her wonderful illustrations
that have brought some of my characters to manga-style life

To Keith Morrison, for his images and
videos that made parts of the Arena live

And to my wife Kathleen, for giving me the time.

Dedication

First and always, this Arenaverse novel is dedicated to the man who embodied the Sense of Wonder that I seek to evoke in the Arenaverse: E.E. "Doc" Smith, creator of the original Marc C. DuQuesne in his *Skylark* series, and the even more influential *Lensman* series.

Second, to the readers themselves, whose emails and messages have shown me that—at least for a few—I have managed to bring forth that wonder that was given to me.

And lastly to all the other creators—of books, of movies, of television shows, of games and songs and music—whose creations have provided both foundation and inspiration for the creation of the Arena and all of its inhabitants.

CHALLENGES OF THE DEEPS

What Has Gone Before

In *Grand Central Arena*, the Solar System of 2375 is a near-utopia, with limitless energy, nanotech replicators and AI freeing people to work, or play, as they wish, and the most minimally intrusive government humanity has ever seen; only the Wagnerian tragedy of the secretive Hyperion Project justified the need for a minimal military force. Dr. Simon Sandrisson believed he had found the key to one of the last great dreams of humanity: faster-than-light travel. Due to some odd anomalies with unmanned tests, Dr. Sandrisson gathered together a crew to perform the first manned test of the Sandrisson Drive, beginning with enigmatic but skilled power engineer Dr. Marc C. DuQuesne and ending with the recruitment of Ariane Stephanie Austin, a daredevil pilot for the Unlimited Space Racing league. With multiple redundant automated systems, Ariane's presence was more a matter of form than anything else; aside from sports such as her own, human beings simply *don't* pilot or drive vehicles in a serious context.

But when the Sandrisson Drive was activated, every AI system—including the implanted AISages, self-aware companions that almost every adult human being has as a matter of course—shuts down, as does the nuclear reactor, and only Ariane's racing reflexes prevents their ship, the *Holy Grail*, from colliding with the gigantic, impossible *wall* that appeared before them.

The crew of the *Holy Grail* quickly discover that they are inside a huge, generally spherical construct twenty thousand kilometers across ... with a moving replica of the Solar System in its center. No AI-level automation works, or indeed any automation above the extremely

3

primitive. Despite all systems and conditions appearing normal, no nuclear reaction can be triggered. The *Holy Grail*, unfortunately, requires immense amounts of energy to activate the drive; unless they can find a source of power, they may never be able to return home . . . and may not live more than a few months at best.

Because she is one of only two unaffected by the loss of an AISage (the others in conditions ranging from shock to full-blown coma), and because she is the only crewmember without defined duties outside of piloting the ship, Ariane is made temporary Captain of the vessel, and they attempt to explore this alien structure. The others, with the exception of biologist Laila Canning, who remains unconscious, eventually recover from the loss of their AISage companions and are able to assist.

Soon, they discover there are illuminated, livable areas within the construct . . . and suddenly find themselves forced to choose a side in a conflict between two seemingly-identical alien "Factions." The humans manage to face down the group calling themselves the "Blessed To Serve," partly due to the appearance of a mysterious cloaked figure called a "Shadeweaver," and rescue the target of the Blessed, a green-and-black semi-insectoid alien called "Orphan."

Orphan proves to be a useful, if not necessarily trustworthy, resource, through whom the humans discover the true magnitude of the problems facing them. They are trapped in an otherspace, another universe that is simply called "The Arena" by its residents. In Orphan's words: "It is a place where we all meet and challenge, where bargains are made and broken and avenged, where an alliance may be built on blood and fortune. It is a place where faith is lost, and where religions are founded or proven true. It is where you shall confront, and be confronted by, truths and lies, enemies and allies, belief and denial, impossibility and transcendence."

Any attempt to use an FTL drive in our native universe transfers the vessel to the Arena; the Arena has a Sphere for every solar system, a replica of every existing and possible native world for any species across all our universe, and some very strange—and equally incontestable— limits placed on all species in the Arena. No AIs. No nuclear power or similarly intense power sources (with some very limited exceptions). Any conflicts between species to be resolved by formal, or sometimes dangerously informal, Challenges whose stakes can be literal worlds.

And humanity must win at least one such Challenge if they are to be accepted as citizens of the Arena, and have the chance to trade for the energy they need to return home. To somewhat counterbalance this, the Arena provides full and detailed translation capabilities to all, meaning that newcomers ("First Emergents") are not handicapped by needing to learn to communicate, and there are certain limitations on Challenges which prevent a newly-arrived race from, for example, losing their entire homeworld in a Challenge; Challenge costs are directly proportional to the resources of a Faction, so a Challenge whose stakes might cost Humanity a ship could cost a Great Faction many hundreds of Spheres.

With no other choice, Ariane, DuQuesne, and Simon accompany Orphan to Nexus Arena, where all species eventually meet and where the majority of the politics, and most Challenges, of the Arena are carried out. They meet several other important beings and species, ranging from Nyanthus, leader of the religious Faction called the Faith, to the militaristic and xenophobic Molothos, Ghondas of the Powerbrokers (who could provide the energy needed to go home), and Relgof Nov'Ne Knarph of the knowledge-focused Faction of the Analytic.

The successful travel to Nexus Arena has opened what Orphan calls the "Upper Gateway" of Humanity's Sphere, which opens onto the "top" surface of the Sphere. This is actually a crucially important event, because the top of a Sphere is not a dead surface in vacuum; the interior of the Arena is filled with (mostly) breathable atmosphere, and every Sphere's top surface is a livable area that is compatible with the native, dominant species of the solar system that it represents. By exploiting this surface, the stranded crew of *Holy Grail* can survive, and perhaps over time even find a way to generate their own return power, even if success in the Arena eludes them.

It is decided that DuQuesne will return to the Sphere and, with controls specialist Carl Edlund and possibly medical doctor Gabrielle Wolfe, perform an initial survey of the part of the Upper Sphere surrounding the Upper Gateway; DuQuesne had recently been "outed" as a former result of the ill-starred Hyperion project, which made him much more physically and mentally capable than the vast majority of humanity, so his choice as the front-line explorer seems obvious.

But their exploration hits an unexpected problem; the Molothos have—apparently by coincidence—found Humanity's Sphere and are attempting to colonize the Upper Sphere themselves. DuQuesne and Carl Edlund are captured by the war-like aliens, but when they threaten to torture Carl to get DuQuesne's cooperation in gaining access to the interior of the Sphere, DuQuesne releases all the controls he has on his Hyperion nature and destroys most of the small force of aliens that had captured them; with Carl's help, he is able to devise a desperate but effective strategy to also take out the ship from which the Molothos had come, thereby protecting the secret of exactly *where* Humanity's Sphere is from the invaders.

It turns out that the Arena considers such a situation to be equivalent to a Challenge, and so DuQuesne's victory makes the small human contingent full citizens of the Arena . . . at the cost of making one of the most powerful and dangerous Factions their enemies.

Still, the crew of *Holy Grail* have little to trade. They need to find some way to convince or bargain with other Factions to get the energy needed to go home and tell the rest of Humanity that they are no longer alone in the universe, and dangerously so. Ariane soon finds herself first present at a strange ritual of the Faith that shows there are powers here they do not understand, when she sees a young member of the Faith named Mandallon elevated to the rank of Initiate Guide and manifesting energies that none of her instruments can make sense of. Shortly afterward, on her trip home, she encounters Amas-Garao, one of the enigmatic Shadeweavers, who also have apparently-magical powers and unknown motives and interests.

Mandallon is committed to assist Humanity due to their status as First Emergents, and specifically to perform a service for Humanity if he can; Ariane, after ascertaining that such service isn't enough to re-power the Holy Grail, asks if the Faith can help the still-unconscious Laila Canning. Mandallon performs a ritual which brings Laila back to consciousness and seems to have healed her . . . although for just a moment, Ariane thinks she sees something else in Laila's gaze . . .

Their first encounter with the Blessed had, of course, not left the Blessed To Serve positively inclined to Humanity, and this is demonstrated when the Blessed orchestrate a Challenge to Humanity. Ariane accepts and maneuvers the venue to Arenaspace racing, and despite some unfamiliarity with conditions, manages to win with an insanely risky tactic that takes her through a "Skyfall"—a cascade of debris found at the edge of the null-G areas of Arenaspace and the directed gravity surrounding every Sphere.

Before she can claim the reward in the form of energy to return, Orphan is able to inform her that there is another catch: all of them cannot return. There must always be at least one person present in their Sphere from now on, or else their status as Citizens of the Arena will be revoked. Given this, Ariane chooses to have their Sphere secured against any unwanted intrusion by the Faith—a service to be paid by the Blessed, who have lost the Challenge.

This choice of course severely disappoints the others, and precipitates the first real internal crisis, with the others arguing that Ariane had no right to *make* that choice without them. She points out that they *made* her Captain, and were perfectly happy to dump many other decisions or interactions onto her head, and if they didn't want her to *be* the Captain they shouldn't have done it in the first place.

The others realize that Ariane is correct; DuQuesne, particularly mortified that he allowed himself to react against her that way, leaves to give himself a chance to cool down and figure out an appropriate way to apologize. But while walking, he encounters Amas-Garao, who invites him to see the Shadeweaver Faction House . . . and invites DuQuesne to join the Shadeweavers. The Shadeweavers like to have at least one member of every species, for this gives them great knowledge and insight into all species' history and behavior.

Unfortunately, when DuQuesne rejects the invitation, it becomes clear that Amas-Garao has made an "offer you can't refuse." The running battle through the Faction House demonstrates to DuQuesne's shock that even a Hyperion is no match for a Shadeweaver. Fortunately, his first attempt at a distress call had gotten partially through, and Ariane has led a group to rescue him, arriving just in time. The ensuing battle is only won when Orphan—who had been thought to have fled in fear—returns and, somehow, partially negates Amas-Garao's powers sufficiently to allow them to escape.

The Shadeweavers' influence makes things difficult for Humanity, despite some assistance from the Analytic and the Faith. Partly to take their minds from these issues, Ariane and company watch a Challenge between two expert Champions of Challenges, the immense yet nimble Sivvis of the Daelmokhan, and the tiny but powerful Tunuvun of the Genasi (a species native to the Arena, and not considered citizens). The ending of that Challenge showcases both creatures' capabilities and their honor as well, leaving a strong impression on Ariane.

The "difficulties" culminate with an assault by the Blessed on Gabrielle, who was supposed to be with Orphan; when a furious Ariane Challenges Sethrik, the Leader of the Blessed, it turns out to have been a setup; Amas-Garao emerges as the selected Champion for the Blessed. Orphan and Sethrik were both used by the Shadeweaver as they both owed the Shadeweavers debts. Moreover, Ariane herself had been subtly mentally influenced to become angry enough to give the Challenge without thinking the implications through. This is the second time the Shadeweavers have done this to her; their initial conflict with the Blessed on the side of Orphan had, it turns out, been partly the Shadeweavers' doing as well.

Ariane is forced to face Amas-Garao in the Arena in single combat, with the stakes being Ariane herself; if she loses, she must join the Shadeweavers. Despite some initial and startling success due to careful tactics and preparation, it becomes clear that the Shadeweavers' inexplicable powers are utterly beyond Ariane's ability to oppose, and she is beaten to near-unconsciousness.

Then, hovering on the brink, Ariane suddenly sees a tenuous but just-possible connection between things she has witnessed or heard about, and invokes the same ritual she heard when attending the elevation of Mandallon—and the power of Shadeweaver, or Faith, or perhaps both, explodes from her with uncontrolled force, pushing Amas-Garao literally to the wall and leaving him no choice but to yield. Both Shadeweaver and Faith join together to seal her power away temporarily.

Before she can demand a price from Amas-Garao, DuQuesne informs her that he made a bet—on her winning—which will now give them the energy needed to return. Thus, Ariane instead demands that from thence forward, no Shadeweaver ever be able to influence or affect the minds of humanity or its direct and close allies. The Arena agrees that this is a just and equitable demand, and Amas-Garao accepts.

Even this victory is not without problems, however. Both the Shadeweavers and the Faith demand that the now-Awakened Ariane join one of them. The Faith see the Shadeweavers as wielding powers more demonic than heavenly, and while the Shadeweavers do not profess to having any holy ambitions or sources, they have little love for the Faith. Ariane has no intention of joining *either* faction, since she *is* the Captain—and, by default, the Leader of the Faction of Humanity. But the temporary seal is weakening and if it is not either renewed, or Ariane taken in by Faith or Shadeweaver and trained, her uncontrollable power could be incalculably destructive.

Once more the Shadeweavers and Faith must join together, this time to create a permanent seal on Ariane's powers, with the assistance of the other humans in a strange symbolic array that requires seven individuals of the target's Faction to focus the seal on the target. This, of course, means that all members of *Holy Grail's* crew must participate; the Arena agrees to temporarily allow them to empty their Sphere for this purpose, and this purpose only. During the sealing ritual, a momentary imbalance causes the powers of all three—Shadeweaver, Faith, and Ariane—to intersect on Simon, giving him a momentary vision that seems similar to the one Ariane experienced upon her Awakening.

With the Sealing complete, things seem to be resolved; but it turns out that Molothos have closely observed comings and goings and have guessed that Humanity's Sphere is currently unoccupied and that if they cannot return in time, they will lose their citizenship. The Molothos therefore have arranged for nearly all of Nexus Arena's Inner Gateways to be in use—making the wait to return to Humanity's Sphere be too long. A last-ditch inspiration by Steve Franceschetti, the design expert for *Holy Grail*, gives them one last chance and DuQuesne literally *throws* Steve over the heads of waiting sophonts through an Inner Gateway, just in time to return him to Humanity's Sphere.

The *Holy Grail* returns at last to the Solar System, carrying Ariane, Marc DuQuesne, Simon Sandrisson, and Gabrielle Wolfe . . . and evidence of the impossible. "*Kanzaki-Three*, this is Experimental Vessel 2112FTL, *Holy Grail*, reporting back." She grinned at the others, as she continued, "Control, you will not *believe* where we've been!"

In *Spheres of Influence*, the Space Security Council and Combined Space Forces (SSC and CSF) have just begun to absorb the enormity of the events of *Grand Central Arena*, but it is already clear that for the first time in a long, long time, politics are really, *really* going to matter . . . and there is a powerful and clever politician named Oscar Naraj who has been waiting for such an opportunity for decades.

While Simon and Gabrielle prepare *Holy Grail* for a return to the Arena (including gathering trade goods worth bringing), Marc DuQuesne embarks on a mysterious, high-speed trip through the Solar System with Ariane—a trip to recruit, if possible, other Hyperions to the cause. His travels are roundabout, revealing that even Marc DuQuesne is afraid of *something*, something that may be following him.

They reach his ultimate destination, and DuQuesne—after momentarily believing has failed—successfully reaches and reawakens Sun Wu Kung, the Hyperion version of the legendary Monkey King. With Wu Kung in tow, they return to join Simon and Gabrielle, who have just been informed by Saul Maginot that Oscar Naraj's maneuvers have succeeded in ousting Saul as leader of the SSC, replacing him with Naraj, and putting Naraj's chosen right-hand person Michelle Ni Deng in charge of the Arena Task Force which will soon send its own expedition to the Arena.

At the same time, Simon and Gabrielle have detected *another* transition to Arenaspace that isn't tied to either group; it is not long before DuQuesne realizes that this was the work of one of his compatriots, the Hyperion named Maria-Susanna . . . a Hyperion who is dangerously, unpredictably insane and who is responsible for the deaths of hundreds of people, including many Hyperions. She was the one DuQuesne was afraid had been pursuing them. Now she is loose in the Arena.

This reinforces DuQuesne's main reason for having recruited Wu Kung: he is to serve as a bodyguard to Ariane, something she accepts after a short period of protest. Ariane's own AISage, Mentor, discusses the possibility that a Hyperion AI may have escaped containment, and Ariane gives Mentor permission to stay behind (which is, technically, illegal, as high-powered AIs are supposed to always be secured by human oversight) and search/watch for such a renegaded AI.

With little time to lose, the main group returns to the Arena, finding that Maria-Susanna passed through quickly, gaining whatever information she needed without trouble and disappearing into Nexus Arena. She did visit Orphan and even offered to join his Faction, the Liberated; despite Orphan's desperate need for recruits, however, Orphan declined her offer, as he found he simply did not trust her.

Instead, Orphan makes an offer to Humanity: several fully-functional Arena vessels, including warships, in exchange for a trustworthy crew to accompany him on an expedition to the Deeps (the reaches of the Arena that lie beyond easy travel via Sky Gates). Ariane agrees, though she warns him that it may be some time before they can *find* such a crew.

Meanwhile, Simon Sandrisson completes negotiations with the Analytic, hoping to obtain the information necessary to create sensors to locate the Sky Gates that will be now active around Humanity's sphere, and which will give Humanity access to multiple other points throughout the Arena's volume. Instead, the Conclave of the Analytic gives Simon what appears to be a priceless yet useless gift: complete free access to the Archives of the Analytic for a year and a half . . . but no access to the *Index* of the Archives. But Dr. Relgof, who sincerely considers Simon his friend, says he allowed this only because he has faith that Simon, who *invented* the Sandrisson Drive, can find those answers on his own, and access to the Archives itself might turn out to be more valuable in the long run.

And then, on his first search of the Archives, Simon finds himself struck by a bizarre, phantom sense of *familiarity* . . . a sense that becomes stronger as he makes his way, without conscious understanding of how or why, to specific areas where the information he seeks is waiting. He realizes that something *did* happen to him in that ritual, something that is giving him understanding, guiding him without his own control, and he is both elated and terrified.

Naraj and Ni Deng arrive, accompanied by their own bodyguard, Commander Oasis Abrams—a redheaded woman that DuQuesne and Wu appear to have some past history with. Oscar Naraj is taken aback to discover that there was one very important point left out of his briefings: that Captain Ariane Austin is, from the point of view of the Arena, the Leader of the Faction of Humanity—in essence, the ruler of the entire human species!—and that therefore his political ambitions are entirely at her mercy. He adjusts quickly (perhaps, some think, too quickly), however, and accepts that his current post will be that of Ambassador. Ariane emphasizes that she *does* want to find someone more suited for the job of Leader, but that she's not relinquishing the position until she's sure she's found someone who really understands what they're getting into.

Simon, still unsettled but keeping his strange condition to himself for the moment, believes he has solved the problem of finding the Sky Gates; DuQuesne and Wu accompany him to the Upper Sphere to see that he is well situated. On the return, Wu breaks away and goes to investigate part of the Sphere, and DuQuesne catches up with him to find him, literally, *talking* to the local equivalent of wolves, something that as far as he knows is impossible.

Sethrik, Leader of the Blessed, visits the Faction House of Humanity, along with his second-in-command, Vantak. Vantak is given the responsibility of talking with Naraj, freeing up the two Leaders to converse in private, which includes discussing Maria-Susanna's apparent careful examination of all the major Factions.

Wu Kung and DuQuesne, returning from their expedition with Simon, are returning with good news: Simon's already found one Sky Gate and expects from that that they have quite a few such Gates. DuQuesne goes ahead to let the others know in person, allowing Wu to have some minutes to himself in the Arena. He is almost instantly visited by Amas-Garao, apparently just taking a look at the odd newcomer, but shortly thereafter Wu sees a being he recognizes from records as Tunuvun being harassed by a crowd, and can't keep from intervening. This leads to a literal brawl on one of the Docks, which Tunuvun and Wu Kung win, but the fact of the brawl *itself* is a problem, and one Ariane is *not* pleased with. "Sun Wu Kung. Get your ass back to our Embassy *right now*."

Meanwhile, DuQuesne is diverted from his journey when he sees Oasis finally alone, travelling to the Grand Arcade. When he catches her, we finally discover that Oasis is actually the mysterious "K," another of the Hyperions and one that DuQuesne obviously had a relationship with at some point. But she is not *just* "K;" she is also Oasis Abrams. The original Oasis had beaten one Hyperion but was ambushed by a Hyperion AI villain named Fairchild, who planned to escape Hyperion using her body and brain. "K" managed to intervene, and to save Oasis, took her mind into K's body. The two share the body now and have grown very close, almost a unified mind, in that time.

Ariane rips into Wu Kung for getting into that fight—which could have led to a true Challenge—and manages to extract his word of honor that he will never enter such a situation again without first discussing it with either her or DuQuesne. On the positive side, such a battle has given Tunuvun and his people a very good opinion of Wu, and thus Humanity, and as the Genasi have a chance to become true Citizens of the Arena soon, this could have long-term major implications.

Simon goes to Laila Canning and discusses his problem, choosing her because he knows there has been unspoken wariness of her after her reawakening by Mandallon—and, Laila admits, not unjustified; she knows she has changed *somehow* and she is not sure what the change means. Simon, similarly, is afraid that he is becoming something *else*, as he completed the designs of the Gate sensors without being even fully *aware* of what he did, although in retrospect he can understand it all. The two agree to go to Ariane together to address these issues.

Ariane sees them after finishing a conversation with Naraj, which touches on both the fact that Maria-Susanna has apparently applied to become a member of the Vengeance, and on the difficulties of negotiations when one is already the target of the Molothos; Naraj has assigned Ni Deng to focus on negotiations with the Blessed, who claim to have been ordered to be more accommodating to Humanity following the Blessed's role in setting up Amas-Garao's Challenge.

Ariane recognizes Simon's fears, and points out that if she were honest the group should have the same fears about *her*—having been touched even more directly by the power of the Arena. The misgivings about Laila she addresses directly, by saying that whether or not something has changed her, Laila has done nothing but assist them, so whatever the truth might be, from now on she will be treated exactly as any other member of the team.

Orphan begins the transfer of vessels to Humanity by first taking the group on board his flagship, *Zounin-Ginjou*, so they can bring him to Humanity's Sphere. They learn something of the operation of such vessels, as well as about the diversity of life floating between Spheres in the Arena.

Having returned to Nexus Arena, with the others now involved in ferrying the new ships, Ariane and Wu have an encounter with Amas-Garao, which is more educational than frightening; the Shadeweaver mentions that Maria-Susanna has also been exploring the possibilities of joining their group, and during that discussion gives some details of the way in which the Shadeweavers operate—including how they must eventually give up their powers to make way for the next generation.

After another short meeting with Oscar Naraj, Ariane and Wu go with Sethrik to view the *Thilomon*, one of the Blessed's major flagships. An assassination attempt causes Wu Kung to force both Sethrik and Ariane to take shelter inside *Thilomon*'s airlock, while he attempts to deal with the assassin. However, when *Thilomon* almost immediately begins to move away, Wu realizes this was a setup and manages—barely—to leap onto the departing Arena vessel.

Simon, on *Zounin-Ginjou*, is observing vessels as they approach Nexus Arena after completing ship delivery, and notices Wu on *Thilomon*. It is not hard to deduce that Ariane must be inside—and not of her own accord, if her bodyguard is stuck on the outside! Orphan agrees that he will not permit his friend Ariane Austin to be taken by the Blessed, but they cannot precipitate war in the neighborhood of Nexus Arena and thus must not be *noticed* by the Blessed until they are well away.

Within *Thilomon*, Ariane and Sethrik discover that Vantak has betrayed Sethrik . . . but at the direct instruction of the Minds, the artificial intelligences that control the Blessed to Serve. The Blessed believed that Sethrik might be becoming unreliable. They also have a specific use for Ariane Austin beyond merely demonstrating that the Blessed, and through them, the Minds, are not to be trifled with.

Wu Kung has somehow survived the transition across the Arena at terrific speeds, and is making his way across the *Thilomon*'s hull, when he is suddenly flung off the vessel, to plummet away into the Deeps of the Arena, where the predatorial *zikki* begin to swarm around him.

Seeing this, Ariane demonstrates exactly what Vantak and the Minds were hoping; in the extremity of rage, for a moment, the Seal on her powers slips, and shatters her bonds. The power re-seals itself too quickly to be usable, but that is still enough. The Minds believe that if they have Ariane to study, they will be able to eventually *understand* the powers . . . and be able to use them to allow the Minds *themselves* to enter the Arena, the only AIs to do so.

Zounin-Ginjou follows *Thilomon* and eventually prepares to attack—only to find that there are twenty other vessels waiting, joining *Thilomon* at this point. While individually superior to any of the Blessed vessels, there seems no doubt what the ultimate outcome will be for *Zounin-Ginjou* and her crew.

During the combat, both DuQuesne and Simon Sandrisson find

themselves doing better using unknown technology than might have been expected, and when *Zounin-Ginjou* is heavily damaged, Simon finds himself running to repair a system he doesn't even know . . . and does so. Though frightened, he also realizes this strange access to knowledge is also desperately needed now, so he allows it to grow, giving him a sense of what is, what *could* be, and he knows there is also a possible way to improve their odds.

The battle continues at a fever-pitch, but then both sides are distracted by the approach of numberless targets which burst from a cloudbank—an incredible assemblage of Arena lifeforms, ranging from *tzchina* to *zikki* and a gargantuan five-kilometer-long predator called a *morfalzeen*. The creatures assault and harass *Thilomon*, culminating with an impact that shatters the forward viewport . . .

. . . through which arrives Sun Wu Kung, who proceeds to defeat all the Blessed on *Thilomon*'s bridge, culminating by throwing Vantak out the port by which Wu entered.

Meanwhile, Simon has been desperately trying to modify one of *Zounin-Ginjou*'s weapons, following that strange knowledge within him. He succeeds, allowing far more intense fire at the cost of needing to reload the focus and liner after each shot. But before he can continue reloading, he suddenly finds he is not alone: Vantak has managed to board *Zounin-Ginjou* during the battle. Simon manages, barely, to defeat Vantak with the help of that over-sense.

Following the battle, Ariane refuses to simply wipe out *Thilomon* and its crew. Instead, after the others discuss the situation, it is decided to take them aboard *Zounin-Ginjou* inside of a subsection of living quarters from *Thilomon*, which will be in a cargo deck under weapons and scrutiny. They will then be deposited on the Upper Sphere of a currently untenanted Sphere, where they will be able to live but unable to travel from or contact any others.

Ariane and the others then have Sethrik—who, with Vantak dead and the succession of Leadership still not officially carried out, remains Leader of the Blessed—carry a message to his Embassy to be delivered to the Minds. This is also part of a plan to uncover what they suspect to have been cooperation between someone on the *Humanity* side along with Vantak.

The ruse works; Michelle Ni Deng goes to meet with Sethrik shortly after his arrival and her conversation reveals that Ariane's . . . removal was quite intentional, all for the ostensible good of humanity. His job done, Sethrik returns and abandons his old faction, joining instead the Faction of the Liberated.

Ariane, having realized much of this was her fault for not really grasping the reins of Leadership, prepares to go to the System to confront the political issues head-on, waiting for the response by the Minds (as that will have a significant effect on her plans) and on the determination of whether Shadeweaver/Faith powers work in normal space (because that would have vast implications for what the Blessed's Minds tried to do). In the interim, DuQuesne gets a message that someone hostile appears to be after the remaining Hyperions he was trying to protect back home. It is decided that Marc and Oasis will go back and try to find out what's happening there—and to contact Mentor, if they can, to see if he has information.

Simon, with the help of Dr. Relgof, is able to uncover evidence that the powers of Shadeweaver and Faith *do* work even in normal space, meaning that the Minds' plans were all too feasible.

DuQuesne and Oasis make contact with Mentor as they approach Counter-Earth Station 3, where the dreaming Hyperions have been moved. The station shuts down as they approach, and despite a desperate emergency docking and headlong rush through the Station, arrive too late; Dr. Davison, who was caretaking for DuQuesne, is nearly dead, and the room with the Hyperions is a wreck, with a pile of charred corpses in the center. Mentor barely warns DuQuesne in time to avoid a high-voltage electrical trap.

In the Arena, while in a discussion about Arena biology with Laila, Ariane is alerted to a visitor's presence. Selpa, Leader of the Vengeance, arrives and announces that they have accepted Maria-Susanna as a member; she is with him, and Ariane gets a first look at the deceptively harmless former Hyperion. No sooner have they left than Tanglil of the Blessed arrives and delivers a message from the Minds themselves:

The Minds accept Ariane's price for their attempted kidnapping, and give three Spheres to Humanity in recompense. Ariane immediately and unexpectedly gives one to the Liberated for Orphan's assistance.

Ariane returns to their Sphere for the first time in months, to discover just how much chaos has ensued, with over a thousand new people now living, working, and researching in the Inner Sphere and Upper Sphere. But there *is* some order, being enforced by Thomas Cussler, who has taken up the position of directing activities in the Sphere. Thomas gives them a rundown of conditions in the Sphere, and the defensive preparations that have been and are continuing to be made to protect Humanity's home Sphere.

The group arrives in time to enter a complete session of the SSC, with most CSF representatives present as well, and Ariane addresses them with a summary of what has happened—and why much of it was the fault of politicial maneuvering that assumed from the first that she was the wrong choice for the job. She presents proof of the Arena's power and influence even in their own world and the need to have an actual, effective Leader of the Faction of Humanity.

General Jill Esterhauer, a long-term member of both organizations, is the center of resistance to this idea, and it becomes clear that this is based both on rational principles—a well-founded fear of any single individual holding such power—and on an apparent pattern of Hyperion connections she has noted, making the General wonder if there is more to these events than is being discussed.

Esterhauer's forces are prepared to force the issue, but Ariane keeps her talking as DuQuesne and his allies—including Mentor—come to realize with Simon's help that there is another element at work; the General has been subtly suborned. When the General begins to consider some of the points Ariane begins to make, a hidden connection comes to life and a brief cyber-battle erupts. This is concluded quickly—almost invisibly to most of those present—and the discussion continues.

Dr. Robert Fenelon of the SSC makes a compromise suggestion, derived partly from ancient Roman political structures, that seems reasonable enough. Before the negotiations can complete, however, General Esterhauer collapses, a delayed effect of the hostile force that had been attempting to manipulate her.

Fortunately, the General is not damaged beyond recovery, and ultimately Dr. Fenelon's plan is accepted by her and by the combined SSC and CSF. With her position acknowledged, Ariane lays out a number of broad directives, plans for the future, including the need to create a set of laws governing activities in the Arena . . . and the need, in view of what has happened with the Blessed, to solve the issue of AI rights; Mentor himself offers an impassioned speech as to why it is time for humanity and their artificial children to work as full equals. The speech includes the revelation that the enemy that nearly destroyed Esterhauer was itself a renegade AI—only stopped by other AIs and a Hyperion working in concert. In short, an escaped Hyperion adversary.

With questions of leadership and succession addressed, Ariane and crew can finally turn to the question of what to do next . . . and Ariane already has that planned out: fulfill the promise she made to Orphan . . .

Chapter 1

Ariane Austin felt the peculiar *jolt* that the Sandrisson jump always gave her, and found a smile on her face. "We're back," she said.

"Out of the political frying pan and into the Arena's fire," DuQuesne said, chuckling. "Feels good, doesn't it?"

"Not something I would have expected, if you'd asked me before all this started," Ariane said. "But I have to admit that Arena politics are more exciting."

"Fates preserve us from exciting politics like that last adventure," Simon Sandrisson said.

Ariane looked back at Simon, who was sitting in one of the passenger seats of the shuttle *Century Eagle*, adjusting his hair clip to catch a stray lock of his pure-white hair. "Why, Simon, are you saying you don't want to rescue me again?"

There was general laughter from everyone present—DuQuesne, Wu, Gabrielle, Oasis Abrams, and Simon himself. "I would say rather that I would prefer you never be in a position to require rescue," Simon replied, his smile and wink charming as ever. "Although you and Sethrik did well enough for yourselves at the end."

"With the Monkey King's help, yes," she said, nodding at Wu with a smile. "But yes, I agree. Still . . . we're about to go out and get ourselves in danger again, aren't we?"

DuQuesne looked momentarily grim. "And I really wish I could find a decent argument to keep you out of it, but I can't."

"No, you can't, Marc. I could keep *you* out of it with more justification. The only argument that even has relevance is that the Leader of the Faction should stay home where it's safe."

They all knew *that* wouldn't wash with her, and wouldn't for the other Faction leaders. Orphan, leader and—until recently—sole member of the Faction of the Liberated, often risked his life in questionable ventures, such as the one they would be accompanying him on.

His unique position excused his risk-taking, but the fact was that—despite the Arena residents' overall greater aversion to high risk—Faction Leaders and equivalents seemed quite willing, and capable, of facing dangerous situations personally. Sethrik and his Mind-groomed traitorous successor Vantak had shown that clearly, engaging adversaries directly and without any reluctance in deciding the fate of worlds with guns, swords, or bare chitinous hands. Her impression was that Selpa'A'At of the Vengeance, Dajzail of the Molothos, and even wise, considered Nyanthus of the Faith would all be willing to take on threats to their Factions personally, if need be.

And that's the kind of company I have to run in. Me. Ariane Austin . . . Leader of the Faction of Humanity.

The thought was *still* ridiculous, even though she'd lived with that title for well over a year now. The idea that she—formerly just a high-ranking racing pilot—had ended up as the literal leader of the entire human race was inescapably ridiculous, yet also as inescapably true. She'd nearly lost her life—and cost humanity a great deal more—before she'd not only grasped, but *accepted*, that burden that the nigh-omnipotent Arena had laid upon her.

Now she was going back once more . . . and she already had a challenge ahead of her.

The rest of the trip to the great docking facility within their Sphere's "Harbor" was uneventful, not that she expected anything to happen. Of all the places in the Universe, being inside one's own Sphere was probably one of the safest, at least in terms of threats from *outside* your own faction.

Unlike earlier voyages, there was *traffic* at the Dock. Multiple ships were coupled to the airlocks along the kilometers-long, eerily skeletal structure. "Approaching saturation," Simon observed. "Are we regulating transitions carefully?"

"Yeah," DuQuesne answered. "Checked with Saul on that and a few other things. They've done a few experiments and verified your theoretical limits—minor tweaks that might change the model slightly but nothing major—and there's now a lot of oversight on transitions on both sides."

"So how many vessels *can* we get in the harbor before we get stuck?" Ariane asked as their seats unlocked and restraints retracted.

"For vessels of reasonable size, the limit's twenty," said DuQuesne. "Doesn't seem to matter whether they're in groups or all spread out, either, which doesn't make much sense to me."

They all oriented themselves before entering the airlock; among the other impossible things the Arena did casually was to provide science-fiction-standard artificial gravity within the Spheres and most other living areas. Not orienting yourself before you stepped out was a good way to fall on your head.

"Why's that?" Gabrielle asked. "Seems to me that if you spread 'em all out, they wouldn't interfere with each other so much. Or maybe if you crowded 'em all together the interference wouldn't reach far out."

Simon's head came up with a sharpness that showed an insight. "Ah, of course. The problem, Gabrielle, is that when the ships are close together, the interference resonance is magnified by the multiple coils, so that it in effect 'balloons out,' vastly larger than the individual drive fields would be alone. At the same time, if you distributed the ships widely, each one has a very large interference radius. I suppose you *could* get more in, if you distributed all of your ships *exactly* right, but it would be a difficult process and would involve sending your transitioning ships billions of miles out—in all directions. And, of course, if any of those ships started to move, all bets would be off."

Wu Kung left first, as usual; he would not allow Ariane to enter any location without scouting it himself. The others followed once he waved; exiting, Ariane saw how Wu was studying the bustling groups of workers. "All clear, Wu?" she asked.

"Come on, Captain," he said. "They're just working." The deceptively diminutive Hyperion trotted ahead of her, brown-furred tail waving a counterpoint to his footsteps, gold-tipped staff slung over his back. Wu's gaze flicked back and forth, shown by the slight movement of his head, but despite his alertness he was also moving with the relaxed bounce she knew signaled that everything really was all right.

She noticed a pensive expression on DuQuesne's face as they continued, and a similar shadow pass over Oasis' as well. She let the others go on past and joined them; Wu glanced at her but then looked away, clearly aware of what she was doing. "Are you both okay?"

The immense black-haired engineer looked down at her, started to answer, then stopped himself; the red-haired former CSF officer seemed also at something of a loss for words. Finally DuQuesne sighed. "For what we have to do now, yeah, I'm okay. But losing those four . . ."

". . . losing *any* of them was bad," Oasis said bluntly. "But *four*? And not by accident, not even by Maria-Susanna? She was bad enough, but we . . ."

"You knew her," Ariane finished. "She was . . . a known quantity, no matter how terribly she was broken. This came out of the blue. You don't know what happened?"

"*What* happened, that was fairly easy," DuQuesne said, looking up reflexively as they passed through the immense door that led to the Inner Sphere. "The question wasn't *what* but *who* and *why*. Whoever did this wanted to make sure there wasn't a chance of reconstructing anything, biological or electronic. They were in the process of wrecking Wu's when we arrived, that's why it wasn't completely totaled." He looked surreptitiously at the Hyperion Monkey King, but Wu appeared to be busily leading the way and watching.

"And . . . ?"

He shook his head. "Still not much. Saul's got his best people working on it, but he's . . . well, not hopeful. There's a possibility there's some left in the deep backup data archives—those are hidden inside extra hardware layers embedded in the internal shell supports—but I'm not optimistic."

Ariane tried to keep her expression neutral, but inside she felt the sting of sympathetic loss. *Poor Wu! That would be his whole world they just destroyed—his friends, his enemies, his family and everything he was raised with. Simulated or not, they were real AIs, which means they were as much people as we are. And that would be true of the other Hyperions who died. Whoever did this murdered a lot more than four people.*

"It *has* to be someone associated with Hyperion," Oasis said. "They knew exactly what they were doing and how to do it, and that trap they set for Marc . . . they knew *him*."

"That ought to narrow it *way* down."

"Problem is," DuQuesne said, "none of the known Hyperion

survivors fit this pattern. The only good candidate—at least for *planning* this—would be one of the old Hyperion AI adversaries."

She felt a chill, as if a procession of ants dipped in liquid nitrogen had run down her spine. "And according to Mentor, at least one of them has escaped."

"Right. But that puts us back to square one, in a way, because even Mentor couldn't tell us *which* of the villain AIs it might be, and there are a *lot* of candidates. There were slightly more than a thousand Hyperions, and while a few of them didn't have, well, epic-scale adversaries, most of them did, and some—especially those from long-running fictional universes—had *many*." He looked to Oasis.

"Don't worry, Marc," she said, and put a hand on his arm. Ariane saw, in her gaze and posture, the duality that lived inside that single body—a nearly-merged combination of the original Oasis Abrams, and the Hyperion that was usually just called "K." "You've got your own mission. Leave this one to me."

Ariane didn't hear the rest of the conversation, because Tom Cussler was waving at her from next to Wu Kung. "Hello, Tom," she said, returning his bear-hug and hearing him grunt a bit at the reminder she was probably stronger than him. "Or I should say, Governor Cussler."

He grinned, and Steve Franceschetti, standing next to him, gave him a congratulatory punch in the arm. "Way to go, Tom!"

"So that's the title, is it? Confirmed by the SSC?"

"Confirmed and a lot of other things, too." She handed them each a datachip. "Go over that tonight in detail. You'll have a lot to absorb. Short version, I'm still Leader of the Faction, but there's a mechanism to yank me that I think we can live with. And I'm not going to be around long; got a promise to fulfill for Orphan."

"I hope the details on *that* are here too," Tom said, falling in next to them as they continued onward.

"They are. As much as I know, anyway. *Not* to be spread around outside of our inner circle, though. You people need to know, but most others don't."

"Are you staying?" Steve asked. "I could get things set up for—"

"Sorry, Steve," she said. "Next time, I hope. But I want to get back to Nexus Arena right away and make clear that things have been settled at home. The Leader of the Faction really can't be absent long."

"Right. Of course." Steve's sharp face, topped by curly brown hair, showed his disappointment, but there was understanding there too; he knew exactly how important it was for the Faction Leader to be present and active in the Arena.

The group continued through Gateway Colony, as it was now being called, making their way through the canyon-like roadways to the hexagon-paved center of the colony, then through the next doorway and through a series of corridors to the Inner Gateway, that huge swirling circle of iridescent-sparked ebony that led to Nexus Arena.

The familiar whirling tingle and indescribable, spinning, hurtling sensation seized her as she stepped through that portal and emerged into the kilometers-wide room filled with Gateways that was called Transition, the entryway to Nexus Arena itself.

In all directions were almost uncountable alien figures—bipedal, amorphous, multilegged, tentacular, floating—moving into or out of the Gateways, meeting with each other, avoiding others, and passing eventually out of Transition through a great archway into Nexus Arena proper. A Milluk—the same species as Vengeance Leader Selpa'A'At— was walking with spidery elegance alongside a slug-like Shiquan; a massive Daelmokhan's semi-saurian body maintained a slow, dignified pace in order to continue a discussion with one of the Blessed To Serve. A dozen dozen other species, all intermingling, talking, gesturing, moving in a dazzling and, Ariane admitted to herself, somewhat intimidating array of diversity and mystery.

But the very sight sent a thrill through her soul, and she knew she was *home*. She felt the grin spreading across her face as she stepped forward and headed down the ramp. "We're *back*, Arena," she said.

Welcome back, Captain Ariane Austin, said a quiet, yet somehow profoundly powerful, Voice in her head, a Voice she had heard a few times before: the Voice of the Arena itself, or whatever intelligence hid behind and within the nigh-omnipotent Arena.

She stumbled with the shock. "I didn't expect an answer."

This time there was no additional remark forthcoming, but the simple fact there had been one at all filled her with a vague foreboding. The Arena generally didn't speak unless it had a very, very good reason to do so, and from what she'd heard from other inhabitants of the Arena, she'd already had it speak to her, or in her presence, more times than most people ever would, even full-time residents of the Arena. *So why did it speak now? Just to greet me?*

"Something wrong, Captain?" DuQuesne asked.

"I don't know, Marc," she replied as quietly as she could. They reached one of the giant elevators in the area outside of Transition, a meters-broad shining column of metal. "The Arena welcomed me back. In person, so to speak."

DuQuesne's brow furrowed, and he nodded. There was no need to explain anything to him. "Well, let's get to the Embassy and check in. Then we can think about whatever this little mystery means before we call up Orphan."

Once out of the elevator, it was simple to flag one of the floating, open-carriage-like taxis and tell it "The Embassy of Humanity"; the taxi accelerated smoothly, weaving through foot and vehicle traffic with scarcely a jolt until it finally arrived at the Embassy.

"Well, we made it without anyone trying to shoot us, interrogate us, or otherwise inconvenience us," Simon observed. "That seems an auspicious omen."

As they passed through the doorway into the foyer of the Embassy, Ariane saw the precise lines and features of Laila Canning emerge from one of the interior doorways and stride with perfect rhythm straight towards them.

"Welcome, back, Captain," Laila said formally, and then, with an unexpected grin, stepped forward and gave Ariane a hug. "We've missed you."

After the initial startlement, Ariane felt an answering smile on her face and hugged back. "Well, thank you very much, Laila!"

Nearby, Carl and Gabrielle had completed their own even more enthusiastic greeting. *I wonder if I'll be performing a marriage there. Already did one for Tom and Steve.*

"Can I assume from your arrival *without* Mr. Naraj in tow that we have resolved our issues properly?" Laila asked, after also embracing Simon and—after a split-second hesitation—shaking DuQuesne's hand.

"Well enough, yes. Though Oscar *will* be coming back. We could not prove his involvement in my kidnapping, and he *did* make a lot of progress with other negotiations that we would not want to drop. We'll just have to keep an eye on him, that's all. He will *not* be given the authority he had, I assure you."

"But your position as Leader, that has been confirmed?"

"We worked out a deal. If you'll open a link?"

Unlike most people, Laila took the whole data dump without batting an eye; Carl's eyes practically crossed and he had to sit down hard. *She was the sort who worked with three AISages simultaneously. I have no idea what it must be like to have a brain like that.* "Oh! Quite clever. I look forward to meeting this Mr. Fenelon—he is coming, I assume?"

"Him, General Esterhauer, and several more, yes."

"What about the . . . well, the murders of those Hyperions?" Carl asked, finally recovering.

DuQuesne shrugged. "We've discussed that earlier. Basically . . . too many possibilities, but the investigation's ongoing. You can check out the second appendix for everything we've got; in fact, I want everyone on our crew to do that. Any of us might have some insight, and believe you me, we *all* want the monster behind this caught."

Carl's eyes went blank momentarily. "It'd help if I understood more about Hyperion."

She saw DuQuesne hesitate, then grin. "Yeah, of course it would. I'll give you guys the same summary I gave the Captain. But . . . don't pass this stuff to anyone else, understand?"

Laila nodded, as did Carl. "We will say nothing."

"How have things been here, Laila?"

"Busy," said the brown-haired scientist. "There are at least two or three queries per day for you. No real emergencies *yet*, however. Long-term, the real problem is going to be the Molothos. Everyone knows we are at a war footing with them, and while the major factions have gained considerable respect for us, the Molothos have many thousands of years of reputation—quite deserved, as far as I can tell—for military efficiency, brutality, and an ability to win wars even if they lose an occasional battle. The only losses they have suffered in significant conflicts have been against others of the Great Factions—the Vengeance and the Faith as well as the Blessed."

She gave a rueful grin. "If we could actually tell people what you managed to do to the Blessed, that might change perceptions a bit, but we cannot. So right now, negotiations with other Factions are still quite touchy because they are, understandably, skittish about involving themselves with us and possibly being targeted by the Molothos in turn."

"That doesn't include the Great Factions, I hope," Simon said.

"Not so far," Laila said, looking thoughtful. "While I am sure none of them want to confront the Molothos if they can avoid it, they're not terribly scared of the Molothos either."

"Good. Then our relations with, at least, the Analytic and the Faith should not be affected," Ariane said. "The last thing we need is to lose the allies we already have."

"Speaking of that, our next major order of business is with our first and most interesting ally," DuQuesne said with a grin. "We still have a job to do."

"And one we've put off for a long time," she said. "Let's give Orphan a call!"

"Just a moment, Captain," Simon said. "Before you do that, I would like to—very regretfully—withdraw myself from this expedition."

Ariane could see the regret echoed in the brilliant green eyes. "Withdraw? Simon, *why*? The three of us—"

"Well, you see, that by itself is part of it."

DuQuesne grunted. "He's got a point there. Like it or not, I think people recognize that the real top dogs of our Faction are you, me, and Simon. Taking all three of us out of circulation for some unknown time might not be the best idea."

"Thank you, Marc. Exactly."

Laila nodded. "I would very much not want to run things without one of the three of you here. These last few weeks have not been easy, and I expect—if that mysterious mission of Orphan's is anything like what he implied—you will be gone much, much longer. One of you *must* remain."

I wish I could disagree with that. Still . . . "You said that was *part* of it."

"And not the largest part, no. In our excitement and—completely shared, I assure you—interest in finding out what, precisely, Orphan's mysterious mission holds, I'm afraid we all forgot that I have a time-limited and extremely valuable opportunity."

Ariane rapped herself on the forehead *hard*, just to remind herself how stupid she'd been. "Oh, *God*, how *could* I have forgotten that? The Archives!"

"Give me a smack too, Ariane. In fact, make that *two* smacks," DuQuesne said. "Klono's tungsten . . . dammit, no, not going back to those old oaths." He blushed darkly, as he sometimes did when his old

Hyperion upbringing surfaced. "But how the *hell* could I have dropped the ball that badly? Simon's got one year left on his pass to the largest library in two universes. We could end up away for months, and if he comes with us he's pissing away one of the greatest chances we have to advance our knowledge and understanding of the Arena and everything in it."

"I'm afraid that's my feeling on the matter," Simon said. "I should be spending several hours a week, at least, digging through those Archives, seeing what I can turn up." The Analytic had given Simon the unlimited right to visit the Archives for one and a half years—but had omitted any right of Simon to use the Archives' equivalent of an index or search function.

Simon's as-yet-poorly-understood connection to the Arena, that sometimes provided him with knowledge or insight beyond the ordinary, had allowed him to mitigate this disadvantage to some extent, but didn't substitute for the lack of the index. Partly, Ariane knew, this was because Simon himself was very wary of that capability—which had no known precedent anywhere in the Arena— and did not want to rely on it overly much.

But even pure random searching of a library that, literally, covered almost the entirety of the Arena—its history, its Factions, its technology—was an opportunity of almost incalculable value, and Simon was right—all too right—that it was one they could not afford to waste.

"I hate to agree, but I can't see any possible argument in the other direction," Ariane said reluctantly. "The fact that you'll be seen— regardless of official positions—as something of my surrogate while I'm gone is just the cherry on top." She looked to DuQuesne. "Do we need to choose a replacement, then?"

"I don't *think* so. Orphan said a minimum would be three more, right? You, Wu, and I make three, and a pretty damned competent three at that."

She felt slightly better, though she *really* didn't like the idea of not seeing Simon for months. "True, he did say three was feasible. We'd probably *prefer* more, but unless he changed his mind, three should be enough."

"You mentioned 'official positions,'" Simon said. "Who's actually going to be in charge?"

"While we're gone? I'm making it a dual effort. Laila and Carl will be the nominal bosses, and I think you and Oasis can do the same for them that you and DuQuesne have done for me."

"Advisors and gadflies, yes," he said with a flashing smile. "That makes perfect sense to me."

Carl grinned. "Or Laila and I the figureheads, with the mad scientist pulling our strings behind the scenes?"

Laila gave one of her short, explosive laughs. "Well, that would be satisfactory too."

"Works for me, too," DuQuesne said, grinning. "So are we ready?"

"Ready," Ariane said. "Let's go see Orphan!"

Chapter 2

"Captain Ariane Austin, Dr. Marc DuQuesne, it is an honor to welcome you back to my Embassy once more," Orphan said, giving the full pushup-bow which both the Blessed and the Liberated used as a sign of greatest respect. "And you as well, Sun Wu Kung. I take this to mean that the various . . . issues in your home system have been addressed in a satisfactory manner?"

DuQuesne saw a smile instantly appear on Ariane's face, the smile that she often wore around the flamboyant, devious yet likeable Leader of the Liberated. "They have, Orphan. Though—as I've come to expect—they created additional 'issues' that will have to be addressed in time."

"That is ever the way of things, is it not?" Orphan said, gesturing them to follow. "The course of a Leader is never simple."

"And if it ever *looks* simple," DuQuesne said, "you better believe you're missing something big."

"So very true. Here, seat yourselves, I have provided some of the refreshments you found most palatable on our last meeting." The tall, green-black semi-insectoid creature took his own seat, which was more a resting perch than anything else, and raised a drinking globe. "To our continuing alliance, my friends."

"I'll drink to that," DuQuesne said, raising his own glass. "How are things now? Where is Sethrik?"

"*Things*, as you say, are going very well since our secret victory over my former people. At the moment, Sethrik is in a meeting with the Naquari, a small but very capable Faction, who may be able to assist us in exploiting some of the resources of our new Sphere."

DuQuesne grinned at that. Ariane's inspired generosity in gifting one of the three Spheres they'd won to the Liberated had not only doubled the holdings of the Liberated, it had also sent an unmistakable message to the Blessed (whenever they realized it) that the Faction of the Liberated was considered one of the most important allies of Humanity . . . and thus any action against the Liberated might well bring the unpredictable and unknown forces of Humanity to Orphan's aid. "We might have some more help for you there, too."

Orphan's head tilted inquiringly. "Indeed? Please, continue."

"The story of your Faction is a pretty inspiring one from a human point of view," Ariane said. "We've had inquiries as to whether a human could join the Liberated. I presumed that they could, and that you would have no objections to appropriate humans joining, but wasn't going to say so until we spoke with you."

"Object? Most certainly not, Captain Austin!" Orphan's voice—translated perfectly by the Arena—was enthusiastically emphatic, and he reinforced this with the double-handtap that indicated assent. "Obviously anyone joining would have to be of appropriate . . . caliber, given our situation with respect to the Blessed, and would have to understand that our ultimate goals will eventually put us directly into conflict with the Blessed and the Minds themselves. It will not be a . . . safe choice of Faction."

"We'll make sure any volunteers are fully informed of the nature and depth of commitment. But you may want to hold off on accepting more than one or two at this time."

"Hold off? But I—" Orphan broke off, stiffening. "Captain Austin, are you saying—"

"—we've found you a crew!" DuQuesne finished for him with a grin. "Yes. And so if you took in more than a couple recruits, you'd exceed that limit of four members you mentioned to us a while back—which would mean that Sethrik would be severely limited in where he could go, and also stuck having to either trust, or keep an eye on, new recruits."

Orphan was speechless for a moment, then performed another deep push-bow. "Given your difficulties, I had of course decided not to remind you of this promise for a time; I am honored and touched that you clearly have kept it in mind even through such trying times. When will I have the opportunity to meet this crew?"

"You've already met them," Wu Kung said, his own smile showing his fangs. "It's us."

A handtap of assent. "Of course. Only those I can trust, and those whose capabilities I know."

"And in my case," Ariane said, "someone with a vested interest in this mystery of yours."

DuQuesne saw the tightening of the wingcases that indicated tension or sudden thought. "Ahh. Of *course*. You hope that this mission may shed light on the powers of Shadeweaver or Faith that lie locked within you."

"Do you think it could?"

Orphan was silent for a moment. DuQuesne caught Wu's narrow-eyed glance, but even without that he could tell that Orphan was weighing options, deciding what to say and what to hold back. "Orphan, don't make me suspicious of you again."

Orphan made a buzzing sound, translated as a brief chuckle. "Ahh, Dr. DuQuesne, I doubt that you are ever likely to lose *all* suspicion of me. But here I must tread carefully. There are things I do not speak of even here, in Nexus Arena, that I will only speak of in the Deeps between the Spheres, where even Shadeweaver or Faith would have difficulty locating me, let alone spying upon me."

DuQuesne nodded slowly. *The Shadeweavers can mess around with the Arena's rules, so it stands to reason that someone like Orphan might not trust even the Embassy's security without limit. But what that implies about his secret? That's pretty scary.*

After another moment, Orphan's hands tapped quickly. "In answer to your question, Captain Austin, yes, I do believe it could shed a great deal of light on this most difficult mystery of yours. Not without some . . . risk, but then, risk is not so terrifying for you as for some, yes?"

"I rather enjoy it at times," Ariane said honestly.

Orphan laughed, though the laugh was a bit strained and his color momentarily paler. "I would like to say how incomprehensible I find that, except that I have found myself, at moments, feeling the same way during some of our more . . . perilous moments."

"So, will the three of us be enough?" Wu asked. "Or do we have to find a couple more?"

"My initial preference would be for a few more . . . but in truth,

three capable beings such as yourselves will suffice, and in some ways
. . . yes, in some ways fewer is preferable. Secrets, you understand."

"In that case, it's still too many," DuQuesne said equably.

"How do you mean?"

He grinned. "We've got an old saying back in Earth system: 'three
can keep a secret . . . if two of them are dead.'"

Orphan burst into buzzing laughter. "Ahhh, yes, how very
appropriate, Doctor! It so truly reflects the way of the spy and
manipulator, does it not?"

"It wouldn't have lasted so long if there weren't truth in it, that's for
sure. So, can you tell us how long this jaunt will be for?"

Orphan took a drink, obviously thinking. "The precise length of
time depends on many factors, as one might imagine. But . . . months,
certainly. The journey is not short, and of course we must first travel
there, and then return, and I cannot say precisely how long my . . .
business, so to speak, will require before I may return."

Months . . . we've had some experience now with travel in the Arena.
That means . . . "You mentioned only talking within the Deeps about
certain things. Does that mean . . . ?"

"Ah, Dr. DuQuesne, you are as perceptive as ever. Yes, our journey
will take us through the Deeps indeed, far from mapped Sky Gates
and well-trafficked routes through the Arena's skies. You are, I
believe, well-familiar with one of the reasons for my sobriquet of 'the
Survivor,' yes?"

"Yeah," DuQuesne said, "and that's actually one of the things that's
got me worried. You've been on at least three expeditions to the Deeps,
expeditions of which you were the only survivor."

Wu Kung stood slowly. "I did not know that."

"It is true. And it is also true that on one of those expeditions I
made the . . . discovery which now necessitates my return. But by that
token, I did learn much of the perils surrounding that particular
location and the, hmm, peculiar approaches one must take to survive
there." Orphan leaned back, his tail bracing him as he regarded the
group.

"I would like to know whether *we* will survive, then," Wu Kung
said, looking much more menacing than someone of his small stature
would be expected to look. "Because if it will put Ariane in too much
danger I will say we are not going."

Orphan's wingcases contracted, then released. "To *know*? All of us would very much like to know, for certain, whether we would survive a given choice, would we not? Alas, I can only give you likelihoods and intentions, not certainty.

"What I *can* say, my friends, is that I know what happened to the members of those ill-fated expeditions, and I know how to avoid those fates. While I give you no guarantees, I have every intention of making this journey as safe as possible. I would *very* much like to return here with my entire crew intact." He gave the broad gesture which DuQuesne interpreted as a smile. "After all, this would also encourage others to possibly journey with me without suspecting that such a trip could be a death sentence."

Wu Kung stood immobile for a moment, regarding the alien narrowly. "There are many things you are not saying."

"Indeed there are. And things I will not say until we are well within the Deeps, I assure you. But I very much mean it when I say that I regard you as my friends, and do not wish to bring harm to any of you."

Wu shrugged and sat down. "Okay, that much was truth. We will go."

Orphan looked over at Ariane. "Had he said no? . . ."

". . . then we'd be staying," Ariane answered immediately. "There's no point in having a bodyguard if you don't listen to him, and Wu's instincts are pretty good."

"Well. In that case I thank you, Wu Kung."

"Do not thank me; it is just that, past all your twistiness, you like Ariane and Marc, and you don't want to hurt them. You were telling the truth there. So that should be all right, and if I'm along, I can take care of them anyway."

Orphan chuckled. "Very good, then."

"So we'll be out for months," DuQuesne said thoughtfully. "We're taking *Zounin-Ginjou*?"

"Yes, my flagship has been repaired, and I will have it appropriately disguised by the time we are ready to launch."

"Disguised?" repeated Ariane.

"Indeed. The more misdirection I can manage, the better. I do not wish to be followed or tracked in any way; minimizing the ease with which others can recognize my vessel is certainly one way to reduce this risk."

"This will be interesting," Ariane said. "All right. Well, we won't lack for space on *Zounin-Ginjou*, so we should be able to take anything we need, yes?"

"Oh, certainly. Bring anything you feel you require or that will make you comfortable. Your own foodstuffs, of course, are recommended. While I will naturally bring food with me, my selections for human palates are of necessity currently quite limited."

Ariane nodded thoughtfully. "Good enough. I still have a few things to do here, though—I have to touch base, as we say, with the other Factions, make sure that there aren't any key issues I have to address before I turn things over to Carl and Laila, and so on."

"Certainly, certainly, Captain Austin," Orphan said cheerfully. "And as I have been waiting a while, another week or two is no great burden. Let us plan on launching on this expedition in two weeks from this day; is that satisfactory?"

DuQuesne considered, then nodded. He was pretty sure it would be easy enough to assemble anything he wanted or needed in that space of time. "Works for me."

"And for me," Ariane concurred. "Orphan, make your plans. In two weeks, we set sail into the Arena!"

Chapter 3

Wu bounced along in front of Ariane, watching in all directions at once. The Grand Arcade, that gigantic area of open-air markets, stalls, and covered collections of shops like mini-malls, was a constant whirl of activity that never stopped—ideal for both an ambush and an escape. He turned periodically, seeing that Ariane was just behind him, that no threats loomed nearby. Then he could return for a few moments to the enjoyment of the moment.

The Arcade was one of the most *wonderful* places Wu had ever been, and seeing and smelling this maelstrom of a thousand species and a million scents lifted his spirits, helped him . . . not forget, really, but push back the loss that still ached, perhaps always *would* ache, behind his heart. *All gone. They haven't* said *it, but I can tell by the glances, the words not spoken . . . if there is anything to be salvaged, it will not be all. It will not be most. A few small things, remnants of my world . . . a world of lies, but they were* my *lies to live with.*

But the Arcade was another world, a *real* world of wonders perhaps surpassing the imaginations of the Hyperion designers, a world within another world within an endless *sky* of worlds. *DuQuesne said it was* made *for us. Maybe he was right, after all. I shouldn't have doubted; he* usually *is* right.

"You're looking better, Wu," Ariane said.

"Better? Better than what?" He was momentarily puzzled.

"Than you have for the last couple of weeks. Happier. There's more of a bounce in your step."

Wow. He couldn't keep from staring at her for a moment. "You could *see* that? I thought I was good at hiding my pain."

"You are," she said, with a gentle smile—one so different from the smile she wore in competition or battle. "But as the Captain with three Hyperions in my crew, I've gotten used to watching for subtleties that I probably would've missed a year ago."

"Ha! Of course you have." He tried to ignore the fact that when she smiled like that and looked at him with sympathy and worry, with those eyes and hair of blue, she looked very much like someone else. "I do not like being sad. I don't like remembering sadness and loss. But . . . I cannot forget, either."

"You shouldn't forget. They were your life. Your *world*. Like you said to Mr. Fenelon, if you don't remember them, who will?"

He nodded, looking around again. They were moving down one of the many rows of food vendors; that made the expected movement of the crowds fairly predictable, which was good. "I know. But I know that S . . . Sanzo," it was astonishing how hard it was to say her name now, ". . . Sanzo wouldn't want me to be sad. If there was nothing I could do, then she would want me to do what I could *here*."

For a moment, he allowed his heart to go black, his voice to drop to a near snarl. "But I will not forget the one who *did* this."

Instead of backing away at the sight of the monster within—as almost everyone, even his old friends, used to—Ariane put her hand on his shoulder, and her touch was warm. "No, Wu. None of us will. And I promise you," her voice was for an instant as level and cold as his, "we *will* find him—or her—one day."

She's STRONG, he thought, one of the highest compliments he could pay anyone. *No wonder DuQuesne and Dr. Sandrisson like her so much.* "Thank you." He glanced around again. "So we are shopping for food?"

"I want to get a good assortment of, well, pretty much everything to take with us. If we're going to be gone for months, I don't want a boring repetitive diet."

"I will agree there!"

For the next hour or so, they did exactly that; Ariane selected multiple foods—meats, unusual grains of purple and green, a dazzling selection of fruits, snacks and alien tubers, all to be sent to the Embassy for packing.

A movement caught his eye and he grinned. "Captain, can we go talk to an old friend?"

"Who are you—" she followed his gaze, and her smile answered his. "Of *course* we can. As long as you promise *not* to get in trouble this time."

"I'm on *duty* this time," he pointed out.

The tiny—even shorter than Wu Kung—white-and-purple figure turned, tail raised halfway, as they approached. "Captain Ariane Austin of Humanity, greetings," said Tunuvun, bowing with wide-spread arms.

"Tunuvun of the Genasi, greetings," Ariane said, bowing.

He turned to Wu. "And my brother warrior, Wu Kung, I am pleased to see you again as well."

"Me too!" He stepped in and clasped hands with the smaller being, feeling the strength of the three-fingered grip. "How are you and your people?"

"Very well, and I thank you for asking. In fact . . ." A scent of trepidation and decisions. "My meeting you here is not entirely accident," he said, looking at Ariane. "I had hoped to meet you in such circumstances—unofficially, where I might ask you a favor without possibly embarrassing us both."

"A favor?" One of Ariane's brows lifted. "I can't imagine anything you might ask being embarrassing. What is the favor?"

"*Refusal* could be an embarrassment, at least for me, if done in an official setting," he said. "And could reflect upon you. I wished to ask . . . would you—and my brother Wu, of course—accompany me to deliver our Challenge?"

"What?" Ariane's scent showed her startlement and gratification. "Tunuvun, we would be *honored* to be present at that event. When would you like to do this?"

"Well . . . now, if it would not be overly presumptuous."

The sharp scent, like lemons and ozone, was clear. "You're *nervous*, Tunuvun!"

The tail twitched. "Of *course* I am nervous! I go to Challenge for my entire people's right to be *people*—to be Citizens of the Arena, to be *part* of the Arena as you are, and we are not. All will rest on my back."

"I don't blame you, Tunuvun," Ariane said, and her smile showed she *did* understand. "And so you want to get that out of the way as soon as possible, so you can just focus on *winning* the Challenge—whatever it ends up being."

"You are a competitor as well, Captain. Yes, you understand perfectly. So . . . ?"

"So let us go issue your Challenge, Tunuvun of the Genasi!"

He bowed again, very low indeed, and then turned and began striding briskly away. "Then follow. It is not too far, and I would rather walk, unless you have an objection."

"None at all. Nothing wrong with exercise." As they began walking, Ariane continued, "So who's the lucky target of your Challenge?"

"I will be issuing Challenge to the Vengeance," Tunuvun replied.

Wu saw Ariane stop in her tracks, and her scent shifted to surprised concern. "Tunuvun, you're going to Challenge one of the Great Factions?" Ariane said slowly.

"Of course he is," Wu answered; it had been so obvious to him that he hadn't realized it *would* surprise Ariane. "The rules said they had to choose one with enough Spheres that the loss would not be great, and honor dictates that such a solemn and important Challenge must be given to one truly worthy."

"Wu Kung sees truly," Tunuvun said. "This Challenge must leave none in doubt of who we are, or what our worth is."

A few minutes later, they stopped before the doorway of one building that thrust itself like a dagger into the sky, pointing towards the distant ceiling of Nexus Arena.

"*This* will be interesting," muttered Ariane.

"Selpa'A'At of the Vengeance, come forth!" Tunuvun said, and one of the green comm-spheres appeared before him as he spoke. "I, Tunuvun of the Genasi, must speak with you here, before my companions."

A moment passed, then the sphere brightened. "With such formality I am called; I answer you, Tunuvun, and say to you, wait, then, and I will be there in moments."

Wu waited, tense. *I really hope Maria-Susanna isn't with him.* He missed the golden-haired woman terribly, but he now knew what she had become, and seeing her so hurt and changed was a fresh pain he did not need.

But Selpa'A'At emerged alone, to Wu's great relief, spherical body seeming to float level between its spidery legs. "I am here, Tunuvun of the Genasi. What is so urgent and so public that you must call me here, before my own Faction House?"

Tunuvun drew himself up, somehow looking tall and proud. "In the name of my people, I Challenge you, Selpa'A'At of the Vengeance, by the right and power of the Arena itself; you must accept, there is no refusal for this Challenge."

The globe of a body rose and fell. "So. Before I respond, might I ask why you have chosen the Vengeance?"

"I offer you a chance to best me, who won a Challenge for the Powerbrokers against you under circumstances that I know did not entirely please you. It is an honorable chance for you, and an honorable Challenge for me."

Selpa chuckled; the actual sound, which Wu could hear underneath the translation of mirth, was a rasp as of wood on wood. "So. The Vengeance accepts your Challenge, then. More, it is our right to select the nature of the Challenge."

Tunuvun tensed. "It is," he agreed.

Wu Kung felt himself tensing as well, for along with the sharp smell of the Genasi's trepidation he could detect the far more worrisome scent of amusement and confidence. *Selpa knows something or has thought of something Tunuvun won't like, I'll bet.*

"We could select many contests that would be ill-suited to Genasi; still, you could then select a Champion who was skilled in such areas. Instead, we will select one that has aspects appropriate to both sides. It will be Racing Chance, with the race an obstacle course."

Instantly, Tunuvun began to relax. "This is an acceptable selection," he said.

No! Wu didn't know what, but that smell of triumph told him a trap had closed.

"And our Champion," Selpa'A'At said, his voice smooth as silk, "for the racing portion, at least, will be Tunuvun of the Genasi."

Wu found his mouth had dropped open, as had Ariane's. "Wh . . . *what?*"

Tunuvun had gone rigid as a statue, and Wu began to realize just how artful a trap Selpa had laid.

"You . . . you can't do that!" Ariane snapped.

"Captain Austin of Humanity, you are, I am afraid, completely incorrect," Selpa said. "Not only is the general rule clear that I can select any Champion; it is also the fact that following the loss to which he refers, the Vengeance immediately made a contract with him and his people to provide us with at least one such Champion at our discretion. This was, in a way, our recognition of his performance in that Challenge."

Ariane shook her head. "Well . . . fine, then. But all he has to do in *that* case is sit down at the start line and let the other guy win."

"No, he can't do that," Wu said, seeing Tunuvun turning towards Ariane with outrage writ large in his posture. "Ariane, this is his *profession*. If he ever is seen as doing less than he could, he'd lose face—lose *tremendous* face."

"My brother understands," Tunuvun said, his voice filled with leashed anger and chagrin. "In fact, to forestall any accusations that I might lose the match on purpose, I will have to run this race better than any I have ever run, with no reserve held back at all, so that there is no doubt I am running to win for my patrons."

But then Tunuvun's scent changed, and though his face looked little different, Wu Kung sensed a broad smile. "But the same rules apply to me. Whoever is to race against me—and who must beat me, if the Genasi are to win their citizenship in the Arena—will have to be my equal, or perhaps even my better, and though I have, rarely, lost, I have met only one such. So I ask you, Sun Wu Kung of Humanity: will you be *our* Champion?"

Selpa stiffened, all six legs locking.

Wu Kung glanced uncertainly at Ariane, but then saw the savage grin spreading over her face and felt a burst of gratitude. "Wu Kung, as Leader of the Faction of Humanity, I give you full permission to accept this request."

"Then I will *gladly* race against you, Tunuvun!" he said, and grasped the smaller creature's hands again. "If you'll forgive me for beating you!"

"My brother in combat," Tunuvun said, and that sense of a smile was all around him, "I will only not forgive you if you *lose*."

Chapter 4

"That might not have been the best choice, Ariane," DuQuesne said somberly.

Simon was puzzled by the gravity in his voice. Reflexively, he glanced around the meeting room, but there was no one present except the members of the "core group," as Simon thought of it—DuQuesne, Ariane, Simon himself, Laila, Carl, and the newcomers Oasis and Wu Kung. "Do you think Wu might lose? Or is there some other reason?"

DuQuesne looked down; the brows were lowered, and Simon could tell that his friend was thinking furiously.

Finally, DuQuesne looked up, meeting Ariane's gaze first before looking to Simon. "Yes, he might." He held up a hand to forestall Wu's protest. "Wu, I know that no one here knows what you're like when you actually go all out—and that we're both finally back in shape for real. But 'Racing Chance' is only about half the 'racing' part. The rest of it—as Carl described to us," he nodded to the tall, slender controls specialist, "and as I verified by checking in our records, is a game of chance and skill. That's the section of the challenge still to be hammered out, but it throws a *royal* wrench in the works compared to a straight-up race."

"On the other hand," Laila said, with her usual analytical calm, "was there a reasonable alternative? We want the Genasi to win their Challenge, correct?" At the nods around the table, she continued, "Then what alternative was there? Speaking honestly, is there anyone else here who could possibly be a better choice than Wu Kung, at least for the racing portion of this Challenge?"

43

Oasis tilted her head. "Well, Marc and I could . . . but no, not *better*. Not for something as relatively straightforward as an obstacle race."

"Something else is bothering you, Marc," Simon said flatly. "Or something else is relevant that you don't want to say."

Ariane's quick look showed that she'd come to the same conclusion.

The big Hyperion pursed his lips, then gave a short, explosive laugh, followed by a quick grin that subsided all too swiftly. "You've got me pegged pretty well, Simon. Yeah, there's a couple things that've got me chasing my tail. One . . . well, I'd like to take Orphan's route and wait until we're in the Deeps, but then we'll be on Orphan's ship, which wouldn't do us any favors in security. I *like* that exoskeletal joker, don't get me wrong, but I can't *trust* him all the way."

He drew in a deep breath. "It . . . has to do with some of the things I guess about the way the Arena operates. And it's pure dynamite, if I'm right."

DuQuesne paused again, looking around the table, and Simon was struck by his hesitation. *He just doesn't have this kind of . . . indecision.* "Marc, what *is* it?"

"Sorry. Look . . . No offense to anyone here—and I mean that—but I can only discuss this with Ariane and Oasis." He caught Wu Kung's gaze. "And that means not with you, either, Wu. Sorry."

Ariane frowned. "Marc, I trust Simon—everyone *here*, in fact—with anything. If—"

"This isn't a matter of trust. It's a matter of *need to know*, and I think no one else *needs* to know, yet." DuQuesne held up his hands. "Now that *will* be your call, Ariane. If you decide you want to let the whole crew know, that's up to you, and I'll back you on whatever course you take. You *are* the Captain, and that's the pure-quill truth; you've proven it to all of us, and my *not* accepting that damn near got me killed once. I will try to *never* second-guess you again like that. But you can't decide *to* keep it a secret if I let it out to begin with."

Ariane looked over to Simon.

Well, now, she's obviously giving me a chance to object. It was highly gratifying, really; she was basically saying, without words, that if he raised an objection she'd override DuQuesne, which was something she was very reluctant to do (and for extremely good reason, given their history in the Arena).

Simon was tempted. He *really* wanted to know what sort of secret was so desperately important, and how it involved Ariane and Oasis but *not* Wu or himself. But at the same time, he trusted DuQuesne implicitly. Marc DuQuesne hadn't been the most approachable of people to begin with, but in the year and more since they'd become crewmates, he'd found Marc's insight and advice invaluable—even before they first launched *Holy Grail*.

"If Marc thinks this is the best choice, I'm not going to second-guess *him* either, Ariane," Simon said. "But before we all leave, is there any more to discuss that *doesn't* require we leave the room?"

"Thanks for the vote of confidence, Simon," DuQuesne said, and Simon could hear the sincerity in his tones. "Yeah, we need to talk a little about strategy and timing. Tunuvun and the Genasi decided to go all-in with Humanity—they've turned the whole Challenge over to us."

"Really?" That startled Simon. "I would have thought their pride would require otherwise."

Wu Kung shook his head. "They're proud as warriors, but Tunuvun said to me that this is more important than pride. He's their best Challenge-warrior and now the Vengeance has him. He knows all the Genasi's other candidates *cold*, but no one really knows *us* that well, so we've got an advantage." He grinned, fangs glinting sharply. "And after our victories, we're making people nervous. A good thing in an opponent. Tunuvun said we were on a winning streak."

"More than he knows," Simon murmured; the rest of the Arena didn't know about the kidnapping of Ariane and the subsequent utter humiliation of the Blessed to Serve, making that *three* of the major powers—Molothos, Shadeweaver, and Blessed—that Humanity had managed to defeat soundly in less than a year.

"Like Wu said," DuQuesne said, "we're on a winning streak, and they're betting it holds. In any case, Selpa's not going to give us too much time before we choose our representative in the *Chance* section of the Challenge, and then we have to all agree on the exact details of the game—we went through this before, with Ariane's Challenge against Amas-Garao. We'll want an Advocate—I'm thinking either Nyanthus, if he'll do it again, or maybe Orphan."

Simon nodded. The Advocates mediated the decision-making process between the Challenge parties, enabling, at least in theory, a fair and reasonable compromise to be reached with respect to all aspects of the Challenge; they also watched for any inherently unfair aspects of the Challenge. From that, Simon deduced that only in extreme cases did the Arena itself intervene directly. "Nyanthus would be my preference initially, but I think he would be a poor choice, given that the Faith and the Vengeance are well-known to be opposed."

"Technically, pretty much everyone's in competition with everyone else here," Oasis said. "Even allies seem to think it's a good idea to keep their friends on their toes, you know what I mean?"

"Right," Carl agreed. "But Simon's got a point. We don't know what the Vengeance's second Champion will be, and even less do we know who they'll choose as Advocate, but picking an Advocate specifically known for hostility towards the Vengeance—is that a good idea?"

Ariane shrugged. "The Advocate's *supposed* to be on our side, just not part of our Faction or—I'd guess—so heavily associated with us that they might feel pressure to bend the rules in our favor. The latter might put Orphan out; we're well-known to be about his *only* reliable allies."

"Point taken," DuQuesne said. "We'll leave him out of it, then. Any other candidates?"

Oh, here's a thought. "If we want to stick with the high-profile sorts," Simon said, "then I propose Dr. Relgof."

DuQuesne brightened. "I could go for that. He's friendly towards us, not hostile towards any faction—except maybe the Molothos, which goes for pretty much anyone still breathing—and he's sharp as a box of razor blades."

"I like it," Ariane said. "He's been one of our supporters, but no *commitment* to do so."

"I approve," Laila said emphatically. "If, of course, he will accept."

"I would be willing to bring up the question," Simon said.

"Please do, as soon as we're done here," Ariane said, after her quick survey of the conference table got nothing but approving nods. "What else, Marc?"

"Well, we'll probably want to take a few days to practice whatever the game is that we end up with, but we don't want to delay Orphan's trip, either."

"I've already contacted Orphan," Ariane said. "His response was 'My dear Captain Austin, such a Challenge takes precedence over anything. And in truth, I look forward to watching this one. Your friend Wu Kung versus Tunuvun? Alas that I cannot sell admissions!'"

Simon laughed along with the others, at least as much from the way in which Ariane managed to capture both the intonations and the posture of Orphan perfectly in her quote. "So who will be our other Champion?"

"Marc," Ariane said instantly.

Simon nodded. "That makes sense, but why are you so certain?"

"Any of us might make good players of a game of skill and chance—sounds like it could be the equivalent of a game of poker. *But* with Wu Kung involved, and—per Carl's description—the fortunes of the game being able to directly affect the obstacles and difficulty of the racing course—that pretty much argues that whoever's playing the game be someone *very* familiar with Wu Kung's habits, capabilities, and limitations. That means really only DuQuesne and Oasis, and—being honest here—I understand Marc's capabilities a little better than yours, Oasis."

The redhead tossed back her long ponytails. "No offense taken, Captain. I'd make the same choice; Marc's beat me at cards more than once."

"All right, then that's settled." Ariane looked up at the rest. "Now, I'll listen to whatever Marc has to say; if we need you again, I'll call you in."

Simon nodded, and he and the others filed out; Wu Kung looked particularly hesitant, but finally he left. "Carl, can we do some sparring?" he said. "I want something to keep me focused instead of just waiting."

"Sure thing, if you'll take a heck of a handicap. I don't mind a little practice, but imitating a punching bag isn't really practice."

"No problem—make it as hard on me as you want!"

"In that case, I've got some ideas that should still make it fun for you. Let's go. Simon, you want to watch?"

"Perhaps later. I'm going to speak to Relgof; that's a time-limited situation, you know."

"I'll watch," Ariane said, coming up behind them.

Simon jumped slightly. "I thought you were having a top-secret secret meeting with DuQuesne."

"I was, but . . . I saw how tense he was, and I asked him if there was a good reason, in his view, that he should keep this a secret from *me* too, as a real ace in the hole. He hemmed and hawed a little but eventually said yes." She smiled. "I trust his judgment, really, and since he was straightforward about trusting me and was going to tell me whatever it was flat-out, I decided to return the favor. Besides, I think I'll just see if I can figure it out myself; I've got some clues to work with."

"Always time for a little mystery in life, yes. All right, I'll see you all later, then."

Ariane nodded and turned to Carl. "Then let's go!"

"Right. Onward to my beating!" He gave a cheery wave and led Wu away, Ariane just behind.

Simon stepped out into the simulated evening of Nexus Arena. The light was just starting to fade, and there were even faint pink shades to the light, a perfectly-emulated sunset behind the various buildings. *Is even that a matter of tailored perceptions? Would I see something different if I were a Genasi or a Tantimorcan? Or is day and night here something very real, and thus seen at the same time and, as much as perceptual equipment allows, in the same way?*

Not for the first time, he was tempted to reach inside himself and *push* for answers—to whether this was real or generated perceptions, for what secrets DuQuesne was telling Oasis, for hints as to what they should consider with this new Challenge, but he shoved the temptation away. *Having the potential to look into the mind of God and be a panopticon at the same time is* far *too potentially corruptive. I'm not taking chances with this.*

With one of the floating cabs to take him, it was only a few minutes to reach the great square-faced headquarters of the Analytic, third of the Great Factions. The door opened for him—his one-year pass to the Archives gave him entrance at any time—and he stopped within the entrance hall. "Relgof Nov'ne Knarph, would you be free to speak with me?"

The green comm-ball appeared even as he began to speak, and floated before him; no red aura appeared, which meant that the call was not being blocked or, as of yet, refused.

A moment later it flickered. "Dr. Sandrisson, it would be my pleasure. You are here in the Faction House, I see. Is this a private matter?"

"Moderately so. Nothing terribly secret, but a request made in person and with reasonable privacy seemed preferable."

"Then come, come. I will meet you in the third conference room, the same one we discussed your fascinating book in."

Simon remembered that discussion well, and found the room without much difficulty. True to his word, Relgof, in his customary white outfit, entered only moments later. "Simon, my friend, it is *good* to see you. I trust you and your Faction are well?"

He returned the handclasp, noting again the peculiar sensation of a second thumb gripping his hand. "Very well at the moment. But we have an issue we believe you could assist with."

"By all means, tell me of your problem," Relgof said, waving him to a seat. His filter-beard flip-flopped in a gesture that seemed to be related to a smile.

"I do not know if you are aware, but the Genasi have issued their Challenge to the Vengeance."

"That much I had heard, yes. The details have not been released by any yet, however. Already you interest me!"

Information, the greatest coin of the realm for the Analytic. "Well, as the Challenged party, the Vengeance chose Racing Chance as the Challenge method. They also called upon the terms of a previous contract and selected Tunuvun of the Genasi as their Champion."

Relgof, who had bent to scoop a bit of the water from the inset flowing bowl in the table, started and splashed himself and his usually spotless uniform. "Silt and sand! Now *that* is a bold and clever move. They seek to use the competitor's own honor and dedication to his craft against him."

"Exactly. So Tunuvun countered by selecting Sun Wu Kung of *our* faction as the Genasi Champion."

"Wu Kung . . . yes, of course! The one who fought alongside Tunuvun in a rather impromptu and unofficial challenge, and won. The bodyguard of your Leader, correct?" At Simon's nod, Relgof rubbed the side of his head pensively. "A most interesting Challenge this promises to be. But there are two Champions in Racing Chance."

"We do not know the Vengeance's second, yet, but the Genasi gave us the option on that as well. I believe they think that our tactics are less likely to be open to the Vengeance. We have selected Marc DuQuesne as the second."

"An *excellent* choice. The very fact that he faced the Molothos and defeated them will weigh heavily in the mind of any playing against him. So, then, what is your problem?"

"We are, of course, still very unfamiliar with many details of these

Challenges," Simon said. "And there are a great many specifics to be nailed down for this Challenge—"

"Say no more. You would like me to be your Advocate—or more specifically that of the Genasi—in the negotiations."

"Exactly. Now, I don't know what sort of fee, if any, is normal and customary—"

"It varies extremely, depending on the relationship between factions and individuals, the interest in the Challenge, and many other factors. In this case, I would *like* to charge you, but honesty compels me to say that I would never forego the chance to observe the process for such a unique confrontation. The only recorded Challenge by native species of the Arena for their right to be First Emergents? It is without precedent. To be an observer first-hand for the Analytic is, itself, sufficient payment. I accept, Simon!"

Simon felt a rush of relief—and gratitude towards Relgof for his inherent honesty. "That's wonderful, Relgof. I will let Tunuvun know."

"Excellent. I look forward to it. Now, before you go, Simon, I have some questions for you about some details of your translated book—and in exchange I may be able to answer a few questions for you as well."

Simon settled back into his chair. "I'd be glad to play 'trading questions' with you. Go ahead!"

About an hour later, Simon waved goodbye to Relgof and began to make his way back to the Embassy. As he boarded one of the taxis, a tall, very familiar form leapt up beside him.

"Dr. Sandrisson, a pleasure to see you," Orphan said.

"And you, Orphan. Are things going well?" Simon realized this couldn't be coincidence; things rarely were in the Arena.

"Well enough. I would like a word with you in private, if I might, Doctor."

With me? Interesting. "I have no objection."

"Excellent." The alien raised his voice. "To the Embassy of the Liberated."

The cab swiftly drove them to Orphan's Embassy. Simon was silent through most of the short trip, trying to figure out what Orphan might want. He couldn't ask any significant questions on the way, though, since the planned expedition to the Deeps was secret. "Ariane," he said to air, and the expected green sphere *popped* into existence. "This is Simon."

"What is it, Simon?"

"Orphan's asked me to stop by and talk with him about something. I don't know what, yet, but I presume it won't take long?" He said the last looking at Orphan quizzically.

"Not too long, no."

"Not long, then. So you can expect me back relatively shortly."

"No problem, Simon."

He followed Orphan into the Embassy and to one of Orphan's conference rooms—the same one, as near as he could tell, that Orphan had previously used to meet with Humanity. "All right, Orphan, I am about ready to burst from the suspense. What is it?"

"Something I think you will find *most* interesting, Dr. Sandrission, if things are as I suspect. You recall, of course, that during our . . . rather forceful negotiations with the Blessed to Serve you not only temporarily repaired *Zounin-Ginjou*, but also improvised a quite impressive weapon that Dr. DuQuesne referred to as a 'primary beam,' yes?"

Now it made sense. A new weapon was something you certainly wouldn't want to discuss in any public area. "That would be difficult for me to *forget*, given that I had to help it fire manually and that I fought Vantak in the same room with that gun." A combination that had very nearly killed him, and one that made Simon wince just remembering it.

"Even so." Orphan ran his hand absently along his lefthand crest, a gesture showing he was thinking and distracted. "Might I ask, then, if you intended to keep its workings . . . proprietary, I suppose is the right term? That is, if you did not intend the Liberated to be able to make use of it and duplicate it?"

"What? Oh, no, Orphan, I am sorry if you somehow got that impression. It was on your ship, and I put it together out of your components, and to make it a *really* practical weapon there would be many refinements. It is certainly as much yours as it would be anyone's. You're welcome to make use of it as much as you like—although I'd very much appreciate you sending the design data over so *we* could replicate it. I confess I didn't really pay exact attention to memorizing what I'd done."

That was something of an understatement. He'd cobbled the clumsy superweapon together using that strange ability of insight and understanding that he'd gained in the near-catastrophe of the sealing ritual that had inactivated Ariane's Shadeweaver-like powers. Thinking back on it, he really didn't remember it all clearly, although he thought he probably *could* if he focused on the problem enough.

Orphan's hands made the twin dismissing gesture that meant disagreement. "You mistake me, Simon. I have already attempted to do so. I examined your revision of my topside turret gun carefully, and applied those modifications to my portside guns." He paused, studying Simon so intensely that the human scientists found himself extremely nervous. "Those portside guns, however, refuse to function. Not only do they not produce the *most* impressive intensity and power of the topside cannon, they do not function *at all*. And my initial analysis of the design is that it *should* not function."

"What?"

"The topside cannon, by contrast, continues to function exactly as before. I have added an automatic reloading option and found a way to store replacement matrices, of course, but I am extremely hesitant to actually disassemble the original—it is, after all, a 'trump card' as you might call it, of inestimable value. But I am at the same time confident that my scans and analysis of the unit are accurate. The portside guns are as near duplicates as I can manage . . . yet they are dead weight now."

The alien leaned forward, and despite the mostly expressionless face, gave the impression of someone with a disquieting grin. "I find this . . . interesting, Dr. Simon Sandrisson. *Immensely* interesting . . . would you not agree?"

Chapter 5

"All, right, Simon; you insisted we have breakfast in private today," Ariane said; per Simon's request, she'd even had Wu Kung stay outside the meeting room. "What is so important?"

Simon was uncharacteristically sober; his usual smile was a shadow of its normal self. "I would have brought this up yesterday, but by the time I got back you were dealing with Arena business, and it was rather late before you were free. This . . . is something best tackled with a fresh mind."

"So stop beating around the bush, Simon." She was concerned now; Simon, while certainly rather loquacious, usually didn't evade answering a question.

Simon looked down at his plate, long white hair momentarily shading his face from view; with an audible sigh he raised his head, looking directly at her. "I had a very disturbing conversation with Orphan yesterday. You remember, of course, the weapon I improvised for *Zounin-Ginjou*?"

She nodded.

"Well . . . Orphan claims that he cannot duplicate it." He went on to recount the exact conversation he had heard.

He copied the device and it doesn't work? "Was he serious?" Ariane was trying to get her head around this idea.

"*Deadly* serious, Ariane," Simon said, helping himself to a samosa. "Oh, he was clearly enjoying the confusion his news engendered, but there was no sign that he was actually joking around."

"Is what he describes even *possible*?"

She felt embarrassment well up within her as Simon laughed. "My apologies, Ariane, but . . . you ask this in the *Arena*. In the *normal* way of things, no. With the tools we have, and that I presume Orphan has at his disposal, if you create the closest replica you can of a device, then the two devices *will* work very nearly identically. To not even come *close* to functioning? No. That makes no sense.

"Yet, if I believe what Orphan said—and I do—then the nonsensical is fact: this device which functions flawlessly cannot be duplicated."

Ariane took a few bites of omelet while she thought. "The Arena."

"Obviously, yes. The Arena itself must be doing this—either allowing my modifications to work despite them not actually being able to accomplish what I thought they would, or preventing a duplicate which should work from functioning." He spread some Arena-local fruit over his pancakes. "The *how* is not terribly relevant—the Arena's capability to switch nuclear reactions and AIs off on a whim shows that it has the capability. What I cannot quite work out is *why*."

"I can work out *a* reason why," Ariane said. "Really, several reasons. Maybe it doesn't want that weapon being used in a general sense. Maybe it just wanted you to be able to . . ."

Simon nodded as she trailed off. ". . . able to rescue *you*. Yes, that thought occurred to me. But if that is the case . . ."

"*Crap*." She couldn't even express the mixed brew of confusion, fear, and even a strange *elation* that this thought triggered in her. But this touched on the question that DuQuesne, Simon, and she had discussed the day after their return to the Arena: why, precisely, had the Arena spoken to her directly? None of them had managed to come up with an answer. But this new fact . . .

"That would mean," she said finally, "that the Arena has taken a direct interest in us—something that seems completely contrary to the way it usually functions."

"If that was the reason, yes," Simon agreed.

Ariane forced herself to consider the situation carefully as she finished what was on her plate and drank some coffee. The idea that the god-like intelligence that controlled the Arena had a direct interest in Humanity—or, even worse, *her* personally—was terribly disturbing. Why would that apparently dispassionate being or power suddenly focus on one newcomer species or individual?

"There is a way we might test some of that," Ariane said after a few moments.

"Which part?" Simon asked.

"Whether it was, in essence, a one-time thing allowed to permit the *Zounin-Ginjou* the firepower it needed to have a good chance to rescue me," Ariane said. *Because there is another obvious possibility.* "Simon, could you duplicate what you did to that gun?"

"Given another such weapon?" He looked abstracted, his eyes gazing thoughtfully into nothing. "I . . . believe I could, yes. I would have to focus myself into achieving that . . . connection again, but my impression, upon thinking about it, is that I could choose to duplicate those actions."

"We have some of the same energy cannon on the ships Orphan has loaned us. I want you to go back to our Sphere and try to duplicate that change. If it works, see if other engineers on *our* side can copy it."

Simon smiled suddenly, a bright flash that helped her relax the timiest bit. "I see, yes. Well thought out, Captain. No desperation or immediate need, so if that was the reason, my new cannon should not work. If our engineers—not of our inner circle—can duplicate it, that would indicate a general favoritism of Humanity, for whatever reason." He paused. "And if my version functions and theirs does not . . . that would indicate . . . ? "

"My guess? That you have the same, oh, what was it that Gona-Brashind said . . . that was it, ability to *trick* the Arena, to bend its rules, that the Shadeweavers and the Faith's Initiate Guides—and probably me—have."

Simon's eyes lit up with understanding . . . and then dimmed with concern that mirrored her own. "But a completely different form of that capability. Even yours appears, from our limited knowledge, to be closely related to, if not identical with, the powers of those two groups; they both certainly believe that is the case."

"But you were an accident," Ariane said, feeling a certainty growing within her. "You said yourself that this happened during the very climax of the sealing ritual, when it was nearly disrupted and all three powers—the Shadeweaver, the Faith, and my own—were connected solely through you. You then saw . . . well, the same thing *I* saw when it happened, the entirety of the Arena at once."

"Yes. And I feel something odd, as do you, whenever we go between the original universe and that of the Arena." He looked at her, raising an eyebrow. "You believe that this is indeed the case."

"I'm betting on it. I think you'll find that you are the *only* one who can build that 'primary beam' variant. And probably other things, if you are using that strange connection of yours to build them, especially under pressure."

"I see. So where you and the others are magicians or, perhaps, empowered priests, I am . . . what? An alchemist?"

"Something like that. Or," she grinned suddenly and gestured to his habitual white outfit, "a mad scientist, perhaps."

Simon burst out laughing. "But I've *already* shown the fools at the Academy!" he said finally, still chuckling. "When we arrived here, after all."

"I know. But it would fit."

Simon nodded decisively. "It might well." He stood, finishing his fruit juice in a single quick set of swallows. "Then I shall commence the experiment today."

"It shouldn't take long, should it?"

"No. I would expect to have a definitive answer by tomorrow, in fact." He looked at her with a warning expression. "I presume I don't have to warn you how sensitive this information is?"

"No. We won't talk about it to anyone outside of our group even after you've got your answer. I suppose," she said, continuing the thought, "that Orphan probably guesses what's going on."

"I am sure he guesses *something* is going on, but as far as I can tell he has no way of knowing that I have this . . . power. However . . . yes, he obviously has made his own guesses and deductions, and he was implying to DuQuesne and me that there were secrets he had guessed about us—about Humanity, I think." He started to turn, then stopped. "On the subject of secrets—"

She knew what he was about to ask. "I have decided to stand by my choice last night. Whatever secret Marc and Oasis discussed . . . Marc has assured me it may benefit us to *keep* it secret; as he would say, it's a trump card that we want to keep *very* close to our vest. The fewer people who know, the fewer who can give it away, voluntarily or accidentally. If he doesn't think I need to know yet . . . I'll trust him to know when I *do* need to know." She stood and looked him in the eye.

"I feel the same way about your ability too. You tell me the results of your experiment privately, and we'll decide who to tell after that."

He hesitated, then nodded. "I won't pretend I'm not a bit put out, and certainly burning with curiosity, but I will leave it to your judgment. I will not push further."

It suddenly dawned on her. "Simon . . . you could just find out, couldn't you?"

He didn't pretend not to understand. "I suspect so, yes. And it *is* a temptation. But if I ever start abusing this power in such a petty fashion . . . well, I would not be the sort of person who should ever *have* such a power." She nodded, as he went on, "I have to accept that you and DuQuesne understand the dangers as well as advantages of secrets, and not get in the way of you doing your job."

He stepped forward and took her hand. "You have always had my support, and you always shall."

The burst of warmth washed away her tension and concern, at least for the moment, and she impulsively pulled him closer, hugged the slender form tightly. "Thank you, Simon."

He returned the hug, then pulled gently away, smiling. "My pleasure, Ariane. Before you go on Orphan's mad expedition, though, promise me one thing?"

"Depends on what it is," she said with an answering smile.

"I take you to Mairakag Achan's restaurant for that dinner we were supposed to have, oh, almost a year ago? But this time without getting interrupted."

She laughed. "You have a deal, Simon!"

"Then I am off. I have, as Orphan would say, a *most* interesting experiment to conduct!"

She finished her own breakfast and then got up. "DuQuesne," she said into the green comm-ball that appeared, "are you ready for the Challenge negotiations?"

"I think so. On my way, we can talk face to face."

DuQuesne met her a few minutes later in one of several lounges in their Embassy, this one projecting a view as though they were a hundred meters above the floor of Nexus Arena, looking out over the other Embassies and out at the Grand Arcade, with the Great Faction Houses looming in the distance. "Nice view. Gives you a grasp of the *size* of this place."

"Yes, it does. So what's the situation with the Challenge?"

"Talked to Relgof while you were off talking to four different Factions last night. How'd that go, by the way?"

"Well enough. They recognized that as First Emergents we're still reorganizing our politics to handle the Arena, so our absence wasn't as bad as it might have been otherwise. The Tensari are very much attached to Oscar Naraj, so I've had to agree that he will continue to be a liason. The others also spoke well of him. Regardless of his connection to Ni Deng's actions, he really *was* doing the rest of his job well."

"So he's coming back soon?"

Wu Kung growled slightly.

She glanced at Wu with a wry smile of understanding. "Tomorrow, I think. He *does* understand how very much under probation he is, I assure you both."

"He better," Wu said.

"If he steps even an *angstrom* out of line, Wu, I will have him shot back to Earth so fast that he won't need a Sandrisson Drive to go faster than light. And," she continued as DuQuesne opened his mouth, "I've already given Laila and Carl full authority to do that too."

He grinned, and Wu Kung's smile showed his fangs. "Fair enough," DuQuesne said. "I figure you're right; he knows just how close he came to a trial for treason, and besides, he's lost his main play for power anyway. His best chance now *is* to play the game our way."

DuQuesne sat back in a chair that was apparently a classic leather recliner; Wu was standing in a corner that gave him a clear view of the door. "So, the Challenge negotiations. Relgof's on board all the way, gave me a rundown of what I should expect; it seems pretty similar to what you went through in preparation for yours with Amas-Garao, although at least in this case it should be more straightforward; we're not dealing with Shadeweavers and their wonky powers."

"Do we know who their second Champion is?"

"Yeah, and I'm relieved as hell. They picked a Dujuin who's a known master of these kind of games, I guess something like their equivalent of a top gambler and poker player."

She raised an eyebrow. "And you're relieved about that . . . why?"

He grinned, with a humorless glint in his eyes. "Because I was damned certain they were going to pick Maria-Susanna."

She winced. The renegade Hyperion multiple-murderer was, according to both DuQuesne and Oasis, fully the equal of any of the others. "Of course. Why *didn't* they, I have to wonder."

"That's the part that *isn't* a relief," DuQuesne admitted. "She's a part of the Vengeance now, so she'd seem a natural choice. And she would certainly be a natural to match up against me." He shrugged. "Well, she was always hard as hell to predict."

"Could she just be . . . well, playing the Vengeance? Using them to get something?"

"I'd bet a whole stack of vals on it, to be honest. Sure, the Vengeance fits her general outlook, but there's nothing to hold her there specifically. The way she was . . . designed, she's supposed to be a co-star, so to speak, with a hero, and no one at the Vengeance is going to fit the role. Since she went crazy, she's been a solo act, and I don't see that as changing. There's something she wants from the Vengeance, and once she's got it, she'll move on . . . to what, I haven't a clue." DuQuesne frowned, black brows drawn down and sharp-pointed beard adding emphasisis to the grim expression. Finally he sighed and relaxed. "Never mind; for now, I'm glad we aren't facing her."

"So am I," Wu said, with the sadness that always touched his face whenever the subject came up. "She would be a hard opponent . . . and I do not want to fight her anyway."

Ariane gave him a smile of sympathy, then looked back to DuQuesne. "So do you have a clearer idea of the actual Challenge procedure?"

"Yeah. We're going to be hammering out the details of the actual game that'll be the 'Chance' part of the deal, but basically what happens is that the two racers start out on the same course and start running. The course has a base set of obstacles on it, and it's long enough so that even someone moving *real* fast will leave time for a good deal of play—think a lot of hands of blackjack or at least several hands of poker. The game ends when one of the racers crosses the finish line.

"The racers themselves are *not* allowed to directly interfere with each other—that is, they can't injure each other, or push each other off a cliff or something—but they *can* themselves arrange to make the course harder."

"How?"

"Well, it depends on the course, but say that part of it goes through a forest, one of them could knock down a small tree across the path if they were ahead of the other guy, slow them down a bit. That kind of thing."

Ariane nodded. "All right. Go on; what about the other side of this Challenge?"

"The Chance players start playing at the same time. Each of us has a set of Obstacle points that we can choose to either use as bets, or to have an obstacle of our choice placed in the way of the opponent, or possibly remove an obstacle from in front of ours—those mechanics are part of what we're discussing tonight.

"Anyway, the *level* of obstacle you can buy, so to speak, depends on how many Obstacle points you pay for it. So you could spend, say, one point to put a rock right in front of the racer's foot where he'd probably trip on it, or forty points to have a wall suddenly appear in front of him, stuff like that. Choices are basically limitless, as far as I can tell, except that you're not supposed to choose lethal obstacles, and even ones that injure are *really* expensive. Past versions of this have had people throw obstacles ranging from a sudden dust-devil throwing sand in the racer's eyes to calling one of the Adjudicators in against the opposition."

"Adjudicators? You can call in the *Arena's enforcers* to be an *obstacle*?"

"In theory. Apparently it happened once, about nine thousand years ago, when one side was just totally outmatched in the Chance section and the other could accumulate insane amounts of Obstacle points. Naturally that pretty much ended the race."

Wu looked up with interest. "They are *that* dangerous, DuQuesne?"

DuQuesne seemed surprised, then grinned. "That's right, you've never run into them yourself. Yeah, they sure are. They don't *hurt* people, but they're apparently boosted up past whatever other people, even the Molothos, can manage, and they've got this impediment field that makes movement like wading through mud; that pretty much ruins any fighter's day."

Ariane remembered that mired-in-glue field that an Adjudicator seemed to radiate at will, and the complete confidence they emanated. "I'd think so. But you're good at this kind of thing, right?"

DuQuesne grinned. "Ariane, I used to play poker for money with the best Hyperion had to offer. If I can match Slippery Jim, Giles Habibula, Hannibal Gunn, and Dave Strider, I'm pretty sure I can handle the Arena's best. Remember, too, these guys are a *lot* more risk-averse."

Ariane remembered how she and Simon had discovered that, and the reactions of various Arena denizens to the humans' perception of acceptable risk. "True. If you can push the game to something like what we're used to in odds . . ."

"That is indeed the plan. They'll still play, but if I keep pushing them into their discomfort zone, it'll *have* to throw their game off."

Ariane nodded. "I hope so. It's not *so* important for us, not immediately, but remember there's a whole *species'* hopes riding on this."

"I know, Ariane," DuQuesne said soberly. "Believe me, I know. And it *is* important to us. This is the first time anyone's publicly put their trust in us. Sure, the Genasi aren't technically full citizens of the Arena, but everyone knows them, and the fact that they're trusting us newcomers to somehow give them victory? That's *big*, Ariane."

The truth sank in. She didn't like it, but DuQuesne was—as usual—right. "Then you and Wu had damned well better win."

"We will," Sun Wu Kung said. "*I* will. I promise you, Captain, no matter *what* obstacles they throw, no matter how fast my brother in combat Tunuvun is, I *will* win this race—for him, and for you.

"By my honor, I will win."

Chapter 6

Simon stood on the bridge of *Paksenarrion* and gazed outward. *I do not think I will ever grow fully accustomed, let alone jaded, to this.*

The great warship—one of several gifted to Humanity by the Liberated—was cruising now many thousands of kilometers away from the Sphere of Humanity, so far out that the Sphere itself was but a shadow in the gloom, its Luminaire a fuzzy circle of dimmed brightness. On every side flowed and eddied incredible banks of cloud—white and gray, green, pink touched with lavender. The darker clouds flickered, internal lightning discharging, sometimes arcing across unguessable distances to strike a neighboring cloud or to shatter some drifting rock or other debris. There was nothing to give a clear scale to the scene, nothing on which the ordinary human mind could seize and use to build a model of the incomprehensible. But Simon *could*—just barely—grasp it, partially with that vast, though currently tenuous, connection to the Arena itself, and that vista stunned him with its majesty and grandeur, storms large enough to lose even an entire *world* within.

He shook himself. "This should be far enough. Even the best remote sensors, operating in an atmosphere so extensive, will not easily tell one sudden discharge of energy from another."

"As you wish, Dr. Sandrisson," Commander Joani Cleary said. The trim young woman—no older than Simon himself, he was sure, with moderately long red hair on one side of her head and polished baldness on the other, suddenly smiled at him. "It's good to see even you veterans get caught by the Arena. I was wondering if I'd ever get used to it."

"I certainly haven't yet, Commander. Although calling us *veterans* is somewhat misleading; only a year or so ago even we didn't know the Arena existed. When did you come through?"

"About five months back. They were looking for people with experience in warship command who met the other Arena qualifications. That . . . cut way down on the candidates."

"It would, yes. We have to discourage embedded AISages, and any extreme biomods; we know that there are some limits the Arena enforces in the latter case, and in the former, well, a sudden shutdown of AISages nearly got us all killed when we first journeyed here."

"Upshot was, only me and five others from the SSC got cleared through all the requirements, and one of them couldn't hack it when his AISage got shut down. So since we have a lot more than five of these babies," she patted her control chair fondly, "all of us got a ship of our own. Thanks for choosing *Paks* for this test of yours; the more we get to do, the more experience we get for whenever the real trouble starts."

"You're welcome, Commander Cleary. But I hope you won't take it amiss if I say that I hope the real trouble *never* starts."

Joani Cleary shook her head. "Someone wishing that we don't get shot at is *never* taken amiss. Now let me get to work here. "She nodded to the others of her bridge crew. "All engines stop; hold position."

Simon braced himself by gripping one of the seat backs as *Paksenarrion* slowed to a (relative) halt. "Thank you, Commander. Now, I'd better get to the lab."

"Good luck. Will you need us to do anything else? You did say this had to do with weapons development, yes?"

"Well, yes. When I am ready, I will be asking you to activate various weapon emplacements in a sequence I will supply. Even if a weapon fails to function, simply continue the sequence; any damaged or malfunctioning weapons will be repaired before we leave."

"Understood, Doctor." She gave him a respectful nod, which Simon returned before leaving for the weapons emplacements.

"Been waiting for you, Simon," Robert Hampson said. The somewhat older-looking man had the slightly wrinkled look of someone who had lost a lot of weight and whose nanos hadn't quite caught up with cutting down on the extra skin. "I'm still not clear why you chose *me* for this test. I'm not an engineer."

"That was quite deliberate, Robert," he answered, as he walked over to the massive cylindrical form of the Liberated energy cannon. "I chose you because you aren't going to even *try* to second-guess what I'm doing here. I don't want someone who's trying to analyze the work, just follow it and copy it."

"All right. It's for sure a biochemist isn't qualified to critique your weapons design. Though I thought you were mostly a theoretician?"

"Mostly, yes. But . . . well, it would be a long story, and some of it I cannot discuss. I *am* glad you were able to make the transition here."

"So am I. Wasn't so easy to give up Vanney, but he'll keep things going back home, anyway. Now, what do you need me to do?"

"First, just observe what I do to this weapon. In detail—I want you to commit every single thing I do to headware, because what you're going to do later is try to duplicate everything I do."

He raised one gray-shot brown eyebrow. "Okay. I don't quite get the point, but I guess that *is* part of the point."

"Exactly. Now, let me concentrate a moment."

Simon closed his eyes, reached deep within himself to that alien sensation.

The vision of complete and total clarity came far more easily this time, as though it had been merely awaiting his call. Simon could perceive, as though they were laid out before him and labeled, every element of the energy cannon, the control and power runs; he could *see* the entirety of the vessel that Commander Cleary had named *Paksenarrion*; he could perceive Robert Hampson's heartbeat and the operation of his brain. Farther, he could envision the slow twining of the surrounding storms, evaluate the probability and vectors of lightning bolts . . .

Focus. One thing at a time. With difficulty, he pushed away the nigh unlimited vision and comprehension, focused directly on the cannon. *Remember.*

Suddenly it was there, the sense of desperation, the memory of a heart beating, *hammering*, hands wrenching the cover plates away. He found his body responding, following those long-ago actions in an eerie replication of fear and determination and inspiration. He removed power and control elements, modified circuits, replaced components with others, ran a new feed outward, to a loading and fire control subsystem.

As with the first time, it did not take long at all before he slapped the cover shut. He slowly forced his mind to clear, the detached, Olympian perspective to fade away. As always, he felt a momentary depression at returning to himself—to a mind he had once thought incisive, quick, brilliant, but now felt dull, slow, almost empty compared to the grandeur and scope of the vision of the Arena. "Did you get all of that?" he asked, consciously keeping a light, unaffected tone to his voice.

"Got it in the can, yeah," Robert said. "Have *no* idea exactly what you were supposed to accomplish, though."

"Good. You *can* duplicate it, can't you?"

"Sure I can! That's why you hired me, right?"

"One of the reasons. You aren't a military pro, but you've tinkered with all sorts of things, including pretty much every type of weapon. That should allow you to do this reliably."

"Should, yeah." Hampson hesitated. "But, um . . . it'll take me a little longer than you. You were *flying* there, Dr. Sandrisson. Never seen anyone working like that."

I suppose I must have been. I did that fast enough to make a difference in a battle, and therefore could not have taken much time. "No time limit, Rob. I was trying to duplicate something I *had* to do very fast. Now, I don't want to have any additional chance to bias how you do this. Go to Turret 2 Starboard and perform the *exact* same modifications on that gun."

"Got it."

Simon sat down on one of the storage bins at the side of the turret and waited. There wasn't, after all, much else to do; *Paksenarrion* was doing a deep patrol, and he devoutly hoped nothing would happen that would require the supercargo scientist to lend a hand.

And he *did* have a lot to think about. The use of that power was clearly seductive. He didn't *think* it was, inherently, sinister or a trap. But for anyone with an inquisitive mind and an interest in grasping the truth of the universe, it was a temptation of almost unbearable intensity. Perhaps it wouldn't—quite—allow him to see the actual *origin* of the Arena, the power behind it, the "Voidbuilders"—but it certainly seemed capable of almost anything else.

The thought countered the elation with caution—*no, Simon, be honest: fear. Sometimes almost terror.* Information was power, and this . . . *connection* to the Arena was a source of information literally beyond his dreams.

In a way, I suppose this confirms that this peculiar power was *an accident. Any Faction that had and used this power regularly . . . it could dominate the Arena easily.*

And for that very reason, Simon knew, he had to minimize his use of that connection. *Addiction takes many forms, and* this *would be the one that could destroy me.*

The dull ache in his heart at the loss of that omniscient vision just emphasized how very true that fear was.

His headcomm pinged, startling Simon enough to make him jump. *Good Lord, I* was *in a brown study there.* "Sandrisson here."

"Doc, I think I've got it finished—but I have to tell you, I have *no* idea how you did some of those things with the tools you had on hand. I had to go fetch a much more diverse and capable toolkit to get this job done."

Really? The expert tinkerer couldn't do it with the same tools? Simon shook his head. *Think about that later.* "You have compared it carefully with the original, correct?"

"Three times. All checks out as exactly the same."

"Good. Then it's time for the field test. Please evacuate the turret immediately."

"Yes, sir."

He pinged Commander Cleary. "Commander, are you ready?"

"Nothing showing on any of our instruments, none of our observers report anything. We're clear. So yes, go ahead, Doctor; you're in charge."

"Thank you. First, I'd like you to fire a volley from Turret 1 Port." That was an unmodified energy cannon. "Make sure all firing is done in a direction that will *not*, I repeat, *not* even possibly intersect with any of the Spheres equivalent to our nearby stars."

"Yes, sir." Her voice became slightly more distant, as she was speaking to someone else. "Spriggs, unlock turrets and prepare to fire. Greenwood, I want you to find an appropriate firing solution as far from any likely Sphere as possible."

Simon stepped outside of the turret and locked down the door. *No need for a repeat of my most unpleasant experiences on Orphan's ship.*

"All turrets unlocked and ready to fire, Commander," Lieutenant Spriggs reported.

"Firing solution complete, Commander," Lieutenant Greenwood said immediately after. "Coded and locked in."

"Thank you, gentlemen," the Commander said. "Turret 1, portside—fire when ready."

"Firing," Lieutenant Spriggs answered.

Simon felt a very faint vibration through the ship, thought he could hear a distant whine. "Firing of Turret 1, port, complete, Doctor," Cleary said.

"All functions normal?"

"All green."

"Very well. Now, please fire Topside 1." That was the one he had modified.

"Topside 1, roger."

Even through the shielded, sound-proofed door, the blare of sound was almost deafening, the concussion enough to jolt him.

"Holy Jesus!" Commander Cleary said, and her other bridge crew echoed the expression. "What the *hell* did you do?"

"At the moment, that's need-to-know, Commander, and per Captain Austin, you do not need to know."

"Understood."

"Now, please fire Starboard Turret 2," Simon said. He felt his gut tensing. *This will be the real test.*

"Roger, Starboard Turret 2. Lieutenant Spriggs, you may fire when ready."

Silence followed the command. "Commander, Starboard 2 does not respond; telltales show it is inoperative."

"You heard that, Doctor?"

"Yes," Simon said, feeling a chill go down his spine like a slow-moving drop of liquid nitrogen. "Yes, Commander, I heard."

Ariane was right. It wasn't favoring her. It isn't something just favoring humanity, either.

It's me. I—and only I—can do this.

But how—and most importantly, why—I have no idea.

Chapter 7

"I yield the play, Dr. DuQuesne; once more you have outmatched me."
Orphan tipped his remaining cards into the dump-bucket. "Anyone
else still in?" he asked the others, looking around the conference-
room-turned-simulated Arena. A shadowy holographic display
showed several simulated runners speeding along a course,
overcoming various obstacles.

"Not me," Oasis said promptly. "I know Marc too well to keep going
on a losing streak."

"I yield too," Carl said, throwing his cards after the others'.

Ariane's blue eyes regarded DuQuesne coolly. "I'm still in play. I
think you are bluffing, Marc. I'm taking ten Obstacle points and
throwing a block in front of your simulated runner in the form of a
patch of swamp. The rest I'm betting on my hand."

DuQuesne grinned darkly. *Yeah, that's the way she plays.* "*All* the
rest? You sure about that, Ariane?"

"She said it, that's how she's playing it," Carl said. "In the real thing,
you're not going to give your opponent a chance to reconsider, are
you?"

"He might. It's a classic bluff tactic. Or a *non*-bluff that you're
hoping the other guy thinks is a bluff," Ariane said. "But yes, I'm
sticking with that decision. All in, no draws."

"Show 'em," DuQuesne said, doing so himself. "Then read these
and weep, Captain; three Spheres, two Gates, two Shadeweaver Faction
Cards, and one that doesn't matter."

"*What?* But with your outer cards that's—"

"Triple Triples, Shadeweaver Controlled," he finished, grinning at her stunned look. "You had a Triple with two Doubles—good, but my Shadeweavers dominate your single Malacari Faction and negate one of the Doubles anyway."

"Extraordinary," Orphan murmured. "I have seen a startling number of improbable plays during this round of Arena Chance."

DuQuesne shrugged. "Not *that* improbable. There's several of most cards, and their interactions are fairly predictable, though the circulation of the cards through the dump and exclusion of shown cards for a few rounds can complicate the odds. Not to mention the Draw die to add a really random element. It's similar to a mashup of several card games I'm familiar with, in any case. I made a lot of money in college from teaching people odds, so to speak." He raked in his winnings. "And I'll put three swamp areas on *your* simulated runner, a bargain at twenty-five points. Time for another play?"

"I'm up for another few," Ariane said. "Our simulated runners still have a ways to go."

"Perhaps," Orphan said, "we can just leave it to the two of you. In the real Challenge it will be a two-person contest, after all."

A green comm-ball popped up in front of Ariane as the triangular cards were distributed in front of them by an automated device. "Ariane, I am back," came the voice of Simon Sandrisson. "I would very much like to speak with you as soon as I reach the Embassy."

"Of course, Simon." She looked up. "Oasis, Orphan, Carl—would one of you take over for me?"

DuQuesne raised an eyebrow, but he knew that she and Simon had a secret already. *I'll trust her to know when to tell it.* It wasn't as though *he* hadn't kept secrets—and sometimes kept them too long. "Okay, who's up?"

The three conferred in a corner of the room, then all three came and sat across from him. "We shall *all* play against you," Orphan said cheerfully. At that statement, three of the phantom runners stopped and vanished from the course, leaving only two—DuQuesne's, already considerably in the lead, and Ariane's former runner, the only one in striking distance.

"All of you on *one* play?" He grinned, and by Orphan's expression he knew they all could see the challenge in that smile. "Fine. All the helpers in the world won't change luck."

As play progressed, he proved himself right; for every play they won, he won three, and by the end of the simulated Challenge his racer had crossed the finish line fully fifteen minutes ahead of his competitor.

Orphan rose and gave a push-bow. "A *most* instructive game, Dr. DuQuesne. If you play so well tomorrow, I have little fear of you losing. I will say, however, that Byto Kalan is an *excellent* player—better than I at this variant of Arena Chance, I am certain—so you should be very wary."

"Believe me, with this much at stake I am not going to just give it a lick and a prayer," DuQuesne said.

As he said that, another comm-ball sparked emerald before him. "Marc?"

"Who—Saul! You've made it over?"

An image of Saul Maginot appeared, hair if anything a little whiter but otherwise looking well—if he disregarded the tight lines on his face. "For the nonce, yes. This is really just a short jaunt, to accustom me to the novel and, I must admit, most disquieting sensation of Elizabeth being gone."

"No surprise there; even those of us who don't have our AISages in our heads had a hell of a time getting used to being without them." He noted the others had already started clearing the room; they knew there had to be something more. Once the door closed, he nodded. "Okay, Saul, let's have it. You didn't ring me up just to say hello."

He saw the flash of a smile at the antiquated expression "ring me up"—like his occasional fits of colorful and unique swearing, a legacy of Hyperion—before Saul's face went serious again. "We completed our analysis of the remains of the attack, including Wu Kung's station."

Damn. I almost wished it would take longer. "And . . . ?"

"We were able to recover some of the world. Not, I am afraid, nearly all of it. Many of the . . . people inhabiting it are gone. But not all of them. Several of his friends remain."

"What about his family?"

He saw the steady gaze drop for a moment. "The two youngest boys were recoverable. Sanzo . . . according to Sha Wujing, who we were able to partially interface with, she was reinitialized by the destruction of the main system."

Reinitialized? Damnation. "She doesn't remember a thing."

Saul sighed. "Nothing past her upbringing in the temple. Apparently she doesn't even remember being sent out on the Journey to the West, and her physical parameters are back to those of the girl who started the journey. And before you ask, no, there's nothing left to check for a backup. We've taken the structure apart down to the atomic level and probed for quantum storage. Nothing."

"Dammit. I mean . . . that's better news than we were prepared for, but still . . . *Damn* them. Whoever they were. Did we get any clues?"

"None. Whatever happened was abrupt and provided no input from the outside; from Sha's point of view it was a sudden racing wave of destruction that he was barely able to outrun, carrying the two boys with him."

"Blast it. Whoever this is, he's a *real* Big-Time Operator, that's for sure. No surprise there—if Mentor's on the beam, we're up against one of our worst adversaries." *And the worst part is that it's really likely that our enemy's nemesis died fifty years ago.* "Thanks, Saul. I'll break the news to Wu myself."

"Good luck on that, Marc. And on your Challenge, that I was just briefed on."

"Thanks. I'm going to need it, I think."

The door opened just as the comm-ball disappeared, and Ariane stuck her head in. "Marc? Could you join us, please?"

One thing after another. "Be right there."

He followed Ariane to one of the smaller conference rooms, where Simon was waiting. "All right, I'm here. But before we get into whatever you've got on the stove . . ." He quickly went over his conversation with Saul Maginot.

Ariane and Simon wore expressions that probably mirrored his own. "Oh, poor Wu. I mean . . . it *is* better than we thought, but . . ."

"Yeah. And we didn't get a single damn clue. Unless the fact we didn't get a clue is a clue. Anyway, I'll let Wu know in private. You didn't call me here for this, so what's up?"

Ariane hesitated, clearly still thinking about the tragedy to Wu Kung's world, but then shook it off. "Simon came to me with a very . . . interesting piece of information from Orphan." She summarized the discussion she had previously had with Simon. "So that's why Simon's been away a few days; testing our theories."

He looked over to the tall, white-haired scientist. "And? What's the results?"

"It appears that I—and *only* I—can replicate the weapon you called a 'primary beam,'" Simon said after a moment. "I was able to duplicate the changes to the weapon on board *Paksenarrion*, but another person present, performing the exact same modifications, created a completely inactive, nonfunctional weapon that required a fair amount of work to repair."

Well, well. I kinda suspected this, after what happened in that battle. Still a bit of a surprise to get it confirmed. "And the primary worked just the same?"

"Yes. Extremely powerful and coherent beam, with both energy and range vastly increased. I left the modified unit installed—I hope that meets with your approval?" Simon turned to Ariane with an air of contrition. "I know I did not check with you—"

"It's *fine*, Simon. Don't make excuses for something like that. Actually, I think we'd very much like you to go around our little fleet and improve everyone's firepower. Yes? No?" She looked at Marc.

DuQuesne thought a moment. "Yeah, I think so. Fact is that we'll need every edge we can get when—not if—the Molothos get here."

Simon winced. "I really wish I didn't have to think about that. But no point in evading it. Yes, if you authorize it, Ariane, I will spend time while you're gone upgrading the weapons."

"I wonder if I might be able to do it too," DuQuesne said slowly.

Simon looked uncertain, then suddenly nodded, white hair shifting like a curtain. "You know, I hadn't *thought* about that, but yes, you have shown some odd capabilities—and around the same time. The way you handled the weapons?"

"Cross-connecting them in a way that even Orphan hadn't figured out how to do? That's sure one of the things on my mind."

"Well, you'll have a chance to find out. Take a look at the one on *Zounin-Ginjou* and see if you can replicate it."

Ariane frowned. "Won't that be revealing something?"

DuQuesne thought a moment. "Not much. He knows I talk to Simon a lot, and so for all he knows, together we figured out what makes ours work and his fail. To an extent, he'd be right, too. And since we're heading out into the dark Deeps, making sure there's more firepower on our transport probably isn't a bad idea."

Another thought occurred to him. "You know, Ariane, Simon— Orphan clearly has some kind of theory about us. He's made some damn cryptic comments from time to time, and the *way* he looks at us—"

"You're right, Marc," Simon said. "I remember during the battle, he said something to the effect that he had become used to being surprised by us, and that the recent events confirmed a hypothesis he had formed."

Ariane nodded, thoughtfully. "He's said a few similar things to me. Maybe this is one of the things he will discuss with us when we're in the Deeps."

"Maybe," DuQuesne conceded. "Though that joker keeps *his* cards close to his vest. And he doesn't *wear* a vest. Still, if he's got an idea about us that could be useful, he'll *have* to tell it to us sooner or later if we're going to exploit it."

"Try nudging him about it," suggested Simon. "His reaction might at least tell us whether he *intends* to tell us. I would like to at least know that much."

"Why me?"

Ariane's lips quirked upward. "I should think that was obvious, Marc; he sees you as by far the most kindred spirit in the crew. He *likes* me, and respects me. He seems to feel the same way about Simon, and have a decent regard for the rest of our crew. But I think he finds that you and he have the most in common."

"Klono's . . . heh, never mind. All I can say is I hope I'm not *that* devious."

"For this next Challenge?" Ariane looked at him seriously. "I hope you're *more* devious. Because the Vengeance are one of the Great Factions, and they didn't get there by accident. So we can use all the 'devious' we can get."

True enough. "I'll admit I've been a little worried about that myself. They've got the resources and experience to basically get the absolute *best* for this Challenge, and Hyperion or no, gambling experience or no, that's gonna be hard to make up for when the other guy's probably been playing this game for years. This version of Arena Chance is actually *harder* for someone like me than a completely unfamiliar game would be, honestly."

Simon's eyebrows rose. "In what way? It would seem that *any* familiarity would be an advantage."

"Sure would. And that's the trap." He saw Ariane nodding. "*She* gets it. Thing is, any time it's *close* to something you know real, real well, it's blasted easy to find yourself thinking that it *is* that same thing, and then you make some choice that makes perfect sense for the game you know well, but is the *wrong* choice for the one you're playing now."

"Oh. Yes, I see. Rather like playing or humming a tune that is very much like one you have known from childhood; it is *too* easy to find yourself suddenly humming the childhood tune rather than the newer one."

"You got it." DuQuesne couldn't keep a grim tone from his own words. "Except that then, you just sound stupid. In this, I could end up giving away a world for a song."

Chapter 8

"Boy, Tunuvun," Wu Kung said, "This is going to be *fun!*" He couldn't keep from bouncing up and down on his feet, staring out at what Ariane had pronounced in disbelief to be "a triathlon on full enhancers!"

He and Tunuvun stood at the top of a mountain—that ended abruptly at a wall behind them!—and looked out upon a racecourse that could only be *possible* in a place like the Arena. *Or,* he noted with a momentary pang of sadness, *at home.* The bittersweet news DuQuesne had given him resonated with that thought. *Sanzo is alive, but it's the Sanzo I first met. And my firstborn, Jing . . . gone.* Fury started to rise, but he controlled it. *Jai and Gen, at least, are still there. Sha Wujing. Cho Hakkai. Liu Yan. Not all is lost, not all are gone.* And that was better news, far better, than he had feared. He looked out again, and gazed upon that wondrous course, imagined his friends with him, and finally smiled again, feeling the bounce returning to his step.

The cool, pine-scented forest below extended down the mountainside for a kilometer or two; then a sheer cliff descended—for a distance he couldn't see on this side, but guessed it had to be several hundred meters—to a relatively level, grassy plain another couple of kilometers; without transition, there was suddenly empty space, filled with drifting rocks and moving dots that Wu's more-than-human eyes could resolve into flying creatures he remembered from his prior adventure in the Arena. *No-gravity space, then.* On the other side, a vast forest, a jungle of massive and alien-looking trees, followed by a strip of gray-gold desert sands, a glittering stretch of water, another wide gap of no-gravity, shining white of polar ice with the dull green-gray of tundra interspersed, a mass of tumbled terrain like some of the worst badlands Wu had ever seen with tangled forest sandwiched in between, and finally a massive building of some sort.

He couldn't be sure without being able to see into the building, but he *thought* that if everything else was the way it looked, he could probably traverse the whole thing in less than an hour if DuQuesne let him go all-out, but DuQuesne had taken him aside just before they came:

"Listen, Wu. We're going to try to run this race—and win it—without showing off. That means you can show everything you let Orphan see, and not one bit more. That'll be *more* than enough to impress the hell out of them, and it's better than anything Tunuvun should have—right?"

"Right. I don't think he was holding anything back that time on the docks, and I was." He still felt a little guilty about that—not doing his best in a fight was *hard*.

"Okay. That means we *should* be able to do this straight. But *if*—and I *mean* 'if,' Wu—I decide we *do* need to go all-out, then I will tell you. You understand? No matter *how* bad you think things are going, you wait for *me* to call it."

He'd nodded. There weren't many people he'd take that kind of talk from, but DuQuesne was one. "My word on it, DuQuesne. I'll play the game exactly your way."

So it looked like this course was going to take a lot longer than an hour. A *lot* longer. Still, it *would* be fun. He'd also *stuffed* himself last night, causing the others to stare incredulously at the amount of food he put away, which meant that the special reserves the Hyperion designers had built into him were now topped off; if DuQuesne *did* ask him to go all-out, he would be ready to match what he'd done the day Hyperion fell, but for a much brighter cause.

Tunuvun looked over to him; he could smell an effort to be cheerful. "Indeed, it seems to be a very entertaining course. Forgive me if I cannot quite enjoy it as I should."

I'm so stupid sometimes. He can't have fun with this with his people's freedom and rights at stake. Wu bowed and extended a hand. "I am sorry, Tunuvun. Of course you can't. But we will both do our best, and—Heavens willing—I will win for you."

"See that you do. But . . ." Tunuvun took his hand and shook it in human fashion. ". . . enjoy the course for both of us, then."

He laughed, showing his fangs. "I will, I promise!"

"Racers," the quiet yet powerful voice of the Arena said, "your attention please. The rules of this race are simple, but it is important that you adhere to them.

"Your two courses will often be closely parallel; upon occasion, the courses will cross or temporarily become one. The course for each is indicated by the green sparks for Sun Wu Kung of Humanity," a line of brilliant emerald points of light suddenly appeared and streaked away down the mountain, a dotted line of pinpoint suns, "and by red sparks for Tunuvun of the Genasi." The second line blazed its way down the mountain, a trail of ruby fires.

"These markers are not visible to any creatures who might be on the course, only to the participants and those observing this Challenge," the Arena continued. "The racers may not directly interfere in each other's performance: that is, there may be no physical contact between the racers, they may not throw, kick, or otherwise propel any materials, objects, or other interfering phenomena directly at their opponent.

"Racers may, however, indirectly interfere in the performance of their opponents, by creating obstacles ahead of them or otherwise causing something to indirectly interfere in the racer's performance."

So I can't throw sticks at Tunuvun, but I could drop a tree on the path in front of him.

"If an obstacle causes a racer to leave the path, they must return to the path as near as practically possible to the point of departure. This return shall *not* cause a racer to have to repeat a given obstacle; for example, if a racer falls into a river and is swept downstream, they may return to their path on the opposite side of the river so that they do not need to cross the river again."

A line of white dots appeared next to each racer's path. "These white sparks will appear if a racer is significantly off their course, and will lead them back to the appropriate point to rejoin the race. The other racer cannot see these sparks.

"From the racers' points of view, the race—and the Challenge—is completed when either one racer crosses the finish line, housed in the building visible to the west, or one racer is unable to continue the race for any reason. Are these rules understood, racers?"

"Yes, Arena," he responded, hearing the words echoed by Tunuvun. *"Unable to continue" covers the fact that some of the obstacles could break legs . . . or necks. This isn't a safe little game.* He smiled to himself. *Which is what makes it* really *fun!*

"We proceed to the rules pertaining to the Players. Players of Chance, please verify that you can communicate with your racers."

Seemingly from right next to his ear, DuQuesne's voice spoke. "You hearing me, Wu?"

"Loud and clear, DuQuesne!" Nearby, he heard a muttered response from Tunuvun to his unseen handler.

"The Players are allowed to communicate with their racers at will. They may give encouragement, and general guidance, but may make no specific suggestions—for example, they could suggest 'You are ahead, try to slow the other person down,' but not 'See that tree ahead? The branch is rotten, drop it down behind you.' They may, however, give specific warning of an obstacle that they are deploying, to allow their racer to avoid it while the competitor does not."

"Got it," DuQuesne said; Byto Kalan, the Dujuin player for the Vengeance, said something similar.

"You will each begin with ten Obstacle points to be used for wagering or for placing obstacles in the way of the other side's racer. The use of Obstacle points is only allowed on the player's turn. Additional Obstacle points will accrue from random chance of the Draw die, for particular combinations of cards, and of course from winning a play, which gives the winner all points bet on that play. Prices for specific Obstacles will be instantly provided to the Player upon consideration of the Obstacle; neither the other Player nor any spectators will be able to see the contemplated Obstacle or the price.

"If at any time a Player has no Obstacle points, they may request a Stake; there are three Stakes available to each player, each for ten Obstacle points. If a Player has no Obstacle points, no bets can be made on a given play; if that Player has no remaining Stake opportunities, they will forfeit the game regardless of the condition of the race at that time."

Wu did *not* like that one. Sure, DuQuesne wasn't likely to have luck *that* bad, but bad luck *could* strike anyone, and the idea that Wu could run the best race ever and still lose the Challenge . . . sucked.

"Each Player also has three Freezes—the ability to put the race on hold while they think about an option, plan a strategy, and so on. Each Freeze lasts one minute and fourteen seconds of Player time; the Racers will not notice anything."

It was hard to imagine being frozen in time like that, but it wasn't his problem. He just had to race.

"Do both Players understand the selected version of Arena Chance, or should the rules be reviewed?"

Please *don't do that now, I will end up going to sleep.*

"I'm good," DuQuesne said.

"I am thoroughly familiar with this variant of Arena Chance," Byto Kalan said.

Wu couldn't have said he was *entirely* familiar with it, even though he'd played a bit. It really was rather like one of the variants of poker that DuQuesne and Giles had taught him, with the various unusual combinations of cards being ranked mainly due to how rare they were, and two chances to add or discard cards in between betting, but there was also the Draw die, which could have a lot of random effects on play, and he had no idea how that changed proper play. But as long as DuQuesne had it firmly in mind, that was another thing that didn't matter.

"Racers, ready yourselves. This Challenge will begin in ten minutes."

Wu Kung settled into a long-familiar stretching routine. *Slowly prepare the body for the race or the war. Stretch the muscles in careful sequence, to the right degree, a carefully building progression . . .*

As he stretched, a green comm-ball materialized. "Good luck, Wu," said Maria-Susanna's voice.

Just the voice *hurt*. He had read what she had done since the Fall of Hyperion, and Wu just could not understand it. She had been so kind, so gentle. She still *sounded* as kind and gentle. Yet she had killed so many. "You are with the Vengeance. Why wish *me* luck?"

The laugh was sad. "Oh, Wu. I don't have anything against these poor people trying to get recognition—I *applaud* them. That's really why I refused to take the Vengeance's side—though the reason I told them was that I thought DuQuesne's familiarity with me would give him an advantage, and that I was—honestly!—too fond of you to really want to go all out to defeat you. So good luck."

"Thank you," he said after a moment. It still hurt to talk to her, but it would hurt more to ignore her. *Maybe she can still be saved. DuQuesne doesn't think so, but . . . he's been wrong before. Not often . . . but he has.*

A few more comm-balls and well-wishers, the most emphatic being Ariane herself. "Run Tunuvun into the *ground*, Wu," she said.

"Do the best I'm allowed," he said, grinning widely. He stood up slowly. *A few seconds more.*

The Arena's voice spoke again. "Racers, take your places. Players, prepare for first cards. The Challenge between the Genasi and the Vengeance begins in five . . . four . . . three . . . two . . . one . . . GO!"

Sun Wu Kung *leapt* from the starting line, a flying jump that would have cleared two meters in height on the level. Tunuvun, seized by the same impulse, gave a matching jump, and the two landed at the same moment, more than thirty meters downhill from the start point, and practically *flew* down the hill, Wu Kung's longer legs moving just slightly less quickly than Tunuvun's shorter strides, so the two racers remained neck-and-neck.

Match him for a while, make sure I know where I stand with him. I don't think *he was holding back in that fight, but I could be wrong. He might have wanted to hide some of what he could do from me.*

Faintly, in his ear, he could hear, "First cards dealt. Dealing outer show cards." *Their game's begun. Obstacles could start showing up at any time.*

The pine woods were getting thicker, so Wu Kung took to the trees directly, bounding from one to the next, running along branches as though they were level ground. He heard and, from the corner of his eye, saw Tunuvun making similar maneuvers. *He's maybe not* quite *as good as me, or as the "me" I'm being now, in the trees, but I'll bet that's because he evolved for no gravity. Those two null-g parts of the course will be his best.*

Without warning, one of the branches beneath Tunuvun gave way, sending him dropping towards the forest floor. A grunt of distant satisfaction told him that had been DuQuesne's doing. *Time to start opening up a little distance.* While he might have wanted to keep it closer for the sake of making the race look more exciting, Tunuvun wouldn't thank him for the added worry.

The Hyperion Monkey King kicked off his current tree and practically *flew* through the next three, now moving at a speed that only his friends—and Orphan—had ever seen before. From all around he heard indrawn breaths and murmurs. *Ha! They are letting us hear something of the crowd's reactions! That is fun too!*

He broke out of the woods, saw the edge of the cliff a hundred meters ahead. Behind him, Tunuvun's swift movement was audible, trailing by several dozen meters. Wu Kung turned, back to the cliff, dug in his claws, and felt the ground disappear from under his feet *just* as he was stopping, letting his clawed hands drop securely to the edge.

The cliff below was solid basalt, rough but still vertical—a quite noticeable challenge for anyone. But with ring-carbon reinforced claws he rammed ten anchors home into the stone and began swiftly clambering down, a cat descending a four-hundred-meter scratching post.

Wow! Tunuvun's just about keeping up! His claws must be like mine! He remembered the battle in the sky. *Natural ring-carbon must be in a lot of Arena native species. No wonder he's so tough!*

Still, Tunuvun was behind; he had to do more than just "keep up", and since they both knew that the luck of obstacles could turn at any time, and that—at least as far as Tunuvun was concerned—they were nearly evenly matched, neither could afford to play too much of a long game. *He's probably not going to push it here on the cliff, but at the bottom . . .*

As he thought that, a hundred meters from the bottom, an entire section of the cliff face suddenly cracked, and Wu Kung found himself flailing in midair, plummeting towards the ground below. *Well, at least I'll get there faster,* he thought, even as he kicked off from one of the fragments, bouncing back towards the cliff face. His claws dug in, ripped free; he spun in midair, tried to reach the cliff again, *I need to slow down—*

WHAM!

To Wu's groggy astonishment, he'd actually lost a second or two; he could hear Tunuvun's feet dashing madly away across the plain. "Wu! Wu, you okay?"

"That *hurt*, DuQuesne. But I am all right," he said, hearing murmurs of astonishment from the audience as he rose and sprinted after Tunuvun.

"Thank our Dujuin friend for that one."

"I like Tunuvun, but could you drop him in a pit for me?"

"As soon as I get the points, I'll slow him down, I guarantee it." The plains were streaming by now, the green-gold waving grass-like plants hissing like a waterfall of sand as he tore through them.

It suddenly dawned on Wu that they were actually more handicapped than their opposition. *We don't want to hurt Tunuvun. Certainly don't want to take a chance on crippling or killing him. But that obstacle showed that Byto and the Vengeance don't have that problem with* me.

Halfway across the plains now, and he'd closed the distance so that Tunuvun and he were once more even, racing up their lines of airborne sparks in arrow-straight paths.

It was then that a pack of scale-armored, fanged creatures like a cross between a small dragon, a lion, and an eagle erupted from the underbrush and attacked.

Even as he dodged, blocked, and flipped, he realized that Tunuvun was speeding away, unimpeded. *Another obstacle!*

There were only twelve of the creatures, so it didn't take *too* long to deal with them, but even so, Tunuvun was a hundred and fifty meters ahead now.

Wu Kung gave vent to multiple curses and sprinted forward hard. He was very, *very* tempted to start letting himself really go, but he remembered DuQuesne's emphatic instructions. *I gave him my word. I can't do that unless he gives permission.*

But even at the level he *was* allowed, he was still faster. A hundred fifty meters was a long lead in a short race, but this was not a short race and most of it was still ahead.

First no-gravity section coming up, though. I'll have to push what I'm allowed to make up distance there; that's where Tunuvun's got to be at his best.

They leapt from the plains into the void, Tunuvun first and Wu trailing by eighty-seven meters, and immediately Wu could tell he'd been right. The tiny white-and-purple Genasi bounded from one floating rock to the next, spun and smacked aside an encroaching *zikki*, and skittered around a hundred-meter-wide boulder at lightning speed, as effortlessly as ordinary people might walk through a light crowd.

Still, I am the Monkey King*, and this is the kind of thing* I *do, too!*

He laughed as he bounded weightlessly through space, ricocheting from stones and outraged inhabitants with reckless abandon. *Have to keep closing the distance!* He was only fifteen meters, more or less, behind Tunuvun now, three-quarters of the way across this weightless space, and—

He saw it out of the corner of his eye, rapid movement all *down* relative to the fixed parts of the course, and there it was, a waterfall of dust and rocks incalculably high, driving down to unguessable depths. *"Hells of boiling souls!"* he cursed, as the Skyfall roared towards him. "DuQuesne!"

"Hang on, Wu—it's about four hundred meters thick!"

Even as the Skyfall reached Wu, he heard the Arena's distant, dispassionate voice: "Warning to Player DuQuesne: do not provide precise guidance. First of three allowed warnings."

Wu found himself scrambling for dear life, jumping from one tumbling fragment to the next, evading randomly crashing boulders, knowing that he was caught in the associated gravity field and thus dropping down, down, down even though he fought desperately to stay at least somewhat level.

He burst from the Skyfall finally, blood trickling from a dozen small wounds. "What in the name of . . . of *Hyperion* is going on?" he demanded plaintively. Tunuvun had disappeared over the edge into the forest, and with all the speed he dared muster Wu knew he was going to be at least three hundred fifty meters behind, maybe as much as five hundred—half a kilometer down.

Tunuvun was far in the lead of a race he must not win . . . and dared not lose.

Chapter 9

"Draw two," DuQuesne said, evaluating his cards. *Nothing impressive in this hand. I need a break.*

The two cards passed to him turned out to be a Sky Gate and a Nexus Gateway. *With the Inner Gateway and Outer Gate I have, that at least makes a decent run.* "Bet five points," he said, not without trepidation. *That's half of what I've got left.*

He could see Orphan, absently stroking his high head-crest in a nervous fashion, sitting near Ariane; Laila Canning sat on his other side, with Simon on Ariane's left. The Players themselves were in the center of a large circular amphitheatre—maybe even the same one that Ariane and Amas-Garao had dueled in—and around them was a ghostly image of the racing course.

Unlike the racers, DuQuesne could also see inside the huge final building, which contained a winding maze that was at least three kilometers long—a lot more of the race than the building's external appearance would imply. *Have to mention that to Wu—without being specific, of course.*

"Match five points," Byto said in his gravelly, deep voice. "Rolling draw die."

The eight-sided die rattled across the table, to come up with a single-line symbol. *Damn! That's the fourth time!*

"Line of Transition," the Arena announced. "Accrue two more Obstacle points and may draw up to three cards."

Byto's gained points almost every play so far, and I've barely stayed even. DuQuesne saw his opponent choose to take three cards. *At least that means his hand wasn't that strong—*

The twitch Byto gave was incredibly subtle, but DuQuesne's Hyperion-built senses picked up on it. *Damn. He's got something now.* As he'd delved deeper into the game, it had become clear it was indeed more like a mash-up of three or four games, ranging from standard poker to collectible card duel games, but that wasn't really helping. There were more ways to win, or lose, and different types of winning plays or hands.

Wu Kung and Tunuvun were dashing through the forest now, the Genasi racer considerably ahead of Wu—and, DuQuesne saw, was taking advantage of the lead to drop large tree branches across his competitor's path. *If my luck doesn't turn . . .*

He rolled the Draw die; it came up as *Emergent*, which at least let him draw three like his opponent. He decided to only take two. *Okay, that makes a Gateway run and Dual Shadeweavers, that's not a bad hand. Still . . .*"Bet three points."

Byto rocked his head from side to side, rolled, drew two cards, discarded two into the dump, and matched the bet, spreading out his cards. DuQuesne also saw him muttering instructions to Tunuvun. *Can't hear them, of course, any more than he can hear what I say to Wu.*

Huh. I don't see any triples or doubles, or a run of . . .

The murmuring from the crowd started just before it dawned on DuQuesne. "Hand of Arena," the Arena announced. Every one of Byto's cards was different, and represented one of the major facets of the Arena, including the Arena card itself as the high card. It was technically a *losing* hand in Arena Challenge—but in a Racing Challenge such a hand gained the player twenty Obstacle points. Since the total bet on the hand by Byto had been eight points, this was a big win overall for him.

On the positive side, DuQuesne was at least now up by eight points, and it would also be his turn first on this play. Still . . . "Wu," he said.

"Yes, DuQuesne?"

"Open it up just a hair. You're way back and it's not getting any easier from here on out. By the way, the course in that building is a lot bigger than it looks." That should be sufficiently nonspecific.

Apparently he was right, because the Arena said nothing, as Wu answered, "Okay, I'm stretching my legs a little. But only a little, right?"

"Right. Not *quite* ready to hit the panic button."

* * *

The murmurs rippled around the stadium again, with Ariane showing a hint of a smile instead of concern as Wu Kung raced along the branches of the network-like trees, ducking *under* the branches to evade the obstacles Tunuvun had dropped. He was closing the distance, slowly but surely, between him and his opponent.

DuQuesne and Byto finished the next play as Wu Kung burst from the forest and began racing across gray-golden desert sands, pursuing the faint dust trail that showed where Tunuvun was scrambling like a lizard ahead of him. "I'm getting closer, DuQuesne. Two hundred thirty meters, I think. Still keep going at this speed?" Wu didn't even sound winded yet, which—if anyone other than DuQuesne could have heard it—might have been a dead giveaway about how much Wu was holding back.

"Throttle it back just a hair, to the top we agreed on before. You'll still catch him about the time you guys hit the water, I think."

This time Byto obviously thought he had something, but DuQuesne knew he had a major hand, too. *Arena card for me. Only two in circulation, and the one he had is still going to be in the dump, but more importantly I've got three Faction Leader cards—and not small ones, either. Vengeance, Molothos, and Blessed—only two of each of those in circulation, too. The Arena can be counted as a Faction, a Construct, or a Leader, so that gives me almost a Great Leader Run, which is something close to a Royal Straight Flush. Plus with two Spheres in my show cards and the single Sphere in my hand I've got a triple.*

"Bet eight," he said. Byto matched him without a pause, rolled, got to draw one card. Again Byto tensed in that way that signaled he thought he had something big. *But by now he might guess I've started reading him and be trying to use his tell to throw me off. Hard to know if he realizes what his tell is; maybe no one but a Hyperion would notice it.*

Byto glanced up, then nodded. "Bet eight."

Ow. That's a big bite. Must be confident. DuQuesne wasn't going to yield this one that easily, so he matched and rolled the die. *Ha! Finally luck's turning my way! Line of Transition for me. Two more points and I get to draw up to three. Real good chance of drawing at least* some *Faction Leader in that, even if not a Great Faction. Time for me to make up some ground too.* "Draw three."

Staring at him from the middle of the two new cards was *Faction Leader: Tantimorcan. Not all Great Factions, but definitely a very high Leader Run . . . and I've got another Sphere, too!* He dumped one of the draw cards—a Sky Gate—and also dumped the Challenge card from his show cards, replacing it with the Tantimorcan Leader card. *I've got sixteen points left. This is a huge hand, though.* "Bet ten."

Byto looked up at him, expression on the rhinoceros-like face unreadable. "Match and increase six."

That's the most allowed—he can't raise beyond what I can match! "Are you *sure* you want to do that, Byto?" he asked, levelly.

The other hesitated only a fraction, then waggled his ears in what was clearly assent. "Match and increase six."

Too late to bail now. Okay, that's the sunk cost fallacy, but still . . . "Match with six. Beat this: Leader Run, Arena high, and a Quadruple Sphere," he said, laying down his cards.

Murmurs chased themselves around the audience; Byto sat back slightly, surprised. "Indeed an impressive hand," he said. "And an interesting coincidence." He spread out his hand. "Great Leader Run, with Quadruple Challenges."

DuQuesne stared in momentary shock. He couldn't even think of an appropriate curse as his count of Obstacle points went to zero. Out of the corner of his eye, he noted that Orphan looked, if anything, *more* shocked. *Wonder why* that *is. Probably the whole improbability of the thing; chances of* both *of us getting all those same cards is ridiculously low. But this is really bad; I'm broke and he's thirty-two points up in one play.* "Arena, I need my first stake," he said, and saw ten points appear in his account.

I've really got to win the next plays. At least I've got a good read on his style, his tells—I don't think he knows I can read them—and I know what's in the dump and how fast it recirculates. There's still time.

But Wu, nearing the edge of the desert, suddenly vanished into the sand. "DuQuesne! Dry quicksand! This really annoys me!" The image showed Wu now effectively *swimming* through the sand, looking for an edge where it turned solid enough to burrow upwards. *Ordinary human wouldn't stand a chance, really, but Wu and Tunuvun ain't ordinary in any sense of the word.* Still, that was dead-slow movement compared to Tunuvun, who was now speeding through the water part of the course, his tail lashing back and forth and helping propel him rapidly through the water. *Looks like . . . it is! That damn tail actually shifted shape, it's got fins top and bottom!*

That was going to be too much of a pain. DuQuesne used all ten of his points to have a bunch of predators converge on Tunuvun, letting the Arena give him another ten stake. *If I lose so badly again that I need the* third *stake, it's not going to matter much that I used up the first this way.*

Wu burst from the sands and dove into the water ten seconds before Tunuvun finished dispatching his adversaries. Wu had only lost thirty meters, but it was clear he was going to lose more for the rest of the swim; Tunuvun was just too well adapted for swimming. "DuQuesne . . ." Wu murmured pleadingly.

"Just a bit. Like you did before."

That didn't *completely* keep him from losing ground, but once they hit the second no-gravity section Wu started eating up the space between the two . . . until an unexpected flurry of *zikki* intercepted him in mid-leap. Wu managed to beat them down with his staff and claws (since no inter-competitor combat was allowed, apparently the Arena didn't object to either Wu's staff or the chain-link belts that Tunuvun wore), but by that time Tunuvun was scrambling across the ice and tundra, seven hundred meters and more ahead of Wu.

And it kept *happening.* Every good hand DuQuesne got, somehow Byto had a better one. He couldn't bluff or trick his opponent. *Reading a guy's tells doesn't help much when all it tells you is that he's going to hand you your head on a platter.*

At the same time—ominously—Byto had stopped throwing obstacles at Wu. Wu was slowly making up ground, but by that time it was looking *very* grim. Wu was almost a full kilometer back and the two were toiling their way across the badlands, with Tunuvun—wearing a desperately focused, yet despairing expression—about to enter the immense building for the final stretch.

"I am very much afraid," he heard Orphan say, "that our friend is going to lose."

DuQuesne looked up, and finally grinned. "That would be a really bad bet to make." He lowered his voice—even though he didn't need to. "Wu, this guy's kicking my ass, luck's on his side every moment. So it's time to stop playing around."

"You *mean* it?" He heard the excited tension in his friend's voice, and chuckled.

"I mean it, Wu. Go, Wu, GO! Go all-out and show them what Sun Wu Kung can do!"

Wu laughed aloud with delight, and there was suddenly a murmur, a rumble, a *roar* from the crowd, an outcry of stunned disbelief as the Hyperion Monkey King *tore* his way across the remaining badlands at a speed that made Tunuvun seem to be standing still. Ariane's jaw dropped, and then she began clapping furiously, the other members of Humanity joining her.

Byto made a noise that DuQuesne was *sure* was something obscene, then turned his head to his cards.

But, DuQuesne noticed with concern, he still did not call for a single obstacle.

The building-maze was now visible to everyone, and Tunuvun sped through corridors, along perilous cables suspended over drops, through narrow tunnels, always at speeds to put a human runner to shame. But behind him Wu Kung burst through the entrance and ran so fast that as he turned a corner of a corridor he was running on the *wall*, then bounding back and forth between the walls enclosing an otherwise empty space, spurning the tightrope there as too trivially easy, satisfying the Arena's requirements by constantly re-crossing the path of green sparks.

DuQuesne made another play, lost, saw his last stake appear in his account. *I have no idea how many points Byto has now.* He heard an incomprehensible mutter, saw Tunuvun stiffen and re-double his efforts, leaping from isolated pillar to pillar in yet another room; but halfway across, Wu Kung streaked into view, jumping not from one pillar to the next but clearing half a *dozen* pillars in a single impossible jump, then another and another, passing Tunuvun as both reached the far side of the room.

The Genasi leaned forward and, somehow, wrung another burst of speed from what had seemed to be his ultimate effort, but he was still falling behind at a ludicrous pace. Wu was ahead by a hundred meters, two hundred, four hundred, outdistancing his opponent effortlessly, closing in on the final room: a huge cylindrical room, two hundred meters across with two narrow golden paths leading to the white-sparkling finish line; twenty meters below the paths was a circular platform a hundred fifty meters across, and below that the room dropped away immeasurably.

And then he heard Byto say "Arena, I request my first stake."

Holy Mother of God. That means he's just—

As Wu Kung entered and began the final sprint, the golden path *dissolved* beneath him, sending him plummeting to the flat, silvery platform below. Even as he struck, four shapes materialized at the cardinal points of the circular floor, four shapes clad in unmistakable armor: Adjudicators.

"We have lost," Orphan said quietly.

Chapter 10

Wu Kung landed in a crouch-and-roll, came to his feet in the precise center of the platform, saw the figures—one Dujuin rhino-like creature, two Daalasan like armored frog-men, and one spidery Milluk in the silvery Arena armor—appear from nothing around him. *Adjudicators! The Arena's own peacekeepers!*

Then he heard Orphan's quiet despair, and rose to his feet, grinning savagely, baring his fangs to the Adjudicators as they raised their own weapons. "I gave my *word* to Tunuvun and Ariane that I *would* win this," he said, and his own speech echoed across the chamber and was repeated throughout the great amphitheatre beyond, its murmurs resonating back to his own ears. "And Sun Wu Kung has *never* broken his word!"

He leapt towards the Milluk, and suddenly felt as though the air itself had condensed, become a mud-thick sludge that dragged at his limbs. *A trap, like the hidden swamp of Numachi no O, the Kappa King!*

This would make it a *challenge!*

Now he dug deep into his reserves, feeling strength and speed *flooding* into him as he unleashed everything. *DuQuesne said I didn't have to hold back!* With a lunge he sped towards the Milluk, ducking under a bolt of energy from the Duijin and outdistancing the two Daaalasan. Two of the Milluk's legs crossed, blocking his strike, but the creature was driven back almost a full meter, approaching the edge of the suspended floor.

But the others were closing now, their weapons shimmering with energies he was sure were meant to stun and disable their foes on contact. *But I still have Ruyi Jingu Bang!*

He spun about, whirling the great red-enameled, gold-ended staff in a blur that made the speed of the Adjudicators sluggish, parrying strikes of three of the four. The fourth, a narrow-pointed trident, slid past his guard and hammered directly into his chest.

The impact was startling, a strength he hadn't felt in years except sparring with DuQuesne. *These Adjudicators are* good.

The field did not seem to impede him skidding across the floor, tumbling towards the opposite side, yet it *did* slow his arms as they extended out, as his feet's claws reached out and dug, and he saw drops of blood trailing in the air, slowly falling to his perceptions as he sought to stop his swift career towards the precipice. *It works against me, and only against me.*

Claws struck and gripped the platform surface, sending a shrill, ear-piercing shriek like a thousand nails drawn across a thousand blackboards, slowing his progress *just* enough. He rebounded from his crouch, met the two frog-like Adjudicators halfway across the platform, moving through the impeding field as though it were thin air, and heard the gasps finally echoing from the unseen audience, the rustle of them slowly, slowly rising to their feet, leaning against the spectator rails, as they realized something extraordinary was playing out before them.

In the distance he could hear feet running, closing in, and knew that he didn't have long before Tunuvun arrived.

Ruyi Jingu Bang ducked down and then up, clotheslining both Daalasan beneath their armored chins. Wu Kung pressed forward, the impact and Wu's strength tearing the two Adjudicators from their feet, dragging them forward with the Hyperion Monkey King and forcing both the Milluk and the Dujuin to brace for collision. Wu braked, flipped up, and came down, aiming a blow for a precise point on the Milluk's armor. *If I guess its anatomy right . . .*

The creature tried to turn, even as it fended off the momentarily incapacitated Daalasan, but it was just one hair too slow. The golden ball on the end of the Monkey King's staff crashed into its armored carapace with enough force to dent both the armor and the golden ball—a ball made of ring-carbon composite. The creature spasmed, legs clenching inward like a stunned spider, and fell, rolling back and plummeting into the unguessable void below.

Now Wu Kung faced the three remaining Adjudicators and matched staff and feet and fists with their weapons, limbs, and armor. A blaze of blue energy from a silver bludgeon made his limbs momentarily seize up, and the Duijin took the opening, grabbed him, slammed him with groundshaking force into the shining platform, then lifted him to hurl him into space.

But Wu Kung's tail seized the rhinoceros-like head about the neck, used the power of its own throw to jerk it savagely forward, then Wu flipped around and used a double-heel kick to send it spinning helplessly into the void.

Two left, and these worked as a team, taking him deadly seriously; he could smell they knew these victories were no flukes, no lucky accidents; disbelief rose high, almost as high as determination in their scents, disbelief that he could move as he did in their field of solidified air. Tunuvun's footsteps were closer now, approaching the entrance and the final path to victory.

The Daalasan pursued him relentlessly, pushing their own speed and strength—obviously boosted by the Arena—to match his own. But strength and speed were only as good as the *skill* to use them, and was he not Sun Wu Kung, the Great Sage Equal of Heaven? Wu *laughed*, laughed at the sheer joy of finally, *finally* finding an opponent in this world to test him to the limits, even as the two at last passed his guard with sheer determination and strength to momentarily match his skill and guile, striking his head with force enough to snap it around, blood spraying from his mouth, pain shocking, hot and urgent as the footsteps that were approaching above.

But he tumbled away, a fall turned into a handspring, a lightning-fast succession of somersaulting leaps that sent him springing into space, rebounding off the far wall, and diving back, bouncing from the floor to sweep one frog-like creature's feet from beneath it and then grappling with the other, gritting his teeth and ignoring the shocking pain as he grasped the energy-charged staff and tore it from the Adjudicator's shocked grasp, hurled it away, and then sent the third Adjudicator plummeting after his weapon.

Above, Tunuvun's feet were on the final path, sprinting at full speed across the gap, as Wu faced the last Adjudicator. With none of his allies to concern him, the Daalasan unleashed a torrent of electrical bolts, a network of destruction and shock that should be impassable, invincible.

But Wu could *see* the writhing of the bolts, follow the Daalasan's intent, his weaving of his tapestry of thunderbolts, and duck under one, leapt through a hole, brushed off the cramping shock of one bolt, and brought down Ruyi Jingu Bang to be parried at the last second by the wide-eyed Adjudicator. The roar of the crowd, distant though it was, was still nigh-deafening, and Wu strained to hear the final footsteps above, charging hopelessly towards the goal that honor demanded Tunuvun reach and his people prayed he would not.

Five seconds, he thought as a machine-gun-fast exchange of staves ringing against each other sent both of them staggering back for an instant. *Four seconds,* and the Adjudicator fired a wide-bore blast of force that would have sent Wu hurtling away into space had he not read that motion at the last possible moment, tumbled to the side. *Three,* and he retaliated, knocked the Adjudicator's staff aside and rammed his elbow home at a point just below the throat that stunned the creature. *Two seconds,* and the Adjudicator tumbled limply away and slid over the edge as Wu Kung turned, judging distances, seeing Tunuvun only a scant few meters from the far doorway and the finish line.

One second, and the crowd had gone silent, breaths and movements, even *thoughts* being held as the final moment of the race had come; Wu shouted the command, and Ruyi Jingu Bang *extended,* doubling its length in the blink of an eye, catapulting him up to the doorway at the very instant Tunuvun reached his, and past it, over, through, breaking the white-sparkling line of victory.

Chapter 11

Even as Wu crossed the finish line, he was suddenly *there* in front of Ariane, skidding to a halt not three meters from the table at which DuQuesne and his opponent were seated, surrounded by rank upon rank of spectators, silent, staring, frozen in disbelief and shock. Even though she had been warned, Ariane was herself still in a state of utter awe. *DuQuesne had said Wu was better than him. But this . . .*

And then the silence broke and a roar of applause, of furious curses and mighty cheers, broke over the Arena like a wave. Tunuvun caught up Wu Kung in an embrace that must have made even ring-carbon supported ribs creak, and his words were incoherent but needed no translation to hear the joy and gratitude.

Orphan was moving forward along with Ariane, and she saw his body's pose echoed a new emotion: *vindication.*

Wu escaped Tunuvun's grasp only to be swept into a bear-hug of victory by DuQuesne. "Dammit, Wu, you scared the crap out of me! Don't *ever* cut it that fine again!"

The Hyperion Monkey King was grinning, blood trickling from the corner of his mouth. "Those Adjudicators were not playing, DuQuesne! I really had to *work*! It was fun! Lots of fun!"

"It was a most . . . *artistic* finish, Sun Wu Kung," Orphan said, with a full pushup-bow. "Such a victory will be remembered long indeed."

That strange expression remained clear on the alien's face and form, and Ariane wondered what it meant. *You learned something there. You were looking utterly disappointed before, almost crushed really. Now you're riding high.* "Did you have a bet on this match?"

"Ahh, Captain Austin, I think you have come to know me well. Yes, a *most* interesting result, and most profitable as well." His black eyes seemed to twinkle at her. "But we shall speak of this later. It is time for the victor to receive his prize."

The crowd which had begun to flood the center of the ring fell back—or was gently *shoved* back by the glittering golden light of the Arena. **"Sun Wu Kung,"** the calm, quiet yet thunderous voice of the Arena began, **"Step—"**

"*We object!*"

The voice was the rough bass of Byto, echoed by the higher-pitched precision of none other than Selpa'A'At, who had reached the side of his selected champion. "Arena, we object!"

The entire crowd went deathly silent, and Ariane looked around nervously. "What's going on?"

Orphan was studying the Leader of the Vengeance with a clinical air. "While it is rare, it is possible for a Challenger, or Challenged, to object that some aspect of a Challenge was unfair or that somehow the result was rigged against them. These objections are rarely sustained—the Arena is, after all, the overseer of the Challenges—but it is their right and it *has* been known to work."

After a moment's silence, the Arena spoke. **"Your objection will be heard. However, only the relevant parties shall be involved in the discussion."**

Without even a blink, Ariane found herself in a smaller—but still huge—room with only DuQuesne, Wu Kung, Tunuvun, Byto, and Selpa. Even the far more experienced Leader of the Vengeance looked startled and disoriented. **"State your objection, Selpa'A'At of the Vengeance."**

Recovering from his startlement, Selpa lifted his manipulators and pointed to Wu Kung. "He has been enhanced to a degree that reveals malfeasance in this contest. Either a Shadeweaver or an Initiate Guide has provided him with capabilities beyond those allowed any of us in the Arena."

"You are saying I *cheated*?" Wu Kung began to lunge forward, tearing free of even DuQuesne's attempt to restrain him; without warning he was pinned to the ground by a force beyond even the Monkey King's ability to oppose.

"Violence will not be tolerated," the Arena said dispassionately.

"There was no cheating or manipulation, Leader of the Vengeance."

"Do you think *I* would have tolerated cheating?" Tunuvun demanded. "I do not know *how* my brother Wu Kung did what he did, but you—"

"Is it not true that the Shadeweavers and Initiate Guides have powers to sometimes conceal their work from even you, Arena?" Selpa said, ignoring Tunuvun's anger.

"It is," the Arena conceded calmly. **"But this is irrelevant to the current instance."**

"We *know* the rules, Arena! Any species may enhance its individuals only so far beyond their natural level! We have seen what the other humans can do, and there is no possible way in which this—"

DuQuesne raised his hand. "Hold on. Arena, there are . . . elements of our security here that may be relevant."

"Understood."

Tunuvun stopped and gave a narrow stare at DuQuesne, and then at Wu Kung, who met his gaze with a swift nod.

Ariane thought she was finally getting an inkling of what was going on—of what DuQuesne was implying—and it sent a chill down her spine . . . whether of fear or excitement, though, she wasn't sure.

"Show them."

Everyone suddenly stared at Wu Kung as he rose, slowly, from the floor, glaring furiously at Selpa and Byto. "Wu, are you sure—" DuQuesne began.

"*SHOW THEM!*" shouted Wu Kung. "Show them and bind them to never speak of it, but *show* them, so they will *know* that my honor remains!"

"Ariane Austin, do you give permission?"

Ariane looked from Wu to DuQuesne. "Marc? What am I giving permission *for?*"

Marc's brows were drawn down, but not in anger; in pained sympathy. "To show these two why Wu's so far beyond everyone. Why it's *right* that he is. To show them . . . Hyperion."

"What?" Ariane was stunned. "Arena? You could *do* that?"

"Yes."

She saw DuQuesne start to speak, then close his mouth with a visible effort. *He wants to say something more, but he's not. He's letting me figure it out on my own.* "Can and will you do as Wu asked? Show them, but not allow them to tell anyone else of secrets learned here, in any fashion?"

"Yes."

Great. Now I just have to decide what to do. "What happens if I say no? Selpa, you have the Arena's word that there was no cheating. You have Tunuvun, your selected champion, saying there was no cheating. You also have my word, if you care to take it, that there was none, and that the reason for Wu's abilities is a secret of Humanity's that just *knowing* is more valuable than I can easily imagine. Can you let it go at that?"

The Leader of the Vengeance swayed uncertainly on his spidery legs, looking even more like a harvestman than usual. "I wish I could, Captain Austin," he said finally, and the regret in his voice sounded genuine. "But this is an entire *Sphere* that hangs in the balance."

"One Sphere of many, which would go to a species that *deserves* one. You of *all* people should understand and sympathize with these people, the worst victims of the Arena's usual rules!" At her words, Tunuvun gave a complex look—both grateful and pained. *He hates having to have others stand up for his people . . . but also is grateful if anyone does.*

"I *do*." There was actual pain in Selpa's voice. "And were the Sphere truly mine to do with as I please, it would be different. But I *am* the Vengeance and I must do as the Vengeance requires. I cannot simply let this go on the word of the force that is—as it well knows—an agent of our Adversaries, and that of a still-new species which is not even fully understood. You must understand *this*, Captain Austin. I am sure you do."

She sighed. "I wish I didn't. But yes, I understand." She looked up—even though that was silly, the Arena wasn't really *in* any particular location. "Arena, if I refuse, what happens?"

"The results of the race will stand and the awarding of the prize will commence. There will be political and personal issues that you will be forced to confront due to this unusual event."

Translated: there'd be a lot of people who suspected some kind of underhanded trickery, maybe even, now that she thought of it, believe *she* had somehow managed to do it using the powers that were still locked away inside her. And Wu Kung, who was now staring at her with pleading emerald eyes wide, would forever be under a shadow of suspicion.

And for him, honor's one of the most important things in the universe.

It was that—and, possibly, a tiny bit of her own curiosity—that decided her. "All right, Wu. Arena, I give permission. With the restrictions mentioned, show us all the truth that Sun Wu Kung wants us to see."

"By your command."

Suddenly she floated in an omniscient void, looking down and through, as seven young people sat around a table, and joked and laughed, and one had an idea, and the others started discussing it . . .

. . . the same seven, and more people, both virtually and physically present, and the talk becoming something more serious, examining possibilities, designs which could be made, what could never be achieved, and what *might* be possible.

A shimmering tracery of girders, nanoassemblers and automated machines spinning a web, girdling it with cables and reinforcing ring-carbon, steel and aluminum and titanium, an immense shining colony . . .

And now images, so fast she could barely grasp them, yet could sense the *emotions*, the *impressions*, the *gestalt* that each image represented: a blond man in a gold uniform, stripes meaning "Captain" on his sleeve; the ebon skin and flowing indigo hair of Erision, facing the Unreality Effect for the first time; a familiar red-headed girl leaping from a building and gliding to safety on a parasail; DuQuesne staring up at the *Skylark* with his friend Richard Seaton; a tall, dark-haired figure in red and blue, streaking into the sky with a thought; her old virtual friend and first crush Tarellimade, staring through greenery at the woman he would one day marry; a blonde girl facing a monstrous vampire, wooden stake in her hand; Wu Kung, emerging from his sealed stone prison, startled to see a woman's face beneath the hat of a monk; and dozens, hundreds more, each a figure of legend large or small.

Then the impression of rage, of betrayal, and of shadow was cast over the brilliance, and the sound was of screaming and fighting, guns and swords and fists in the dark, and more flashes of single scenes: the red and blue standing back-to-back with one wearing red, white, and blue and holding a shield; the gold-uniformed man standing straight, holding a salute, as in the screen before him a woman, dark-haired, wearing a beret and eyepatch, saluted him, and then Maria-Susanna, screaming as she held the gold-uniformed man's body; eighteen men, all different yet, somehow, all the same, poised for combat around a strange blue box.

And still more; four children in strange costumes fighting alongside an assortment of gray-skinned, orange-horned creatures that were, themselves, children, and the blood all around was purple, blue, green, brown, and even red; Wu Kung staggering forward, drugged and slow, to be beaten down to the ground; a tall, slender man sitting in a Victorian dressing-gown, immobile, waiting in a cluttered apartment with a strange pattern of bullet-holes on the wall, an apartment that suddenly disappeared, and in that moment the man raised a pistol he held in one hand . . .

Without warning they were back, the room now too bright, sterile and cold, and the glory and madness and anguish of those two decades compressed into moments almost brought her to her knees; she swayed and was caught by DuQuesne, whose face was white, with tears leaving shining streaks behind. "Not again," he was murmuring. "Not again." Nearby, Tunuvun was half-collapsed, his gaze flickering incredulously between Wu Kung and DuQuesne.

Wu Kung was standing now, shaking, glaring at Selpa and Byto; the Leader of the Vengeance had sagged to the floor, his legs vibrating, and the rhinoceros-like Byto uttered a gasp of disbelief and pain. "What do you say *now*, Vengeance-ones? What of my honor *now*?"

Trembling still, Selpa rose and then bobbed before Sun Wu Kung. "I . . . retract the implication." The translated voice was raw with horror, disbelief, revulsion. "You . . . your people . . . this was *true*?"

"Every last bit," DuQuesne said, voice rough. "And you didn't see the half of it."

"Do you understand?" the Arena asked.

"Yes," Byto spoke finally, with the same disbelieving horror in his voice. "These . . . people. They . . . those *were* their native worlds. So whatever enhancements were made to them . . . were natural. By the Arena's own decrees, they retain all they were made with . . . for they did not know they were made, or even that there was another world in which they *could* have been made."

"**Then do you withdraw the objection?**"

Selpa rocked so his eyes stared full at DuQuesne and Wu Kung, horror still writ large in that pose. "Yes. It is withdrawn." The tilted gaze turned to her, and Selpa tightened with what had to be not merely horror but revulsion. *Why?*

Even as she asked the question, she understood. *Because now he knows that we were capable of creating Hyperion. He knows just how far human beings can go even in their own system, against their own species.*

"**You will retain this knowledge, Selpa'A'At and Byto of the Vengeance, as well as you, Tunuvun of the Genasi, but you will be incapable of conveying this knowledge to any others. You will also recognize that none of those responsible for Hyperion are present, or likely to be present in the Arena.**"

"Understood." Selpa's voice was finally dropping to its normal controlled register; Byto echoed the agreement. Tunuvun simply bowed.

Instantly they were back in the amphitheatre. Once more the golden light cleared a path, and this time Ariane could see that a tall raised platform lay before them, with a stairway winding to the top. "**Sun Wu Kung,**" the Arena intoned, "**the objection has been withdrawn, your victory untainted and uncontested; step forward, and receive the prize.**"

That's right, she remembered. *The selected champion claims the prize first.*

Since the prize was an entire Sphere, she wasn't sure how this was going to be handed out; strong as Wu was, she suspected lifting twenty thousand kilometer-wide Spheres was a little out of his range.

The cheers had begun again as Wu Kung, once more proud and happy, stepped jauntily forward, barely keeping himself to a semi-dignified walk rather than the all-out sprint she could tell he would prefer. Strains of music echoed around them, a fanfare or tribute to a winner that, while alien, still managed to evoke a kinship with other, similar ceremonies on Earth, including her own experiences in the Winner's Circle back home.

Finally the four of them—Wu Kung, DuQuesne, herself, and Tunuvun—reached the top of the platform. A beam of pure white light touched Wu Kung as he stretched out a hand, and something glittered within, a something that floated steadily downward, sparkling like a jewel, until she could see that it was a perfect crystal sphere, with a white-glowing symbol within.

"You have won Racing Chance in Challenge, Sun Wu Kung, and thus the prize is yours. This token is yours. Whoever presents it to the Vengeance, they shall be given a Sphere and all the privileges of the Arena that are the right of every Citizen of the Arena."

Wu Kung caught the jewel and held it in wonder. "A Sphere . . ."

She saw DuQuesne stiffen.

"A Sphere that becomes a home," Wu murmured, staring at the sparkling crystal, enraptured. "DuQuesne! It could be . . . it could be *our* home!"

Oh, no. No, Wu. But she understood exactly what Wu Kung was thinking: a home for the Hyperions. Perhaps, just possibly, a home for their friends, too, the friends locked away as patterns in quantum states. Wu came from a place that believed in such miracles, and with the power of the Arena . . . was it entirely impossible?

And could anyone in Wu's position not be tempted—*terribly* tempted—by that possibility?

DuQuesne swallowed hard. "Yes. Yes, Wu. It *could.*" She could tell that Marc did not dare push Wu Kung one way or the other. The Arena had given *Wu Kung* this treasure, and it was his, and his alone . . . and pushing Sun Wu Kung would probably end poorly anyway.

Tunuvun stood, rigid as steel, staring in mute fear. *The Monkey King is also known for his caprice . . .*

And then Wu grinned. "We have to get one for ourselves!" he shouted, and then tossed the priceless gemstone into the air, so it came down perfectly into a stunned Tunuvun's hands. "Now—we have a *celebration!*"

The cheers that erupted around them were nearly deafening, and a swarm of Genasi sprinted up the column and caught up Wu, lifting him high. "A celebration for our rights and our victory, Sun Wu Kung," Tunuvun said, and his translated voice was thick with near-tears of joy, "and for you, who gave it to us when we thought all lost. And you, who I now know never had a true home . . . You were my brother before, now you are brother to us all. You are *Genasi* now and forever, no matter what else you may be, and forever will our home be *your* home as well!"

Wu Kung laughed as they flung him high and caught him again.

"Then I have gained *many* brothers and sisters today! A wonderful thing to celebrate!" He grinned down at the rest of them. "Time for a party!"

"Yes, Wu," she agreed, smiling her relief and echoing his excitement. "It is *definitely* time for a *big* party!"

Chapter 12

"As always, a fine celebration," Orphan said, observing Wu Kung trying to imitate a whirling dance by three of the Genasi, while a laughing crowd of a dozen species watched the performance. "Afterward, however, would I be correct to hope that you and Captain Austin will be free?"

"You mean, to go on your little jaunt into the back end of nowhere? That's the plan," DuQuesne answered. He had noticed the tall alien had a particularly cheerful demeanor—even more, in his estimation, than the simple fact of the victory would have been expected to cause. *He's definitely got another secret that's amusing the hell out of him.* "Barring someone else throwing an emergency curveball at us. Which I hope won't happen for a few days, so that we'll be well gone and leave the others to deal with it."

"So you have already made most of the necessary arrangements? Excellent. Might I ask who will be serving as Faction Leader in Ariane's absence?"

DuQuesne thought a moment, but didn't see any harm in telling him; it wasn't as though the information wouldn't be general knowledge soon enough. "Carl Edlund and Laila Canning," he said, reaching out and grabbing a mini-sandwich from a nearby platter. "Simon's going to advise them, too, but he's got other work to do that we don't want interrupted."

"Research in the Analytic Archives being a large part of it, I would presume," Orphan said with a handtap, and helped himself to a crustacean of some sort.

DuQuesne ignored the faint but audible *crunch* as whatever piercing mechanism Orphan hid inside his mouth-proboscis penetrated the shell, and looked narrowly at the green and black alien. "Just *how* did you know about that?"

"Oh, I was able to deduce it from conversations with both Researcher Relgof and Simon himself. An *extremely* interesting situation, if I guess aright. How long does he have access?"

"Sorry, that's need-to-know, and you don't need to know," DuQuesne said with a grin.

"Of course. No harm in asking, however."

"None at all, as long as you drop it like that whenever we say it's off limits—and to your credit, you always have, so far."

Orphan laughed and gestured vaguely around him. "But of course, Dr. DuQuesne; as I told you when first we met, the Arena is *built* on secrets; asking about them, and knowing when to *stop* asking, is the true lifeblood of Arena interactions." His wide black eyes studied Wu Kung. "For instance, I would *dearly* like to know what was discussed in that interim when the five of you vanished, when old Selpa first objected, and then withdrew his objection. But I know for certainty that *that* secret must be one of *considerable* value, and if you ever wish to convey it to me, you will decide it on your own."

Yeah. More value than you know. "Just like I'd be real interested to know what's got you looking like a cat that just busted into the cream warehouse, but I figure you're telling no one until you're ready."

"Dr. DuQuesne, you have some most *refreshing* turns of phrase, though I have a great suspicion that what I heard there bears relatively little relation to what you actually said. And yes, I am not yet ready to discuss that issue with you. But soon, I promise. Very soon indeed, with luck."

A movement caught his eye and he turned to see the rhino-like Byto coming to a stop nearby. "Byto? I'm a little surprised to see you here."

The shift of the head and body was somehow equivalent to a nod. "I had not originally expected to come . . . but I wished to speak with you for at least a moment."

Orphan maintained his position, and while Byto glanced at the Leader of the Liberated, he made no indication that Orphan should leave. "Well," said DuQuesne, "I've got no objections to that. What about?"

"I wished to say that you played an extremely good game—with, as far as I could tell, absolutely *terrible* alignment of chance against you."

DuQuesne grinned. "And *you* played a hell of a game yourself, *with* the devil's own luck."

The massive form relaxed fractionally, and a snort was translated as a laugh. "DuQuesne, I have *never* had such a run of fortune in all my years. I was *certain* we would win . . . and at the same time, I felt it was almost unfair. If you have the opportunity . . . I would very much like to play you again, hopefully when the random factors are more equally distributed . . ." another snort, ". . . and you have no impossibilities waiting to save you at the end."

"I'd like that, Byto. Tell you what, I'm going to be busy for a while, but as soon as I get a chance we'll set up a game and choose some matched racers, and maybe do some less-apocalyptic-sized betting on the outcome."

"So let it happen!" Byto bobbed his huge head in what seemed the rough parallel of a bow, and moved off.

"That was auspicious," Orphan observed. "Byto is one of the best players of most games of skill and chance combined in the Arena. Having him on friendly terms with you cannot help but be a good thing."

"That's my take on it. He's still wound up over exactly what happened there, but I guess the game's more important to him. Selpa didn't come, and I'm not sure we'll see him for a while."

"Someday," Orphan said with that tilt that indicated a wry smile, "I would *very* much like to know what the objection was (though I could guess that much), and how, precisely, you managed to counter it."

Given that it's one of our biggest secrets? Not likely. "Don't hold your breath, Orphan. That's a secret worth more than you're likely to offer."

"Unsurprising," he said with equanimity. "The objection being what I suspect, anything that could counter it would be . . . extraordinary."

Across the room, DuQuesne saw Ariane finally disengage from what had been a long conversation with Nyanthus and Mandallon and start making her way towards DuQuesne.

"Orphan," she said with a cheerful nod. "Enjoying yourself?"

"Greatly, yes," Orphan replied. "But I noticed your most direct approach to our location, and suspect you wish to speak to Dr. DuQuesne rather than myself."

Good eyes as usual; that's what I figured.

Ariane gave a half-smile. "As usual, you're right. But you don't have to move. Come on, Marc, I want to talk with you somewhere quieter."

DuQuesne nodded and followed her out of the Embassy ballroom and down a hall that led to one of the smaller conference rooms. "What's up, Captain?" he asked, as the door slid shut.

"Hold on." She went around the room with a device in her hand, scanning carefully. DuQuesne, recognizing what she was doing, stayed quiet.

Finally, she straightened, then gave instructions to the Embassy directly that included both electronic and sound insulation, as well as physical security (i.e., locking the door against intrusion).

"That secure, huh?"

"Did I do the job right?"

"You mean checking? Yeah, looks like you should have covered pretty much everything. You're a quick learner. So, what's the deal?"

She sat down, gesturing him to join her. "Marc, this is one of the few times I'm separated from Wu without having to order him away, so I wanted to get a few answers from you now."

Right. I kinda expected this. "Go ahead, Captain."

"I think I've finally put two and two together. What happened today—what Wu had the Arena show us—and the discussion afterwards, plus a couple other things, tells me what that secret is you were telling Oasis—" K "—in private."

"And that is . . . ?"

"Well . . . we heard what Byto and Selpa said, and it echoed in more detail something we heard from Orphan way back when—that there's a *limit* to how much individuals could enhance themselves. And we even have some more direct evidence for it—a couple of the top commando soldiers we brought in found that their enhanced capabilities were way below spec here in the Arena, and nothing they could do would bring those capabilities back. But when they went back home, everything worked fine."

Startled, DuQuesne gave a nod and a grin. "You know, I didn't pick up on that little test at all. You managed that right under our noses and no one caught on?"

"I did. Well, with Saul and the CSF helping set it up on the quiet. They wanted to verify that guess. They weren't happy about the results, either."

"I can imagine. Go on."

"Well, back when the Blessed had kidnapped me and you guys rode to the rescue, we thought we'd lost Wu—and then he showed up at the head of a living armada and kicked the crap out of practically a whole *crew* of Blessed. And that made me think about Wu Kung really hard, and even more so after this race. Did *you* know he could actually communicate with Arena animals? I wondered if that was just something anyone could do—I mean, the Arena does all that other translating for free—but I couldn't get any other creatures to react when I tried it out on our Upper Sphere."

"Yeah, I knew. He showed it the first time we visited the Sphere together, and I had a gut feeling it meant something important."

"Something like an extension of what Byto described, right? About Hyperion being the *world* for your people."

"You've got it," DuQuesne said. *I think she really does.* "And yes, I think it does mean what you think it does, for Wu, maybe for Ki . . . Oasis, and probably for me, too. I'm not going any farther than that, even here. If we're right, it's the biggest ace in the hole humanity *has*."

"And you don't trust Wu to keep the secret?"

"It's not a matter of *trusting* Wu," DuQuesne said. "It's knowing what Wu's *like*. He can keep a secret like, oh, a surprise birthday party, or a prank he's going to pull, for a few days, but a secret this big, and one that affects *him*, for what might be months or years— since ideally we don't want to let that set of felines out of their containment units until we absolutely *have* to? No, he'd never manage that. He'd get put in some situation where he got really mad over someone being mistreated and let it all out. We *saw* that within the first few weeks we were here. Sure, that worked out fine in the end with Tunuvun, but . . ."

She nodded. "I understand. And I understand why you didn't even want to drop it on *me*. You couldn't be *sure*, and even if you were, we don't know the nature and extent of . . . this issue."

"Right."

Ariane nodded again and stared abstractedly into the empty air of the conference room. "Can I ask you something, Marc?"

"You can always ask. And I'll try to answer."

"When you . . . in your original life, I mean . . ." She rolled her eyes, a flash of blue below the sky-blue hair. "Argh. When you were in Hyperion, you and Richard Seaton were best friends, right?"

"Pretty much from the time we met, yeah. We were a lot alike, but just enough different that the other guy sort of filled in gaps the first one didn't know he had, if that makes any sense."

"It does. So . . . I read the original Skylark books, of course. He must have married Dorothy Vaneman, if they kept anything about him the same."

"Sure did. I was best man, of course."

"So you . . ." She actually blushed slightly. "Did you meet anyone? If you were replacing Crane, then you would have—"

He looked down. "No, never did, quite. There were . . . well, *could* have been, maybe, a couple women, but the chance never quite came. See, I wasn't quite the original DuQuesne, so Stephanie De Marigny wasn't really the match for me, I wasn't Crane, so they didn't put Margaret Spencer in, and I wasn't exactly Kimball Kinnison either, though our adventures were in a universe that combined the two series, so I never had a Clarissa equivalent." He felt his smile touched with sadness. "The old bastard admitted that he and his friend never could quite figure out the right person to match me with, and said he wasn't sure if he should be sad or grateful, since it would've meant I lost even more when . . ."

"I know," she said quickly. "There was nothing left of your . . . world, then?"

"No," he said heavily. "The five of us were the main targets of the counteraction at first, and the AIs driving the countermeasure figured—probably rightly—that depriving us of our whole basis, our world, was the best chance of breaking us."

"So . . . who was 'the old bastard' you mentioned?"

"My personal Frankenstein, Dr. Timothy J. Bryson (though he didn't actually rate the title of 'Doctor'). The guy in charge of making the Doc Smith Hyperion—and honestly pretty much the only one so interested in Smith's old work that he pushed through my creation."

"Are you saying he's *still alive*?"

"Yeah. Not many of them left, after Maria-Susanna got through with them, but . . . well, after I got over being furious at the whole mess of them, I decided I at least owed him my existence so I helped him disappear—with a little assist from Saul. Gave him another warning before we left about our new problem—the renegade AI. Maybe it's not going to give a damn about the so-called experimenters, but I didn't want to take chances."

The look she gave DuQuesne warmed him through. "Marc, that was . . . noble of you."

"What? No, I . . . look, okay, it was more than some of the others would've done for their creators, yeah. But mad as I was about what he'd done, he was one of the ones who decided that the whole thing had gone too far. I never found out for sure . . . but I think he—and Nat, his AISage and fellow researcher—might've tweaked the security feeds enough to give us the slack we needed. I *do* know he was one of the ones that tried to help *both* groups get out of there when it came apart. And the two of them *had* created me. I wouldn't be here, wouldn't have any memories real or false, if he hadn't reached back three centuries and tried to breathe life into some old author's pulp fiction."

"So you helped this Bryson and his AISage escape?"

"Just Bryson." He shook his head. "Nat . . . Nat got wiped out making sure Bryson and a couple others got clear. Don't know who got him, but it was one of the villain AIs, I'm pretty sure. Maybe even the one we're dealing with now." He looked up, although he wasn't seeing the far side of the room now; just the old man's face, and the shadow of Hyperion. "Anyway, why'd you ask?"

"Well . . ." She blushed. "Never mind. We had better get back to the celebration, and tomorrow we'll have a lot to get ready for."

"As you say, Captain." He could not keep a broad smile from his face as he rose and gestured the door open. "After you!"

Chapter 13

"Not taking *Zounin-Ginjou*?" Simon asked, looking at the relatively small craft—no more than fifty meters long—that was sitting at the end of the berth the Liberated were assigned.

"Later," Orphan said, carefully checking the exterior of his ship. "If all three of us took *Zounin-Ginjou* from here, too many eyes would note the departure; this is a short-range vessel, the sort used for brief jaunts from point to point."

"With your permission," said Sethrik, watching as DuQuesne dragged a large case into the shuttle's loading door, "we intend to allow a 'leak,' as you call it, of information, which will lead people to believe that the Liberated were donating some very valuable materials to your cause, and this was the mission to transfer it out of sight or range of those in Transition. Sensitive material is often transferred in this manner. Decoy missions as well, of course, so they will wonder whether the real material is in some other shipment through Transition at about the same time."

"And in actuality you are just transferring Orphan, Marc, Ariane, and Wu to *Zounin-Ginjou*?"

Sethrik gave the swift outward flick of the hands that indicated negation. The former member of the Blessed and only other member of the Liberated continued, "Our story will have a core of truth, and you *will* be receiving something very useful to your current efforts. Details can be leaked later, so that suspicion will be kept to a minimum until it is far too late for anyone to even attempt an effective investigation."

117

Simon shook his head, smiling. "Everything you do in the Arena seems to have three more layers than one sees."

"And *that*," Orphan said, leaping back to the loading dock, "is why the Liberated still exists. Three or four layers are the minimum."

"I think we're ready, Orphan," said Ariane, Wu shadowing her closely; Simon saw his eyes darting everywhere.

Ahh. The last time they were on the Docks, Ariane was kidnapped. I doubt Wu Kung will ever forget that. And this is *an open, and thus potentially dangerous area, and one that we know has far less restrictive rules on violence.* "So you have no idea when you will return?" he asked again.

Ariane shook her head, making the dark-blue hair ripple. "Afraid not. A pretty long time, though, so I'm going to be trusting you to keep things under control here. Laila and Carl are in charge, but you're going to be my eyes while I'm gone, you know."

"I know." He took her hand. "I will miss you. Perhaps a dinner when we return?"

She grinned. "Perhaps!"

"C'mon, Ariane, let's get inside and give Wu a chance to settle down," DuQuesne said, emerging from the door. "Everything set, Orphan?"

"All is in readiness, if all of your cargo is loaded."

"I don't see any travel bags," Simon said, looking around.

"Everything's in one of the crates," DuQuesne said. "That way doesn't instantly look like we're going on a long cruise."

Sethrik gave the compress-release gesture that approximated a shrug. "When your Leader is no longer seen, they will realize she is gone."

Ariane raised a finger. "Not so quickly they won't. Credit Oscar Naraj with this idea: anyone watching will see me and DuQuesne emerge from Transition, go back to the Embassy, and then a little while later see both of us go join Tunuvun and a bunch of Genasi on a clearly Earth-designed ship. The rumor there—and like yours, it will also be true—is that we're making an official gift of an Arena-capable vessel, with a lot of normal-space tech and information, to the Genasi."

"Ah, of course," Orphan said, with his oft-amused tone. "And *these* decoys will not be seen again. But then the questions about where you have gone will center, not around the Liberated, but the Genasi. Who have an honor debt of immense size to you, so keeping the secret is a given. Well done."

Ariane gave Simon a quick hug, and didn't hesitate to include a swift but emphatic kiss before pulling away. DuQuesne shook his hand, as did Wu Kung.

Simon waved as the four disappeared inside the small Arena ship, and watched alongside Sethrik as the sleek transport—something like a Victorian-designed bullet with wings—pulled away and accelerated smoothly towards the area of the Sky Gates around Nexus Arena.

"So," he said to the tall, green-and-black alien as they began walking back, "do *you* have any better idea than I do as to what it is that Orphan's all secretive about?"

"Unlikely," Sethrik said. "While he has given me many details about the history of the Liberated, about our resources—surprisingly large, given how much the Faction was reduced—and so on, he has remained extremely quiet about his personal secrets. And this one seems even more personal than most."

Simon nodded. "I rather expected as much. Although you would also have to deny it if he had told you but wished you to keep it secret, I suppose."

"You begin to understand the way of the Arena, yes." Sethrik looked into the distance; this part of the Docks was actually rather empty today. Simon wondered if there was some sort of day/night cycle in loading and arrivals, or if it was merely the random chance of schedules. "Of course, even with the distractions you have planned, it will eventually become clear to watchers that Orphan and your Leader are gone, and they will reach the correct conclusion that they left together on this day."

"But that shouldn't pose an immediate problem, correct?"

Sethrik's buzzing chuckle was somewhat disconcerting. "What *should* be, and what *does* happen, these are often different things in the Arena. As I have occasion to know. Still, no, I would expect that Orphan will have gained enough time so that the chances of any tracing his passage or learning his destination will be extremely small."

They passed from the Docks to the interior of Nexus Arena, and Sethrik waved down one of the automated hovercabs. "Are you returning to your Embassy?"

"No, Sethrik—I actually have business at the Analytic today, so you go first."

Sethrik gave the handtap of assent and directed the cab to bring them first to the Embassy of the Liberated, before carrying Simon on to the Analytic's Great Faction house. Simon jumped down and walked into the huge, soaring edifice of polished alloy, glass, and stone that was the home of the Faction dedicated to pure knowledge.

Having been there multiple times previously, it was simple to make his way to the Archives. Not so simple was keeping his breath from being taken away upon entering. The vaulted ceiling, a hundred meters above, with arched windows streaming sunlight—or a perfect facsimile thereof—into the cavernous space filled with rank upon rank of shelves, the shelves themselves fifty meters high, and each row dwindling away into unguessable distance, fading into the softness of mountains on the horizon. *Here* was the sum-total of the knowledge of the Analytic, one of the five Great Factions, the knowledge of a hundred thousand years and more, of species beyond counting, of Challenges as vast as the stars of Earth's sky, of secrets from a million worlds.

And I have nearly a whole year to roam it at will. It seemed a terribly short time, yet the opportunity was beyond price. Simon Sandrisson could not restrain a wicked grin. When the Analytic's board had agreed to give him this access, they had clearly believed they had by far the better end of the deal, because the access lacked one crucial element: access to the *indexes* of the Archives, the searchable database-equivalent of the incomprehensibly huge morass of data, prototypes, samples, and other accumulated knowledge held within the Archives. Thus—as far as they knew—Simon had no way of knowing where to find data that he truly *wanted*, nor of translating finds that were not recorded in any known language, for the Arena's translation did not work for such data, only in general for the spoken word.

Had they known about that nigh-omniscience that Simon could tap, they might have thought very differently.

"Ahhh, Simon! I had heard you had come to visit!" The rough tones of Relgof Nov'ne Knarph interrupted his reverie. "And I see you cannot yet enter the Archives without feeling the impact of a thousand generations of knowledge."

"Can *you*, Dr. Rel?"

The semi-humanoid alien's filter-beard rippled with a chuckle. "No, truly. The immediate impact has somewhat lessened, but never have I come here without a moment of awe and reverence. Let others have their gods; I have this temple of knowledge."

"Have you come to watch me wander the stacks?"

"That is a *fascinating* turn of phrase, Simon, given the circumstances," Relgof said, with a near-human tilt of the head. "Come, let us examine a section of the Archives."

Climbing into one of the egg-shaped floating carts used the way old-fashioned library ladders were—to reach any part of otherwise inaccessible materials, the two set off; Relgof allowed Simon to direct the course of the cart. *I wonder what he meant by that bit about circumstances.* Since he didn't have a particular question in mind at the moment, Simon chose a direction at random and sped the cart down it for four and a half kilometers, stopping at a set of shelves with assorted memory crystals and some models and skeletal exhibits. *A record of a civilization? An archaeological record?*

"So, are you going to clarify that comment, Rel?"

Relgof did not bother to pretend he didn't understand. "Simon, the Analytic can, of course, observe any activities within its own House. You have visited several times. Now, we are both well aware that you were denied the use of the Great Index and other search tools.

"It is rather difficult to imagine how, then, you managed—on your first visit—to unerringly locate key records on detection and uses of Sky Gates, and based on your reactions and subsequent events, were able to *understand* them, despite at least one source being in an ancient language with no known remaining members."

Simon kept his face expressionless with an effort. *Of course, since the Arena seems to even sometimes translate expressions from body posture, I cannot be sure some of my surprise or concern was not also translated.*

"Now," Relgof went on, reaching out and picking up one of the models of a strange house with oval doors and hexagonal windows, "It so happens that—at the moment—I believe I am the only one who knows about that most unbelievable event, since the others were not inclined to monitor you. And I do not wish to alert them to this. I *am* however genuinely curious and wonder if you might be willing to enlighten me."

Simon raised an eyebrow. "I don't suppose you would accept 'coincidence' as an answer."

"Would you, my friend?"

"No. I admit that I don't have nearly your experience with the Archives, but even my few visits have given me some impression of its vastness." Simon thought for a moment as he took memory crystals and fit them into a visualizing device built into the cart, scanning the images and text therein. _History, looks like. Might be archeological work on a long-vanished species._ Relgof watched patiently.

Finally, Simon shrugged. "I won't deny that I have found a way around that limitation, but the value of _that_ secret—in all honesty—is a lot greater than a mere year's access to the Archive."

Relgof's filter-beard froze, and the entire creature weant rigid. After a moment he relaxed. "Yes, I suppose it must be. Either you have—in a manner we find undetectable—managed to gain access to the Index, which insofar as I am aware would require assistance directly from a Shadeweaver or Initiate Guide, or you have found a method that allows _you personally_ to find what you wish without any recourse to the Index."

Technically, without any recourse to the Archives at all. But I am far too cautious and—in honesty—afraid of using this power to that extent. "That seems to be roughly correct, Relgof. What do you intend to do about it, if anything?"

"Hmmm. Well . . . I would be willing to not mention this to anyone—and to steer the rest of the Analytic away from analyzing your visits, if any show such interest—if you have some unique piece of information, something useful to impart to me."

Simon pursed his lips. "I suppose friendship does have limits when such secrets are involved."

"When I am, myself, the Chief Researcher, the Leader of the Faction? Alas, yes. I must receive value for that offered. I have allowed considerable latitude already, partially for the uniqueness of your situation as First Emergents, and partly because I feel we truly are kindred spirits. But _this_ . . ."

"I understand. Not like our prior after-hours research where the information we uncovered was something of interest to us both."

Relgof tilted his head. "To what do you refer?"

Simon blinked in puzzlement. "Rel, to that rather long-drawn out session of research on the background of Shadeweaver and Faith capabilities, culminating in your discovery of that old story about the Ryphexian 'Master of Engines'?"

The gangly alien's posture and voice were replete with utter confusion. "Simon, I confess that I have not the slightest idea of the event to which you refer."

Suddenly it all made sense. There had been *no references* in the Index to Shadeweaver or Faith powers being used outside of the Arena. The two had found it necessary to perform many hours of research in order to find a single confirmation.

If you want to keep a secret like that . . . you need a way of making people forget.

But Ariane Austin's victory over the Shadeweavers in direct Challenge against Amas-Garao meant that the Shadeweavers *could not affect* Simon or any other human. That didn't hold true for the other species and factions, however.

Simon suddenly smiled. "Then I have something to trade, Rel— your real problem is going to be keeping it in mind long enough to make use of it!"

Chapter 14

"Orphan . . ." Ariane said apprehensively. "Are you *sure* we want to get any closer to that?"

"My dear Captain Austin, we are going to get *far* closer," Orphan replied with a chuckle.

The immense vessel loomed ever larger in the suddenly-tiny shuttle's viewport. *Just about an old-style mile long, and looks it,* DuQuesne thought, as he saw a brilliant line of light that widened, became a massive pair of doors into a huge landing bay. "Almost like coming home, isn't it?" he said.

"In some sense it *is* coming home, Dr. DuQuesne," Orphan said, his wingcases relaxing, showing that he was indeed genuinely happy to be returning to *Zounin-Ginjou*, the flagship of the Liberated. "I have spent at least as much time in this wonderful ship as I have in Nexus Arena, or on the Liberated's Sphere."

"*That* is *Zounin-Ginjou*?" Ariane demanded incredulously. From Wu's expression, he hadn't recognized the ship either.

"Indeed it is," Orphan replied, with an amused tone in his translated voice. "Yet truly, I cannot fault you for being surprised."

"I would've been, if it weren't for the fact that I knew you'd never land on any other ship, and I could tell you were heading for this one from way back," DuQuesne said.

In truth, it did *not* look much like the quasi-Victorian work of art that was the flagship of the Liberated, replete with brassy-golden trim and fittings, rich wooden hull hiding battleship armor, and vanes and fins to make the most avid Vernian steampunk fanplayer cry with joy.

The sleek spindle-shaped vessel was no more; a much broader, duller outline, one completely utilitarian, efficient, massive, with lines and angles that DuQuesne thought were all too familiar.

"It looks like one of the Blessed's ships," Wu said, putting DuQuesne's thoughts into words.

Ariane nodded. "That's exactly why I was nervous; I thought it *was* a Blessed vessel."

"Quite deliberately so," Orphan said. The shuttle passed through the doors and DuQuesne felt the artificial gravity slowly take over, allowing Orphan to bring the vessel to a soft landing. "The exterior of *Zounin-Ginjou* is now identical, at least to any ordinary inspection, to that of a *Madon*-class Arena freighter, a common vessel type for the Blessed to use in intra-Arena trade."

"Ha! I see!" Wu Kung grinned with his sharp fangs showing. "You *look* like the Blessed, so you can pretend to *be* one."

"I *thought* you would understand quickly, Wu Kung. Exactly; I can play the part of my former people very well—I *was* one, after all, for a long time before changing sides. With luck, any confrontations would be ended by simply identifying the vessel as one of the Blessed; very, *very* few wish to risk the wrath of any of the Five Great Factions, after all, and the Blessed is probably the second-worst to offend."

"With the first being our hair-trigger xenophobes the Molothos, yeah," DuQuesne said. "I like it. You've made her into a Q-ship; looks like a freighter, registered to a dangerous power, and if someone *is* stupid enough to try to hijack you . . ."

". . . they find out they're attacking one of the most powerful warships in the Arena," Ariane finished with a grin. "I like it. And now that we're inside, I can *definitely* see this is really *Zounin-Ginjou*. What cabins will we have?"

"I see no reason you cannot have those you used previously. In fact, when I was conducting the rather *extensive* repairs necessitated by our prior argument with the Blessed, I performed a few more modifications to that entire suite of cabins to make them better suited to the use of Humanity."

"I'm sure we'll appreciate that," DuQuesne said, as he made his way to the cargo area. "We've got a lot of stuff to unload here and get to our living area."

Orphan, already making his way down the ramp extending from

the forward section of the shuttle, gestured toward some shapes on the far side of the bay. "You will find cargo handling equipment there—I believe you recall how to use it from our prior adventures, yes?"

"Not helping out, Orphan?" Ariane asked with a faint smile.

"Many apologies, but I wish to get us underway immediately. The less time we remain in this part of Arenaspace, the less chance for any to notice this vessel's departure—or the fact that the little shuttle we rode in has docked here."

"No worries," DuQuesne said. "Get us going; this is your party. Me, Wu, and Ariane can get everything moved pretty quick."

It was not all *that* quick; moving the provisions for what might be up to a year wasn't a trivial exercise, especially when the food and such had to be brought to the galley, while clothes and other personal baggage had to be brought to the living quarters. Still, they were almost done when DuQuesne felt that subliminal shock that told him they'd made a Sandrisson jump, presumably through a Sky Gate. "We're really on our way now," he muttered.

"And I don't have a *single* meeting to go to!" Ariane said, grinning broadly.

"Yeah, but we have no idea what we're heading *into*," DuQuesne reminded her—not without an answering grin. "We might be in a battle three days from now, who knows?"

"Battles are *fun!*" Wu Kung said, emphasizing that with a sharp rapping of his staff on the deck. "Meetings with talk-talk-talk, *that* is danger!"

"You know, maybe I need to reconsider; is it a *good* thing that I'm agreeing with Sun Wu Kung?" Ariane asked.

"There are worse choices, but yeah, agreeing with him usually leads to an *awful* lot of heads getting busted."

"Only *bad* people's heads," Wu pointed out.

"Generally, I'll grant you that." He straightened up. "I'm going to go check up on our host on the bridge."

The other two followed, Ariane moving up to walk next to him; *Zounin-Ginjou*'s corridors were more than wide enough to make that possible. *Orphan sure didn't skimp on comfort on this ship.*

Of course, that was partly from necessity. If Orphan had been able to make use of top-of-the-line automation, he could have used every cubic inch of space for more armor, weapons, stores, and so on, leaving himself only as much space as he wished to keep for his own comfort and any anticipated allies. But with the Arena restricting automation to the point that he was stuck somewhere around the early twenty-first century, Orphan ran into a different limitation: how much he could actually *control*.

Without intelligent automation, there were only so many bells and whistles he could hang onto *Zounin-Ginjou* before they became useless distractions. Paradoxically, even though the ancient-style automation took up a lot more space per system, he ended up with a huge amount left over because he couldn't install nearly as many systems; some of that volume was of course used as additional cargo space, but he had apparently decided that a large luxury suite might one day be useful, and turned a hundred cabins' worth of space into about twenty.

Even so, *Zounin-Ginjou* packed a fantastic amount of firepower and resources into its hull compared to any similar vessel, and DuQuesne approved. *When you're alone in the Dark, carrying the biggest guns you can helps light things up, so to speak.*

"Relaxing while you can?" he asked Ariane.

"As much as I can, yes. It's not easy; I'm always worried about what's going on back at Nexus Arena. It's only been six days, but . . ."

". . . but we know how a few days can change everything. But you were *right* about this trip. I can feel it, somehow."

"So can I. But I'm still worried."

Wu Kung grunted behind them. "I worry a little, but mostly that's a waste of time. We just have to be *ready*."

"Yeah," agreed DuQuesne as they arrived at the bridge, "the problem is, ready for *what*?"

"Oh, wow," Ariane said, looking up.

"Ahh, Captain Austin, I see you already appreciate some of the wonders of the Arena."

Wu Kung bounded up and pressed his face against the near-indestructible transparent ring-carbon port, staring in a combination of joy and awe.

Before *Zounin-Ginjou* was a vast canyon of clear air, with gargantuan, rolling walls of cloud to either side, extending unguessable kilometers above and below their current course. Streaming twilight-lavender and grey-touched black, rolling deep green and mountain-waves of deepest blue, the clouds formed a dark corridor with faint yet white-tinted light streaming from behind the massive ship.

A barely-visible cone of shadow preceded them, a shadow against shadows where *Zounin-Ginjou* blocked the light of the Luminaire that must be almost directly aft. Periodically, blue-white, brilliant scarlet, or burning orange arcs of lightning would streak across the impossibly huge clouds, swift yet traveling so far that the eye could sometimes follow them into the distance ahead or above or below. Other lightning strokes, deeper within the clouds, would illuminate the interior, turning the dark cloud momentarily to a wall of frosted crystal tinted with all the colors of the rainbow.

"Wow," Ariane said again, reverently. "Orphan, do you ever get tired of it?"

"One grows *used* to anything . . . but with your eyes, I see it anew, and am once more uplifted and humbled. Humbled by the vastness and the grandeur of the Arena . . . and uplifted by the thought that I, Orphan of the Liberated, am one of those who may travel these skies at my own will."

He does "talk purty," as Rich would've said. Wonder if his own people would hear language this flowery? "Where are we?"

"That, Dr. DuQuesne, is actually a most interesting and perplexing question. I can describe the location, if I wish, by the directions needed to *reach* it, but can I truly say I know *where* it is? I do not know. For instance, I cannot tell you whether Nexus Arena lies in the direction we are heading, or behind us, whether it is a mere twenty million kilometers to our port side or five light-years distant to starboard. Without an active, inhabited Sphere in this area of space, with inhabitants to tell us from which galaxy they hail, we cannot even guess where within the vastness of the Arena we may be."

"Are we in the Deeps yet?" Wu Kung asked.

"We begin to approach them. But our destination is still a great distance away . . . or, at least, a great deal of *time* away, even though for all I know our destination lies just on the other side of these clouds."

"So where are we going right now?"

"There is another Sky Gate here," Orphan answered. He studied various instruments; DuQuesne saw lines flicker on the viewport. "If my navigation is correct—and I am reasonably confident that it is—the Gate lies just inside of the wall of cloud to our starboard side, about two thousand kilometers ahead and down, relative to our current orientation. If we detect no other vessels here, then we will pass through that gate."

"And if we do detect other vessels?"

"Then we will continue on, pass through another gate that is ahead, above, and just slightly to port. I will then have to take another roundabout route to return here again, taking us another several days."

Ariane nodded. "So that gate you want to go through is one *you* know about, but no one else does."

"You have the essence of it, yes. Though there *may* be others who know. I have no knowledge of any others living who do, however."

"You sensing any ships now?"

"None whatsoever. And, with luck, we shall detect no others. This is a very little-traveled route."

"And then we will be in the Deeps?"

"For a while, yes. Then another short leg of the journey through somewhat-explored territory before we reach our true destination."

DuQuesne nodded. Wherever Orphan was taking them clearly had to be reached a very specific way—which fit with what he knew of the Arena. *There must be a lot of places that can only be reached one way— one sequence of Sky Gates in or out.*

Zounin-Ginjou, disguised or not, was still very fast, and it was not long before they were approaching the area of the secret Gate. Orphan spent the last few moments watching his monitors tensely before finally turning the vessel and sending it darting straight for the clouds a short distance below them.

A blaze of pearlescent light started at the forward end of *Zounin-Ginjou*, and DuQuesne knew another had started aft, the two light-circles racing to meet each other. That undefinable, tingling *jolt*, and suddenly the scene outside the port *changed*. A majestic maelstrom of silvery cloud spread out below them, turning with ponderous, lazy power beneath a sky of gold.

Orphan rose from his seat and turned. "Welcome to the Deeps of the Arena, my friends." He bowed deeply. "And now . . . now there are none to hear us as far as any can imagine, and at last I can tell you the *why* of our little journey."

Chapter 15

"Leader, an urgent communication for you."

Dajzail looked up from his meal, seeing Kanjstall the Salutant waiting. "*That* urgent?"

"It is from Fleet Master Alztanza, Leader."

Home and Hive, that is *urgent.* With only seven Fleet Masters in the entire One Civilization (that the undercreatures mistakenly called an "empire"), communications from them were rare and always important; and Alztanza himself had been one of Dajzail's friends since they were young. "I will take it now, then."

Kanjstall dipped his respect, came forward, and gave him the message crystal. Without being told, Kanjstall dipped again and left. *That is why he is my Salutant. I can rely on him utterly.*

Placing the crystal in the reader, he was immediately faced by the Fleet Master.

"Dajzail, the Wise and Compassionate," the Fleet Master began, and Dajzail rippled his manipulators in annoyance. *I am not some Hive vaingroom, to be foolishly flattered, especially by a friend.* But he reminded himself that the last Leader, Alethkand, had been far less tolerant, and the Fleet Master had learned his communications protocol in those days, well before Dajzail had ascended. Fleet Master Alztanza continued, "the Strong and Just, I greet you. We have vital news for you."

As he listened, Dajzail forgot entirely about his meal, and felt his manipulators and entire body vibrating for an entirely different reason: fierce joy. Once the message was concluded, he spoke. "Kanjstall," he said, the green-light ball of Arena communication instantly appearing, "send a message to the Fleet Master, the complete text to be: *Report here at once.* Then join me in the conferral chamber with the Master of Forces, Master of Homes, and Master of Trade as swiftly as may be."

Dajzail finished his meal, leaving the bones to be cleaned up later, but he barely noticed the sensation of fullness or savored the taste—a shame, he noted distantly, as Tensari was difficult to come by without inciting difficulty with the undercreatures and should not be treated as mere fuel for a day. But his mind was far too occupied to pay attention to anything else.

The other four Molothos were waiting for him in the conferral chamber as he entered. Kanjstall, small but quick on his claws, dark carapace showing the touch of that green peculiar to those from the original homeworld; Malvchait, Master of Forces, massive, almost completely red with highlights of space-black, a warrior and strategist without equal; Elshuti, Master of Homes, mediant sex currently, a steel gray, hir eye damaged across nearly a quarter of its circle but the rest shining clear and sharp; and Master of Trade Peryntik, fresh from her latest molt, her regenerated forelimb still white-soft.

The four dipped low, their lower carapaces touching the floor; he gestured impatiently with one claw and they rose and locked legs for comfort. "What matter is so urgent, Leader?" asked Malvchait.

"The War of Purity moves forward," Dajzail said simply.

The others froze momentarily, and then a great hungry screech of fierce joy rose from all four. "We have word, then?"

"Fleet Master Alztanza finally broke the mystery, yes. His analysts sifted all of the data gathered from the high colonies, and finally discovered that the Twinscabbard-class vessel *Blessing of Fire* had failed to report back after more than four full revolutions. This was of course only one of several lost in that general period, but the timing was good; it would have been out more than one and a quarter revolutions and due to turn back, thus well out into the Deeps on exploration. Fortunately, there were records for the gene-codes for the Masters and Salutants on *Blessing of Fire*, and once Alztanza had received them, he was able to match them with the body the undercreature DuQuesne taunted us with."

"We do not know their home-star's exact location, then?"

Dajzail's laugh rippled around the room, a sound he knew would sound far from pleasant to most undercreatures. "Oh, but we *do*, Elshuti. We know—to within a very small degree—the time at which the conflict must have taken place. Thus, Alztanza was able to determine, within an equally small margin of error, how far *Blessing of Fire* could have traveled in that time, and what the general planned heading of *Blessing of Fire* was.

"This leaves only one candidate star, a green-central single-unit star not drastically different from our own, which fits with the human-undercreatures' known illuminance preferences."

"Are there Forces available on the nearest high colony?" asked Peryntik.

"A Seventh-Force is stationed there."

Malvchait bobbed up than down, obviously pleased. "Three hundred forty-three warships? That should be *more* than sufficient for this. I will take control personally, if you so order, Leader."

"I do wish you, and Alztanza—since it *was* his discovery—to direct this operation militarily. I will, myself, take command of the Master warship of the operation. *However*, I do not agree with your initial assessment."

The leader of the Molothos' military forces scissored his claws in apologetic confusion. "Truly? I know they have gained some warships—"

"I have *watched* these undercreatures *very* carefully," Dajzail said, and rapped his own fighting claws hard on the table to reinforce his emphasis. "They are *dangerous* animals. Fortune has favored them multiple times. The warships they were given are from the Survivor, and he is not one to take lightly. The Arena's announcement showed that *two* of them managed, in some manner, to defeat the entire complement of *Blessing of Fire*, perhaps even to destroy the ship itself. That may be—almost certainly was—an event that involved great fortune as well as, or even in place of, great skill, but we cannot *know* that.

"All we *do* know is that the human undercreatures have won *every single challenge* they have faced thus far, defeating the True People, the Blessed to Serve, the Vengeance, and the Warpers of Reality, the Shadeweavers themselves." He vibrated in violent negation. "No, we shall take no chances. Assemble a full Force at Zeshezan-Katrill, Master of Forces, all seven Sevenths. No, *two* full Forces. At the same time, assemble a *complete Fleet* for quick deployment to lowspace. We will not permit them the luxury of safety anywhere. We will assault and take their Upper Sphere. We will secure their Sky Gates for our own use. We shall bring an entire Fleet thence."

The others rose higher in anticipation.

"And then we will—regardless of cost or time—send that Fleet through their own Sky Gates, come to their very home system, and crush their worlds, and make these undercreatures either the slaves of the True People . . . or one final, cautionary tale in the history of those who have insulted us!"

Chapter 16

"To use a human expression that's probably going to be interesting in translation, Orphan, we're all ears," Ariane said.

Orphan tilted his head. "That . . . *was* an interesting expression indeed. But I get the gist of the meaning." He stood, leaning back against a railing in front of the actual viewport, silhouetted against the planet-sized whirlpool of cloud and storm ahead.

"It begins many, many years ago, when I signed on for an expedition to the Deeps headed by a consortium comprised mainly of members of the Vengeance and the Analytic. As I am sure you recall from our prior conversations, the Deeps are of vast interest because they may hide almost anything; in particular, they may conceal remnants of the Voidbuilders, or some of the earliest residents of the Arena, information of great interest to both of those Great Factions.

"Now, one of the things one looks for in these explorations is unknown Sky Gates. While we know that Sky Gates will appear around Spheres of worlds owned by any faction, it is also known that sometimes there are Sky Gates associated with other locations, but not predictably so. Thus, such exploration expeditions will have sensors for the disturbances of Sky Gates and hope to pass close enough to one to detect it. This is naturally a very rare event; even if such Sky Gates are quite common, the Arena is vast beyond easy grasping and the range of detection makes detecting them a random affair indeed."

He turned and looked out of the port; Ariane could see the tightening of the wingcases. "But on this trip we found one, an unknown Sky Gate far from any Sphere. The captains conferred and decided to venture through—not that there was much chance they would decide otherwise, in truth.

"Alas, we emerged in the very center of one of the great storms, a massive tempest that seized our vessels, assaulted them with lightning large enough to span a world, sent us spinning out of control. I managed to reach one of the emergency launches, just as a veritable *wave* of rocky debris hurtled from the depths of the storm and battered both vessels furiously. A shard of metal embedded itself in the base of my right wing, nearly shearing it off, and piercing deep into my back, but I made it inside. The launch fired thrusters automatically and shot me from the doomed ships; I watched with horror as they began to break up, and then the storm sent me hurtling beyond sight of the disaster.

"Such a small vessel has some advantages in surviving storms, even if there are many others where size would be a great comfort. I could not control the launch, but though I was sent hurtling hither and yon, and occasionally rapped violently by a careening boulder or random *zikki*, the launch survived reasonably intact; I was somewhat less than well, but my wound would not be swiftly fatal. I could not remove the shard, but there were field dressings in the emergency launch which would prevent infection."

Orphan began pacing slowly back and forth, not even apparently aware of his motion as he continued to speak. "At last, I broke out into clear air, a space where I could get some idea of my bearings and no longer be out of control within the storm.

"To my immense surprise, there was . . . *something* already there. Not a Sphere (although I later discovered a Sphere sat very nearby), but an immense and complex structure, many thousands of kilometers in extent." He glanced to them and tilted his head, a gesture that made her think of a wry grin. "I was, as you might imagine, somewhat reluctant to approach this unknown installation; a Faction that constructs something so large in an isolated portion of the Arena is almost certainly hiding *something*, and if they were one of the more . . . intolerant Factions—"

"Like the Molothos," Wu Kung put in.

"Precisely, yes, if they were of that sort of Faction, they would be likely to do something extremely rude and final to me." Orphan seemed to look up through the hull of *Zounin-Ginjou*. "Still, I had no idea of where I might be, how far away the Sky Gate we had entered by was, nor very many provisions to keep me alive. And it *is* a general rule of the Arena that stranded people are to be assisted; is this true on your world?"

Ariane nodded emphatically. "Yes. Whether on sea, land, air, or space, a distress signal is expected to be heeded and anyone capable of effecting a rescue in the indicated region is expected to render assistance immediately, regardless of the nationality or associations of the distressed vessel or people. There are some exceptions—it's not a *legal* requirement for most people—but there's a *very* strong tradition."

"Excellent; this is of course true with most civilized groups. So, I decided that I had little to lose and headed for this structure as best I could, transmitting one of the standard Arena beacon signals for help." The wingcases drew in even more, and Ariane saw a vibration of the tail that gave her the impression of a shudder.

"Without the slightest warning, my ship was seized by some . . . unknown force. There was no sign of another vessel or any activity near the huge structure, but my ship was suddenly borne towards it with remarkable rapidity and complete precision; we travelled, as near as I can tell, in an absolutely straight line from my location to a bay at one side of the structure. I attempted to use my ship's thrusters to affect the motion, but to no avail; it seemed to have no more effect than if I had pitted my own wings against the power of *Zounin-Ginjou*'s engines.

"My little vessel landed in the bay, and immediately shut down— again without the slightest act on my part. Seeing that my choices were minimal, I exited the launch. I will not deny that I was not merely mystified, but frightened. There had been no communications of any sort, and in this landing bay was no sign of any other ship, or even any living thing. It was a grand and chilling isolation, a place absolutely devoid of living presences . . . and yet I *knew* I was watched, that my slightest move was being noted by whatever force had chosen to bring me thence."

Orphan's entire body swelled and shrank, with a whistling sound from his spiracles—clearly the equivalent of drawing a long, uncertain breath. "My friends, I still find myself shaken merely *recalling* those moments."

"Can't blame you, Orphan," DuQuesne said. "Sounds like some of our experiences when we first got into the Arena. As Ariane used to say, 'creepy' was the word that came first to mind."

"'Creepy'? Yes, most precisely, *creepy* is the right description, if the translation holds true." He expanded and rattled his wings, then closed them tightly. "So, I stepped out, and a door across the bay opened. With no little trepidation I made my way across the polished and utterly *empty* floor to the corridor thus revealed, and was directed in similarly . . . creepy . . . silence through several other twists and turns, until I found myself before a set of immense doors; tired and injured as I was, I waited immobile a moment, trying to decide whether to move forward or not, when the decision was taken from me. The doors parted, folding up and away, and I knew I had no choice. I stepped into a room nearly complete in its darkness. Then, slowly, the darkness began to lift, and there was a figure standing there."

From the tone of Orphan's voice, and the slow-rising tension of his narration, Ariane felt a tingling, cold thrill edging down her spine.

"All at once the light came up . . . and I found that I was face-to-face with . . . *myself.*"

Ariane glanced at the others; DuQuesne was staring, riveted, and to her surprise she saw gooseflesh standing out on the former Hyperion's arms. Sun Wu Kung's posture was taut, his eyes narrow, but his mouth curled up in a smile, as though the unknown were just one more challenge to assault.

"Holy Mother," DuQuesne muttered. "*Creepy* doesn't get the half of that." She recognized a particular tone in his voice and realized that Orphan's story must touch on something else, something in DuQuesne's Hyperion past. "Wasn't a mirror, was it?"

The buzzing, low laugh was filled with Orphan's own apprehension. "Ahhh, Dr. DuQuesne, that might almost have been comforting. No. My other self gave me the tiniest of bows, and welcomed me to his home. I asked him, of course, who he was, and he said he was *Vindatri.* Did you hear that in your language or mine?"

"Yours," Wu Kung answered.

"Hm. Yes, because it was used as a name. But it is also a word, and the word itself was suggestive." He said the word again; this time Ariane heard what seemed half a dozen words or more, all said indistinguishably together. "You do not understand? Perhaps the exact concept is not easily translated. It means something like 'watcher,' 'observer,' 'monitor,' but with hints of 'guardian,' 'protector,' and also 'judge.'"

"Sentinel, maybe?"

"Perhaps, although that loses some nuance." Orphan flicked his hands absently outward, then continued. "Vindatri then bade me stand still, and walked behind me to look at my wound. I felt a shock as the fragment of metal simply tore its way back out of my wing, and I saw my right wing and case drop to the ground; I collapsed myself, and lost consciousness."

Orphan, clearly still nervous, seated himself, though that seemed almost useless as he almost *vibrated* in the seat. "When I awoke, I sat up—and realized I was no longer in pain. I reached back with my tail . . . and found that both wingcases were there, intact. The room I found myself in—provided with furniture and other accoutrements perfectly appropriate to our species—had a mirror, and—as you can see now," he turned in his chair slightly, "my back was utterly unmarred; no sign of a scar, no sense of injury, only my memories to tell me that I had ever been injured."

"Damn. So this Vindatri pulled you in, yanked the metal out of you, and fixed you up perfectly?"

"Yes. Rather than draw the remainder of the story out—for it would be long indeed—Vindatri kept me there for some time, discussing what I knew of the Arena and its people. He seemed particularly interested in the Faith and the Shadeweavers, but in my own story as well. Finally, he said to me, 'I have rescued you and healed you. Would you agree that you owe me a debt, Orphan?'

"A very great one, Vindatri, if you can also return me to my home; else my gratitude and debt will mean little, I fear."

"He laughed, and tapped his assent, and said, 'True enough. And there is little you could do directly for me, even then. You have already done me a service by telling me of the Factions I have myself not seen in a very long time. So I will return you, in my own way. You have spoken of the strange powers of the Shadeweavers and Faith, and how you fear their abilities; I shall give you something to protect you from them. For this, I will ask only two things: first, that if ever truly *new* factions appear, you come, and tell me of them.'"

Orphan stopped, tilted his head. "The second condition, alas, is a secret. Perhaps one day I may tell you. I hope so." He spread his wings. "But now, I think, you understand."

"No doubt," DuQuesne said. "You promised to tell him of new factions, and here we were. And as it turns out, you've got *two* to talk to him about."

"Exactly," Orphan said. "The fact that you *are* members of one of the new Factions, I believe, will directly interest Vindatri, and perhaps give you some chance of asking him some very interesting questions."

"Such as," Ariane said, "How he can make a gadget that stops the powers of the Shadeweavers cold, and if that means he can tell me what I can do with mine."

A quick handtap and bob-bow. "*Precisely*, Captain Ariane Austin." That tilt-headed smile. "I believe you will find this . . . a most *educational* trip!"

Chapter 17

I am completely exhausted, Simon thought. *Refitting an entire ship with the "primary beam" weapons was not easy.*

That wasn't *entirely* true, either. It had become easier and easier to perform the changes as he moved from turret to turret; his body moved almost of its own accord, the Arena-born knowledge and inspiration guiding his fingers as they flew across the complex interior of the energy cannons and readjusted, shifted, added, changed.

And that still frightened him; he could feel how *simple* it was to access that god-like knowledge, how many other things he could know, could *do*, that perhaps even the Shadeweavers and Faith could not.

And he was, as far as he knew, the *only* person with this power. *With great power comes great temptation. I do not wish to prove the old saying about power corrupting, but I can understand how easily it* can *corrupt.*

Still, he *was* exhausted. Superhuman understanding driving his body was still draining his physical stamina. The Embassy of Humanity loomed up before him, and with relief he stepped through the doors.

With a start, he saw that Laila Canning was already walking towards him.

"You have excellent timing, Simon," Laila said without even so much as a greeting. "We have an emergency, and both Carl and I very much want you present."

Bugger, as one of my father's friends used to say. No rest yet. "Why didn't you call me, if there was an emergency?"

142

Laila smiled briefly, but the smile did at least touch her eyes, light them momentarily. "Because the emergency literally just walked in the door a few minutes ago. I was going to call you if you weren't on your way down the street."

Simon sighed. "I presume it cannot wait?"

"The Leader of the Tantimorcan Faction is here, and he's already *very* distressed that our Leader isn't available. Took a few minutes to convince him that we were completely empowered to act—we had to play that recording of Ariane's delegating that authority to us before he would."

"All right. I guess we . . . wait. He's *here*?"

"Yes. In the second conference room. I told him we would be with him as soon as possible."

"Right." Simon sighed. "Would you by chance know what the *subject* of this emergency is? I would prefer not to be entirely caught unawares."

"He insisted it was something appropriate to discuss *only* with the Faction Leader, and judging by the way his manipulators vibrated, he wasn't exaggerating."

"Definitely wasn't," Carl said, joining them. "Glad you made it, Simon."

"I suppose I should be also. Very well, let us not keep the Leader of our fine shipwrights waiting."

The three of them reached the conference room and the door opened to admit them. Sangrey Vayhen, the Leader of the Tantimorcan Faction, immediately raised himself as a gesture of respect. He was a squat creature, something like a giant toad with a multi-eyed head and twin manipulator tendrils that split into many individual fingers sprouting from near the corners of a wide mouth.

"Leader Vayhen," Laila said, "our apologies for making you wait on what is obviously urgent business; I felt it was important to have Dr. Sandrisson here as an additional representative of the Captain's will, since you impressed on us the urgency of your problem."

"No apology needed," Sangrey answered. "Indeed, I must thank you all for seeing me so promptly." Behind the formal wording Simon could sense a huge amount of nervousness. That subliminal over-sense allowed him to read the alien's posture, scent, and motions. *He's actually afraid of something.*

"Now, please, tell us the problem, Leader Vayhen," Carl said.

"Ah, yes. Of course." There was a thud-click from inside the creature—a sound that he knew had to do with the way they breathed, and one that sounded very much like a nervous swallow in context. "First . . . I must inquire as to whether I am correct in understanding that the name 'Austin' is a line or clan designation?"

What in the world . . . ? "It is what we would call a family name, so yes, in a way," Simon answered. "That is, in general, someone with that last name had at least one parent with that name, and will probably have other relations with that name—although not all of them will."

If anything, Vayhen looked more tense; his manipulator tendrils were stiff and moved in a jerky fashion. "Oh, dear. You see, I have to come here to both demand an apology from your Faction, and possibly to present an apology as well."

Well, that is certainly a most . . . interesting way to present one's situation. "Sangrey," Laila said, "if the Faction of Humanity, or any of us, owe you an apology we will most certainly give you one, but we *must* ask you to please clarify what is going on! None of us have any idea what *either* of us would have to apologize for!"

"Ahh. May the mud rise above me, I am too nervous!" A vibration of color rippled up Sangrey's flanks. "It may seem strange to you, Dr. Canning, Dr. Edlund, Dr. Sandrisson . . . but your faction has been most terrifyingly spectacular in your arrival and success, and the thought of confronting you is most daunting to one such as myself." He raised a manipulator. "Display relevant events at Docking 5."

An image formed in midair, of a group of people—people of multiple species—on one of the docking platforms of Nexus Arena. The group was following a lone human being, and was clearly agitated, shouting angry imprecations at the human, who was retorting in multiple human languages, wearing a broad grin all the while.

"This . . . individual had entered into discussions with several of our people over various political events, but . . ." Sangrey seemed at a loss. ". . . but he did not *discuss*. That is, he seemed . . . intent on finding opportunities to *insult* people, to twist their words in dialogue, not arguing in good faith. And he continued this in a manner that was quite maddening, causing a number of our people and others to follow him, trying to shout him down or force him to be reasonable. Yet he continued."

Simon winced. *Oh, Good* Lord. "Sangrey, as a member of Humanity I *do* apologize. And I believe that all three of us apologize fully in Ariane's place."

Laila rolled her eyes. "I knew we'd get some of his type in sooner or later, but I had thought the screening that was being done would be . . . but no, I suspect this was not included in the original specifications. Our laws don't stop you from being deliberately rude, at least not reliably."

Simon caught a clearer fragment of dialogue and blinked in disbelief. *Did he . . . he* did. *He actually said "I know you are but what am I" while taunting an alien mob! How is that even being* translated?

"But I am afraid it is not over," Sangrey said, and his eyes were positively *wincing.*

Abruptly, the mob lunged forward. Simon remembered: on the docks, many of the Arena's usual protections against violence were relaxed or ignored entirely. There was a short struggle, and suddenly a single figure—a bipedal, human figure—fell, or was pushed, and plummeted away into the endless void below.

"We were informed, alas, that his last name was Austin, and so I was afraid that . . ."

Simon found himself suddenly laughing. "Oh, heavens, Sangrey, I understand. You thought your mob might have just killed off a relative of our Leader!"

Despite the nonhuman appearance, Simon could see Sangrey starting to relax. "Then we did not?"

Carl shook his head. "Ariane doesn't have *that* many relatives, and I know most of them. I didn't recognize that guy. See, while last names *can* indicate family, in most cases there's a *lot* of different families with the same last name. And 'Austin' is a pretty common last name in the area of the world Ariane came from. I'll check up just to be sure, but I'd bet money on that troll not being related to Ariane in any way."

The Leader of the Tantimorcan Faction relaxed even more visibly. "Troll?"

Not translated, or translated too literally? Really, the Arena seems almost arbitrary *in its translation.* "A term that can mean a certain sort of monster," Simon said, "but in this context means a person who derives amusement by bothering others in exactly the manner you describe, harassing them to get a response. Unfortunately our civilization doesn't do much to stop such people; at home, you can just block people from contacting you. I am afraid that does not work so well here."

While it was in the abstract sad to see anyone die, Simon found he could not summon much sorrow for the man who'd brought the violence of the mob down upon him. In truth, Simon simply found it incomprehensible that some people would take joy in making others angry and upset. And now someone had died at the hands of a mob, and the late Mr. Austin's habits had now caused a serious issue that had to be dealt with at the highest level.

"You wouldn't know this guy's first name, would you?" Carl asked.

The large toad-like creature was sagging down slightly; Simon thought this indicated relief, a relaxation after facing something terrifying. It was bemusing to think of *humans* as something terrifying, though. "The other name was Terry, I believe."

"I *thought* so!" Carl said. "This guy was *notorious* for this kind of stuff back home; I've actually heard of him before from Ariane, who was pissed that they shared the same last name. And you're in real luck, Sangrey; according to a quick check of the records, he didn't have any family of his own, doesn't even have anyone in the 'in case of emergency, contact' slot of the form. So there probably won't be too many people terribly broken up by the news. Maybe quite a few celebrating."

I would dearly love to leave it at that, Simon thought, but he knew he couldn't—and a glance at Laila confirmed that she was already on it. "While that is something of a relief," Laila said briskly, "your people *did* take the law into their own hands. I can't just ignore that."

"This is most certainly understood, Dr. Canning. It is not entirely clear what happened at the end—it may have been at least partially an accident, but it may also have been as deliberate as it seems. We do not wish this to lie between us; what can we do as recompense?"

"I presume there *was* an attempt to recover him?" Simon asked.

"An alarm was given and some fliers dispatched by us and others, but . . . there were only some *zikki* found."

Simon could not keep from wincing himself. *Zikki* were fast-moving Arena predators, something like armored flying squid. If Mr. Austin had fallen into a group of those, well . . .

He took a deep breath of his own. "Leader Vayhen, would you give us a moment to confer?"

The manipulator tendrils spread wide. "Oh, certainly; do you wish me to leave?"

"No, no, just give us a few moments." The other two followed him out.

Once the door closed, he looked at them. "Technically, it's your decision, not mine."

Laila gave a dismissive sniff. "*Legally* perhaps, but we all know that you and DuQuesne are the ones she leans on, and she left you to give us the same backup." She flicked a glance to Carl, who nodded.

"What do you think, Simon?" Carl was clearly uncertain. "This is a sticky situation any way I look at it. I mean, that guy may have been a total asshole, but even being a world-class asshole doesn't mean you should get killed."

Simon closed his eyes and frowned. "That rather depends on location and time, Carl. In many past civilizations, being an . . . asshole could, and often *did*, carry a penalty up to and including death. I am not entirely sure that in the setting of the Arena—where offending the wrong person could lead to a *war*—it is not in fact completely *appropriate* that we look at things in that light."

"Still," Laila said thoughtfully, "we don't want to set a precedent that our people can be disposed of by mobs."

"No. But Leader Vayhen has already accepted that there is wrongdoing on his side." Simon was suddenly certain what Ariane would have done. "Laila, Carl, what do you think of this . . ."

After he'd explained, he saw both Carl and Laila nodding. "Works for me," Carl said. "I think it's probably the best compromise."

"I concur," Laila said. "I was thinking along similar lines; this confirms it."

"Then shall we?" The other two followed him in.

Sangrey raised himself slightly as they entered. "You have come to a decision?"

"We have, Leader Vayhen. The fact is that we, as Humanity, must accept a large part of the blame. It is imperative that we start screening *all* our people for such tendencies and keep those sorts at home where they won't cause trouble. We *should* have done so already, and this event is a result of that oversight. Laila, we can have people start on that right away, yes?"

Laila nodded. "Not a problem."

"And," Carl said, "The fact is . . . Showing that vid to people back home just might get *through* to some of those types that there's limits on what they can do. The Arena's filled with *consequences*, and there's nothing wrong with hammering that home."

He did *work for someone who raced in a potentially lethal sport; I suppose that gives you an appreciation for the less forgiving aspects of reality.* "Obviously, Sangrey, we expect you will mete out appropriate punishment to the perpetrators, by your own standards, but insofar as our *official* reaction? The Faction of Humanity is willing to simply let it pass, as long as the Faction of Tantimorcan is also willing to let this pass."

Sangrey squished himself low to the floor, apparently his equivalent of a bow. "The Faction of Tantimorcan accepts. May this incident be forgotten."

"May it be forgotten," the three of them chorused.

Once Sangrey had left, Simon turned to the other two. "We *do* have to make sure this sort of thing *cannot* happen again."

"No argument there," Carl said. "I found this guy's file and I can see why he was let in—he's really good at inventory management, creative, good at leading people in the right circumstances. But he is . . . *was* also really good at finding weak places in people's mental armor and pushing; it was more than a habit, it was an *avocation* with him."

Laila smiled—a cold smile that Simon was rather glad was not directed at him. "Then I suppose he achieved his life's goal. I would presume that we could get the AIs working on sorting out these people *before* they come through."

"Naturally," Simon said. "It might be as simple as looking at how many blocking lists an applicant is on. However, I think that will require some more CSF/SSC work. Restricting where people go is not normally permitted when it's not conflicting with another individual's rights. I am afraid a lot of our laws are going to have to be revised."

"I will send a summary to Thomas Cussler," Laila said. "It's really the sort of thing he should be watching for. As you say, we *will* have to adjust our screening, and perhaps our laws, to deal with this."

"And fast," Carl said, looking more serious. "Trolls are usually just nuisances, but there's other people who have more sinister motives, especially now. But you're right, that's Tom's and the SSC's problem; we'll send 'em our recommendation and let them figure it out. The fact someone's gotten killed should give them a good kick in the pants to move forward."

Simon stretched. "Well, now that that's settled, I want to get myself some dinner and go to sleep. I feel, as DuQuesne might say, like I have been pulled through a knothole." The others waved as he left.

However, now that he'd had to deal with another crisis, he found he wasn't yet ready to relax. *Blast. Well, then, I'll go out and eat. That should work off the extra nervous energy.*

The Grand Arcade was—as at almost any time—a whirl of scents, sights, and sounds uplifting, dizzying, and, in a way, comforting; here there might be a thousand different species, enemies and victims and allies, and yet they were all here to do things so very much the same— shop, haggle, eat, entertain, gamble. It was here that you could see that in many ways we really were all very much the same.

Simon found a restaurant that he'd seen before, run by a Daelmokhan. Despite their rather inhuman appearance, the Daelmokhan had biochemistries quite close to that of humans and their restaurants tended to have a large variety of edible, and even quite tasty, selections. Armed with his headware references to make sure he didn't choose unwisely, he quickly made some selections and sat down.

Yes, this was the right call, he thought, as he cracked the shell on a creature that looked like an almost spherical crab with circular frond-like appendages on two sides. *I can feel myself relaxing. Once I'm done, I know I'll be able to go to sleep by the time I'm back at the Embassy.*

"Hello, Simon. Would you mind *terribly* if I could sit down?" said a light, musical voice, a voice with just the perfect undertone of huskiness to make it completely arresting.

Startled, he glanced up.

Hair gleaming like spun gold, eyes like pure sapphires, Maria-Susanna looked down at him, smiling, with just a hint of uncertainty that made her look startlingly vulnerable. "Honestly . . . I need to talk to someone."

Chapter 18

"The idea is tempting, Dr. DuQuesne, but . . . are you certain it will *work*?"

"Not *certain*. But . . . say eighty percent chance it'll work," DuQuesne answered. "And if it *does* work, your firepower just went *way* up."

"It will *drop* if you fail, however," Orphan pointed out. DuQuesne could tell that the protest was, at least partially, purely from Orphan's instinctive need to be cautious.

"You'll still have the top turret that Simon modified in the first place," Ariane said. "And from what I saw of that thing in action, you could lose a *lot* of turrets and still be ahead of where your ship started."

A buzzing chuckle accompanied by a handtap was Orphan's reply. "You indeed have a point, especially since that weapon no longer requires someone to stand in the turret reloading it. And having *another* such weapon . . . or three . . . yes, that is definitely a gamble worth taking."

"Three? You wouldn't want *all* of them converted?"

"Alas, I do not have nearly enough channel assembly reloads to reasonably make use of that many. But up to three, yes, I have the supplies to make useful."

"Okay, then we'll get to it. On one condition."

"That is . . . ?"

"You don't watch. If I'm right, and I've got the secret, I'm not giving it away. Giving you a SAMPLE, yes, but not the technique."

The green and black alien chuckled again. "Doctor, I have gone over the one Dr. Sandrisson created many times, and failed to find the secret. If you have that secret, then it is your Faction's by right. The gain of such weaponry will be more than adequate to salve the complaints of my curiosity."

DuQuesne grinned. "Okay, then. C'mon, Ariane, I'll need your help."

Ariane looked puzzled, but nodded. Wu turned to follow them. "Hold off, Wu."

True to his training and promise, the Monkey King looked at Ariane. "Do you want me to come?"

"If I'm not safe with DuQuesne, I'm not safe *period*. If he doesn't want you there, he'll have a reason."

"All right. But I will be even more bored then."

"I have an idea, Wu Kung," Orphan said. "While I now know you were . . . oh, what was that term I heard one of you humans use . . . *sandbagging*, that was it! I know you were sandbagging during our little match, I think some sparring, and perhaps discussion of combat traditions of each others' civilizations, could reduce your boredom."

"Ha!" said Wu, his tail coming up with more interest. "You have a good idea there! All right, while DuQuesne and Ariane waste their time with machines, we will have some fun!"

"Just don't have *too* much fun, Wu," Ariane said with the smile that often showed up when Wu Kung was around. "We need Orphan in one piece."

"Yes, please; I like keeping my limbs intact," agreed Orphan.

"No dismembering, agreed," Wu said with a grin. "But a warning: I think *you* were sandbagging a little too."

DuQuesne saw Ariane's eyebrows go up. "Really?"

Orphan looked, somehow, *too* casually innocent as Wu Kung replied, "Not *much*, maybe, but he's the tricky type. I didn't find out until *years* later how much Sha Wujing was holding back, and Orphan's like him. Only with a better sense of humor!"

"That's not hard to manage," DuQuesne said, remembering the grim gray river-ogre from Wu's home Hyperion world. "Okay, guys, we'll see you later." DuQuesne led the way towards the main starboard battery.

"All right, Marc, can you tell me what *my* role in this is? I know you're testing to see if you can do what Simon did, but—"

"Wait." DuQuesne took out a handheld scanner and observed its responses carefully; then he set it to give an alarm if anything changed and returned it to his pocket. "Sorry, wanted to double-check that Orphan wasn't monitoring us. Yes, I *probably* don't need help to do this. But no reason to tell *him* that. He knows Simon did it . . . somehow. He also knows he can't figure out *how*. So if this time it's two of us (and it works), he'll have even *fewer* good clues to go on. As far as I know, aside from the *Holy Grail* crew, Nyanthus, Mandallon, and Gona-Brashind are the only ones who know what happened at the ritual that sealed your powers, and thus the only ones with even a *chance* to guess that there's something strange about Simon. Without that, he'll be shooting in the dark."

"I feel kind of guilty for working so hard to hide things from him," Ariane said.

DuQuesne reached the door, unsealed it, let Ariane enter first and then closed and dogged the hatch down again. "So do I—a little. But friend or not, that joker's *always* got his own agenda in mind, and he's got us in trouble before. So I don't feel *that* guilty."

Ariane looked up and an expression of momentary awe flickered across her face. "Wow. That's a *big* gun."

"It is that. Even without these mods, it's *nothing* you would want to mess with. Shooting hundreds of kilometers through sea-level thick amosphere, that's not a popgun by anyone's standards."

"So—being a devil's advocate here—why are we going to just *give* Orphan these super-guns?"

DuQuesne nodded in appreciation. "That *is* the question. And I'll bet you can answer it yourself, Captain."

The blue-haired woman nodded, watching as he started to take the cover plates off the energy cannon. "Well, first, we're on board and could end up in a fight, so it's just covering our own bets to make sure he's got the best equipment."

"Sure a good point," DuQuesne agreed. He concentrated, thinking back. *Me and Richard . . . working on the* Dauntless *before launch . . .* "Go on."

"Hmmm . . . well, he'll *owe* us something. Something pretty big, since he couldn't get this anywhere else. And keeping an ace in the hole like this is something that's second nature to him; he's not going to blow the secret for us."

"You've got it. Most of it, anyway." *Simon routed these power leads here, then . . . oh, yeah, now I see it!* The modifications suddenly made *sense* to DuQuesne, were clear and straightforward. He began working faster, feeling himself getting into the flow.

With an abrupt shock, he realized Ariane had been addressing him, with increasing concern. "DuQuesne! Can you even *hear* me?"

"What? Sorry, Ariane, I got really immersed there."

"Scared me a little; your hands were *flying*, and before you looked like you weren't even quite sure what you were doing."

"I wasn't," he admitted. "Then all of a sudden it just *clicked*. What'd I miss?"

"Not much, really. I just asked you what the *rest* of it was."

"It? Oh, why we're giving these to Orphan." He adjusted another setting, tested the connections. "Simple: I want to *keep* him in debt to us. The one thing he's *scrupulous* about is keeping his word and paying his debts; that's something everyone in the *Arena* cares about. So as long as he knows he owes us, we're not just relying on his sense of friendship, but on his sense of . . . well, honor, I guess."

"I wish I could let my idealistic side argue, but I remember the way he helped Amas-Garao get me in the ring. Good work, 'Blackie.'"

He chuckled. Somehow, having someone use that old, old nickname while he was there with his arms buried in a starship's guts . . . somehow it felt like *home. Is there an afterlife for AIs? I hope so, Rich, because I really feel like you're watching me, somehow.* "Thank you, Captain."

"No problem. On the subject of 'he's gotten us in trouble before' . . . what do you think about the condition he couldn't tell us?"

"You mean the other part of his bargain with this Vindatri?" He frowned, arranging his thoughts. "Well, first, no point in trying to pry it out of him. Obviously he gave his word not to tell, and we're relying on that characteristic of Orphan's nature."

"Agreed. Any guesses?"

Hmm. Yeah, these go . . . here. "A few. You know I can read even alien body language pretty well—which fits with our other deductions. And . . . you're right. I think it's potential trouble. No hostile vibes from him, but he showed just a touch too much tension in his stance. Not as bad as the time before he set Gabrielle up, but not good."

Ariane was silent for a few moments as he worked. Then, "So . . . is there anything we should be doing to prepare for . . . whatever it is?"

"Damned if I know. I know there's *something* he didn't say, that he knows we'd really want to know. What, exactly? Not even a guess. On the other hand, we've got a *massive* trump card that—even if he somehow figured it out—he'd have a hell of a time countering."

"*Orphan* might have a hard time countering it, but what about Vindatri?"

"*That* is the question of the hour, and I hate to say it but I haven't got a clue. Orphan doesn't know who or what Vindatri is, he's in debt to the guy, and he's scared to death of him, too."

He could see her stiffen. "He is?"

"Not a doubt about it. He wasn't just creeped out from the meeting; he was still scared to this day. Not all that surprising—Orphan's the kind of guy who wants to have a handle on everything, and Vindatri obviously was out of his league in pretty much every direction." DuQuesne thought about it a while, inserting new circuitry into the control ring. "But honestly? Unless this guy's one of the Voidbuilders themselves, and I kinda doubt it, I think our ace is still good insurance."

Ariane paced slowly around the turret, her path marked by the clicking of her boots on the deck. "But that story still creeped *you* out, too. Why?"

He paused, looked up. For a moment he couldn't speak; habits of silence decades old still had a hold on him, even in Ariane's presence.

Finally he sighed and sat back. "Hyperion again."

"I guessed *that* much. It echoed something that happened to you there?"

"Yeah. Our first encounter with Mentor, actually. Not *your* Mentor, of course."

Not for the first time, a tiny voice in the back of his head asked, *Are you sure?* Ariane's AIsage sure *sounded* like the one DuQuesne had known. *He* could *have escaped, somehow. It'd explain why he was able to track down other escaped Hyperion AIs once the possibility was raised. Crippled, of course—he's in a T-5 housing now, not a T-10+ like the . . . well, the original Mentor.*

Aloud, he continued, "We needed support for the fledgling interstellar community we were setting up, and we already knew we were up against *some* kind of hostile interstellar power, one that already had agents on Earth even before we got the *Skylark* off the ground. One of those agents was the one that hurt the original Oasis so bad that K had to transfer her consciousness gestalt into her own body."

"Fairchild, right?"

"Dr. Alexander Fairchild, yes. And I hope to God he isn't the AI that escaped . . . not that any of the major bad guy AIs would be a picnic. Anyway, the way we ended up meeting Mentor was by following clues to a particular location in space and, well, getting drawn in just like that. And met Mentor in pretty much the same way, him choosing to manifest an appearance appropriate to each of us."

Ariane—who had actually *read* the originals he was based on, unlike about ninety-nine point nine nine nine percent of humanity—nodded slowly. There was a faint smile on her face. "So you weren't just a sort of Seaton-Crane cross. You were . . . what, Virgil Samms, too?"

He blushed. "Sort of. Kimball Kinnison, too. Not quite the model of perfection Samms was. Put me and Rich together for that. And yeah, put both series in a Mixmaster and fast-forward for the plot. Anyway, that's why it creeped me out; sounded *waaaay* too familiar, and I know *this* is the real world."

She took his hand and squeezed it. "I can't blame you, Marc. It creeped *me* out too, and I sure wasn't in Hyperion."

He nodded, squeezed back, and then straightened up, started working on the next section.

"Marc," she said after a moment, "that subject reminds me of our 'trump card.'"

"Not surprised. What's on your mind?"

"Well . . . speaking as the Captain and Leader, I'd like to know . . . how *sure* are you of it working, and to what extent?"

Wondered when she'd ask those questions. And when I'd have to let myself think about them again. I'd shoved them way to the back for damn good reason. But she's also got a damned good reason for asking. "Given what we saw with Wu, I think we've got a hundred percent guarantee of *something*. As to the extent . . . that's the $64.00 question." He checked his sensor again, then sighed. "Okay. Ariane, you've pretty much backed me into a corner here, so we've got a mini-crisis on our hands."

She blinked. "A crisis? Of what?"

"Of secrets and leverage, basically. See, this Vindatri—he could make something that trumped the Shadeweavers' powers, do other things that creeped out even our favorite opportunist Orphan. So I *have* to assume he could do a lot of the same things the Shadeweavers could."

She nodded after a moment. "Okay, I follow, and I think you're right. He told Orphan that device would work to protect him against *either* Faction, so we can take it as a given that he understands their powers very well, and can probably use at least some of them. What's the crisis?"

"Once I really started to think we Hyperions might be able to use our Hyperion-world capabilities, I did a few quick tests. And the answer was *yes*. They worked. The powers of the mind that I got from my Smithian mash-up Hyperion-verse? Working. Telepathy, perception, the whole nine yards." He gestured to the energy cannon. "This is just another demonstration—the wonky physics and technology tricks that shouldn't work, do. For me, anyway. And apparently for Simon, maybe for a different reason though."

She was staring at him in awe. "They really *work*?"

"Yeah. Don't know their limits—how much can the Arena give me? How much does it *want* to give me? What can people like this Vindatri do? Not a clue. But that's not the key point here. The point is that with those abilities I of course got the capability to *wall off* that knowledge. I know it's *there*, but even *that* is shielded. A Shadeweaver—or this Vindatri, or the Faith if they ever tried—would have to force his way in. It's not like that trick the Hyperion designers came up with; I'm pretty sure that once they *recognize* that trick exists, the Shadeweavers could find a way around what amounts to a mental checksum, and Amas-Garao sure throught so too. But these things . . . they're genuine mental shields, complete with surface thoughts that hide what's there."

Ariane suddenly closed her eyes and smacked herself on the forehead. "*Duh!* Pushing you like this, and getting the information from you, means *I* am now going to be thinking about it. And that makes me a potential security risk."

"Basically, yeah. Problem is that while the *Shadeweavers* promised not to mess with our heads, this Vindatri sure didn't. A trump card isn't much of a trump card if the other people can *see* it."

"And," Ariane went on, "if you weren't hiding it from *yourself* most of the time, you might give it away in your behavior. Right?"

"You can bet those legendary ninety-seven rows of little green apple trees on it, especially when you're dealing with Big Time Operators like Orphan or this Vindatri."

Ariane stood there for a few moments, obviously thinking, and he saw her grow a shade paler. Her eyes met his again. "And now that I know the potential extent of your—and Wu Kung's—abilities, *I* am the big security risk. It was bad enough before that I had suspicions, but with you confirming it—"

"About the size of it. Yes."

"Then . . ." she hesitated, and he wasn't surprised. *I'd damn well hesitate before suggesting what I think she's going to.* "Then could you . . . do something to either make me forget, or shield any thoughts I might have?"

"If I'm right? Yes, I can do that. If you—"

"Do it," she said sharply. "Until I know how to use the power the Faith and Shadeweavers locked up in me, I've got *no* defenses against beings like that messing with, or reading, my mind. We can't take the chance of someone finding out key information because I pulled it out of you and can't keep from thinking about it."

DuQuesne could see that she was absolutely certain. "Yes, Captain," he said. *Arena, you damn well better be* picture-perfect *in making these powers work, because I am about to mess with someone else's mind.*

He put down the tools, seated himself comfortably, gestured for Ariane to sit as well. "Main thing is for you to be as relaxed as possible," he said. "Had to do something like this for some of our allies like Dorothy—Rich couldn't quite bring himself to touch her head but he knew it had to be done."

She took a deep breath and let it out slowly. "I'll try. What's it . . . like? Will it hurt?"

He concentrated. *Shouldn't hurt at all,* he thought, projecting towards her.

"*YOW!* Oh my *GOD,* that's weird! I mean . . . I've had stuff sort of like that in the simgames, but it's been a long time, and that's *real.*"

"Think of it as a simgame effect, if it makes it easier," DuQuesne said. "This may be physically real, but the Arena's running the show. The show's just *really* convincing."

He closed his eyes and entered the surface of her mind. *Ariane? I'm here again.*

A sensation of nervous excitement. *Yeah, I can hear that. Or think that? Vocabulary for telepathy isn't really there, you know?*

He grinned, knew she "saw" a mental representation of the smile. *Yeah, I know. Now, I don't want you to forget what you knew, so I'm going to do something a little trickier; build a sort of mental camouflage around that part of your knowledge. I can't really build in a mind-barrier that'll protect you from a direct push by someone with any kind of mental power, but if he or she doesn't suspect there's something to look for, they're not going to see it.*

So how will that work? If I think about our trump card—

It will use your own knowledge of the surroundings and situation to emphasize whatever other *thoughts you might have. People's minds flicker from one thing to another pretty quick, and they're usually thinking at least two or three things in fast succession even when they're only conscious of thinking about one. It'll be a little disconcerting for you at first, because it'll be a little like hearing yourself talking about two things at once, but you'll get used to it. That's what I've got up around my own mind.*

He started constructing the mind-block. It was something like a mirror, something like a blind, something like a false-front, but really not like any of them because it was a *mental* construct.

It was not, of course, possible to ignore everything *about* Ariane's mind while he was there—though he tried very hard to keep focused only on the task at hand. *A person's mind is the only place they should be guaranteed to have privacy, and telepathy violates that. Even with permission . . . and dammit, I shouldn't even be getting* hints *of what she thinks about me or anyone else!*

But he kept on, weaving a cloak of thoughts that he could implant and layer over particular concepts and knowledge in Ariane's consciousness. *Got to be careful as* hell *here. The idea is to hide stuff, not to touch anything else.*

He felt, distantly, a bead of sweat going down his back. *Now I know why Rich didn't want to do this for Dorothy; too much riding on it for me, personally. And doing it here in the real world, in a world where I haven't spent years mastering these powers, where I'm just starting to think about it again—I could really mess it—*

Relax, Marc. A flash of a confident smile, a warmth and absolute trust.

He was startled. *You heard that.*

Another flicker of humor despite tension. *Marc, I almost didn't need to. I know what you're like by now, don't I? I could* guess *what you'd be thinking.* A sensation as though she had laid a hand on his shoulder, even though neither of them had moved. *You've never failed me yet, and I don't think you ever will. Trust yourself. You know what you're doing, and you're not going to mess anything up.*

Her absolute confidence startled him . . . yet at the same time it was something he realized he had known all along. *All right, Ariane. Hold on and this'll be over in a few minutes.*

A weave of thought and intention, anchored to her will and the conditions around her. Connections to the secrets, connections that shielded, deflected, turned away; it was as though a part of her mind was becoming blurred, shadowed, harder and harder to see, and he placed another layer on it, and another.

Finally he sat back. "Done!" He wiped his forehead and reached into the toolbox for the bottle of water he'd brought along, drained half of it.

She rubbed her head thoughtfully. "I don't feel much different."

"That's the whole idea. Just try not to think on the subject *too* much; don't want to put strain on the coverup."

She looked askance at him. "You *do* know that's like telling someone to *not* think about pink elephants, right? Suddenly they're thinking about nothing *but* pink elephants!"

"Yeah, but better that I get to see how it acts under stress right now than find out it's falling apart the moment we meet up with Vindatri."

"A test run under stress? Okay, I get it." She blinked. "You're right, that *is* strange. It's . . . it's like being in a big empty room with one other person talking at the same time you are, the echoes bouncing around each other. I can hear . . . or see, or whatever . . . the thoughts that the people *outside* would get, and my hidden thoughts, too."

After a few minutes he nodded. "Seems to hold up pretty well. I can see it by scanning, but I *know* it's there and I know *exactly* what to look for. If I think about it from a surface-scan point of view I don't think anyone short of the real Mentor or another Stage Three mind— as we used to call them—would catch it unless they were already suspicious and poking hard. It's not going to protect you from a direct forceful scan, but it's good enough for now."

Ariane nodded thoughtfully but said nothing right away. He turned back to the gun and started working again.

After a while, DuQuesne became aware that she wasn't saying anything, just watching him; it was distracting for a moment, but then the silence became . . . companionable. She was just there watching, not intruding nor impatient. He smiled again, and let himself focus completely on the work, hearing ghosts of old conversations and banter from the lab and the ships he and Rich had shared.

Finally she did speak, and the question was an echo of questions fifty years old and more. "So, do you think that gun's going to work?"

"I'll bet on it. Ariane, I can *feel* it. I can see how to rework this thing to fire the way that Simon did, and how to improve on it—since Simon wasn't an engineer. Difference between a guy who had the world's best instruction manual, and another guy who knows when to *ignore* the manual."

"But what you're doing . . . really *wouldn't* work, right?"

"Not by the *normal* rules of the Arena—or back home—no. But it *will* work by the rules I grew up with—and we just proved that my other abilities are working here. Which means that Orphan's ship just got a lot more dangerous."

She grinned up at him. "You look *happy*, Marc."

Do I? I guess I do . . . Yeah, I do. DuQuesne looked down and smiled. "I am. This . . . brought back the *good* part of the memories, and having you here . . ."

Her smile faded but did not go away, her eyes were serious, no longer laughing. "There's a conversation I've always avoided with you," she said finally.

He could have misinterpreted that, but he wasn't going to let the invitation pass. "But not now?"

She shook her head. "Not this time. The two people I'm actually interested in are *both* my closest advisors. I'm not going to escape that problem either way."

No, I guess she won't. Technically she's designated me second in command, Simon not really being in the chain of command near that level, but we've been the two she relied on most. "Does that mean you'll always have to keep a distance, or not?"

She rolled her eyes, then without warning reached up, pulled herself up by his shoulders and *kissed* him, open-mouthed and eager.

DuQuesne was caught completely off-guard, but he knew how to respond to that. The kiss lasted for something like forty-three years, but oddly the clock said it was only about thirty or forty seconds when she dropped her feet back to the deck. "Wow," he said, which was utterly trite, and completely inadequate, and he found at the same time there was no better word. *Haven't done that since K and I separated. And for someone fifty years my junior, she's good.*

She laughed and gave him another quick kiss. "No, Marc, I'm not keeping my distance. I'm betting that our friendship—yours and mine, and ours with Simon—is strong enough that we can work this through without disaster."

"And what *about* Simon?"

Ariane shook her head and laughed again. "Honestly, Marc, I don't know. You're both incredibly brilliant, capable, and courageous. Simon's beautiful and charming and debonair, and you're tall, dark, brooding, and angsty. And now both of you have awesome and mysterious powers, too."

"I'm not *angsty!*" It was surprising how much of him rebelled at the characterization. *Which might just be proving her point, dammit.*

"Sometimes, my favorite Hyperion, you *are*. You can't help it and I don't blame you. And it's kind of cute in someone as massively omnicompetent as you." Ariane kissed him again before he could recover from being called 'cute,' which—as far as he could recall—was a word *no one* had ever used to describe him before. "But like I said, I don't know, Marc. I *thought* I would be a one-man woman eventually—I wasn't comfortable thinking about my parents' multi-relationship arrangement. But . . . maybe not. At least not when I'm presented with two such awesome people who think *I* am awesome, too."

He managed to finally catch up and laugh himself. "Well, you *are*, Ariane. If you weren't, do you think you could boss me around? And you *do*, no mistake."

"I do, don't I? And that's always a shock, you know. Anyway . . . I know *you* are a one-woman kind of guy, if you were raised to be a Doc Smith hero."

"Sure the way I always thought of it. But . . . well, I'll have to think about the whole situation." He slammed the panels shut. "But . . . I do love you, Ariane. I think I have since . . ." he grinned, "since the time you shut us all down and told us that if we called you 'Captain' you were going to *be* the Captain, by ninety-seven rows of the proverbial apple trees, and we had better just sit down and suck it up."

She returned the grin with a startled guffaw. "What? Well, that's not the romantic memory *I* would have expected."

"Oh, I *liked* you a hell of a lot before, but that was the point where I *realized* just how much you meant to me. It's only gotten worse since." He looked along the energy cannon. "Well, I think we're done here. Better tell Orphan he can do a test firing once he gets his automation rigged."

She hooked her arm into his, and he felt a weight lifting from his heart, even with all the complications he knew this would bring. "Oh, yeah, speaking of complications, which we sort of were, Captain, I should warn you, you have one other problem."

She looked up as they stepped through the hatch. "And what exactly is that?"

"Sun Wu Kung. He's kind of prone to developing attachments to the one holding his leash, and like I told you a while back, you look a *lot* like Sanzo."

"What? You mean . . . *Sun Wu Kung* might be—oh, for God's sake, no!"

He could not keep from laughing as the door swung shut behind them.

Chapter 19

Simon stared incredulously for a long, long moment, before his natural politeness asserted itself. "Pardon me. Of course, please sit down." *I've just invited a known mass-murderess and part of another faction to eat lunch with me. But perhaps a wiser course than rejecting her.*

Relief was visible on the perfect features as Maria-Susanna sat down. "Thanks *so* much, Simon. I . . . know you probably haven't heard good things about me."

"And some of them are true," he said. "Most of them, I suspect."

For just an instant he saw—or, perhaps, *sensed*, through that strange connection with the Arena—a flash of agony, remorse and anger and confusion. It was gone almost before he saw it, and she simply said, "I . . . suppose, yes. At least in some sense or another. I won't argue with you, not now."

Her eyes were downcast, and he heard a trace of shakiness in the breath she drew before gesturing, with too casual a movement, for the menu to appear before her. *She's worried. Frightened? A Hyperion?* He found a part of him wanting to reach out, take her hand and ask what was wrong.

Oh, this is dangerous. She may not assault me physically here, but already I can feel *her effect on me.* He recalled her prior appearance, how she had charmed even Ariane, to her confusion . . . and the furious anger he'd sensed in her, when no one else had seen it.

In that instant he understood. *Of course. I had not yet fully admitted the existence of this strange ability, and it was active without my awareness. It gives me a perspective beyond the human, and here, against a woman who is herself beyond human, I am afraid I* need *that detachment.*

Simon concentrated, allowed that god-like perception to trickle in, to elevate his senses and knowledge above those he owned naturally. As he did so, he could suddenly see layers of tension within the woman across from him. *It does not let me read minds, but perceiving external signals that I would ordinarily miss, that it can do.*

More importantly, he felt that preternatural attraction and sympathy becoming more distant. He could still *feel* them, but they were no longer gaining a hold on his deeper emotions and perceptions. *But they are* real. *There is an attraction, a fascination, that goes beyond any ordinary emotional reaction.* He could, somehow, *tell* that, even though he could detect nothing objective that would explain the attraction.

But none of that changed the fact that in front of him was a woman who was worried, afraid, a woman to whom such fear would be alien, perhaps was the trigger to make her into the monster he had heard of.

Or . . . just possibly . . . the lever to find a way to curing *her. Is that possible?*

"You could have called me—or anyone—if you wanted," Simon said finally, as she scanned the menu with the air of someone only half-seeing what was before them. "But you did not. Why?"

Her eyes met his, a flash of deep-sky blue more intense than Ariane's, and even through the Olympian detachment of his connection to the Arena he could feel the heartrending impact of that sad gaze. "The contact through the Arena . . . is impersonal, Simon. You know that. No one would have met with me without first preparing, formulating their suspicions, their fears." She sighed. "And I'm not a danger to you. I'm *not!* I don't *agree* with DuQuesne and some of the others on everything, but I want to *save* humanity, protect it . . . it's . . . it's my *purpose.*"

That much was true, and at the same time trembled on the ragged edge of disaster. *To admit she* has *a real purpose is probably dangerously close to recalling that she was* created. "I am not arguing with you, Maria-Susanna. What brought you to me, then, Maria-Susanna of the Vengeance?" He thought it best to remind her that despite her protestations, she was no longer *with* humanity.

She laughed, and there was a *bitter* note in that laugh that sent a jolt through Simon. "Just 'Maria-Susanna' now, I am afraid. I am no longer a member of the Vengeance."

My God. "What? But . . . why?"

"I don't *know!*" she snapped. Then she blinked, clenched her fists, and took three deep breaths. To Simon's oversight, a roiling crest of emotion rose and was just as suddenly damped down. "I don't know. SelpA'A'At called me in, said that the Vengeance felt that my presence was no longer a benefit to the Vengeance, and removed me from the Faction."

She shook her head slowly, confused, angry, sad, all at once. "He seemed . . . *horrified.* By *me.* Or something associated with me. But I had told him a version of the truth, and he had seemed not to *care* as long as I posed no threat to his people. Now, suddenly, without warning, I am disposed of."

"Just like that? Now you have no home, nothing?"

A wan ghost of a smile rose on her face. "Just like that. Oh, I am not a beggar on the streets; he did not begrudge me a very large number of vals for both my service and to pay for the insult and injury of dismissal. But I am now . . . nobody in the Arena."

"I am *certain* there are other factions that would accept you," Simon said.

"But not my own homeland, I suspect."

Simon paused, and drove himself higher, looking at Maria-Susanna as he had Vantak during the battle. *Is there a solution here? A chance? A way to draw her back from the brink?*

Even as he did that, he *saw.*

Saw the woman before him, younger, without the signs of care or anger, alongside a man in a gold shirt whom she looked at with absolute adoration. She traveled with him, fought at his side, tended him in injury, and was in turn tended when she had fallen.

And then the same woman, screaming in horror and denial as she cradled the man's body in her arms. Denial turned to rage, rage to murderous fury and the first cold-blooded killing, hunting a woman whose features echoed her own through the increasing chaos that had to be Hyperion Station during its fall. The loss of others, hundreds of others, and the mind made to be a support and hero and defender *broke*, and he could see the pattern of the madness within her, bent inward, self-supporting, self-destroying.

Yes. It could be done. But not by me. Only by someone who knew her well, whose voice could reach *her . . . and only if they said the right words.* Still, he now had a grasp of what could be said, what could be done, even if it was very little.

"Perhaps," Simon said, after what must have been only a fractional pause to Maria-Susanna. "But if you return, you will have to answer for everything you have done. You know that. Even if you justify it to yourself, the law will not have the same view."

"Yes . . ." her eyes blanked for a moment, then refocused, with another of those flashes of madness or pain. "Yes, I know. And so I cannot come home. Not now."

"I'm sorry, Maria-Susanna."

She looked at him then—*really* looked at him, not through the lens of her own worries, but with the wide-eyed blue gaze that he had seen in the younger girl. "You mean that. You really *are* sorry for me, for this . . . situation." She smiled, an expression with the force of a cannon of sunshine, and reached out to squeeze his hand. "Thank you, Simon. And . . . I'm sorry, too. For having misled you, and *especially* for taking your research without permission. I needed it . . . but that's not really a good excuse." A moment of pained self-awareness. "I'm . . . good at excuses, though."

"Given your situation . . . I won't hold a grudge," he said, with a smile and a nod. "Don't do anything like that again, though."

"I won't. I promise, Simon; you're safe from me—you and your marvelous brain and whatever it invents." Again another flash of self-awareness, and her other hand convulsively tightened. "*You* aren't associated with *them*, so I can promise that."

"Them" being Hyperion, I have to assume. The thought of Hyperion triggered another recall, and he suddenly found himself trying to weigh the dangers of exposing something.

She leaned forward. "What is it, Simon?"

Well, there's no way I'll convince her there wasn't something. And . . . in all honesty, I would not want to keep this secret from her. "I just remembered something very important that I need to tell you."

"Important? For *me*?" She was, for the moment, honestly startled. She knew no one in the Faction of Humanity would have anything they wanted to say to her, barring "you're under arrest," or possibly something worse. "What is it?"

"Someone's killing Hyperions, and it isn't you."

Maria-Susanna went pale, face now alabaster white. "What? Who?"

"We have not yet identified the culprit. But we do know that he, or she, or it, is responsible for the deaths of at least four Hyperions, and nearly killed DuQuesne as well."

Her perfect brows drew down and he could suddenly *see* the resemblance between her and DuQuesne: there was an implacable rage there at any who harmed people she thought of as *hers*. "Who did this . . . person kill?"

"I wasn't given the details—probably wouldn't recognize their names. DuQuesne and Oasis said it was . . ." he checked his memory of the conversation to make sure he got it right, ". . . Johnny, Telzey, D'Arbignal, and Giles."

I was wrong; now *she's gone white.* The beautiful golden-haired woman sagged back in shock. "No. No, not *Johnny!* Not funny old Giles! I didn't even know . . . I thought they were dead already! Oh, DuQuesne, you were *hiding* them from me, and now they're *gone*?" Her color was starting to return, and a hard, cold light was rising in her eyes. "But this enemy found them, even when *I* hadn't?"

"Our top suspect . . . is an escaped Hyperion AI."

She froze. Not only pale, her hands suddenly shook. "*No. No.*"

Simon couldn't ignore that horror. He rose and gently put an arm around her.

Maria-Susanna leaned into him—just for a moment—shuddering. She pulled away, but did not move far enough to take his hand from her shoulder. For long moments, she sat there, still, gazing into an unseeable distance.

At last, she swallowed and nodded. "Thank you, Simon. Thank you *very* much. Not just for telling me . . . but for being here, for me, when you owe me nothing. I won't forget this."

She rose, taking his hand and squeezing it. "They . . . might be right about me," she said, in the quietest whisper. "I . . . sometimes ask myself if they are. But . . . I can't think about that. Not really."

"Maria—"

"No, don't. Just . . . take my thanks. You've been very kind, Dr. Simon Sandrisson, and I haven't had—or earned—much kindness of late." Her eyes were misty for a moment, then she blinked the incipient tears away. "And thanks to you, I know what I have to do. Again . . . thank you."

Without another word, she turned and strode away, quickly weaving through the crowd until she completely disappeared.

She knows where she's going now. He had no idea how he had led her to the decision, but clearly something about their conversation had given her the direction she had lacked. *What Faction will she approach? What is her goal now?*

And am I EVER *going to get to relax enough to go to sleep?*

Chapter 20

"Orphan, we're being followed."

The tall alien was beside her almost instantly. "Are you certain, Ariane Austin?"

"Pretty sure. See these returns? And using the rear telescopes I thought I saw a couple glints where that cloudbank thinned out."

Orphan straightened, stroking his headcrest in the way he often did when thinking. "This *is* an excellent place for an ambush. We are actually heading for another of the Sky Gates that—as far as I am aware—only I know of. But we will be passing quite near the usual gateway used by traffic in this region of the Arena."

"Prep the weapons, then?"

"Best to do so, yes. I would rather not fight anyone, but please, ready us. I will take the main board, Ariane. If you would be so kind as to take the secondary, there? Yes. I will give control of the vessel to you, so that in the event of emergency you can use your superlative piloting instincts to our benefit."

She grinned, feeling a surprisingly welcome tension spreading through her. *Good* Lord, *am I so bored that potentially being in another Arenaspace battle sounds* fun *to me? I guess I am. That's pretty pathetic, Ariane.* "On it, Orphan."

Wu Kung bounced up. "I will take one of the turrets, DuQuesne! These are not as fun as a real fight, but at least I can do something."

"You have indeed learned how to operate them," Orphan agreed. "However, I *must* impress upon you the need to minimize your impulsiveness. As I said, I wish to *avoid* conflict if possible."

169

"I understand," Wu answered. "I will not *touch* the weapons unless you say it is time. I promise."

"Good enough," DuQuesne said. "You take this panel, I'll take the other."

For a few minutes, they continued cruising through Arenaspace, now in a skyscape of red-and-purple clouds dimly visible in the wan light of whatever luminaires might be hidden in the far distance. A massive accretion of sky-rubble, accumulated from the castoff materials of who knew how many Upper Spheres, drifted in the middle distance, a jagged, irregular silhouette of black against the magenta and crimson background. A layer of white cloud lay below, streaming slowly across their course. Ariane thought she could see faint, darting movements in the distance—perhaps *zikki* or one of their smarter relatives.

Then the faint shapes on the radar display began to close in, their outlines to become sharper. Even as she turned to notify Orphan, she saw another set appear on the *forward* radar. *They're jetting out from behind that accretion!* "Ambush, Orphan! Forward and aft, spreading laterally." Another set of returns. "Crap. Some coming out of the cloud layers above and below, relative to our own orientation."

"Well-organized pirates, indeed," Orphan said. "If so, however, they will contact us shortly. Pirates, after all, prefer to take their prizes intact. How many do we have, and estimates on size or class?"

"Let me take a look," DuQuesne said. At her glance, he winked. "I've got a little more experience in this than you, Ariane."

Orphan gave him a puzzled look. "A single prior battle, impressive though it was, is not a tremendous amount of experience, Doctor."

"Who said it was my only prior experience?"

Orphan began to reply, stopped, studied him, then did the expansive wing-shrug. "Carry on, then."

"Lessee . . . total count is . . . eight vessels. Judging by size, maneuvers they're making, I'd put five of them in something like a swift attack boat class; they're not very big, but they're fast and maneuverable and probably pack a punch. One of the ones coming out ahead is hanging back quite a bit, she's a *lot* bigger than the others, probably the mothership or at least a mobile HQ; not maneuvering fast so a carrier-type, probably a converted cargo ship, looks about half to three-quarters the size that we are, or that our disguise looks to be anyway. Other two aren't small and they're in between in acceleration, so I'm guessing they're frigate or destroyer class—hope that's translating well for you."

"Eminently well, Doctor. Two powerful but smaller military vessels, several much smaller attack craft, and the main vessel. Ranges?"

"The main ship's about fourteen hundred kilometers away," Ariane answered. "The destroyer-types, about five hundred kilometers—one above and below. The fast-attack boats started farther away but they've accelerated, they'll be within four hundred kilometers very soon."

"Very good." Orphan's head tilted, then he gave his assenting handtap. "Exactly as expected, I see a transmission. Now, all of you, remain silent. The onboard transmitters will focus on me, and make the rest of you look like members of my species, but do not strain this rather stupid automation any more than necessary."

"Got it," said DuQuesne, and Ariane nodded. Wu Kung acknowledged the command by miming a zipped-lip motion and grinning silently.

Without a pause, the display area of the forward port lit up, showing a powerfully-built creature with a head reminiscent of a monitor lizard, but with eyes on the sides of the head and a horizontally-opening jaw. "This is Shipmaster Bos Arbsa, on the *Jewel of Night*. If you are uncertain, that would be the large ship nearly directly ahead of you on your current course. My fleet has you completely boxed in. Please reduce your current vector until you are at rest with respect to *Jewel of Night*."

The transformation that came over Orphan in that instant was startling. With scarcely a movement, somehow the fluid, dramatic Leader of the Liberated was suddenly rigid, cold, expressionless. His wingcases showed neither tension nor excitement. "This is *Dranlu*, a *Madon*-class freighter of the Blessed to Serve. You will stand aside. You will not attempt to board or approach this vessel. The Minds of the Blessed will not tolerate piracy upon our vessels."

Ariane had gained enough cross-species experience to recognize the momentary discomfiture of the Shipmaster; as one of the Great Factions, the Blessed were not to be crossed lightly. However, it was, indeed, only momentary. "We recognize the power of the Blessed. But I put it to you that even the Minds themselves cannot seek revenge when they know nothing of the crime." The jaws parted in what somehow looked to Ariane like a cruel grin. "Which—to your great misfortune—means that I can make no offer to spare your lives. I am completely familiar with the capabilities of the *Madon*-class freighters, and their armed variants. Formidable, but insufficient. Make your farewells to your crippled computational masters." The transmission cut off.

"So much for talking," Ariane said. "They're closing in to weapons range. Orders, Orphan?"

Orphan sighed. "Alas, we *do* wish our presence here secret. Yet I cannot see any way to defeat these pirates without revealing that this ship is far more than it is."

DuQuesne nodded. "So we take 'em apart as fast as we can."

"Primaries?"

"Not immediately," Orphan said. "If by poor fortune any of these escape, I would rather they not also carry news of our new weapons." Ariane saw his pose shift and knew that Orphan was, in his own way, smiling with a sharp and deadly certainty. "And it is *they* who do not realize what they have ambushed."

"Missiles inbound!"

"Activate point-defense cannon emplacements . . . seven and twelve," Orphan said. "These would fit with a *Madon* military transport variant, and should protect us sufficiently for the first salvo or two, before the remainder of their fleet gets in range."

"You want to sucker them in," DuQuesne said in an approving tone. "Get them close so that when our disguise comes apart they're way too close to get away."

"Perfectly correct. For now, return fire with main turret four, Wu Kung, and DuQuesne, missile batteries three and five. That accords with the expected armament, and if you use them well, our adversaries may already be significantly damaged by the time they realize that their trap has become ours. When I give this sign," Orphan gestured widely with both arms and wings, "you may open fire with every weapon at our disposal except the 'primary beams,' as you call them."

Ariane was already maneuvering to avoid the incoming fire, to confuse enemy targeting. In keeping with their assumed identity, she was throttling the acceleration and maneuverability of *Zounin-Ginjou* down drastically. This wasn't easy; it was like trying to make one of Grandfather's old classic sportscars behave like a broken-down clunker when the steering, engine, and transmission were all tuned for high performance. She concentrated, imagining that she was steering not a ship but a whale, a slow, majestic creature that would respond to her commands only with the same ponderous, considered movement.

The fast-attack vessels closed the distance, but even her comparatively slow maneuvers were enough to force them to adjust their courses; this was not like space, where vacuum would allow nigh-infinite range and where stealth was impossible; *Zounin-Ginjou* under Ariane's guidance found drifting haze ahead that blurred her outline, made the smartest missiles that could work in the Arena confused, forced them to go to infra-red tracking that could in turn be confused with tailored flare signals.

Point-defense cannon whined and spat their own shotgun-defense of destruction at incoming missiles, shredding or vaporizing the weapons. Two passed the point defense but were thrown off-course, exploding some distance from *Zounin-Ginjou*; even so, Ariane heard the detonations faintly, felt the vibration in the hull. "They're getting the range, Orphan!"

"Understood, Ariane Austin. But their vessels are nearly in position!"

She could not restrain her own fierce grin as she saw Orphan was right. As the fast-attack craft began their next attack run, the destroyer-sized vessels launched a large salvo of missiles, far larger than their two embattled point-defense assemblies could manage; but they were now less than two hundred kilometers away.

Spears of energy cut through the thin armored shell that formed the disguise around *Zounin-Ginjou*, and hypersonic cannon shells stitched a line of holes along the false engine housing. "Surrender," came the voice of Bos Arbsa. "Your main engine is damaged, and you are—*Voidbuilders' Curse!*"

Orphan had given the signal, and DuQuesne and Wu Kung's fingers flew across their boards, then gripped and tightened on firing handles.

A fury of incandescent destruction lashed across the heavens, a full battery of main guns targeting each of the seven luckless vessels that had reached close-combat distance even as the multiple secondaries and point-defense emplacements raked the sky with fire and screaming hypersonic metal to erase incoming salvos without a trace.

The five fast-attack vessels stood no chance at all; Ariane, no longer needing to maneuver for the moment, sat open-mouthed as the gunships were literally *erased*, firepower sufficient to put holes through full-sized battleships focused on vessels not even a tenth the length or a thousandth the mass of *Zounin-Ginjou*. The destroyers did not *disappear*, but the combination of triple beams of main energy cannon and a salvo of missiles shattered them to useless, lifeless hulks in mere seconds.

Shattered, too, was the fragile disguise covering Orphan's flagship, now falling away in tattered fragments. "Bring all three primary turrets to bear on *Jewel of Night*, Dr. DuQuesne, Sun Wu Kung."

"Who *are* you? The Blessed do not send stealth vessels against pirates!" The pirate captain sounded *outraged*, his translated voice practically screaming *this isn't fair!*

"Alas, Captain Bos Arbsa, you have had the most terrible misfortune to fall afoul of *Zounin-Ginjou* and the Survivor," Orphan said, and his light words were spoken in a cold tone that sent a tiny shiver down Ariane's spine.

Bos Arbsa froze. "Oh *no*," he said, a completely human reaction from such a monstrous face. "My apologies, Survivor! We will withdraw!" Even through the blurring of everything but the creature's face, Ariane could see he was making quick, desperate gestures to his unseen crew.

"I was *attempting* a quiet, unmarked transit through this area of space," Orphan continued, not even directly acknowledging the other's words. "Now you have forced me to destroy my—you will admit—*most* convincing camouflage."

Ariane saw that *Jewel of Night* was moving away—but not directly away, diverting to the side. "Orphan . . ."

"I see, Ariane Austin. *Very* interesting." He looked back to the screen, and his voice was still light, empty, and cold. "I am afraid, Captain, that—like yourself—I can afford no witnesses to this conflict." DuQuesne's face was set in stone, as was Wu Kung's; she saw that they had directed *another* salvo of fire at the remains of the two destroyers, which disintegrated to nothing but clouds of debris, no fragment large enough to show individually on the radar.

Ariane suddenly guessed what Orphan obviously already had; the reason *Jewel of Night* was maneuvering in the direction it was *had* to be that its captain knew of an uncharted Sky Gate, one close enough to afford a chance of escape if *Jewel of Night* could stay far enough from *Zounin-Ginjou*. With concealment no longer an issue, she swung the battleship around with such acceleration she could hear faint creaking noises transmitted through the hull, and let the engines roar to full power, *Zounin-Ginjou* now thundering through the air of the Arena at an ever-increasing pace.

The other captain's voice was still shaken, but regaining some of its bravado. "A good disguise, and a costly one, but you won't get my own flagship, Survivor. You are faster, but you will not close the range fast enough."

"I must, regretfully, disagree. Goodbye, Captain." Orphan nodded to DuQuesne.

A triple salvo of intolerable brilliance annihilated the darkness of the Deeps, blazed its way in a fraction of a second to, and completely through, *Jewel of Night*. For an instant the stricken pirate mothership shuddered, faltering, and then with an eye-searing detonation, vanished as damage reached its main superconducting storage coils.

Orphan stood still, watching the explosion and fire fade away, blazing pieces of wreckage careening through the endless deeps. He hesitated, then sighed, a sound amplified by his spiracles into a mournful hoot. "Gentlemen, if you would . . . complete the job."

DuQuesne and Wu nodded and the unstoppable fire of the primaries eradicated all traces of *Jewel of Night*.

"You seem . . . bothered by this, Orphan," Ariane said finally.

"Hm? And you are not, Captain Austin?"

"Well . . . yes. You know that from our last engagement. Fighting back is fine, but wiping out every trace, even possible survivors . . ."

"Your feelings are commendable, Captain. And not unexpected, given the outcome of our last battle together. But in this case . . . I dare not let this secret out, neither the secret of my possible destination, nor that of our weapons. I can take no chance on even a single survivor."

"You've been at war with the Blessed—and sometimes others—for thousands of years, Orphan," she said. "I'm not asking why you're doing this—though I'd have a hard time giving that order—but why you are *bothered* by it. They *did* attack us, and after they thought you were Blessed, were going to wipe us all out; you had little reluctance before about vaporizing all the Blessed survivors."

"Ah. Yes, I see the dissonance." He looked out the forward port. "Continue on *Jewel of Night*'s prior course. I would like to mark the location of its Sky Gate for later investigation. It is, of course, *theoretically* possible that its last maneuvers were meant to distract us from a more distant observer craft, but I would lay immense odds against that for many reasons."

Orphan turned back to her. "In answer to your question . . . In that long struggle you have referred to, Captain, I have done many things. That included being a pirate, to be perfectly honest with you, a pirate who targeted Blessed vessels. I know exactly the fears and hopes that drive such beings, and the horror they must have felt to know that they had so terribly underestimated their prey. And even more, the despair of knowing that this time, their quarry would not be satisfied with anything other than their complete annihilation." He looked out the port again, but Ariane had the impression he was not seeing anything. "But more . . . we cannot stay here and quarter space for days, examining every trace of these vessels for any sign of life. It is thus possible, though unlikely, that there *are* a few survivors, ejected or otherwise escaping the annihilation sent against their vessels.

"In *that* case, Captain, they will be drifting alone in the endless Deeps, with scarcely a hope in a trillion that there will be rescue or anything but slow death or sudden awaiting them behind the next deceptive veil of mist." His eyes shifted back to her, and they were dark wells of pain. "And *that* fear and despair I have *lived*, once, and would not wish upon even the Minds themselves."

Chapter 21

"I am glad, *tremendously* glad, that you were able to resolve that situation so well, Laila, Carl, Simon," said Oscar Naraj, his deep, rich voice resonating in the comfortable meeting room. "The Tantimorcans were appreciative of your tact and sympathy, and I have thus concluded a *most* advantageous negotiation with them."

Simon still found it somewhat uncomfortable to sit in the same room and talk civilly with a man he still suspected of being the prime mover in Ariane's abduction. From her expression, Oasis Abrams felt the same way; Carl and Laila had been working with Naraj long enough that any remaining dislike wasn't visible. Still, Naraj had accepted the rulings of the SSC and CSF as far as anyone could tell, and had thrown his full energy into his duties as Ambassador and negotiator.

And he *was*, beyond any doubt, very good at that. The other species of the Arena generally responded well to his approaches, and he had negotiated numerous "advantageous," as he said, deals with various smaller Factions.

His powers were, of course, *strictly* limited. "I presume you have a copy of this agreement?"

"For your review, and the approval of our duumvirate *Leaders Pro Tempore*, certainly. The gist of the agreement is that we will provide or procure Champions for their next three Challenges, and in exchange they will design and construct full prototypes of five Arenaspace vessels for our complete use, including all data to allow us to begin full production of the vessels."

"That *does* sound like a bargain," Laila said. "But what if—despite our record thus far—our Champions do not quite make the grade, so to speak?"

Oscar nodded gravely. "A concern, of course. Two of the five designs will not be completed unless and until we have won one Challenge for them. If we lose all three, by some terrible mischance, there will of course be penalties. The details are in the contract. Please review them as soon as convenient."

"Definitely," said Carl. "We're learning a lot about ship design in the Arena from studying Orphan's ships, but we still need some better tailored designs for operations other than big military patrols. The Arena and Warship SFGs have produced some decent designs, but I don't think they're quite up to the level of factions that have spent centuries doing this stuff."

"And we *do* need more ships," Simon said. "The Sim Focus Groups' work will do for the interim, but I am becoming more and more certain that time is running out for us. The Molothos have not forgotten about us, and if they ever find out where we are . . . they will *crush* us."

"Believe me, Dr. Sandrisson, I completely, *completely* agree," Naraj said. "You may recall that I approached their Leader with the naïve belief that some form of negotiation would be possible, and was swiftly disabused of that notion." He frowned, an expression that made his broad face look sad rather than angry. "Negotiation *might* be possible with them—I refuse to believe that it is utterly impossible—but only if one was in a position of vast strength."

Laila Canning shook her head swiftly, bobbed brown hair following the motion. "Perhaps, but irrelevant for now, Ambassador. It will be a very long time—if ever—before we are in such a position."

"I think we're all agreed on that. But do we have any other, well, *Hyperion* Champions around?" Simon asked. "After all, DuQuesne and Wu Kung are not available, and we'd like to have such a trump card available."

A (reasonably) gentle punch stung his arm. "Um, *hello?* Earth to Simon? I'm sitting right here!" said Oasis Abrams, AKA the mysterious "K" of Hyperion. The redhead's smile took the sting from her words, and lessened the sting in his arm, too.

He smiled. "I meant in *addition* to you, Oasis, but yes, I should have phrased that more clearly. My apologies."

"No problem," she said. "And yes, we've got at least one more. Vel just made the jump here; he's being checked out as a pilot for some of our Sphere defense ships, but he'll be available."

"Vel?" Simon sorted through memory and briefings. "Ah yes, Velocity Celes. But I thought he was a *ground* racer, not a space racer like Ariane's friend Hawke."

"He is, but he's a *Hyperion*, Simon, and one designed as a driver and pilot. Believe me, he'll be one of the best we've got in just a few *days*." Oasis' grin held absolute confidence. "Trust me on this."

"I wouldn't dream of doubting you, Oasis," he said. "But as I understand it there are at least a few more; I think we should find a way to recruit as many as possible; as DuQuesne put it, the Arena was almost tailor-made for them." As he said that, he caught a momentary, almost subliminial *shift* of Oasis' expression; it vanished in the instant he saw it, but he was certain it had been there. *Interesting. What does that mean?* "From what we know, all the Hyperions enjoy some rather unfair advantages over regular Arena citizens. And Lord knows, we could use all the unfair advantages we can get."

"True, *very* true indeed, Doctor," agreed Naraj. "On the subject of gaining unsuspected advantages, I also have a summary of our actions in what your Captain whimsically named 'Operation Dandelion.'"

Simon chortled. "Let us have it, then!"

Assured that they were prepared, Oscar Naraj transmitted a quick data dump from his own headware. Simon found that his experiences with the Arena had, at least, made assimilating large amounts of information far easier. He quickly sorted out the salient features of the report.

Operation Dandelion was, in Ariane's words, "Our plan to grow like *weeds* in the lawn of the Arena." Having obtained two other Spheres—completely unbeknownst to anyone else in the Arena except the Liberated and the Minds (both of which had strong vested interest in *keeping* that deal a secret), Humanity had every reason to establish and expand its presence on those Spheres . . . and the worlds they represented.

"As you can see, reconnaissance of the Spheres and their associated solar systems has been very successful. The first Sphere, named *Tellus* by Captain Austin, is associated with a solar system with eleven major planetary bodies, one brown dwarf orbiting at a considerable distance from the primary, and two Earth-type habitable worlds. The second Sphere, named *Gaia*, is associated with a solar system with seven major planetary bodies, two asteroid belts, and one Earth-type world. The most interesting fact about both of these systems is that while we know they belonged to the Blessed to Serve and were, therefore, presumably colonized by them to one extent or another, there is no trace of any prior colonization or exploitation."

"That's . . . frightening," Oasis said after a pause, red hair exaggerating the awed shake of her head. "I know that some of our prior conversations with Arena residents implied something of the sort, but . . ."

"I concur," Simon said. "This is perhaps the most complete demonstration of the Arena's capabilities. If we are in any way correct, it removed vast numbers of former inhabitants from the Spheres and the planets and solar systems associated with them, relocated them safely to some other appropriate Spheres, reworked any aspects of the planet to fit Earth-normal requirements, and . . ." he thought a moment, ". . . and must have rearranged the planets including physical distribution of ores and such to make the system appear completely untouched."

Even Oscar Naraj—normally focused more on the political and social than on the physical issues of the Arena—looked daunted. "A truly, *truly* awe-inspiring capability. And I must also wonder how the Arena determines the location of those removed; surely it does not simply dump, perhaps, billions of people onto another world?"

"I asked Relgof about that," Simon said. "The Arena distributes the refugees as evenly as possible—apparently taking into account things like family and friend associations, resources at the destination, and so on. And in the event that a simple relocation is not practical—for example, a small Faction with two Spheres whose systems have large populations—it has apparently created appropriate habitats for the refugees."

"And does this in what may be a matter of hours, presumably, depending on how the Sphere is claimed and how quickly the claimants may go to their new possession," Laila said. "Impressive does not *begin* to cover it. But," she said with a brisk air, "we are off the topic. Have we begun colonization efforts to Tellus and Gaia?"

"Initial exploration and preparation efforts are underway," Naraj said. "As expected, AI and nanotech capabilities are in full force in the normal-space solar systems, which will give us a tremendous ability to begin construction and expansion."

That reminded Simon of one of the other crucial issues. "Has the SSC moved forward on AI Emancipation?"

"Forward, yes. Swiftly, no. As you can imagine, it is a tremendous, *tremendous* challenge to address the potential issues in a manner that even a plurality, let alone a majority, of the Council is comfortable with."

Simon knew that Naraj was one of those *not* comfortable with the idea—and the knowledge of the existence of the Minds of the Blessed and their total re-engineering of their creators gave a *very* concrete weight to the concerns of fully-unleashed computer intellects. "Would it help if any of us were to go and try to push things along?"

"Yeah," Carl said. "I'd point out to them that when Ariane gets back she's going to expect something to have been *done* on this, and if it hasn't been she'll raise all kinds of hell. And every one of us will back her to the hilt."

Oscar's face wrinkled in thought. "It may be necessary for *someone* to apply pressure. But allow me to convey your concerns on my trip tomorrow. If I feel there is no inclination to hurry things along, then one or two of you might put in an appearance."

"You're not really enthusiastic about the idea, though," Oasis said.

"Not a bit of it, no. But I have agreed to perform my job to the best of my ability, and I know the group of you are indeed—without any doubt—speaking with the full authority of, and complete consistency with, Leader Ariane Austin's position in these matters; I have no intention whatsoever of incurring Captain Austin's wrath *ever* again, I assure you, so thus *my* beliefs are not relevant." Naraj smiled, and Simon could see a rueful edge on that smile. "I cannot earn back trust unless I am absolutely reliable, after all."

"And for a long time," Laila said bluntly. "All right, we'll wait until you get back. But you should know we'll have other sources."

"Dr. Canning, I would be *extremely* disappointed by you if you did not. Trust is only a part of it; for domestic and foreign intelligence it is *desperately* important to have multiple resources providing you with information."

"Don't worry, *I* am running that part of the operation!" Oasis said with a grin. "It's like going home, in a way."

Naraj's eyebrows rose. "Truly? Then with a *Hyperion* running your intelligence, I have no further concerns." He nodded. "In any event, I expect to begin serious colonization movement in the next . . . oh, month and a half. There are already a large number of applicants, and as these are merely to be new human colonies they do not need to be screened to nearly the degree as new entrants to the Arena need be."

Simon felt a touch of his internal omniscience stirring, allowed himself to perceive what urgency drove it. *Ah.* "I would caution people to construct *nothing* on the Upper Sphere that can be detected, not until we have formidable system defenses and are ready to deploy equally strong defenses around the Sphere. While it seems *unlikely* that we will have another encounter with the Molothos or other hostiles at our new homes, we do not want to give away our presence inadvertently."

"Noted, Dr. Sandrisson. I concur, and I will convey these instructions myself," Naraj said. "Now, there are a few other issues that I must review . . ."

Simon finally extricated himself from the meeting; Oasis followed him out. "Lordy, he *does* like to talk, as Gabrielle would say."

Oasis laughed, green eyes sparkling. "He sure does. But hey, not like there wasn't talk-talk on both sides." She fell in next to him, matching him stride for stride; she was somewhat shorter but her legs were long. "I'm starved after all that, though. Want to go get something?"

"I would *love* to. I need to get out of the Embassy."

While the Grand Arcade was the center of Nexus Arena's commerce, it was far from the *only* place of commerce, and Oasis led him to a restaurant actually *on* Dock 4; it was a tall spindle of a building with a broad, glassed-in deck atop, something like pictures of the ancient Space Needle or some of the delicate towers in some of the more popular space sims.

"The view is *stunning,*" he said as they were seated.

The immense Dock stretched many kilometers out from the side of the incomprehensibly huge cylinder that was Nexus Arena. Hundreds—*thousands*—of vessels of every size and description were docking, loading, casting off, maneuvering near or far from Dock 4 and the many other Docks visible to one side or the other. A flock of *teirann*—which DuQuesne had named "aetherbirds"—streamed by, their crystal bodies and wings a ripple of rainbow and diamond, while in the distance the many-colored clouds turned and streamed slowly, majestically, occasionally lit from within by lightning.

"It *is* gorgeous, isn't it?" Oasis said, smiling broadly. "Privacy screen," she said to the apparently empty air, and a faintly-visible luminous curtain surrounded them. "I *love* this place. Great view, get to watch the life of the Arena going by, and still have a private talk with someone."

"*How* private?" he asked. Given the kind of subjects that might come up with Oasis, he felt the question was important.

"Contracted from both the Analytic and the Faith. So as private as anything gets, really, aside from what Orphan mentioned once about going into the Deeps. Or maybe going back home. And the *food's* great—as long as you don't mind some spice. Lots of different spices, actually."

"I have tried to be quite adventurous, at least in the cuisine area," Simon said. "Bring it on, as DuQuesne might say."

Her face flickered through a number of emotions in an instant at the mention of the other Hyperion—fondness, melancholy, a misty-eyed reminiscence—before returning to a more immediate good cheer. "All *right*, Simon! I like a guy who's willing to try things that bite back."

"As long as they're not venomous," he said with an answering smile. As he examined the menu that materialized before him, he asked, "So you were a . . . what, intelligence agent before? You said that it was like going home."

Oasis' face flickered, and the expression . . . shifted. It was a tiny shift, but he had seen it many times now. Oasis Abrams and the Hyperion known to him only as "K" were not *quite* fused. That shift happened when one or the other of the women sharing one brain was slightly more dominant, and the expression told him that this was "K."

She nodded, even as her fingers made a selection on the menu; he did the same. "Technically for both of us, actually. I . . . Oasis . . . did a fair amount of intelligence work for Saul and others once we got over the fall of Hyperion enough. But I . . . K, that is . . . been doing spy stuff since, well, about the time Marc was trying to decide which college to apply to. Before that, really."

"I imagine it was rather different than such work *here*, though, unless your . . . er, world was like ours."

She laughed again, though with the same touch of wistful sadness that the other Hyperions often showed when thinking of the past. "Like this? No, *totally* not much like this. Either the Arena or modern Sol System. But a lot of the basics don't change, just the tricks and the targets." She looked back at him; those amazing green eyes almost matched his own in color, but he was sure his never managed a tenth of the intensity in hers. "Now *you*, you've always been a scientist, right?"

"Well, I was always *interested* in being one, but you can't call yourself a scientist right away," he answered. "But yes, that's always been my profession. I have found myself sometimes acting in other capacities since we arrived here, of course."

"Oh, sure! DuQuesne told me you saved *Zounin-Ginjou* and fought the would-be Leader of the Blessed one-on-one!" He knew this woman—regardless of which persona he regarded as active or central—was older than he by a factor of nearly two, but she was looking at him with a wide-eyed excitement that made her seem scarcely eighteen. "We all got the summary, but tell me the details— what do *you* remember about it?"

Simon cast his mind back, a bit bemused by the conversation's turn. "Mostly? Being terrified, I suppose. I mean, there was a great deal more to it, but once I realized there were actually people trying to *kill* us I assure you my heart was doing its best to pound its way out of my chest."

"Were you *just* terrified?" she asked, leaning a little forward.

Remembering that battle—the flare of missiles' jets passing scant meters away, the staccato hail-rapping of hypersonic cannon rebounding from armor, the incredible body-shattering concussion of the primary beam firing within a turret, the long, cold glint of his sword pointing at the green-black form of Vantak—Simon felt as though he were, momentarily, back on board *Zounin-Ginjou*, and . . . "No," he said finally, hearing his own startled, incredulous tone. "No, I was . . . excited. Exhilarated, at times. Determined. *Transported*, in more ways than one."

He looked up to see her smile, sharper, knowing, but the green eyes were warm and sympathetic. "I *knew* it. There's nothing like that feeling, is there? The *Edge*. Running on a bridge as it's falling apart under you and not knowing if you're gonna make it, facing someone trying to kill you and wondering if you're good enough to take him, hearing the countdown to disaster and seeing you have twenty-nine seconds to stop it or everything blows. You know the *Edge* now, don't you?"

He felt the chill of gooseflesh along his arms, saw the hairs standing up, remembered the fear of his own omniscience warring with the exaltation of the *prediction* of the future, of combat against a chosen warrior of the Blessed to Serve, and nodded slowly. "Yes, if that is what you call it, I cannot argue that I do not know the 'Edge.'"

She laughed joyfully. At that moment, their servers entered, placed the first plates in front of them, then withdrew. Once they'd left, she smiled again. "*Fantastic*, as another lost friend of ours would have said; you love the running, deep down, like all of us do. I couldn't really hang out for long with someone who didn't."

Simon liked to think he had gotten a *bit* better at picking up on personal interactions over the years. "Oasis, pardon me very much if I am wrong, but are you making a pass at me?"

"Would it bother you if I was?"

"Not . . . precisely. I did think you and DuQuesne—"

"Ah. Marc. Yes, we did have something. Still do, sort of . . . but I'm not the woman he knew then, and that really does throw him way off. And me; Oasis never knew Marc, and he's not entirely her type."

"And . . . no one else?"

The distant look came back. "There was . . . when I was a lot younger. But . . . Hyperion. He was part of my world, and we couldn't salvage it." She smiled with only a hint of sadness. "And besides, even before Hyperion fell, we'd . . . drifted. That's why DuQuesne and I got together."

He frowned. "You know, I get a bit puzzled about *time*. It sounds like you and Marc were together for quite a bit, yet you could not have met until that grand-scale crossover that led to the disaster."

She shook her head, the brilliant red hair rippling like flame in wind. "Remember, they could control perceptions and events in-universe—and they had the technology to do things like speed up or slow down metabolisms, too. So while in the real universe we weren't even twenty, Marc was physically and intellectually well over thirty, and I was well into my twenties. The investigations, discovery of the truth and all that, from *our* point of view, covered a few *years*, while it wasn't more than a couple of months from the . . . researcher's point of view."

"Good Lord. Every time I think I grasp the depth of that project, I learn something that shows me I was wrong. A bit like the Arena, I suppose."

"*Too much* like the Arena," she said forcefully. Then she closed her eyes and sighed; when they opened again, she was smiling once more. "Anyway, hell of a diversion for an answer that really was yes, I *am* making a little pass at you, or flirting anyway to see if *you* are interested."

You know, I honestly don't think I was such an attention-magnet before. For a moment he *really* missed Mio, his AISage, who would have had some sort of witty and incisive remark on the situation; the silence in his head was sometimes too much. "I would have to be both blind and deaf to *not* be interested, I think. So this is a date, then?"

"If you like. I know you've been dancing around with Ariane, and Laila, too."

"But no commitment on either side yet; in the case of Ariane, of course, there is also DuQuesne and the fact that all of us tend towards monogamous pairings if we were to be serious." *And as both Ariane and DuQuesne are off on a journey of undetermined length . . .*

"Great!" She grabbed his hand, squeezed it, then grabbed up one of the strange multifaceted fried objects in her appetizer and bit into it. "Wow, spicy indeed. Here, try one!"

From the crunching sensation and the strong, complex flavor and texture, he was sure this was some sort of meat, fried in hot oil of some type. And spicy it was, with hints of cinnamon, pepper, and capsicum . . . and maybe a touch of something like lemony cardamom? "Very good. I like it. Here, try my . . . um, marinated *uljuru*, which I *think* is some kind of worm-type creature."

He watched with seeming casualness as she scooped one up, popped it in her mouth, and chewed. Her eyes flew wide, but she did finish swallowing before she went for her glass. "Holy *cow*, that's hot! HOT hot!" She paused, then suddenly laughed. "Well, *that* will teach me to underestimate you! You've got a more asbestos-lined mouth than *I* do!"

"My best friend when I was young, Marisol, had a heritage of Indian-Mex cooking going back generations, and she would *try* to give me something I couldn't eat—it was a sort of friendly contest. For my part, of course, I refused to admit that anything she brought was too hot, so I developed quite a cast-iron palate."

"Holy *cow*," she repeated, now on her second glass of water. "You could've probably given Sydney a run for her money." The wistful note was very faint, but he could still hear it. *Another Hyperion memory.*

That rang another bell. "May I ask you something?"

"You can *ask* anything, Simon. Can I have another of those?"

"Of course," he said, taking one himself and enjoying the tingling burn. "Back in our little conference, I was quoting DuQuesne in saying that the Arena seems almost tailor-made for your people, and I noticed a little . . . change in your expression. What was that about?"

She seemed to be taking the second *uljuru* much better; perhaps the first had numbed her mouth. "*That*, Simon, is . . . something we might actually want more privacy for. Back at our Embassy, if not all the way back to Earth. Let's just say that it's maybe more the other way around."

That they *were made for the* Arena? *Yes.* That fit with his internal sense, even though he did not have that Olympian perception active. "Very well, we can discuss that at a later time. But perhaps you can tell me something of what you've done *since* Hyperion?"

"I could bore you for *hours* on that topic, Simon," she said.

The rest of the meal passed swiftly, and Simon found he was very much enjoying it. Oasis had a quick wit, a ready laugh, and despite her warning of boredom had lived an exciting life, helping Saul Maginot clean up the occasional but often very dangerous fringes of the otherwise peaceful Solar System of the late twenty-fourth century.

Finally, the two of them rose and went to the overlook, gazing out over the Dock several hundred feet below. She had taken his hand and was talking about what she saw. ". . . and that's actually a Tensari cruiser; they're not much into military stuff, but they do have a few— I think it's still Tantimorcan design, but the decoration's pure Tensari. That little one in between the two big cargo transports, that's someone's personal flyer; the general design looks like it could be Vengeance but I can't be sure. Now, looking down towards Nexus Arena, we can—"

She broke off, and her face had gone stark pale.

Following her gaze, he had a quick impression of a tall figure, human or very humanoid, wearing a white suit of some sort. But before he could get a better look, the figure was swallowed up by the crowd.

His hand was empty, and she was already halfway to the stairs, *at* the stairs, running down them, *flying* down them at a speed he simply could not match. "Oasis!" he called, trying to catch her, "Oasis, what *is* it?"

She was a blur, leaping from one side to the other of the spiral stair, sliding down the banister and then bounding to the other side, making the other patrons going up or down the staircase seem frozen in place. Oasis reached the bottom before he—fast as he could run—was more than a quarter of the way down.

Panting with the exertion, he finally burst out onto the Dock, looking around, searching the crowd. He saw a flash of red hair in the distance, forced his now-aching legs into a sprint, weaving between Daelmokhan workers and Milluk tourists and a Chirofleckir businessman, until he finally came into sight of her, slowing down, feet unwillingly going to a walk and, at last, a stunned, immobile stillness.

"Oasis, what is *wrong*?" he demanded as he finally reached her.

"I . . . don't know," she said after a moment. "Did you . . . see anything, when I was looking?"

"A person—which could have been, or not been, a human—in some kind of white outfit, clothes and hat. But I could not even confidently say *what* kind of outfit, let alone whether it was being worn by a human being."

"I *swear* it was . . ." She trailed off. "But that isn't possible."

"Why? Who did you think you *saw*?"

Her smile was fragile now, like a cracked crystal goblet. "Someone . . . someone who not only should be dead," she said in a shaken whisper, "but technically wasn't even ever alive."

Chapter 22

Wu Kung found himself feeling an incredibly rare tinge of apprehension, as well as awe, staring at the thing that had just become visible through the mists of the Arena's Deeps.

Silhouetted against a backdrop of dull crimson clouds, it was black as night, an angular shape of incomprehensible vastness. An ebony stitching of criss-cross darkness that looked like monstrous girders, great arching curves with hints of fluted, organic shapes rising about a central assemblage of contours that implied some gargantuan onyx flower of alien and unsettling aspect.

Ariane's voice echoed Wu Kung's own nervousness. "Orphan? Is *that—*"

"—our destination, the home of Vindatri? Indeed, Captain Austin." Though his voice was relaxed and controlled, Wu could smell a great deal of nervousness from him. *He may have a duty to fulfill here, but this Vindatri guy doesn't make him comfortable.*

"And he lives there *alone?*" DuQuesne asked. The tones and DuQuesne's posture showed how wary his fellow Hyperion was. "That's an awful lot of house for one guy."

"Not alone, entirely. Later in my . . . stay with Vindatri, I did see and meet others who were apparently his servants. And as I said, there is a Sphere not far away." He gestured, and Wu could see, through the clouds a faint hint of form, a curve of an artifact larger than Earth. "I believe that Sphere to be inhabited, although I have never actually landed upon it."

Ariane was studying the huge, shadowy assemblage. "Where exactly am I heading? There's an awful lot of that thing—if I'm getting the scale right, it's something like three or four thousand kilometers across!"

"Larger than that, Captain. If I recall correctly, I docked at—"

A quiver ran through *Zounin-Ginjou*, and Wu tensed, seeing that the position of the distant shadow had shifted slightly in the forward port. "What was *that*?"

Orphan's wingcases had compressed, and his stance was rigid; the scent of tension and even fear was suddenly sharper. But he answered in his customary relaxed tones, "Ah. I believe the decision of how to approach and dock has been taken out of our hands. Note that *Zounin-Ginjou* has already altered its course."

Wu felt very little other motion, yet the . . . Castle of Vindatri, as Wu Kung had to think of it, began to swell before them at astounding speed, as though Ariane had set the engines on full power and was driving them towards collision. "Crap," Ariane muttered. "I sure hope this Vindatri doesn't fumble the ball at the last minute, or we're just gonna go *splat* when we hit."

The alien structure rushed closer, expanding beyond the width of the forward port. Glints of light—diamond-white and emerald green, shimmering ruby and sapphire, warm amber—became visible, dotting the forbidding megalithic blackness with jewels set on a crown of night; Wu could now pick out hints of detail, of scalloped planes and oval ports and sharp-edged lines of decks or floors.

A cavernous opening yawned before them, six lines of white light guiding their uncontrolled, headlong rush down the center of a landing bay so huge that it seemed to Wu that it could have held a *fleet* of ships like *Zounin-Ginjou*. Without more than the tiniest jolt, the massive warship of the Liberated came to a halt, its incredible speed reduced to nothing in less time than needed to draw a breath, and settled into a cradle that rose from the massive deck, a structure of dark metal and glinting crystal that enfolded *Zounin-Ginjou* as though made for it. Wu heard both his human companions exhale shaky breaths, and Orphan's spiracles whistled once more.

"It seems," Orphan said after a moment, even his voice wavering with uncertainty or fear, "Vindatri is *very* eager to meet with us."

"Have you ever returned here before, Orphan?" Ariane asked, rising slowly from her pilot's seat.

"Once, long ago . . . in part, I must admit, to verify to myself that he and this place truly existed. I had the . . . item that I used in our confrontation with Amas-Garao, yes, but I had never yet used it—nor had good reason to at that time—and that experience was so unheard-of in the annals of the Arena that I had to remind myself that I had truly experienced it."

"I get that," DuQuesne said with a touch of humor. "We felt a little like that about the Arena."

"Indeed." A wing-snap of decision and, Wu thought, a touch of bravado. "Well, friends, shall we greet our host?"

Ariane and DuQuesne nodded. "No time like the present," Ariane agreed.

Wu immediately stepped in front of her. "Bodyguard, remember?"

She smiled. "I remember," she said. "Do what you have to."

Orphan led the way. DuQuesne took the rear, which made Wu feel slightly more comfortable; this would let him focus mostly to the front and sides. Ariane made no protest about being in the middle.

The main lock from *Zounin-Ginjou* opened to reveal a wide platform already in place outside of it. Stairs led down to the dark-polished deck of the massive installation. *It is all dark; it feels like a fortress of one of the underworlds. Even the Dragon's Palace was brighter-lit, and* that *was at the bottom of the sea!* He reached back, touched Ruyi Jingu Bang, reassuring himself that the mighty staff was still there. *Though it is not a thousandth as mighty as it was in the real-dream of Hyperion,* he thought sadly. *Against this Vindatri it may be of less use than the floating drift of a dandelion.*

The dim-lit volume was silent save for the echoes of their motion. Orphan stopped a short distance from the bottom of the staircase and looked around, then raised his head and arms. "Vindatri, you have guided us thus far; where must we go?"

The echoes of the question had not even died down when four lines of fire sketched themselves through the air, arrows of brilliance leading across the great landing bay and then splitting to follow separate paths. Each line was a different color, and all four started in the air scarcely three feet in front of Orphan: a line of red, a line of green, a line of blue, and a line of pure white.

"Wonder which is which—or whether it matters," DuQuesne said.

"I have little doubt that it matters," Orphan said. "But it may be that the selection is nonetheless up to us."

"In that case, I'm taking blue," Ariane said. "Always been one of my colors."

"I refuse to choose another color," Wu said. "I am following Ariane. I am responsible for her."

"I agree with the principle, Wu," said DuQuesne, "but my guess is that you're gonna find out it's not that easy. Me? I'll take green; has a little resonance for me in the space-exploration context."

"I see," said Orphan. "White is, I believe, for me."

"Still not taking red," Wu said.

The four of them made their way across the deck, echoes of footsteps chasing themselves around the nearly-empty room. Finally, they reached the point where the paths split, and Wu could see that there were four separate staircases; one turned and went straight off to the right into blackness, the second bent right for a short distance than turned back to go ahead through a dark archway, the third similarly went left for a short distance and then turned back ahead through a different archway, and the last turned left and also faded into darkness. Ariane's blue took the strong righthand turn; the neglected red line turned to the far left, while green and white took the middle paths.

Wu Kung continued up the blue line, glancing back to make sure that Ariane was following. When he turned his attention back to the glowing line of light before him—a delay that was no more than the blink of an eye—he saw a brilliant scarlet streak leading into distant darkness.

He spun around, to see Ariane and the others staring at him; Ariane stood with one foot in the air, frozen in the act of following.

Wu Kung growled faintly and started for Ariane again—

—to find himself marching with the same angry determination up the red line of fire.

Now the growl was a snarl. "I am her *bodyguard* and *you* do not get to take me away!" He whipped Ruyi Jingu Bang off his back and commanded it to extend; DuQuesne and Orphan ducked out of the way as the pole streaked out to place its one end in front of Ariane. "Grab on, Ariane!"

"Wu, I don't think this is going to work," Ariane said reluctantly. "But . . . okay." She grasped the golden ball at the end of the staff tightly.

"Good!" He retracted the staff slowly, following along until he reached Ariane. "Now keep hold, okay?"

"All right," she said.

"*Now* we can go!" he said, confidently stepping forward.

The line of fire was suddenly red, and he felt no other hand supporting the great Staff. His cheeks burned under his fur with embarrassment. "All right, you coward sorcerer! Come out here! You are mocking me? I will beat your *face* in!"

"Wu!" Ariane's voice was sharp, although he could hear a note of sympathy too. "We are visiting *his* stronghold. He seems to want us to play by his rules. Please, try not to antagonize our host, no matter how . . . peculiar his behavior is."

He snarled again and stamped his foot, causing an echo like a gunshot to chase its way around the room half a dozen times. Then, seeing DuQuesne's remonstrative look, Wu swallowed, closed his eyes, and forced his breathing to slow, his meditations to begin. It was not easy; besides his anger, other, unsettling thoughts insisted on intruding. *Like Sanzo. So like Sanzo. Even the same* commands *as Sanzo, sometimes.*

Finally, he felt a semblance of balance and calm returning. "As you command, Captain. But I will *still* be angry with this Vindatri!"

"Be angry all you want, but *behave*, Sun Wu Kung. Do you promise?"

He rolled his eyes. This was all so *unreasonable*. But it was not the first time he had had to deal with unreasonable people . . . and this sort of negotiation had been part of the Journey to the West, and he had learned that, often, Sanzo was *right* about not starting fights. *And Ariane probably is too.* "Yes, Captain. I promise I will behave myself."

Decision made, he turned and began loping down the direction indicated by the red fire. *The faster I finish whatever is ahead of me, the faster I can go back to guarding Ariane!* He gritted his teeth. *She had better be all right, or I will* somehow *teach this "Vindatri" a lesson!*

The darkness ahead was not so dark to his own perceptions, and he could see that there was an archway through which the leading line of light passed. The light shrank before him at the exact speed of his own progress, so the line always started just a short distance in front of him. *That's a nice trick. I remember how one of Guyamaoh's underlings could trace lines of smoke and flame sort of like this.* He had to admit it was pretty, a bright crimson shimmer that receded ever before him like a rainbow.

Up another set of stairs and finally the light ended at a door, an oval affair set in the metal wall, with a wheel in the center. He tested the door, found it did not move, and so grasped the wheel and turned. It yielded smoothly, and with a *clack* he heard a lock or latch disengage. The door swung easily back now, and Wu Kung stepped through into a pitch-black space. He advanced cautiously, on guard, all other senses extended; he heard nothing, smelled nothing but faint traces of oils and metals and old, alien scents of things long gone.

Abruptly the door behind him slammed and the latch engaged. At the same instant, lights blazed on, illuminating the room as brilliantly as day, and in the glare before him was a tall figure. As his eyes adjusted and he could make out the figure before him, Wu Kung felt his jaw dropping and the staff in his hand sagging down.

"Took you long enough," said the towering gray-skinned form of Sha Wujing.

Chapter 23

DuQuesne stared narrowly at the man before him. He knew the patrician, lined face, the graying hair that had once been brown, the sharp brown eyes looking levelly into his own, the half-smile of the lecturer and scientist so familiar to him.

"I had expected to end up talking with myself," he said finally. "Not you, Professor Bryson."

Clearly this couldn't be the man he looked like; this had to be one of Vindatri's guises. At the same time, it was almost impossible to think of him as anyone else, when the man lit up a cigarette and took a swift puff, raising one eyebrow. "Indeed, Mr. DuQuesne? And why would you expect to have a conversation with yourself? Admittedly, this would allow you to have a conversation with someone on your intellectual level, but I would expect, a rather boring one."

DuQuesne moved forward a bit closer—warily, because he had no idea what this . . . manifestation of Vindatri's was supposed to accomplish or what might trigger a less innocuous reaction. "Oh, I've had some pretty interesting arguments with myself, whenever I've been of two minds on a subject. As for why, Orphan's story ended up with him facing himself."

"Ahh, Orphan. It was exactly as appropriate that you meet me as it was for Orphan to confront himself. And I hope you are aware that Orphan neglected to tell you various details of that encounter."

"Suspected it, yeah. He's been a stand-up ally in some ways, but I don't think that guy even tells *himself* everything that's going on."

Bryson, or the image of him, chuckled in the same dry-leaf way

DuQuesne remembered. "A particularly apt characterization, I am forced to admit. The question remains, then, why are you speaking to me, in particular?"

"Technically, I'm speaking to Vindatri, and don't think I'm forgetting that," DuQuesne said. "And I bet you're not going to trick either of my companions, either."

"As another acquaintance of yours might say, do not indulge in such loose and muddy thinking. *Tricking* is not the point of this interview, not in the sense you mean it."

"Hm. So it's an *interview*, is it? A way for you to . . . what, examine our reactions to some particular stimulus? Interesting that you'd need to do that when you can obviously read our minds in detail."

"What is obvious, Mr. DuQuesne, is quite often not the truth— something I believe I mentioned more than once in class, yes?"

Damn, he's got that "superior professor" attitude down perfect. "That your doppelganger's doppelganger mentioned, yeah. The Hyperion Bryson never got old enough to go all gray. So, you want me to answer the riddle here? Fine." He thought a moment. "Okay, I think I've got a line on it. Orphan's more self-defined than just about anyone else you'll ever meet. He was built to be a weapon against a faction that he then personally converted to; in a pretty short time after that, he was the *only* member of the Faction, and he's been defining his Faction as himself, and himself by being his Faction, for so damn long that he's pretty much the *only*, let along biggest, influence on his life. So who else was going to be used to play mindgames with him, but himself?"

"Full marks, Mr. DuQuesne," said the fake-Bryson. "And why me?"

"That's a much more interesting question," he muttered, looking at Bryson carefully. *I'm impressed. Every detail's just as I remember it.* "You . . . you were the nexus. You were the point that brought me and Rich Seaton together, the guy who got both of us pissed off about the same thing enough that we clicked and teamed up to humiliate you. And then you helped make us *grow up* enough to become the people we were supposed to be."

Bryson nodded slowly.

"Key influences. What made us who we are. And Bryson . . . you're the *real* Bryson. Well, a reflection or image of the real Bryson, the Hyperion researcher that . . . designed me. So you represent what shaped me on both sides of the glass."

"Precisely."

"*And*," he said with sudden conviction, "you didn't even know why, not right off. Because what you—Vindatri—*did* is to trigger a reaction in *us* that generates the illusion. That's why you implied you don't read minds; you can find the right way to trigger a memory or a reaction, but until we *live* it, see it, experience it, you don't get the details; we make those *for* you."

"Oh, excellent, Marc," Bryson said, with the rare, broad smile he remembered well. "Truly, you live up to your designer's intent, and then some."

"And *from* that, you start to get a real, personal handle on who we are, what we think is important, what we're really *like*." DuQuesne nodded, then frowned. "Not that I like it, or approve of the method. I've had a *bellyful* of being manipulated before."

"Understandable," Bryson said. "Yet you would, I think, agree that actual mind-reading is much more of an intrusion, and disapprove even more, while I think you would also understand that a being such as Vindatri has good reason to be cautious."

"Maybe. I don't need to be cautious around babies, and power-wise you sure seem to have that level of divide on us."

"Perhaps. Perhaps. Yet in the Arena things are rarely what they seem, Mr. DuQuesne."

DuQuesne suddenly became aware that his surroundings had slowly, subtly, but completely shifted; he was now in what appeared to be Professor Bryson's office, complete with stacks of papers waiting to be graded and the same slightly-battered wooden chairs with green leather-cushioned seats for students looking for additional help. "That's impressive. Don't know if I *like* it, but it's impressive."

"You don't find a familiar setting comforting? Interesting, Mr. DuQuesne." Bryson seated himself in the larger swivel-chair behind the desk, and stubbed out the cigarette which was now burned almost to the filter.

"Okay, that actually counts as evidence you *don't* read minds, unless you're just playing a really deep game. Because if you read minds, you'd *know* that this stopped being a comforting setting for me about fifty or so years ago."

"Yet these images are also what you produced under the stimulus you theorized I have created. Even more interesting."

It *was* interesting, and DuQuesne found he had to stop and consider the situation. If he was right, this was a sort of self-generated illusion; "Vindatri," whatever and whoever he really was, just sort of poked your brain and then gave it the tools to generate one hell of a hallucination that Vindatri could participate in—but much of it was provided and directed by DuQuesne's brain, not Vindatri's. So why, exactly, was he seeing this particular setting?

He found himself involuntarily glancing over his shoulder, and the answer was obvious. "Blast it. Because seeing you, talking with you . . . thinking about all of that . . . I keep thinking Rich is going to walk through that door. Part of me would like nothing more. Except I don't want a shadow play of him, I'd want the real thing, and he's *gone*."

Bryson nodded slowly, pulling out his cigarette pack again absently and proffering it to DuQuesne in the same gesture DuQuesne had seen a thousand times and more. He saw his arm, almost against his will, reach out and take one of the white cylinders; Bryson lit his first and then handed the shining metal lighter to DuQuesne.

The sharp, warm taste of the smoke was the same, too. DuQuesne felt a sting in his eyes that wasn't from smoke. *My aunt's cat's kittens' pants buttons, as Rich might've said, this is just too* damn *good an illusion.*

"Why are you here, DuQuesne?" Bryson-Vindatri finally asked.

"Here—your office, or here—Vindatri's home?"

"Oh, Vindatri's home, I meant."

"Orphan needed someone to help him run his ship; from what he told us later, we're also sort of exhibits to help him fulfill an obligation to you to tell him about any true newcomers to the Arena." DuQuesne figured Vindatri would know the details; if he didn't, his questions might tell DuQuesne something about the things Orphan might be hiding.

"That is . . . a rather *surface* explanation, Mr. DuQuesne—"

"If you're going to keep being all formal, I've been *Doctor* DuQuesne for fifty years and more now."

"Humph," Bryson snorted, but then shook his head and smiled. "Old habits, eh, Doctor? You were my students and then adventurers for a while before you ever officially finished that degree. But in any event, *Doctor* DuQuesne, that was a surface explanation. I asked why you were here, not why *Orphan* would want you here."

Interesting question. Let's see how this dance goes. "Pain in the ass or not, we owed Orphan a lot, and so we're fulfilling a debt." He debated internally for a moment, but realized that holding back the next piece of information would be pointless; it *was* in fact one of the major reasons they'd come. "And since we know about Orphan's little toy, we wanted to come here to find out what you know about the powers of the Shadeweavers and the Faith."

Bryson's façade cracked for an instant; the brown eyes were suddenly strange, unreadable, and the figure was rigid and motionless. Almost instantly, however, it resumed the more natural motion. "Does that mean that Orphan has had occasion to use my gift? Interesting. I had reached a tentative conclusion that he would likely *never* use it as he did not know its limits and would always argue with himself that there would be a moment of greater need . . . later."

"Used it and maybe burned it out. Might want to give it a maintenance check and replace it if it's still in warranty."

The Bryson-illusion smiled. "I may have to do that, yes. Now . . . somehow it does not seem to me that *you* have any direct interest in these powers, other than the quite natural curiosity of a scientist trying to understand a power that seems to violate some of the basic principles of science."

"Ha! That's the whole of the Arena in a nutshell. But until we're all together, I don't think I want to discuss the rest of it. You want to talk about other things, hey, great, but our mission and my purpose or lack thereof? Wait until me and my friends are all together, and you've taken off all your masks."

"An interesting requirement," he said, and the tone was not *quite* Bryson's any more. "How, precisely, would you know I *had*, as you say, taken off all of my masks, when you do not know the truth of what I am?"

"Trust me, I'd know," DuQuesne said. "I'm real, *real* good at telling real from fake. You might say it's one of my absolute defining characteristics."

"Still, I would *very* much like you to tell me a bit more about your interest in the powers of Shadeweaver and Faith."

DuQuesne had been tense and waiting for it, and so he sensed it instantly; a disturbance in his mind, a sudden awareness that part of him was not thinking in the direction that it should. He shot to his feet and slammed his fist down on the desk so hard that the illusory wood cracked from one side to the other. "Stop it *right now*. Understand this, Vindatri or whatever your name is, I'm giving you *one* chance, and one only, to *back off*. You don't touch our minds. It's one thing to do what you did here—and I still don't like it—but the *microsecond* I catch you poking around trying to *change* my mind, or anyone else's, again, that's the microsecond I'll make you regret it."

The sensation vanished instantaneously, and the figure across from him only looked like Bryson the way a doll of Bryson would have. "You *sensed* that. You *resisted*. Extraordinary. Utterly unheard-of. Yet you do not truly think you can threaten *me* here, do you?"

The last thing DuQuesne wanted to do was trigger a conflict here and now; yes, he had his trump card in the form of the fiction-made-real powers the Arena was granting him . . . but he had no idea what Vindatri's real power level was, and even back on Hyperion DuQuesne had known there were people out of his league. Still . . . *You gotta double down on stuff like this. Can't let him get the complete upper hand, think he can push us around.* "Maybe. Maybe not. But sure as God made little green apples you'll find out if you *ever* try messing with any of our heads again. Do you follow me?"

Slowly animation returned to the figure; Bryson stood and bowed slowly. "You are a *fearsomely* interesting arrival, Dr. Marc DuQuesne. So be it. I will refrain from testing your capabilities in so dangerous a fashion."

He gestured, and the door of the office opened, showing—instead of the brick corridor of the school—a long, well-lit passageway of metal. "I thank you for a most instructive meeting, Doctor. Please proceed." The smile was neither human nor comforting. "There will be much to talk about . . . later."

Chapter 24

Ariane stumbled to a halt, mouth dropping open, eyes wider than they had been since she was a child.

The old man—who didn't look so old now, to a girl ten years older—smiled broadly at her and held his arms wide. "Hey there, racer girl!"

I thought I was prepared. Boy, was I wrong, a part of her thought. That part, Captain Ariane Austin, Leader, knew perfectly well that this was—*had* to be—just an unexpected guise of Orphan's mysterious "Vindatri."

But the other part of her was starting forward, tears rippling her vision of the man, brown hair sprinkled with gray, smiling lines creasing his face, sharp eyes twinkling like polished wood, wearing the blue jeans and shirt that had been a standard outfit for workers for, literally, centuries. There was even a streak of black oil or grease on one cheek, just as if he'd been working on one of the . . .

Even as she thought it, she realized that she was no longer in a sterile, dimly-lit room of metal and plastic and glass; the Texas sun shone brilliantly overhead, striking hot highlights from the red-painted metal of the ancient truck that Grandaddy leaned against, hood wide open, tools neatly arranged on his mobile rack nearby.

His hug felt the same, too, and the smell—of oil, a touch of gasoline, a little sweat, citrus soap—was enough to make her actually cry. *Don't let him see that much of you!* the Leader snapped, but it was a halfhearted self-scolding.

She let go and stepped back. "You're *dead*, Grandaddy."

201

"Maybe so, Arrie, or maybe not so dead as you think." He wiped his eyes, and she could see the glitter of tears.

A thin trickle of anger finally began to seep in. "I *know* you are. Saw the garage burning, and we'd seen you go in, and they found your body in it. So this, this is all a trick, and a pretty *mean* trick, too, Vindatri."

Grandaddy frowned, but it was a sad frown, an apologetic one. "Sorry about that, Arrie. I never wanted to make you sad, you know that. And . . . well, neither does Vindatri, since you bring him up."

Ariane swallowed the anger. *This is the person we came to see. Whatever he does, he may be the* only *chance I have to understand the power I've got.* "So . . . what *is* the purpose, Vindatri?"

"Wish you'd just call me Grandaddy, like you always did. Y'see, this, well, *everything* around you, that's not actually Vindatri's doing. Not exactly, anyway. He can give . . . call 'em hints, guidance, stuff he wants to see or know or talk about, but the way those questions show up, that's more *you* than him."

"So he's not just reading my mind?"

"Nope. Maybe he *can*, but that's not the way this game's being played. He's getting to see what you're seeing, but only touches of what you're *thinking*—the stuff you're focused on, what's being projected."

That did make some sense. Obviously *she* would know exactly what her Grandaddy's old farm would look and smell like; she suspected that someone just reading her mind and trying to build it from scratch would find it a *lot* harder. She smiled finally, brushing away the last of the tears and feeling less embarrassed by it than she might have been. "I was actually expecting Mentor."

"Ha! Be too predictable. Besides, there's a damn good reason it's me and not him. Bet you can guess it."

"Because he's been . . . more a friend than anything else. He didn't raise me, didn't *shape* me. He's *named* Mentor but he wasn't my mentor, so to speak."

"And you're fast on the answers as you are on the track. Good answer, Arrie, and pretty much spot-on." He reached up and slammed the hood of the truck down. "C'mon, let's get inside. Hot out here, a body could use something cold. Want a beer? Or maybe lemonade?"

It's just like a simgame. Play along. "One of *your* lemonades?"

"You bet."

They walked to the somewhat weathered-looking house in silence, puffs of dust kicking up around their feet until their boots rattled across the wooden porch and into the dimmer, cooler interior. Grandaddy opened the refrigerator—startling in its modernity, shining sharp edges in the midst of centuries-old décor—and got out the lemonade. The pitcher was just the way she remembered it, light shining mistily through the glass, slices of lemon swirling in the water, scattered bits of pulp drifting as Grandaddy poured her a big tumbler full. "Here you go." As usual, Grandaddy had pulled a beer from the back of the fridge and popped the top off easily.

She took a long series of swallows. *My god, it tastes* just *like Grandaddy's.* Tears threatened to well up again, but she forced them back. Once she was sure she had everything under control, she spoke. "So what does Vindatri—you—want?" she asked. It was a huge temptation to just accept what she saw at face value, but that level of escapism wasn't really in her. *It's an awesome simulation, but it's still just a trick, and for some purpose I don't quite know yet.*

"Truth? He's not sure, exactly. To know more about you. Figure out why you came with Orphan. Find out what *you* want, coming this far with someone you must know didn't tell you the half of the truth about what he was doing."

I was afraid of that. "Orphan held something back, yes, but he was, well, up-front about not telling us everything."

"Was he, now? Good for him. Boy's spent years learning how to keep his left hand *or* right hand from knowing what the tail was doing, if you get my drift. Nice to think he's tryin' to get over that." He took a long pull from the bottle. "That hits the spot! Now . . . Orphan says there's been *two* sets of First Emergents?"

So he's already been talking—probably is *right now—with Orphan. Wonder if he plays games like this with him now?* "Well, we're your standard First Emergents, if there is such a thing. The others are natives to the Arena, the Genasi, who just got their first Sphere."

Grandaddy froze—just a tiny hesitation, but that hesitation was like a glitch in a simulation, suddenly bringing home the fact that this was *not* real, no matter how much it seemed like it was. "The *Genasi*? Citizens now? Well, well, well, that's a surprise and a half. Though I can't figure there's anything *standard* about you and your friends, nohow. That DuQuesne's a firecracker, and Sun Wu Kung's just a plain hoot. How'd you get your citizenship? Who'd you Challenge?"

She hesitated, but honestly couldn't think of any reason not to tell him the basics; everyone in Nexus Arena already knew, after all. "We actually got that through a Type-Two Challenge. The Molothos landed on our Upper Sphere, and we kicked them off."

The stare was *definitely* two-edged; in a way, it looked just like her grandfather's incredulous gaze, and yet there was something else, much older, alien, behind it. "*First Emergents* defeated a *Molothos* scouting force on their own Sphere? As their initial Challenge?" The voice had shifted the tiniest bit, but then warmed back to that of her Grandaddy. "Dang, Arrie, you people know how to make an *entrance!* Not that I didn't already know that, having seen you at the races and all. Still, that's one *hell* of an introduction. You've had other Challenges too?"

"Yes. And some conflicts that weren't, strictly speaking, Challenges. But like you said, we came here for a reason, so I'd like *you* to answer a question or two, instead of just me talking."

"Ask away, Arrie. Can't absolutely guarantee an answer, but won't hurt to ask."

Here goes nothing. "Do you know how to teach someone to use the powers of the Shadeweavers or the Faith?"

The imitation-Grandaddy didn't answer right away; he gazed at her with a faint smile on his face, taking an occasional sip of his beer as he studied her. Then, just as she was about to speak again, he said, "Why would you need anyone to do *that?* Both of those groups'll gladly teach anyone who gets the initiation. Hell, they keep the initiation *tight* so that they're the only game in town."

"Usually, yes. But . . ." She concentrated, and in a flash of silver-gold light, swapped her current clothes for the uniform that had been created in the moment of her apotheosis.

The entire simulation flickered, and for a moment she stood again in a shadowed gray room, facing a simulation of her grandfather that stood rigid and blank-eyed. It was a full second or three before the farmhouse reformed around her with its scents of old wood and coffee and barbeque. "Well, dye me pink and call me a pig. You've got the power *without* being either? I will be *dipped.* Absolutely *dipped.* That shouldn't be *possible.*" Another chuckle, touched with the alien tone.

"And that is the second impossible thing I have seen this day. *Fearsome* indeed."

I'll bet he's talking about DuQuesne. "So are you going to answer my question?"

A slow smile spread across Grandaddy's face, a smile like the one he'd worn when she first convinced him to take her for a ride in one of his antiques. "Answer it? All right, Arrie. Yes, Vindatri knows how to teach someone about those powers. He's got the data, archives going back *millennia.* Maybe not the *Encyclopedia Galactica,* but good enough. That what you're here for?"

"Mainly, yes. And paying a debt and a promise we made to Orphan."

"Well, now, that's fine. Good to know Orphan managed to make himself a few friends. Lord knows he needs 'em in his line of work." While the words were very much Grandaddy, the motion was still a little off, and his next words showed that Vindatri must be aware of it. "I have to say, I'm still a little shellshocked by that trick you pulled. Never happened before. Never *heard* of it happening before. I . . . Vindatri . . . will need to think a bit on this. Your other friends, they've had their surprises too, but yours takes the cake. Put your glass in the sink and run along, Arrie—you'll find your friends waitin' for you just down the road."

"Are they all right?"

"Be a poor host who hurt his guests the first hour they were in his house, wouldn't it? They're just fine, Arrie. Maybe a bit peeved and confused—like you—but no real harm done. Go talk it over with 'em, and we'll talk again later, without all the different masks."

She rose and put the glass into the old stainless-steel sink, then looked over at the illusion of her grandfather. "Vindatri . . . this was a very well done illusion. And . . . I guess a part of me really wanted to see Grandaddy again. So . . . it's okay. Thank you, even."

The smile, also, seemed to have two people behind it. "Then you're *very* welcome, Ariane Stephanie Austin. Now go meet up with your friends. See, time goes by differently for each of you in these interviews, so they've been waiting a bit."

That makes sense, actually; he probably wanted to devote most of his attention to each person as he interviewed them, so he had to stretch out the perceptions of the others during that time. Which meant she'd been here at least three, maybe four or more times as long as she'd thought. "On my way!"

As she walked, the sun faded, the landscape went ghostly and disappeared, and she found herself striding quickly down a brightly-lit passageway that ended in a trapezoidal door. The door slid open as she approached, and she saw, seated around a table, DuQuesne, Wu Kung, and Orphan. "Good to see all of you!"

The others leapt to their feet, even Orphan. "Captain! Glad to see you're okay too," DuQuesne said.

"Indeed!" Orphan's voice was emphatic. "I did not, of course, expect Vindatri to do anything . . . extreme, but as you realize I do not *know* him well, so there was a degree of concern."

Wu had already made his way over to her and surveyed her, sniffing. "You were upset, but you are not hurt. Good."

That's an impressive nose he has. "But you look . . . a little scuffed up, Wu," she answered. And it was true; the Hyperion Monkey King's costume was somewhat askew in areas, and she thought she saw darkening under the fur of one cheek.

"Ha! This Vindatri's version of Sha Wujing and I had a discussion . . . sometimes with our fists!"

"Of course you did. Look, can I sit down and we can all talk about what happened?"

"Sure," DuQuesne said. "Though remember that whether he's here or not, Vindatri's probably listening in."

"Yes, I'd expect he must be," Ariane said, pulling out a chair at the table and sitting down. There were three platters of various snacks on the table, one obviously for Orphan and the other two apparently meant for human consumption. "This stuff all checks out?"

"One hundred percent," DuQuesne affirmed, "which tells us one hell of a lot about Vindatri's abilities. He obviously didn't know much about us before talking to us, and I'm pretty sure he didn't know squat before we got to his area of space, otherwise he wouldn't need Orphan to go playing messenger boy. So he managed to get a read on us and whip up quite a spread in the time he was interviewing us—and I'm pretty sure *most* of his attention was focused on us, not setting up a snack bar."

That *did* emphasize that Vindatri's powers went considerably beyond making quick sims and having a very impressive and distant secret base. "So he evaluated us, matched biochemistries, and somehow figured out something about our palates in that period of time. That *is* pretty impressive." She looked at the others. "So what happened to the rest of you? What was your private conference like? Orphan?"

"Mine? I would suspect the least entertaining of us all. I saw Vindatri again and he asked me a few questions about you—after instructing me to tell him *nothing* other than the precise and most limited answers to his questions."

"So he didn't want you supplying any more information than he asked for?" That actually made some sense. "He wanted to evaluate us as much as possible without having any preconceived notions. So what *did* he ask you?"

"Hm. First he asked if all of you were part of the same Faction, to which I answered yes. Then he asked if you were part of the same *species*, to which—after some hesitation—I answered that I believed so, but was unsure." Orphan paused, then gave one of his decisive handtaps and continued. "He then asked if I was here to fulfill *both* of my conditions, to which I also answered yes. And that, I am afraid, was the entire substance of my interview."

DuQuesne studied him. "And you *still* can't tell us the second condition or requirement he had on you?"

"Not as of this moment, no. I am hoping that restriction will be eased soon."

She turned to Wu Kung. "So, did you actually keep your temper?"

"Well . . ." Wu Kung shifted in his seat. "Mostly. As I told you, I met Sha Wujing, or really an imitation of him. The imitation was . . . good, but not perfect. At first I could smell it was not him, but then the smell got closer."

"Hmm. Tells me that Vindatri's not scent-oriented," DuQuesne said. "Visually and audibly his illusions or sims were spot-on from the start, and the only bobbles I noticed were when things weren't going the way Vindatri expected or was used to."

"Most people like you don't use your noses much," Wu pointed out.

"Although there *are* quite a few species with excellent scent capabilities," Orphan said, "and I concur with Dr. DuQuesne's conclusion; Vindatri must not be one of these, or he would have had scent as a focus of your sim from the start."

"Anyway, after I told him I knew he was a fake, I asked him why he was too much of a coward to show his real face."

"This was your idea of *behaving*?" DuQuesne demanded.

"I didn't even *try* to punch him then! I was behaving really well!" Wu Kung said defensively. "He laughed and said he just wanted to take a form that I was more comfortable with and that I could understand. So *I* said that I could understand any form he took well enough, and that all he *needed* to understand was that I was your bodyguard and I needed to get back to you."

Wu's face shifted into a scowl. "But instead he started asking me questions about you and why I wanted to be your bodyguard, and at first I told him about DuQuesne but then I said I liked doing it, and he asked why, and I told him how important you were to Humanity and all that, and then that fake Sha Wujing snorted at me and said that the real reason was that I couldn't handle myself alone so I'd found a cheap substitute Sanzo! So *THEN* I hit him!"

Of course we were going to get to the hitting sooner or later. "And did he hit back?"

The scowl turned into a grin. "Oh, yes! We had a *fine* sparring match, and I got to kick him through some of his simulated trees and he mashed my face in his phony dirt." His green gaze was suddenly sharp and focused on her. "But I remembered to do it just like when I sparred with Orphan, so neither of us got really hurt."

That look had a *lot* more meaning in it than just the words, and in a moment she'd fished it out. *He's not just saying he didn't fight to kill; he's saying he held back a lot to hide what he can really do. Orphan might blow that lie out of the water, of course, but it's still the right move overall.* She smiled. "Well, that's *good*, Wu," she said, catching his eye and nodding for emphasis to show she understood. "Wouldn't want to hurt our host. Go on, though."

"So we traded a lot of punches—and kicks and throws and all—but finally he admitted he might have sounded a little insulting, and he apologized, so we stopped fighting. He asked me about why I didn't seem to be quite the same species, and," another glance at both her and DuQuesne, "I told him I'd been genemodded a lot before I was born."

He's saying he kept presence of mind enough to not talk about Hyperion. Good work, Wu. "Well, that's certainly the truth. Then what?"

"Well, he said he had a lot to think about and was still busy with the rest of you, so he sent me on to this room. That's it."

"Suggestive," DuQuesne said after a moment. "He probably learned a lot about you by getting you fighting mad, but you surprised him with a couple things too."

Wu looked smug. "I also learned he isn't a fighter."

"Really?"

"His simulation kept . . . what's the word? Glitching, that's it. It kept glitching for tiny fractions of a second during the fight."

"Might be that he's a fighter, but not *your* kind of fighter," DuQuesne said. "Remember, he was trying to simulate Sha Wujing, who'd going to be fighting a damn sight different than Vindatri would, no matter what he's really like. So the sim had to keep making split-second adjustments to keep things working anything like the way you'd expect."

"Maybe. But I think he wasn't used to lots of real combat."

"Still, either way it's interesting," Ariane said. "How about you, Marc?"

DuQuesne nodded. "I'll sum up in words, but since I recorded mine in headware, I'll dump the whole thing to you."

She opened a connection, felt DuQuesne access it and braced herself for the flood.

And then she found herself staring in open-mouthed disbelief at DuQuesne.

He noticed immediately. "Ariane? Ariane, what's wrong?"

For several long moments, she still couldn't speak. Finally, she got a grip on herself. *Of all the things . . . This can't be coincidence . . . but what else could it be?* "Marc . . . take a look at this." She sent him a quick clip of her own experiences.

He went pale beneath his olive skin. "Holy Mother of God. What in *hell*—"

"I don't know either, Marc," she said, voice shaking with disbelief. "But your 'Professor Bryson' . . . is my grandfather."

Chapter 25

Dajzail ripple-walked from the airlock down the ramp; Alztanza himself waited there, holding his fighting-claws rigid in salute. "Guard not," he said to Alztanza, who immediately relaxed his stance. "It is good to see you again, 'Tanza."

The Fleet Master clattered a smile at him and they briefly clasped claws. "And you, Daj. How was your journey?"

"Well enough, though it took me *homeyears*, it seemed, to extricate myself from the Embassy. I have selected temporary representatives, but they all needed individual instruction . . . so in any event it took me a while to get here."

Alztanza rattled his claws in sympathy. "I do not envy you the administrative duties, Daj. For my part, it took me some time to reach here as well, as I traveled with my ships, and it takes no fewer than *three* Sky-Gate transitions to get here, one of them quite a long ride. Oh, greetings to you, Kanjstall," he said as Dajzail's Salutant stepped up near them, carrying the most vital of Dajzail's luggage. "But in some ways, Daj, the time was well spent. I was able to complete arranging the basic strategy and drill our forces prior to your arrival, which is good. You know how the presence of an actual *ruler* can disrupt perfectly good training exercises."

"True enough. So the entire two Forces are assembled?"

"All four thousand eight hundred and two vessels are here, yes. Of the original Force there were five not really suited for deployment, but I have received fine replacements for them. I would be honored if you would take *Claws of Vengeance* as your personal warship."

"*Claws of Vengeance*? That would be a Twinscabbard vessel, yes?"

"It would," said the Fleet Master, clearly pleased he remembered naming conventions well enough to make that deduction.

"Then I accept. A fine symbolism to lead from a vessel of the same class they destroyed, and such ships are excellent combinations of firepower and speed." He saw Alztanza's eye flickering in its scan. "No, I have no one else in my party."

"Really? I had expected the Master of Forces, at the least."

"Malvchait remains on the Homeworld, and is directing the assembly of the Fleet which will take their lowspace system, once we have secured their Sky Gates. That will be a matter of several turnings, I think."

"I would expect so." For a few moments Alztanza was quiet as they walked towards the military docking areas. "Faction Leader, might I ask if the secondary force is necessary?"

"In truth, I hope not," he answered after a moment. "It will mean diverting a significant portion of our current military resources to one target which cannot be engaged for several homeyears at least, depending on how close we can Transition. That Fleet will have to come here and deploy, and deploying it will take a long time as well. If by terrible chance we are defeated here in Arenaspace, we would prefer to merely send near-lightspeed projectiles to destroy their worlds, but . . ."

Alztanza nodded. No military member of the Molothos could be unaware of the limitations the Arena imposed even in lowspace, including eliminating in one fashion or another any cataclysmic-level weapons or simply negating their effects. Fractional-lightspeed projectiles were one such weapon. "Still . . . if I may speak with all bluntness?"

Dajzail felt his head tilt, in the manner of a *savaziene* trying to find the best viewpoint. He and Alztanza had been second-nest friends, and even though they had been separated for a long time, he was startled that his friend would be so formal with *him*, especially in person rather than via official communications such as the one that had started this venture. "Always, 'Tanza. Quicksand, friend, do you need to be so nervous around me?"

"You are not just Dajzail, the lightweight moltling that I kept from being pushed around by my nestmates. You're the *Leader of the Faction of the Molothos*, and that means that yes, I have reason to be nervous—as you will probably see." Alztanza took a breath so deep that Dajzail could hear it, and then spoke. "Daj . . . I am not sure this is a wise thing that we do."

Dajzail stopped so suddenly that Kanjstall almost ran into him. He studied his friend and Fleet Master carefully with the full regard of his eye. "Kanjstall, please carry the luggage ahead and arrange transfer of the rest to *Claws of Vengeance*."

Kanjstall, flicking his attention between them, asked no questions. "As you command," he said, and ripple-walked away as fast as he could.

Once he was gone, Dajzail surveyed the quiet corridor carefully before turning back to Alztanza. "Explain your statement, 'Tanza."

His friend's tension was—just slightly—less, realizing that by ensuring no witnesses Dajzail was also ensuring that there would be no one to tell him that he had failed to act properly. "Daj . . . first, the lowspace intrusion *will* reduce our ability to project force elsewhere. *Especially* in lowspace, since the majority of our forces are highspace-focused. We may be taking only a seventh of our total forces—which still is nothing to take lightly—but closer to *fifty percent* of our lowspace forces."

Dajzail restrained an annoyed retort that *of course* he knew these things. Alztanza would realize that, and so there had to be more to it than that. "Say onward."

"A lot of the undercreatures in our various systems may become restive if they believe we no longer have sufficient resources to control them," Alztanza said bluntly. "Our lowspace military resources are outfitted for invasion, yes, but pacification and security are their other two missions, and we're cutting those forces in half for a significant period of time for this mission."

"But even if our current attack *succeeds*, 'Tanza, we'll need a lot of forces to send in and pacify the humans' star system. Perhaps, I'll grant you, not nearly this many, but it is also a *statement*, one that we will want to make known. But you're right—we could at least wait until we know the outcome of this first strike mission. We'll keep the forces assembling but they won't deploy until we've secured the Upper Sphere and destroyed all exterior resistance. Better?"

Alztanza still did not look entirely happy, but he rocked his claws to indicate some level of assent. "Better, yes, Leader. But . . ."

"Place it all before me at once, 'Tanza! Don't draw it all out!"

"As you say, Daj, but then remember you asked and don't strike at me without thinking."

What in the name of the Homeworld?

Alztanza raised himself a bit higher. "In all honesty, Daj . . . I don't know if this entire thing is a good idea."

"You . . ." He felt his eye flicker. "You mean teaching the human undercreatures a lesson?"

"I mean exactly that, Daj. Remember, you promised!" That last was said with a sharp warning buzz, as Dajzail found his fighting claws rising of their own accord. He forced them down with difficulty as Alztanza continued. "Daj . . . Leader, we already have conflicts with several Factions. None of the Great Factions at the moment, although relations with two of the others are very strained and there are skirmishes, but several others. Speaking as a Fleet Master, I truly do not relish the thought of opening a new war-front without having eliminated at least one of the ones I already have. Especially doing so while drawing down our forces significantly. A single Force, or even two, that's nothing to worry about, but a Fleet is many orders of magnitude more likely to cause problems."

Dajzail waited; it was clear that Alztanza was not finished.

"And . . . we get into these wars so *easily*, Daj. Let us look clearly in the water and see what it reflects, not what we would prefer to see there. These First Emergents came out, found us on their world, and managed—through methods we do not know—to defeat our scouting force. They have won multiple other Challenges and lost none, to our knowledge. I studied what is known of these 'humans' carefully—if I am to lead a force against them I must *know* them. And . . ."

He paused, then sighed loudly, a whistling sound, and continued. "And we *do not know enough*, Daj. We do not know how they defeated a scout force with two and only two of their number. We do not understand how their Leader was able to gain the power to defeat Amas-Garao. Her defeat of the Blessed Leader Sethrik seemed due to utter insanity. And their most recent victory is even more inexplicable, implying that some of their number have learned how to *evade* some of the Arena's most well-known restrictions. Truthfully? I would rather have a less conflicting interaction with them, perhaps to learn some of these truths."

Less conflicting . . . ? Dajzail heard the whistle-shriek of a breath drawn suddenly, knew it was his own. "Alztanza . . . you of all my people, you cannot be . . . a *Beast-Talker?*"

"What? *No!* Daj, I'm *cautious,* not insane!"

He felt a tiny bit of relief. "Well, *they* claim to be sane, you know."

The Nest of Accommodation, more familiarly and insultingly called the 'Beast Talkers,' were a small faction of Molothos who claimed that the undercreatures weren't *really* under-creatures, but actually PEOPLE, hard though that was to believe, and that the Molothos should learn how to "go past" their usual behaviors and start treating these beings as equals. Of course, what they wanted everyone to "go past" was the obvious and inarguable truth that the Molothos were the only truly civilized species in existence and start consorting with undercreatures little better than mindless beasts.

The Beast-Talkers were a splinter movement from the Rational Reward movement, which was fairly radical but had shown some good results from creating a system of more generous rewards and privileges for undercreature slaves, and *they* had been a splinter from the Maintainable Nests, who were perfectly respectable and had created the current system that provided more sustainable undercreature service resources rather than the traditional methods which even Dajzail felt had been ridiculously wasteful. Because of this line of descent, there were a small—but unfortunately increasing—number of people who thought this implied there might be something to the Beast-Talkers' ravings. This was the classic fallacy of the Extreme, similar to someone noting that you needed two milligrams of silicon carbide every day to keep your exoskeleton strong and from that claiming that you could be invincible if you just ate forty grams of it.

"That said . . . I *am* close to converting to the Rational Rewarders. Their results are impressive. But no, my point, Daj, was that we're going up against a species that's got too many unknowns in it and I'd rather try to trick, steal, or buy some of those secrets first before throwing my people into a mouth-grinder."

"The longer we wait," Dajzail said after a moment, "the more the humans will expand and fortify their position, Alztanza."

He could see that his friend had no immediate answer to that, and went forward. "I'm not being overconfident here, 'Tanza. Even the Master of Forces thought we could probably do it with a Seventh-Force, but I told him not to be stupid, and I've made it two full Forces. These are *First Emergents*, Alztanza. They've had a turning and a half in the Arena, and some of that was just getting home. They've got a few allies, and are trying to gather more. Right *now* they only have whatever they've been able to build on their own, which will be *far* from optimal for highspace Arena operations, and perhaps a few loanships from the Survivor.

"But if we wait and maneuver and try to bait them into revealing secrets, they will only be getting stronger. And we *cannot* allow these undercreatures to get away with their prior insults; you must agree with me on that?"

Alztanza stood immobile for a moment, then dipped all legs and his claws. "As you say, Leader. They cannot be permitted to do this with impunity."

"And . . . ?"

The Fleet Master gave a buzzing sigh, then laughed. "And you're right, Daj. A full Force is probably ridiculous overkill, but if we wait a few more turnings we could find that they've made alliance with one of the Great Factions that's willing to fight for them, or they get new Spheres, or something else. Sorry for bothering you with my misgivings."

Tremendous relief washed over Dajzail. *I absolutely feared getting in an argument with him—and if I had, I'd have had to remove him from command, something we might never have been able to forgive each other for.* "Do not apologize, Alz; your points made sense. I just think this is the best course, and you seem to have agreed in the end. So it's just been a good chance for me to face the reflection myself."

He linked claws with his friend for an instant, and the two of them began to move up the corridor again. "Then let me get settled into *Claws of Vengeance* while you give the Seventh-Masters their final instructions prior to departure.

"Tomorrow we begin our mission of purification!"

Chapter 26

"Dr. Alexander Fairchild," repeated Simon, studying Oasis closely.

The Hyperion-born woman was *still* not entirely herself; the strain showed in the stiffness of her arm as she reached out for the water pitcher and poured herself a glass. She drank, looked aimlessly around the conference room that Simon had chosen when they had returned—in haste—to the Embassy. "Yes," she said finally.

The name finally clicked. "*Masaka*. That was the name of the Hyperion AI that nearly—"

"—*did* kill me, Oasis, forcing K to take me in. Yes."

No wonder she's so shaken. Fairchild literally ripped her mind apart trying to take her body. "But . . . K, *you* seem just as upset as Oasis, so to speak. That is, it seems that all of you is terribly shocked—by what has to be a coincidence or misperception."

Oasis' smile was weak and without humor. "You are right, Simon. I *am* upset, and if DuQuesne were here, *he'd* be freaking out, too."

"Why? Oasis," he put a hand gently on hers; she immediately gripped his painfully hard. "Ow. Oasis, *why*?"

"Because Dr. Alexander Fairchild was DuQuesne and Seaton's worst enemy in *their* universe, Simon."

Other people might not have quite grasped the import of that statement, but Simon had been around enough Hyperions to understand. If Fairchild had been a long-running enemy to DuQuesne, it meant he was *at least* DuQuesne's equal. "I see. Yes, that *would* be terrifying. But, Oasis, you know it's *impossible*. Fairchild was an *AI*. Formidable as he might have been, there is absolutely no way he could enter the Arena."

When she did not immediately answer, he went on. "We *know* this. AIs do not *work* here, ever—unless the thing we call the Arena is an AI, and in that case it suffers no rivals. The Minds of the Blessed have spent tens of thousands of years, perhaps more, trying to evade that law of the Arena's, and failed completely. According to both Orphan and Sethrik, the Minds have tried placing versions of their intellects into bodies prepared for them, bodies otherwise perfectly identical to any other Blessed. The bodies collapse upon entrance. The Arena is not fooled.

"So you see, what you saw was a trick of perspective, a chance coincidence of form and color. It *had* to be, because there is absolutely no way that—even if this Fairchild is the renegade Hyperion AI we encountered in our own space—he could possibly be *here* in the Arena."

She squeezed his hand again, then looked up, but her eyes were still haunted. "I wish I could be so sure, Simon. But it's possible that that rule doesn't apply to Hyperion AIs."

"What? Why not?" He remembered something. "Does this have to do with whatever you discussed in secret with DuQuesne?"

She nodded, twirling one of her four ponytails absently. "Yes." Oasis bit her lip, thinking. "Simon, I think I have to tell you. Because honestly, you could probably find it out anyway, if you wanted, and you haven't. Right? I mean, that power of yours could do that, don't you think?"

"Yes. Probably."

"Then . . . why not try? I'm going to tell you anyway, so it's not like you'd be stealing the information." Her voice was more animated, and he could tell she was genuinely curious, and the question at least was drawing her back out of the completely atypical state of tension and fear she'd been in.

Nonetheless, the question made *him* tense, as any serious consideration of using that ability always did. Still . . . he could think of no sensible reason to refuse the test. He drew in a breath, preparing himself. "Very well."

Preternatural clarity rose up within him more swiftly, more readily than before, infusing him with an absolute perception of his surroundings; he could hear Oasis' breathing, sense her heartbeat, observe the tiniest motion of each *hair* on her head, watch motes of dust in their random courses across the room, and hold it all within his head as easily as a three-letter password. *Great Kami, I forget. Every time, I forget what it's like to have this power . . . yet I always remember enough.*

He focused now, focused on a single question: *what was the secret DuQuesne told Oasis here, before they left?*

The answer came to him in a flash.

He opened his eyes, then closed them as he banished that god-like perception once more. His hands shook and he took a moment to calm himself.

This time it was Oasis' hand on his, and his squeezing hers tightly. "What's wrong, Simon?"

"You don't understand, do you?" he asked quietly. "Yet . . . of all people, you should." He drew another breath, let it out slowly. "Even the *fringes* of that . . . power, perception, access to the Arena . . . goes beyond anything a human mind should be able to process, yet I *do*, it seems like mere child's play. I can rise up, see . . . oh, anything, it feels like, expand my perceptions and knowledge so far that, honestly, I have never even *tried* to push its limits. A part of me fears there *are* no limits, even if that sounds utterly ridiculous."

He could see a dawning understanding in her eyes. "And it *feels* so right, so *perfect*, especially for a scientist, someone whose *goal* has always been to *understand the world*. I *want* this power, Oasis. And I am *terrified* of it."

Oasis' eyes were wide and he could see she *did* understand. "Oh, God, Simon, I didn't realize . . . of *course* you would be. One moment you're not all that . . . and then you *are* 'all that.' You can see anything, know anything . . . and that's your heart's desire. And maybe your worst fear, because if you ever *did* know everything, what would be left to know?"

"And if I did know, not everything, but even a measurable fraction of the Cosmic All, as Ariane's Mentor calls it, what would I be thinking then of the people who could not even understand a billionth of it?" he murmured. "Would I still even be *human*? Would I *care* about humanity?"

She suddenly reached out and hugged him. "Simon, your *asking* those questions is one of the best arguments that you would. You have to trust yourself . . . and maybe us, too . . . to keep you anchored to

who you really are, no matter what . . . head-rush the Arena-sense gives
you."

She let go, but the warmth and affection, the *comfort*, of that
embrace lingered, and he felt the fear and apprehension fading.
"Thank you, Oasis. Yes, I'm afraid of all that . . . but you and Ariane
and DuQuesne all seem to think I can handle it. So perhaps I *should*
trust you and use this power more often."

"Well, don't go *too* far. I don't want to have to *deck* you if you go all
glowy-eyed 'A GOD AM I' on me. And I'll do it, you know."

He chuckled. "I am sure you would. And I give you full permission
to do so, if that ever happens."

Her smile answered his, then faded back to a more serious
expression. "So? Did you get it?"

"Ah, yes. I did, I believe." He studied her, replaying the revelation
and what it might mean, and found that even without the cosmic
vision it was an awesome thing to contemplate. "That the Hyperions—
by virtue of having been raised from birth in settings that were
completely real to them, by people whose sole purpose was in making
those lives as real as possible, those *people* as real as possible—may
potentially have the same powers and abilities here in the Arena as
they did *in their Hyperion worlds.*

"The Arena gives to those entering it the abilities that were natural
to them, even to the extent of tailoring environments in all ways. To the
Hyperions, the worlds they were *raised* in were natural—they had not
an inkling that they were not, and their creators had no other thought
in their minds but to fulfill that perception. In other words, they are
not limited by the restrictions of the Arena on other species, and may
even be aided by the Arena in achieving abilities that would normally
be . . . well, utterly impossible, but are natural to them."

"That's it. We already know one big piece of evidence: Wu Kung
gets to talk to, and influence, animals in the Arena. No one else—that
we know of, anyway—can do that. And his winning of the Challenge
proves that he's not subject to the normal physical limits, anyway."

Her brows came down. "And *that* is why I'm not so sure about
Dr. Fairchild. Sure, a normal AI couldn't find a body and move into the
Arena . . . but a *Hyperion* AI who, like his physical counterpart, had
been designed and raised to be a particular person, who *believed* they
were that person, who *lived the life* of that person . . . I'm not so sure

that *they* couldn't pull that off. That the Arena wouldn't see them as legal entries, so to speak. Maybe it would, but maybe not."

The thought gave Simon something of a chill. "I wish I could disagree, but you're right. It fits with what we know of the Arena's rules. As an AI—in a computational chassis—I am sure he would not be allowed. But if he could transfer himself into a human body, *then* . . . yes, it might be something the Arena would permit."

He stood up. "Oasis, this is of course your secret. But I think it has now become imperative we share it with Laila and Carl, if no one else. Because if it is possible that a Hyperion AI—or, as Mentor said, possibly as many as *three*—has even the slightest chance of entering the Arena with their full *fictional* capabilities, *we* are not going to be the only people in danger.

"It could be every Faction in the Arena."

Chapter 27

"Your words tantalize me, my friends," Orphan said as DuQuesne was still trying to wrap his mind around this latest revelation. "It is clear—it has, in truth, always been clear—that there is some great mystery surrounding Dr. DuQuesne, and his compatriots Wu Kung and Oasis and, I believe, Maria-Susanna. I have to believe it also has to do with Wu Kung's *extraordinary* performance in the recent Challenge.

"It seems that these connections now encompass our Captain as well, yes?"

"In a way, yes," DuQuesne admitted. "But we're not going into detail here."

Wu Kung was looking puzzled, unlike Ariane who was still shellshocked. "I'm right, aren't I?" she said, and transmitted an image to him.

The man in the faded denim was undeniably familiar, and the details that DuQuesne could notice—a particular faint scar on one cheek, the pattern of wrinkles around the eyes—confirmed it. "It checks out, Ariane. That's Bryson, all right." He grinned suddenly. "And you know what, it makes a whole lot of *other* things make sense. How many people these days even *heard* of Doc Smith's work? He's not even a fringe thing, he's *ancient history*, older than Shakespeare was in *his* time, and never even vaguely that popular. I never met another person in my *life* outside of Hyperion who recognized my name; hell, he wasn't much remembered only a century after publication, and now it's three hundred fifty-plus years later than *that*.

Your parents let you get half-raised by that old throwback and that's how you came to be this way."

"But . . . but you said he was *alive!*" The dark-blue brows had come together and he could see anger welling up within her. "He *died* in a fire. They even found a *body*, so—"

"Maria-Susanna," DuQuesne said quietly. "Saul and I helped him run to start with, but he had to live his life, or lives, real careful. I'll bet he stuck around a lot longer than was safe, watching you grow up. But finally he knew he'd pushed his luck too much and had to die. A clone body's not hard to get made if you know the tricks to it." He reached out, touched her arm. "Don't be mad at him, Ariane. He did it for his safety and yours. He probably didn't think Maria-Susanna would hurt a kid, but he couldn't be *sure*. She's not easy to predict."

He looked over at Orphan. "Sorry I can't clear things up much for you, Orphan, but the real answers you'd want are way too valuable."

"Quite understood, Doctor. Alas, I cannot guarantee any privacy here."

"Yeah, I know."

Ariane shook her head, and then he saw her eyes widen and her gaze snapped to meet his own. "Marc—"

With a visible effort, she stopped herself. "Well . . . damn. That's going to make it hard to talk about *anything* we don't want to give away."

And I'd really *like to know what it was she just thought of, because whenever she gives* that *expression you know it's going to be a doozy.*

"I can understand your reluctance," said a high, clear voice, "but I assure you that I have no intention of intruding upon any privacy you may require."

Standing in a wide doorway that had not been in that wall a moment ago was a tall, slender figure in robes of pearl-gray, edged with green and gold threads. Its stance and outline indicated a bipedal form, highly attenuated and graceful. The robes had long sleeves which currently fell in a way as to conceal the limbs within, and the hood of the robe allowed only a hint of features to be seen within. It was not quite the utter shadowed void that Amas-Garao seemed to favor; the faint outlines of what seemed a face could be made out.

Ariane rose to her feet as the figure approached; now she bowed;

DuQuesne and, he saw, Wu followed suit, with Orphan performing his pushup-bow. "Vindatri, I presume," Ariane said.

"I am," the figure answered.

"Is this your *real* shape?" Wu Kung asked.

A rippling laugh echoed around the room. "It is a shape that is mine, and not copied from any of you, and a form that should be one you can accept. In that sense, it is real."

"But it's not the shape you were *born* with," Wu persisted.

"No," conceded Vindatri, "but is the form so important? I have worn more than could be easily counted in the ages that have passed since that time. To me, the effort to craft an appropriate shape is less than the effort one of you might put into choosing a set of clothing."

He (DuQuesne decided to stick with that pronoun, as it was the one Orphan had used) gave an extravagant bow and flourish of the arms. "Welcome to *Halintratha*," Vindatri said, and the name or word momentarily had that eerie many-in-one resonance. DuQuesne caught hints of *bastion* or *castle*, of *vault* or *safe*, of *mystery* and *knowledge*, of *quester* or *researcher*, of the Arena itself, and other words as well. *A stronghold of knowledge? Bastion of Mysteries? Not a library, though.*

"Welcome to Halintratha," Vindatri said, "you who have journeyed far through the Deeps to find me. Orphan I know, and have given my first greetings to each of you as well. Now it is time for us to speak together, and understand the ways in which fate and the Arena have brought you hence."

"Wasn't 'fate,' it was Orphan," Wu pointed out. "He's got some sneaky reason for it, too, besides the one he's already told us."

Orphan gave the open-shut shrugging gesture. "And I have admitted that I was not allowed to speak of the second reason, as you know, Wu Kung."

"That is, however, past," Vindatri said. "I give you leave to speak as you wish, Orphan. And if you describe fully, I will be learning as well, so do not be overly coy with your words."

Orphan bob-bowed to Vindatri, but his posture shifted, and his tone was dry and humorous. "Be not overly coy? You remove much of the joy of speaking, o Vindatri."

The half-seen features within seemed to crease in a smile. *Which would be really strange; how many animals on* Earth *do things that are really like smiles? An* alien *doing that? I'd like to see what's really under that cowl.*

But Orphan had now turned to them. "As you know, the first condition was a simple one: bring news of First Emergents, and of course if I could bring one or more such *with* me, that would be a far better form of news.

"However, I had *terribly* specific instructions that I *must* bring members of any First Emergent species with me if they were to demonstrate a particular characteristic."

As usual, Orphan chose to pause at this intellectual cliffhanger. Wu obliged Orphan's need for dramatics. "Well, don't *stop* there, what *was* it?"

"It was something which was both incredibly *broad* in its definition, yet something which, Vindatri assured me, I would *know* if ever I saw it. Specifically, that the First Emergents in question would have 'the blessing of the Arena upon them.'"

DuQuesne thought the phrase was familiar, but it was Ariane who stiffened and stared at Orphan. "That . . . that's part of the *Canajara* prophecy."

"Ah, you know of the prophecy of the Faith?" Vindatri said with an air of faint surprise. "Or I should say *prophecies*, as the *Canajara* is a complex and often contradictory myth cycle for that Faction, with at least four significantly different tellings of the tale—each with of course almost numberless variations. But forgive me, Orphan, continue."

"Of course. I observed your people *very* closely, as you know. You became my allies—rather tolerant allies, I must admit, as I gave you ample reason to suspect me, or even to sever any alliance with you. And the result of those observations was to conclude that indeed you fit this description."

"This has to do with that . . . secret you've been keeping," Ariane said with certainty. "And for some reason you thought it was going south during the Genasi Challenge, and suddenly you were absolutely certain, like you'd been vindicated."

"And when you were all mysterious during the battle against the Blessed," DuQuesne said, starting to see the pattern. "When you said . . . oh, what was it . . . 'Let us just say I believe I have confirmed a hypothesis, and that this is *most* in your favor.'"

Orphan's buzz-laugh was delighted. "Quite on-target, both of you—and a fine memory you have, Dr. DuQuesne!"

DuQuesne grinned back. "Well, I can't take all the credit; that was a weird enough comment that I actually filed the quote in my headware. So out with it. What's this 'Blessing of the Arena?'"

"Surely you can guess, Dr. DuQuesne," Orphan said slowly. "And you, Captain Austin. Perhaps not Sun Wu Kung; he has not been privy to all the relevant events. But let us review the points that impressed themselves upon me, some at the time they happened, others upon deep reflection.

"First, your encounter with me. You happened upon me just as I was cornered by the Blessed, and managed—with the assistance of a rather unexpected visitor—to cause them to depart. Then, having just entered the Arena with my guidance, within *days* you discover that your Upper Sphere has been invaded . . . and repel the invasion with but two of your limited number." His black eyes measured DuQuesne. "Correct me if I am wrong, Doctor, but it would be my contention that it was, specifically, *your* presence that made that possible—and to be even more specific, that your victory had something to do with the secret you share with Maria-Susanna, Wu Kung, and Oasis Abrams."

DuQuesne glanced at Ariane, who nodded. "All right, I'll give you that one. Carl wasn't in any way useless, and he was crucial for some of it . . . but yeah, given the way that all went down, no one else in the crew could've pulled it off without me, and you've got the connection right."

"Excellent. And would I also be correct in assuming that your victory over the Molothos was one involving some . . . oh, desperate improvisation, perhaps?"

"That'd fit, yeah." *Rigging together controls for an alien ship we'd never seen a few hours before and turning it into a kamikaze to take out a full-sized warship? Desperate enough.*

A satisfied hand-tap from Orphan. "So, moving on, there was the *startling* performance of Dr. Franceschetti at the casino, leading to your Challenge by the Blessed to Serve. Your victory over Sethrik in that race was also *highly* instructive.

"And then you attained victory over Amas-Garao of the Shadeweavers—not once, but *twice*, the second time in direct Challenge of personal combat."

Now the tall figure of Vindatri went rigid. "Is this truth that you speak?"

"Oh, it was a *magnificent*—and at times heart-rending—battle, Vindatri. Captain Ariane Austin, a First Emergent but a few scant weeks in the Arena, facing Amas-Garao, one of the oldest of the Shadeweavers, and—ultimately—defeating him with a maneuver that shocked both Shadeweaver and Faith—and required them both to act to preserve their own lives as well as those of most in the stands who had been watching."

Vindatri turned slowly towards Ariane. "You . . . you *Awakened yourself?*"

Ariane's white grin was a deadly, beautiful blade. "I did."

"That is impossible."

"Ahh, Vindatri, I have heard—and spoken!—that word in association with Humanity so many times, it has become a comforting refrain to me," Orphan said wryly. "I am sure you, too, will become *very* familiar with it. Perhaps you already are.

"But we have hardly finished yet, my friends. As you mentioned, Dr. DuQuesne, there was our chase and confrontation with a fleet of the Blessed to Serve. There was the utterly *inexplicable* ability of Dr. Sandrisson to repair—and then *improve*—my own vessel, and your similar ability to make use of my own ship's controls with a skill that seemed barely short of the supernatural.

"And there were other events, several of them . . . but then we reached the Genasi Challenge, and it seemed that perhaps I was wrong, as I saw what was happening. But then I formed a modified hypothesis, and indeed, the Grand Finale of that little race turned out *precisely* as I had guessed."

Turning all the events over in his head, DuQuesne thought he saw what Orphan was driving at . . . and it *was* both impossible and terrifying. "You think . . . you think we're, well . . ."

". . . lucky," Ariane finished. "Naturally—or if you're right about the 'Blessing' business, *un*naturally—lucky at almost anything."

"Precisely," Orphan said. "Random factors *align* for you. The right people are at the right place at the right time. The accidental offense, or the deliberate, turns out to be precisely what you needed. Your own cavalier attitude towards risk itself was another hint—one borne out by several of the entertainment modules your people shared with me. It seems to be a common trait of your heroes to say something to the effect of 'never tell me the odds.' Partly, of course, that is because you have never integrated the same probability-evaluation technology that most of the Arena natives take for granted . . . but it seemed to me that you truly had less *respect* for the threat of random chance."

He looked around slowly, and DuQuesne could tell Orphan was enjoying the reactions he was getting. "Yet if you were truly *anomalously* lucky, surely your people would have noticed it back home; you are not incapable in the areas of statistics, after all. But then, as I watched that final Challenge, I thought that there was one possible explanation, and that Challenge, I felt, confirmed it. Not proof, perhaps, but good enough."

Klono's tungsten . . . "Maria-Susanna."

"*Very* good, Dr. DuQuesne. If you were *all* lucky, the luck would *cancel out* when it was, in short, human versus human, or in this case, human faction versus a faction with one rather unusual human in it. You had your . . . trump card, yes? Yes. Your trump card in the form of Sun Wu Kung, but for once your preternatural luck could give you no headway in the card game, because Maria-Susanna had joined the Vengeance . . . and brought her own luck with her, even though she was not directly playing."

"But that's . . . *how*?" demanded Ariane.

"That's the sixty-four *thousand*-dollar question, isn't it," DuQuesne said slowly. "Though with the Arena involved I guess it's *not* all that hard to explain. As long as you don't need to explain *why*."

"And *that*," Vindatri said, "is of course the question of interest. Why? Why would the Arena favor you? For I do not accept any possibility that this is some kind of natural ability; 'luck' is a spurious concept in normal conversation, a perception that because random factors have aligned well several times that this represents some sort of special phenomenon. But with the Arena's powers? It would be quite possible to influence events exactly in the manner necessary to provide such luck.

"But how this would serve the Arena's interests? That, now, that is a difficult question indeed."

"Does it *have* to serve the Arena's interests?" Ariane countered. "I haven't even been convinced that the Arena *has* 'interests,' in the sense of things it wants to accomplish, rather than rules it has to follow because it's built that way."

Vindatri fluttered his hands in a way that somehow symbolized argument. "The very *existence* of those rules implies some form of purpose. The Factions have debated the *nature* of that purpose, of course, and it is certainly true that it may not be the Arena, proper, that has the purpose . . . but whether it be the Arena or the Voidbuilders of myth, I think we must agree that there *is* a purpose, and thus some number of interests, involved in the operation of the Arena."

"So what's *your* interest?" Wu Kung asked bluntly. "You gave Orphan directions on who to bring back, your own words tell me that you must have some purpose, yes?"

"Yes," agreed Vindatri. "But I will not tell you that purpose. Doing so would fail to serve said purpose."

"Would your purpose mean that you can't help us—specifically, help me?" Ariane asked.

Another hint of a smile. "I can say that no, it would not impede me from providing you with some level of assistance in unraveling the mysteries of these powers. And for my own part, teaching you would perhaps reveal to me something about the powers I have not yet learned; as my own surprise doubtless revealed, I have never heard of a self-Awakening happening, and certainly never in combat."

DuQuesne could see Ariane's expression lighten. "Really?"

"Indeed and in truth. I will be happy to help you unbind the seals the Shadeweaver and Faith placed upon you, and then show you the way in which those powers may be used."

"And what do you want for this help?" DuQuesne asked. "I don't think you just give stuff like that away for free."

"Free?" Vindatri's gaze was coldly speculative, despite the shadowed smile that reappeared beneath the hood. "Oh, certainly not. Yet to some it may appear so. I will consider the price before we begin. To an extent, learning precisely what your Captain *is* would be payment; never before have I heard of a self-Awakening. It is of course assumed among the Shadeweavers that there had to *once* be such, to begin the order, and similarly the Faith presumes there were those touched by the Creators directly to begin the Faith, but in all the records of both there are no mentions of such actually happening."

Yeah, that would *be valuable.* "But that wouldn't pay the whole freight, I'm guessing."

"In all likelihood, no. As I have said, I must consider." Vindatri gestured, and a sparkling white light appeared in the air before them. "Follow, and you will be led to quarters suited for you."

"We *could* just sleep on board *Zounin-Ginjou*," Ariane said.

Orphan made a swift gesture of negation, even as the figure whirled about, tense and menacing. "My apologies, Vindatri! She means it in a kindly way, to not put you to additional effort on her behalf when we already have comfortable spaces aboard my vessel." The undertones of Orphan's voice showed he was very nervous, even afraid. *And the way Vindatri's standing, he's probably got a reason to be afraid.*

Slowly, Vindatri straightened from what had been almost a predatory crouch; his head tilted as his gaze fell on Sun Wu Kung, who had instantly placed himself between Ariane and Vindatri.

By now Ariane had grasped the situation. "Many apologies, Vindatri. I did indeed mean no offense to you in any way."

Vindatri gave a broad, fluttering gesture. "Then I apologize for my anger, which must have been apparent. It is . . . very rude for a host to not provide accommodations for his guests, and similarly exceedingly rude to refuse such accommodations when offered. But I see you did not understand, and thus I thank you for the thought of courtesy, but beg you accept my own."

Ariane glanced at him. Reluctantly, he nodded. *Last thing we need to do is piss this guy off.*

"We would be honored," Ariane said, and Orphan relaxed as they began to follow the light.

DuQuesne was not relaxing, even as Vindatri disappeared through another doorway. *One crisis averted. But this guy's ancient, powerful, and used to doing things* his *way. Working with him's going to be like walking through a minefield.*

And if you keep walking through minefields, sooner or later something's gonna blow up in your face.

Chapter 28

"*Fictional* powers can be made *real*," Laila Canning repeated slowly. Her sharp brown eyes studied Oasis as though the red-headed woman was a specimen on her dissection table. "How certain are you of this?"

"Between ninety-five and a hundred percent sure," Oasis said. "I mean, Wu Kung already demonstrated he's going *totally* beyond the normal limits of the Arena and he can do that talk-to-animals thing that *no one* does, as far as we know."

"That's . . . that's a total game-changer right there," Carl said after a pause. "I mean . . . the Arena giving Hyperions their . . . how do I say it? Natural superpowers?"

"It's perfectly in line with the Arena's normal behavior," Simon said. "Although, based on other events, I *have* to assume that the Arena has a range of discretion it can use in *interpreting* its directives and actions. The real question isn't so much how it *can* justify this . . . but *why* it has chosen to do so."

Laila nodded. "That *is* indeed the question. As Carl says, this potentially changes *everything*—in general, favorably for us, although your possible sighting could be very much *not* in anyone's favor, Oasis."

"Fairchild? He'd be a total *disaster* for everyone. Especially with DuQuesne and Wu off for who knows how long."

She still sounds worried. "Oasis, why DuQuesne specifically? I mean, we still have you, and Velocity, and I presume there must be a few others left."

The woman's long, slender fingers caught at the ponytail dangling near them and began twining the red strands around them, a nervous motion at odds with the cheerfully unflappable Oasis he was used to. "There probably *are* some more—I think DuQuesne said there might be fifteen, sixteen of us still around, so with me, DuQuesne, Wu, Maria-Susanna, and Vel, that's ten or eleven still back in the System. But I didn't know who they were. I didn't *want* to know, remember? I was hiding out as Oasis Abrams, not really ever planning to be 'K' again. I think DuQuesne was the only one with a good idea of who the other survivors were and where or how to contact them."

She took a breath, glanced at her hand, and with a visible effort made it release her hair and drop to her side. "DuQuesne is Fairchild's opposite number. Fairchild . . . wasn't exactly *human*, I guess is the best way to put it, and both he and DuQuesne had a *lot* of powers that go way, way beyond normal human capabilities. Way out of my league, or Vel's. Plus being his *designed* opposite, in a world that assumed the good guys win and bad guys lose? That *has* to give DuQuesne a major edge over Fairchild."

"Very interesting," Laila said. "Eminently logical, if I accept the basic premises. The Arena is accepting their universes as real for the purposes of what powers it gives them; if the universe itself had a clear . . . definition of right and wrong and of victory conditions, you believe that at least some of that would also transfer to the Arena."

"Yes. Or it's at least a real good bet."

"You know, we should be able to get an answer as to whether this Fairchild guy is here or not," Carl said.

"Really? Aside from Oasis, none of us here would even *recognize* the gentleman," Simon said.

"Probably not, but you've got that super-cheat-code in your head, right? Couldn't you just *look* for him that way?"

Simon blinked, then chuckled. "I probably could, at that."

"*Will* you?" Laila asked. "I understand very well your reluctance to abuse that ability, but I think time may be of the essence in at least knowing if we *do* have a Hyperion-born enemy out there." For a moment, he saw unconcealed worry on the former biologist's face. "Honestly, Simon, the idea of someone who is *DuQuesne's* equal out there as an enemy? That *terrifies* me."

"You and me both, as DuQuesne might say," Simon agreed. "Very well, Laila. I will make the attempt; at the least this capability of mine should be used to serve the needs of our Faction Leaders—permanent or temporary."

Once more he drew on that transcendent feeling, the ultimate *clarity* that lay beyond mere mortality. *Dr. Alexander Fairchild*, he thought. *Is he here? If he is,* where?

Almost instantly he felt that sudden wrenching turn of virtual viewpoint, the sensation that presaged his ascension to a pure and detailed vision of his target.

But just as suddenly it *stopped*. He had the vaguest sense of the target and its location—somewhere in Nexus Arena!—and then . . . nothing. An impenetrable gray fog enveloped most of the gigantic construct.

He sat back with such startled force that he nearly tipped the chair over.

"What is it, Simon?" Oasis asked, steadying him with one hand on his shoulder.

"It was . . . the most *disorienting* thing I have ever experienced," he said after a moment. "I had the feeling I was about to see, or at least locate, this Dr. Fairchild . . . and then . . . nothing. I had a sense that he was indeed here, somewhere in Nexus Arena . . . but after that, it was as though the truth were cloaked, hidden in shadows I could not penetrate." He gave a wry smile, trying to hide how startled and, truth be told, upset he felt. "After never encountering a limit with this power, I must say I was unprepared to find one."

Oasis could not hide the fact that she had gone pale. "But you *did* sense him."

He frowned. "I *think* so. But I admit I have never tried to look for an individual before. Perhaps that is not allowed except in a very broad sense."

"Simple to find out," Carl said. "Try locating someone you *know* is around."

"Very well. Let me see . . ."

He rose to the Olympian heights and thought, *Dr. Relgof.*

Without a pause, he felt that *turn*, and his vision sped away from Humanity's Embassy and across Nexus Arena. He found himself looking down on Relgof Nov'Ne Knarph as he engaged in some form of discussion with a number of other members of the Analytic, inside the huge Great Faction House.

That worked. It's terrifying, also, but it worked. He thought for a moment. *Perhaps it doesn't work on Hyperions?*

Easy enough to test. He thought about Oasis, and his perception swiveled and spun, to come to rest above, well, *himself*, looking down upon the red-headed Hyperion. *So much for that theory.*

Perhaps it has to do with that . . . universe of origin? In which case I should be able to find Ariane but not DuQuesne.

But both attempts rebuffed him; he streaked off through vast spaces of the Arena, to a location that would be distant indeed . . . but long before he even got a clear sense of where that *was* within the titanic confines of the Arena, everything dissolved in grayness. *Odd. Decidedly odd.*

The transcendent feeling still remained with him, and a few quick tests showed that he could still hold details beyond human comprehension in his mind. The power did not seem weakened. *But there are particular beings, or locations, that refuse to be . . . remote-viewed, scryed, whatever I might call it.* He tested a few other choices, finding it easy to locate and view Oscar Naraj, Sethrik, and even Mairakag Achan, serving various customers in his restaurant.

But when he tried to look in on Nyanthus, he was once more completely stymied by gray indeterminism. *Then, perhaps, it has to do with particular capabilities. If so, perhaps I could not locate Ariane because she has such powers locked within her.*

Maria-Susanna was also grayed-out. *Now* that *worries me. I did not get the impression she had inhuman abilities* per se. *Why can I not locate her?*

He opened his eyes, letting that sense recede. "I can locate *some* people but not others. I am not yet entirely sure of the rules that determine which I can, well, spy upon and which I cannot. It is not, however, based on whether they are inside a Faction House, or a member of any given Faction, or limited by species. My best guess at the moment is that it reflects people who have some type of Arena-granted special capabilities, but even that is not universal." He looked at Oasis. "I could view you easily enough, even though I know you must have at least *some* special talents or powers from your Hyperion background."

Laila frowned and smoothed back her pageboy-cut chestnut hair. "Nonetheless, we have confirmed the *existence* of Dr. Fairchild. Correct, Simon?"

"I . . . am afraid so. The sensations were the same as the ones I felt for other people I know exist but who were hidden for some reason."

"Damn," Carl said. "That's bad. Do you think we could sort him out of the people who've come through our Sphere?"

Oasis bit her lip, thinking. "I really don't know. He'd want to leave no trail. If we knew *exactly* what he looked like now, maybe. But while I'm pretty sure whatever body he cloned for himself will look *like* his sim image, I'm also *very* sure it won't be identical. He's not stupid. He's a *genius* and he's really, really good at thinking things out a hundred steps ahead."

Someone with DuQuesne's brain and the moral compass of a classic villain—a smart villain—in one of the grandest-scale tales ever written. Very much not *what I would have wanted to hear.* With an effort, he made himself smile. "This *is* bad news, but it's not nearly as bad as it could be. We have at least two advantages over him, after all."

Oasis looked up with surprise, and even one of Laila's eyebrows curved up like a seagull's wing. "Really? What are those?"

"Well, first, he doesn't know we know he is here. If he insists on wearing that outfit you described—a white classic suit—we can make sure many people keep an eye out for him and report; we'll locate him fast enough.

"But more importantly, *we* know that you Hyperions can use your special abilities . . . but he won't. He's undoubtedly read the reports sent back and could tell that none of you were doing anything beyond what your special engineering would allow. He *may* figure it out eventually, but for now, it's a clear advantage."

He was glad to see Oasis' face smooth out a bit. "You're right, Simon. And he's also without a Faction—or else he's stuck under the rules of Humanity's Faction. It will take even *Fairchild* a while to figure out the Arena and how to exploit it."

"And in the meantime we will do our best to locate him and, hopefully, contain him," Laila said. "Carl, if I understand our delegated powers, we have essentially *absolute* authority in the Arena, correct?"

"Basically, yes. As long as we follow the Arena's rules, which are pretty loose when it comes to internal Faction business."

"Good. Then we will do our best to locate him—and capture him when opportunity presents itself. Put him back in regular space and put him on trial for murder—as I believe we can all agree he is the primary suspect for the deaths of the other Hyperions?"

Simon saw Oasis nod, and added his own. "And, quite likely, the one who was guiding General Esterhauer—and tried to wipe her when things weren't following his script. Yes, I think that you not only can use your delegated Leader of Faction powers to capture him, but also have more than enough justification to keep him back home."

"I don't think you can keep him imprisoned forever," Oasis said. "Or even for very long."

"I would think we can keep him busy enough until DuQuesne gets back, at which point, if you're right, we will have the antidote to his poison, so to speak."

Oasis suddenly grinned. "I think you're right!"

"Good," Laila said decisively. "The news was not what we hoped, but we have a plan of action—a *practical* plan of action, I think. Oasis, I know you don't have standard headware, but please generate some images of this Fairchild for us so that we can transmit them to all our people who might be in a position to find him."

"Will do!"

Simon nodded, but somewhat absently. He was still trying to figure out the *rules* of this strange gray blankness. A quick test showed that he could locate the other known Hyperion—Velocity Celes—as he practiced piloting one of the Arenaspace vessels near Humanity's Sphere. Carl Edlund, ditto, just as easy as anyone else.

But there was one other individual about which there were some questions . . .

Even as Simon felt his eyebrow rising in surprise, he realized Laila was speaking to him. "I beg your pardon?"

"I said, I just realized there is one other question you might be able to answer for me. Well, more precisely, for our negotiator Oscar Naraj, although I admit it is important to me as well."

"I'm always willing to help. What is the question?"

"It is more a fact that *poses* a question. You understand that Mr. Naraj is an extremely observant man, and especially so in his specialty of negotiation and diplomacy."

"I would expect so, yes."

"Well, he has of course kept a close eye on the doings of our enemies as well as our allies, and just the other day he asked me if I knew of any particular events that might have affected the Molothos. When I said I did not and asked why, he said that he was fairly certain that neither he, nor anyone else, had seen or heard from their Leader, Dajzail, in quite some time."

"Hmm. Well, I can certainly *try* to answer the question as to where he is." He closed his eyes once more.

He rose above and through the Embassy, and thought the question, *Where is Dajzail, Leader of the Molothos?*

A wrenching turn and a rush of speed, flying through the varicolored clouds and spinning Spheres and innumerable living things of the Arena, until he found himself seemingly floating in air within a compartment that to his eyes was *too* brilliantly lit, and filled with Molothos attending to various duties. In the center sat Dajzail, squatting on some sort of support structure that Simon presumed was a chair. The Leader of the Molothos was examining something on a screen projected before him.

He's on board a ship, *it would seem. But what ship, and where?*

With barely an effort of thought, Simon rose up, through the hull of the vessel, and floated beyond, looking around, trying to sense the *position* of the ship below him.

Wait. There was more than one ship. Simon concentrated, expanded his vision. Two ships. Three. A dozen. Two dozen . . . no. There were hundreds . . . no, *thousands* of ships in this fleet!

And he suddenly knew where they were.

His eyes snapped open and he realized he had already stood. "Laila . . . I believe we have a far bigger problem than a mere renegade Hyperion."

Chapter 29

"So we have an agreement?"

Ariane looked at DuQuesne, who gave a quick nod; she turned back to Vindatri. "We do. You will consider the explanation for my personal Ascension to be payment for training, if it truly conveys to you new information. If not, we will give you some additional in-depth information about Humanity as a faction which goes beyond that available to other members of the Arena." She grinned. "Exactly *what* that information will be we will negotiate later, but we're not writing you a completely blank check on that."

"It is done, then." The slender, still-cloaked form of Vindatri bowed low to them. "Then I would have this explanation, if you would."

Ariane started to answer, then stopped, directed her gaze across the room. "I'm sorry, Orphan, but—"

"No need to apologize, Captain. Your agreement did not extend to giving *me* this information." He rose from his seating perch. "Dr. DuQuesne, I presume you already have this information?"

"Yeah, I do. In detail."

"Then would you care to join me? I have as yet seen only small portions of Halintratha, though more than yourself, and perhaps we could explore for a while—Vindatri allowing, of course."

Vindatri inclined his head—face still strangely shadowed. "You will know when you approach any areas off-limits to you."

"Sure, I'll come with you," DuQuesne said. "Wu'll keep an eye on things here."

Wu Kung grinned from his seat, where he was juggling small fruits

241

somewhat like grapes, letting them drop into his mouth periodically and then replacing them from the bowl nearby. So far he'd gone through half a bowl that way, and was currently keeping ten constantly airborne in a fountain that reached seven meters in height. "Count on me, DuQuesne!"

"All right, Marc, Orphan, I'll see you later."

She got up and looked out the window—or, possibly, viewscreen—that covered one entire wall of the room Vindatri had chosen for their meeting. *The room's . . . over the top. Like a lot of what I've seen so far.* A room didn't need a ceiling almost ten meters high, at least not when your occupants were human beings. The lighting wasn't gloomy—not compared to what she'd almost expected when she'd first seen the dark, eerie bulk of Halintratha floating in the Deeps—but the strangely-curved geometry of the room was unsettling.

But you can't beat a view like this.

Ebony arcs of shadow coiled in frozen motion across a backdrop of dim-lit clouds of crimson, rose, and tangerine, shading as she lifted her head to sunshine-yellow and thence to white tinged with amethyst. In that direction, where the light seemed brightest, she could *just* make out a spectral, looming outline of a circle, a Sphere large enough to enclose the Earth with space to spare. *So why isn't he on that Sphere, rather than just floating around in the sky like this?*

"So, to business," she said, flicking her glance to Vindatri, who had come to stand at the window also, though not too close. "First, I should probably show you that Challenge. It'll be easier to understand if you know what happened."

"I would be very pleased to view it. A *Shadeweaver* defeated by one not of their own, or of the Faith, their opposing force? It has never been done, not in a Challenge of arms at any rate."

"Believe me, I'm not surprised." The handheld projector created a sphere of light which faded to reveal the great colosseum in Nexus Arena, and herself and Amas-Garao facing each other as the crowd roared.

Ariane found herself tensing as the replay of that brutal combat continued. The images and sounds brought with them a wincingly-clear memory of the jolt of electricity, the savage strength of her opponent, the humiliating brutality of the repeated and unstoppable hammering against the limits of the ring.

But she also felt a sharp grin on her face when she delivered an unexpected and devastating blow to Amas-Garao, when he learned to his sorrow what an electric eel biomod felt like . . . and felt again a chill of awe and disbelief as she unlocked the power of the Arena within herself and forced the Shadeweaver to surrender or be destroyed by the energies that she herself could not even attempt to control.

Vindatri was silent for a moment. "A . . . unique performance, Captain Ariane Austin," he said finally. "And I will confess that I, like your opponent Amas-Garao, cannot comprehend how that took place. I can recognize that you invoked a certain . . . ritual, beginning 'Recard iseatin dukwes . . . ,' and that in itself is surprising as I would not expect one not a member of either group to know it."

Got it. Now I know something new about him, *and I don't think he realizes it!*

Vindatri continued, "But the words by themselves are useless; you do not, I think, even know what they *mean*. So resolve this conundrum, and I will count myself paid, even if the explanation, in hindsight, seems obvious as the dawn."

"Do *you* know what those words mean?"

"In a sense, yes. But the explanation?"

She grinned. "When First Emergents appear, both the Shadeweavers and the Faith respond; the Shadeweavers attempt to draft at least one of the new Emergents, and Awaken some others of their ranks, presumably to provide the Shadeweavers with sufficient resources to keep an eye on the new arrivals. The Faith create an Initiate Guide whose job is to be an advocate for the new arrivals, and similarly expand their membership to account for the newcomers."

She studied the waiting Vindatri, then went on. "Well, we don't like to believe in the real supernatural, so we figured that meant that the Arena makes some set of slots open whenever a new species appears. And since we like simpler explanations when possible, we figured that both Shadeweavers and the Faith get their special powers from the same source—the Arena—and thus those slots that opened up probably apply to both of them at once.

"The question was . . . what keeps anyone who knows that ritual from doing it themselves, as soon as they hear of First Emergents? If it's something totally mechanical, like accessing special privileges to Arena systems, then there had to be something like a password, a secure something, that kept distribution of those powers strictly under control."

"Indeed. And the answer?"

"It was really a guess, not really a deduction. I was half-knocked-out at the time, and my brain started doing this sort of free-association trick." Absently, she spun Wrath of God on her wrist with the memory of how disjointed images and sounds had played through her mind. "But I'd seen the *Faith* version of the ritual, and I remembered that it involved the blood of the Initiate Guides doing the ritual, then applied to the one to be Awakened. So the thought of *blood* went through my mind. And I also remembered that one of the names the Shadeweavers use for themselves is 'the Blood of the Skies.'"

"Yes," Vindatri said, slowly at first then gaining speed, "blood would indeed make sense. Something *carried* in the blood, you mean, something that in essence gave you the . . . right, clearance, what have you . . . to access the power." He then glanced at her. "But where would you have gotten the blood in the first place? You never managed to blood Amas-Garao."

"Not in *that* battle, no," she admitted. "But in a *prior* fight, he was hit *hard,* and some of his blood went all over me—some right into my mouth."

Vindatri burst out into an echoing laugh that resonated throughout the huge room. "Elegant and well-reasoned. You had the blood, you knew they intended to Initiate you, so one of these 'slots' was still available, and you had learned the Awakening chant to be spoken by the new Initiate, and you had absolutely nothing to lose by trying. And yes, this reveals details and understanding I had not previously guessed. Well done, and your price is paid."

"Great!" Despite that excited exclamation, Ariane felt suddenly terribly nervous. *And now I have another responsibility to take up.*

A low chuckle that also vibrated the floor beneath her. "Ah. I sense your lightness of word cloaks a seriousness beneath. Excellent. The powers we wield are not to be taken lightly."

Her heart was pounding faster. *Wonderful, Ariane. Now that you're about to get what you came for, you're getting scared of the whole thing.* "Can I ask you something?"

"I have no doubt you will ask *many* things in the coming days. What do you wish to know?"

"What do *you* think about this whole thing? Are we right? It sure *seems* to be working like a machine was running it, and the similarities tell me that the Faith and Shadeweavers probably *are* basically the same."

"It is . . . possible," Vindatri said. "Yet there is little evidence. The words call for certain things to *happen*, they indicate certain directives and limitations, but that does not mean that these words are heard or responded to by the same source of power. Surely your people have worshipped gods of one sort or another in the past, and surely similar words may have been used to invoke many of them for various purposes."

"Yeah, but none of them were real. Or if they were, we never found actual *evidence* for them."

"While the Arena is undoubtedly real. Yes." Vindatri gestured and she found herself stepping back farther into the room; he circled around, half-hidden eyes surveying her carefully. "But the fact remains that none of the thousands of factions, over millions of years, have managed to replicate even the simplest of the Arena's unique tricks. Is this merely, as the Vengeance would have it, because the Arena wishes to maintain a monopoly on this technology? Or is it because, as the Faith believe, there is something greater than simple technology at work?"

Vindatri spread his arms and closed them, conveying the impression of a shrug. "I am old, far older even than your friend Orphan—who is, by the standards of most in the Arena, ancient indeed—and even I cannot answer that question. I prefer to neither believe nor disbelieve in the powers as technology or something more . . . numinous, shall we say, but merely to explore what I and others can *do* with them."

He stopped and looked down. "The seal upon you is startlingly strong and complex. How was it done?"

She hesitated. *Information is power.* "Well . . . it was both the Faith and the Shadeweavers who put it on me." *No need to give details, I think. But a bit more background, maybe.* "Honestly? I wasn't going to commit to either one, since I was Faction Leader, so both of them felt they had to lock me down."

"Ah. So you have had no experience, following your sealing, of the power." Then he paused. "No, you can perform that one *remarkable* trick. I cannot understand how this is *possible.*" He was silent again, staring at her. "Ah. There is, in fact, a . . . crack, shall we say, in the seal." He hesitated, then went on, in a tone that was so low it was clearly murmured to himself, ". . . a crack clearly made from *within*, not a flaw in the binding, which appears nigh-perfect . . ."

He straightened. "In any event, this *does* provide me with an avenue to perform the release, which we must do before any effective instruction can be done. Are you prepared?"

"Me?" She clenched her fists nervously. She looked at Wu. "I hate to say this, Wu, but you'd better get out of the room, if he's going to unseal me here."

Wu saw her expression and did not even argue; he just looked at Vindatri narrowly, then walked quickly to the exit.

Once Wu was out, she turned to Vindatri and gave him one of her best challenging smiles. "*I'm* prepared, Vindatri . . . the question is whether *you* are."

"I have seen more than one Awakening, Ariane Austin," he said, with a faintly-visible smile of his own. "I believe I am prepared enough." A shield shimmered around him as he stepped back from her. "Do not move."

Sigils bloomed across the floor in starlight blue and sunlight white, diagrams of magic or circuitry sketched in frosted crystal across the dark metal floor, growing to a circle of complexity she could not grasp as it completely surrounded her. Vindatri was muttering more incomprehensible phrases as he did so: "*Manigtur enzing tralenzor ul . . .*"

The symbology abruptly spiraled up from the floor, enclosing her in a moving column of runes and letters and sigils composed of pure rainbow luminance. ". . . *merma pezimfel nonash . . .*"

A pressure, an expansion, so painful and yet so wonderful that she screamed—

And the universe screamed with her.

Chapter 30

"Where are we going?" DuQuesne asked. Orphan had been moving ahead of him, leading the way with assured speed that told DuQuesne that the Leader of the Liberated knew where he was going.

"A particular area of Halintratha which I have visited, and I believe you will find of great interest," Orphan said, opening a door and beginning to climb down the ladder thus revealed.

"In what way?"

"You shall see."

DuQuesne reached the bottom and started after Orphan. The lighting here was dim, emanating from strips high on the curved ceilings, and something about the material of the tunnels deadened sound; it was uncomfortably quiet. At a four-way intersection, Orphan halted so suddenly that he nearly bumped the tall alien; Orphan's right arm, extended back in an obvious cautionary gesture, touched DuQuesne's arm for an instant.

In the distance DuQuesne heard a faint movement, but for a few seconds he couldn't focus on it; he was too surprised by another fact:

Orphan had placed *something* on him in that momentary brush; something on his forearm. DuQuesne didn't dare look; if he guessed right about what was going on, giving away that he'd noticed *anything* could be bad news. *At least my mind's shielded. Not that Vindatri's tried anything since that one brush.*

The movement, a faint whispering, rushing noise, was fading, becoming more distant. He waited until he saw Orphan relax, then folded his arms. "Well? What was that?"

"I confess, I am not certain, Dr. DuQuesne. But when I do not recognize something, I prefer to avoid it until I have an opportunity to study it at a comfortable distance. Even here, I should note; Halintratha is safe for *Vindatri*, but I cannot say that this is true for visitors."

His fingers had found the object under cover of folding his arms. It was small, flat, with a feel of metal and plastic; with practiced skill at sleight-of-hand, he conveyed it to a safer location within his clothing. *Check it out later.* "You're saying this exploration jaunt isn't safe?"

"I am saying it *may* not be." A scissoring wing motion. "In honesty, I believe that Vindatri does not, perhaps, fully comprehend the limitations of those of us less ancient and powerful."

"I got you." That wasn't a huge surprise; a lot of people tended to assume that other people were pretty much like them, so extend that attitude for a few thousand years and add in overwhelming power and you'd easily have someone like Vindatri, or even worse. "How far is this place we're going?"

"Not much farther. I hope to reach it and then begin our return before our host has completed his work with Captain Austin."

DuQuesne raised an eyebrow even as he felt himself smiling. "You're hoping Ariane's got him *distracted*."

"If anything could do so, I would expect it to be the Captain and her most *extraordinary* story, yes . . . and even more so her power, if he chooses to release the seals that the Faith and Shadeweavers placed upon her. And this area I have only seen once, with Vindatri, and he only gave me a short glimpse, a few moments to wander and be amazed. Nonetheless, I *have* been there once, so I am hoping that— especially with the master focused on something else—we will be able to enter on our own."

This must be one hell of a thing he wants to show me. Or maybe it's not quite that important, but it's good enough as a cover for him to give me . . . whatever the hell the thing is he gave me. The two emerged from the corridor into a huge, canyon-like space, strata of pipes and cables criss-crossing walls stretching upward to be lost in distant shadow. *Ceiling's at least a hundred meters up, I'd guess, since even using my best vision I can't catch a hint of it. This place's design makes no goddamn sense that I can see, and it's giving me the blue screaming willies, as Rich would've said. Feels like a horror-sim set.*

"Now, where was . . . ah!" Orphan gave a leap, assisted by his wings, and landed on a small platform that had been nearly invisible, ten meters above. The alien glanced down with a challenging tilt to his head.

DuQuesne measured the distance and angle, then took a running jump that cleared three meters vertically, bounced off the opposite wall six meters away and three meters higher, then ricocheted from that wall back, flipping in midair to land feet-first right next to Orphan. "How's that?"

"No less than I would have expected from you—but still, impressive, Dr. DuQuesne." DuQuesne could now see they were standing in front of a door. "We are very near, now," Orphan went on, touching the door; it slid away vertically. "Now—if we do gain access—I would like to first point out that you would have likely never found this location on your own, so if you do find what I show you of . . . significant interest—"

"—we'll owe you some information of equal interest. Or something else. Don't worry, Orphan, I know the drill and you'd love us to owe you something."

"As you prefer having *me* in *your* debt? Naturally, Doctor. Then let us proceed."

The corridor here was smooth and featureless, and had two more doors—thick, heavy doors—across it that also opened at Orphan's touch.

A final door, however, refused to budge. Orphan gazed at it for a long moment, then gave a wing-snap shrug. "Well, Doctor, it appears you will not owe me—"

The floor *shuddered* under them, and DuQuesne felt as though the entire *station*, all of Halintratha, was *tilting* beneath him. A thrumming vibration transmitted itself through the very walls and floor.

"Ah!" Orphan said, a note of hope in his voice. He touched the door again.

This time the door slid aside without hesitation, even as the lights flickered unnervingly. "It appears that our host has unlocked the seal, and I suspect is discovering that—as has so often been the case—your Captain is not nearly so easy to handle as he thought," Orphan said cheerfully. "Come, quickly!"

We're kilometers *from that room. But then, when Ariane first*

Awakened, it shook Nexus Arena *itself.* "All right, Orphan, but this won't do us much good if the whole station comes apart around . . ."

The light had grown brighter—despite occasional flickers—but that was not what made Marc C. DuQuesne trail off in mid-sentence.

Before him—arranged in row upon row, ranks ordered as precisely as a military formation, were alien figures. Hundreds, thousands, maybe *tens* of thousands, all standing, sitting, squatting in perfect poses.

Not ten meters away was a Blessed to Serve, wings tight and arms and legs bent in a combat pose DuQuesne remembered well from their first encounter. Near him was an irregular, rocky *something* that he thought must be one of the very rare silicon-based lifeforms Orphan had mentioned once or twice; farther in he saw a Wagamia, standing with arms spread wide, like Dr. Relgof in one of his transports of enthusiasm; a Chiroflekir with its blue-green translucence was visible nearby. Far to his left he thought he saw a Daelmokhan, massive torso rising high above its neighbors, but while he recognized a good number of these figures, by far the larger number were completely unknown.

Another shudder ran through the structure of Halintratha, and a sparkle of light rippled *through* solid walls and beams as though they were water, a ringing of crystalline bells following the luminance. *Ariane's putting on a hell of a show. I sure hope this show doesn't end with a* BANG, *so to speak.*

But since there wasn't anything he could do about that . . . "All right, Orphan, this is a hell of a museum, but what—"

"Hurry, Dr. DuQuesne!" Orphan was on the move, *sprinting* down the lines toward the far-distant side of the room.

He shrugged and then sprinted after the Leader of the Liberated, easily gaining distance on him. "What's the rush?"

"I do *not* wish to be in this room once his attention can be focused again. Admittedly, he *may* be monitoring this room in other ways, but I do not see any cameras or similar devices, nor do I detect any . . . and it seems counter to the way I know Vindatri does things. It is my hope, therefore, that he will not know we have entered here. Or, at least, that he will feel obligated to *pretend* he does not know."

That fits with my gut. I don't want to be caught anywhere that was locked before he got distracted—because the lock might go back on with me inside.

Even less did he want to get caught inside a room that looked like a futuristic waxworks. *Right now I'm feeling* way *too much like I'm in a space-operatic version of Bluebeard, and we've just unlocked the wrong door. Sure, these are* probably *models,* he thought as he passed a Rodeskri—one of Nyanthus' people—with tendrils spread and symbiotes frozen in mid-flight about it. *But maybe they're a lot closer to life than that.*

Deep-purple sparks writhed down the walls, then back up, vanishing into the ceiling with a smell of smoke and ozone. "That emergency seal in the Arena took what, about four, five minutes?"

"That would fit my recollection, yes. And yes, I am using that as my estimate for how long we dare take." Orphan slowed, as they were approaching the far side, the last ranks of the assembled multitude of silent figures. "There, Dr. DuQuesne."

Marc C. DuQuesne looked, and stumbled to an incredulous halt. At the far end of the assembly—where he somehow guessed this entire array had begun—were two figures.

One was the red-black jagged outline of a Molothos, fighting-claws raised, lamprey-grinder mouth open to scream or rend.

But the other, standing at the very beginning of the line—the first of all, DuQuesne thought—was utterly unlike the rest. Where the others were detailed as life itself, in poses so realistic that they seemed merely frozen in an instant of motion, this figure was . . . a sketch, a smoke-gray glassy silhouette in three dimensions, with only hints of features. It did not tower over the others; indeed, the nearby Molothos loomed above it and outmassed it by several times.

But still DuQuesne stopped, and stared. "Holy Mother of God . . ."

For stylized and bereft of details though it was, the figure that faced him was *human.*

Or human*oid,* he corrected himself. There weren't enough details for him to be certain it was human. But there were hints of eyes—two of them—and other contours that hinted strongly at a human face. There were two arms and two legs and no tail, and the arms had five-fingered hands with opposable thumbs; the feet, too, looked very human.

"You saw this before?"

"I caught a very brief *glimpse* of it on my prior visit," Orphan said. "I could tell there was *something* odd about that figure, but Vindatri called me back before I could go anywhere near enough to be sure what it was. But the *shape*—half-seen—stayed somewhere in my mind. After we first met, I had a vague sensation of having seen your species somewhere before. At first I dismissed it as being associated with the Wagamia or a few other similar species, but eventually I recalled this incident and wondered if I recalled correctly." He surveyed the enigmatic statue. "It seems I recalled even more truly than I had thought."

"To the proverbial ninety-seven decimals," DuQuesne muttered. "This means *something*, and it's *big*, sure as God made little green apples. Question is *what*." He completed a walkaround of the figure, then shook his head. "Whatever, we're not going to work it out here. We'd better head back."

"And quickly. The tremors continue, but I think they are diminishing."

They sped back down the array once more; DuQuesne thought Orphan was right, although there was one more powerful jolt that almost sent him careening into a huge, multi-tentacled octopoidal monstrosity with a single eye encircling its head. He recovered and ran on.

Orphan reached the door and dove through, then stepped aside to let DuQuesne pass and triggered the door's closure. "We have made it," the tall, green and black alien said, beginning a more leisurely walk. "I hope we have not been detected."

DuQuesne caught his arm and pushed him forward. "Don't relax yet. *Move.*"

Orphan did not hesitate, but immediately matched DuQuesne's urgent speed. "Might I inquire why?"

"First, we don't even want to be *near* that area when he starts checking, or he might go over the place with a fine-toothed comb; and with *his* powers, you can bet he'd find *something* if he was looking." DuQuesne dropped off the platform; the landing was a bit of a jolt, but no biggie. Orphan, of course, had his wings to cushion the drop. "Second, if we were on a casual exploration tour, instead of trying to get to some specific goal, what would he expect us to do when the whole *station* started doing the shimmy?"

"I take your meaning, yes. We would be expected to be heading back to see what was going on."

"Right. So let's make good time and play our parts."

And when I get a minute by myself, I'll find out what it was you really *wanted to get away with.*

Chapter 31

I do not like leaving her alone with this Vindatri. He hides his scent often, and when he doesn't he smells sneaky, like Orphan and Naraj.

But he knew *that* look from Ariane—the one that said it wasn't a suggestion, and that she was worried for *him* as much as for herself, and that there was no point in arguing. *Sanzo had that look too, sometimes.*

The door sealed behind him, and he leaned against the wall outside of the chamber. *Maybe they will be done soon. It will be* boring *to stand out here on guard for hours.*

Still, he would do it if he had to. Sanzo—and Sha Wujing and Liu Yan and Cho Hakkai and even DuQuesne and K and Maria-Susanna—had often laughed at him about how he couldn't stay still, but even they knew that wasn't really true. If it was for *honor* he could stay still as the stones for an eternity if he had to, and there was no greater honor than in guarding someone like Ariane.

If only she didn't remind him so much of Sanzo, it would be easier.

The doors and walls were soundproofed, but nothing was *perfect*, and by concentrating Wu could the faintest echoes of sound from within; the dead silence in this section of Halintratha helped. *Some kind of chant in a language I can't make out. He must really be trying to unlock the seal!*

He leaned closer to the door to see if he could make out anything more. *If I can't see* this, *I at least want to* hear *it!*

Then without even a pause he was flinging himself away, down the corridor, the supernal warrior's instinct that was at his very heart *screaming* at him to get away, get away *now!*

255

A sound of shattering crystal as though a palace of stained glass and diamonds were collapsing beneath the iron fist of a titan, followed instantaneously by roaring, howling, crackling thunder that did not dwindle into the distance but *rose*, and the walls, the solid walls that Wu Kung knew were harder than steel, *bulged* outward. The door was blasted from its frame, a seed squirting from between the fingers of a giant, and embedded itself to half its length into the wall opposite.

"Buddha's *Balls!*" he heard himself whisper. Seething, spitting energies of blue and green and violet streamed out of the doorway, hammering against the walls and spreading halfway down to where he had ended up, twenty meters down the corridor.

But he could also hear Ariane screaming. It was a sound of both pain and ecstasy, a sound he knew from old, old adventures, the sound of a power awakened within a body that did not know how to contain it. *And if you fail to contain it . . .*

He charged forward, teeth gritted, staff out and ready.

The fountain of power did not slow him much, at first, but tingles of static sparked within his fur, crawled along his staff and robes; it was a wind, a rising hurricane of fire and ice and thunder and battering stardust. But he had faced the power of the Storm Dragons, and even in this world of the Arena, had survived the hellish winds of an Arena-ship flying headlong through the skies. He held the staff up before him and it helped cleave the flow, reduced the impact on the rest of him.

The pressure increased suddenly as he passed the doorframe, and the unsteady storm of energy ripped and tore at him; but he dug in his claws and pushed his way through.

Ariane was floating in midair, a blazing figure of almost pure light with only hints of structure, of solidity, head thrown back, hair no longer midnight blue but white and gold and violet that blended into the sheer power blasting out from her. Vindatri was behind a curved shield, half-hidden eyes visibly wide, trying to maintain his position, but sliding incrementally back against the absolute force of Ariane's Awakening.

"Ariane!" Wu shouted, but the word was torn from his lips and sent spinning away. *She wouldn't hear that unless I was practically shouting in her ear!*

"How are you *standing*?" demanded Vindatri's voice, sounding as though he were, in fact, speaking from next to Wu Kung.

"Does it matter, wizard? What is important is that Ariane gets control of her power before it kills her—or us, maybe! So if you can speak to *me*, help me speak to *her!*"

He saw the veiled eyes narrow, then close. The shield flickered, a momentary disturbance that forced Vindatri back one step, two, three, but the mysterious being's hand gestured towards Wu, and Sun Wu Kung felt a tingle across his lips. "*ARIANE!*" he shouted.

The glowing, levitating figure started, and eyes of blue-white fire shimmered, shifted.

Encouraged, he forced himself forward, step by torturous step. "Ariane, *focus!* The power is yours, but it is an undammed river, destroying its own banks! You must call upon your discipline, your focus, your own strength and encompass it within you!"

For the first time, the screaming wail paused. "Wu? Wu, it . . . it *hurts* . . . but at the same time I don't want it to stop, I want it to keep going . . ."

"I know!" He remembered the fire of the Peaches burning him away to nothingness, and how he still could not stop himself from eating another . . . and another . . . and another . . . "I know, but you *have* to stop it. Focus on my voice, or on Vindatri, on *something!* Just *focus!*"

Her eyes locked on his, desperate but determined, and the fire-tracery of an evanescent jawline tightened. "Wu . . . you're in . . . danger . . ."

"My job is to *protect* you!" he snapped. "From monsters, from traitors, from *yourself* if I have to!" He took another step forward, felt the pain as the power stripped fur from the hand gripping Ruyi. "If you want to protect me—and Vindatri, and maybe this whole station with Orphan and DuQuesne, too—*focus!* Encompass the flow, *understand* it, *guide* it, like your mind guides your arm! Have you had no masters, no teachers?"

A hint of a smile, a painful ghost of a laugh. "Back to Astrella again . . . maybe I should've paid more attention . . ."

She reached out with trembling fingers of light and shadow and spun the strange, multisection bracelet—itself a faceted ring of evaporating energy—on her wrist, repeating a habit Wu had noticed before when Ariane was nervous. But her eyes closed and the storm of power stuttered, weakened, shifted a moment.

"She must restrain the power more! I must place a new Seal upon her, one that can help her control the power while she is taught!"

"Then do it! Why do you tell *me*?"

"Because—difficult though this is to admit—her power remains too great. She is trying to control it now—and showing excellent signs of potential—but the focus to administer such a teaching Seal will require I all but drop my defenses entirely."

Wu shook his head. "I can't tell her any more, give her any more clues. I don't know how your power *works*. If this isn't good enough . . ."

A thought suddenly struck him, and he grinned. "But I have another plan!"

He let go, allowed the still-rampaging power to push him back, but dug claws in to one side, skidding both backwards and in a curving sideways path until he neared Vindatri. "I will be your shield."

"What? But you—"

"I can do it!"

He brought up Ruyi Jingu Bang and began spinning it, forcing his strength against the cataract of power hammering against him, turning it to a disorganized, weakened spray of energy that barely brushed the alien's shield. He heard what he suspected was a stunned curse, but a moment later detected the sounds of another ritual in that strange alien tongue.

He had no time or focus to actually hear and remember the words, though; Ariane's unleashed power slashed and hammered and shocked him, and his staff and body were the breakwater against the raging elemental flood, the windbreak cleaving the hurricane of force, turning the implacable stream of energy into harmless, chaotic mist, like a spinning fan before a firehose. His claws anchored him and he refused the pressure, ignored the pain as lightning and razor-wind stripped layers of fur and flayed the skin beneath.

The voice of Vindatri began to rise and thunder on its own, echoing through and above the din of uncontrolled fury, and a glow of red and blue radiated from behind Wu. Without warning, the unending pressure ebbed, resurged, dwindled, turning into an erratic and unpredictable series of assaults and respites. Wu staggered and found himself falling. "*Vindatri!*"

"No fear, Sun Wu Kung, for by the Voidbuilders themselves, she is now *SEALED!*"

It was not a detonation but an *implosion*, an incomprehensible pressure that froze power in motion, crystallized energy, and then funneled it inward, backward, compressing the pussiance of that alien power into a single central point. With a shockwave that split the walls about them, the convergence came together at that central point—Ariane Stephanie Austin.

Wu dragged himself back to his feet in the deafening silence, and staggered forward. "*Ariane!*"

But she was already raising her head, an exhausted but triumphant grin emerging. "Calm down, Wu," she said as he reached her and began helping her up. "I've got a handle on it now, I think. With Vindatri's help, and yours."

"A *handle*? I think you are dreaming! You were still out of control! I could put a crank into a waterfall and have that much of a handle on it!"

She laughed. "Seriously, Wu, I was starting to figure it out, Vindatri just finished closing it up."

"There is truth in what she says." There was a note of unwilling surprise in Vindatri's voice. "Near the end, some of those instabilities which unbalanced you so, Sun Wu Kung, were not due to my own work, but to that of Ariane Austin, beginning to truly grasp how to contain the power that came from within. I foresee you being a truly *impressive* student, Captain."

"Thanks," Ariane said. For the first time she seemed to really *focus* on Wu. "My *God*, Wu, you look like crap! Did I do . . ."

"Look *around* you, Captain," he said.

She followed his glance, and stared. "Oh." Then she raised an eyebrow at Vindatri. "I *did* ask if you were prepared."

"You did, Captain. And I must confess I did not take your words seriously. A mistake that Orphan warned me about earlier. I must endeavor to remedy this failure in myself; assume that your human capabilities will be exactly as startling as implied." A hint of a smile within the hood. "And now that you have begun to grasp the power within you, and a seal made that will permit effective instruction, I look forward to many more surprises."

"Wu needs some first aid, though," she said. "He looks—"

He shook his head, uncomfortably. "I will be *fine*. These are a few scrapes, some lost skin, a few burns. They are nothing. I will be *fine*."

"All right, if that's the way you deal with it, I guess it's your business. But for *my* part, I feel like someone just put me through a juicer, so I want to go somewhere and sit down and do nothing, maybe for a *week.*"

Wu grinned and helped her walk. "I do not think you will get *that* luxury!"

Chapter 32

"How close do you estimate we are to the Humans' Sphere?" Dajzail asked.

Alztanza rocked his fighting claws. "We *estimate* about fifty thousand kilometers. Of course, that's—"

"I know." Reckoning distance in unexplored parts of the Deeps was always difficult. Even if you knew, in theory, where your target was, without a beacon you could easily go astray. "At exploration speed in these conditions, that means we still have some small-turnings left to go." A vessel like *Claws of Vengeance* could approach or even exceed the speed of sound, but in unknown regions of the Arena, with clouds and other things to conceal many dangers, it would rarely exceed a tenth of its maximum. "Is their Luminaire detectable yet?"

"We have detected significant lightening near our course. Naturally, it could still be several other things. The question is whether we make the assumption that it is, in fact, the Luminaire, and alter our course accordingly, or continue until we can be certain."

Dajzail gestured and an image of the forward screen was projected in the conference room. *So. The darkness of the cloud before us* does *diminish some, at about ten to fifteen degrees from our current course.* A veteran of numerous Highspace sorties, Dajzail knew how many phenomena of the Arena could mimic or conceal the presence of a Luminaire, ranging from fortuitous arrangements of clouds that allowed far-distant light to pass more easily than that of the target Luminaire to burning spheres of gases or solids, or even deliberate simulations or decoys.

Usually it did not matter; one could take one's time, approach any possibilities slowly and deliberately, leave signal buoys if necessary to allow retracing of one's steps, and so always arrive at the right destination. In this instance, though, misjudgment could be fatal; the capricious nature of Arenaspace's weather patterns, seeing conditions, and transmission phenomena meant that if they chose wrongly, they could end up cruising right into sensing range of enemy scouts while going in the wrong direction. Moreover, the scouts would presumably be able to quickly notify their superiors and know the exact pathway back, while the Molothos would have to either follow their enemies or backtrack.

That would eliminate the advantage of surprise, and depending on how difficult it was to redeploy and come about, reinforcements might be on their way, or the humans able to at least dispose their existing forces in a far more formidable way. True, Dajzail was certain that their victory would still be easily assured. However, the more warning the undercreatures had, the more of them could seek shelter, and the more of *his* people they might manage to kill. He wanted this to be, as much as possible, bloodless on his side, an absolute, crushing victory demonstrating utter superiority. Not a battle; an extermination of a tiny nest of vermin.

No point in bringing my finest military advisors if I do not use them. "'Tanza, what's *your* gut feeling? Is that a Luminaire, or not? If it *is*, it *must* be the Human-undercreatures', and thus our target."

Alztanza focused so much on the projected image that the rest of his eye visibly dimmed. Finally he rapped his fighting claws on the table, quickly. "That is a Luminaire. I will stake my career and life on it."

Dajzail buzzed his satisfaction. "My heart says the same, as well. Give the order."

The Fleet Master touched a control near his head with one manipulator. "Fathinalak?" A buzz of acknowledgement. "Good. Ship Master, divert our course by one thirty-fourth of a circle to port and one two-hundredth of a circle to the apex; signal all other ships to match, and track the light in that direction. Alert me *immediately* if you, or any other Ship Master, have reason to believe that light is *not* a Luminaire."

"Acknowledged, Fleet Master," Fathinalak said.

Dajzail felt the faint motion as *Claws of Vengeance* changed course, and relaxed. *That was the correct decision, I am sure.* "Now, of course, comes the more difficult and dangerous task. How do we deploy for the assault?"

"We do not want to approach closer than, oh, five thousand kilometers to their Sky Gates. While we have virtually no intelligence on their internal activities, such undercreatures are not so stupid as to fail to fortify the Sky Gates *heavily*. Such fortresses will not be significantly mobile, but will have the heaviest, longest-range weaponry available to their species. What little we have learned of their technology indicates they are a reasonably-well-developed species with weapons of at least the same order as those of most Arena dwellers."

"Understood." The last point was, unfortunately, not unexpected; technology usable in the Arena was mostly limited to devices discovered long before a species discovered the stardrive that brought them here.

Another gesture brought up an image of a sphere with stylized mountains and seas atop it, glittering dots of Sky Gates hovering over it. "We have no idea how many Sky Gates they have, correct?"

"No. The only persons who have actually visited their Sphere are either their own personnel, or the Survivor, as far as we can ascertain—and *he* we have less than no hold over." Alztanza looked at him with head tilted.

He gave a buzzing sigh. "Yes, 'Tanza, I know. Not nearly as much information as we would like. Do we have *anything* on which to base strategy, other than the basic knowledge of Sphere and Gate?"

"We *do* have estimates, based on guesses from other sources, that Orphan has gifted them with between fifteen and twenty-five warships. Possibly a smaller number of warships with other more general utility craft."

"These are of Tantimorcan design, yes? That could be difficult."

"But still, outnumbered more than one hundred sixty to one? This will not be a major problem."

"They will undoubtedly fly patrols, unless they are fools, and my research tells me they are very dangerously clever undercreatures. Such patrols will fly perhaps ten, fifteen thousand kilometers out and return. Will they have relay buoys?"

Alztanza buzzed wryly. "Again, as you said, they will unless they are fools."

Dajzail leaned back on his legs, wobbling the prop-seat a bit. "Then it is likely that upon making any contact with a patrol vessel the alarm will be given. And the alarm will be relayed by radio. Thus, as soon as such contact is made, the attack *must* immediately go to full speed to engage before they have a chance to prepare."

"Correct. I am currently planning to commit eight Seventh-Forces to the attack, in the Two Claws, Two Mouths formation, spread wide enough to bracket any likely forces, while the remaining six Seventh-Forces stay in reserve, with comm-buoys being deployed as we separate so that effective real-time communications can be maintained.

"That should give us a numeric superiority of nearly two hundred to one over the largest major force we expect and, with any reasonable luck, complete obliteration of their forces with minimal losses on our side. Then we will bring up the reserves and begin a variant on the Assault Wheel to provide continuous fire on their Sky Gate installations; I would expect us to be able to quickly saturate any defenses and then destroy those installations."

He gestured to the Sphere. "At that point, we will have command of the skies. I will station a Seventh-Force outside of each of their Straits, in case they have any other deployable vessels, and another will be used to secure the Sky Gates. The remaining forces will be used to determine their land-based capabilities and distribution of forces so that we can most efficiently cripple or destroy them and then land our ground forces on the surface.

"Once a significant force has landed and established a perimeter, we expect that our gravity preferences will be established as a sign of our claim to the Upper Sphere. This will *severely* impede any remaining resistance, as the Human undercreatures' biology is clearly intended for considerably lower gravity. We will establish a powerful ground force around their Outer Gateway, in multiple layers so that any attempt to, for example, clear the area using a superconductor bomb will not significantly impact our dominance."

He looked up, manipulators and torso in a satisfied pose. "We can then begin assembling the Fleet, which will also have the added advantage of completely securing our ownership of their Upper Sphere. Even if—for whatever reason—our lowspace assault is not as effective as we would like, their activities in the Arena will be tremendously curtailed, perhaps for decades or centuries."

"Good, 'Tanza. Now tell me what could go wrong."

An amused screech. "Everything, Daj. We don't know enough about our enemy. *Likely* to go wrong? Not much. Could *reasonably* go wrong? Well . . . communications in the Arena are as variable as anything else. We could lose comm with the attacking force, which means that anything *else* going wrong could keep us from responding to a dangerous situation. They could have an alliance no one knows about, so there's many more ships in the defensive force. Mines along our approach, there's another one. Not likely, though, since to effectively mine the approach requires that you know where the ships are going; you can't effectively mine a trillion cubic kilometers all around your Sphere, even if you wanted to."

"What if they *do* mine the approach? Say a scoutship farther out than we expect, that sees us and reports back?"

"Hm. Well, we can put a screen of smaller ships with scanners in front. I'd be reasonably confident that we'd detect any mines they could create that way. Of course, that would mean the smaller ships would be the first ones in range of enemy fire; we couldn't pull them in, especially if we had even a small indication of mine activity, until we could be *sure* we were in the clear."

Dajzail did not like the idea of putting his people out in harm's way, especially in tiny patrol vessels. On the other hand, he liked the idea of ships, including his own, running unaware into mines, even less. "Do that. I don't want to take chances here. What if they *have* been warned?"

A spreading shrug. "Then we'll take more casualties than I expect, but we'll still win. At this stage, Daj? They haven't detected us yet. They *can't* detect us without some kind of scout vessel in range, and I'll put my people's ability to detect a spy up against any number of undercreatures' attempts to spy. They don't have the resources to have put spy ships out this far."

Dajzail inhaled deeply, letting his fighting claws relax. "That was what I hoped to hear. In the end, then, they cannot know we are coming."

"And even if they do, by a miracle," Alztanza said with satisfied finality, "we will still destroy them all."

Chapter 33

"Simon," Laila said, "Correct me if I am wrong, but with our modern manufacturing techniques we could produce several ships such as those Orphan gave us each day, yes?"

"I would expect so, assuming sufficient attention and resources were dedicated to that task. Why do you ask?" Simon answered while checking the compact toolkit. *Another trip to add "primaries," this time to one of the Sky Gate Defense Stations.*

"Because we *aren't* doing that, and given that we now know the Molothos are in fact on their way I would think that adding as many ships to our forces as *possible* would be a major priority. So there must be aspects that I am not considering." She gave one of her brief, bright smiles. "After all, I *am* a biologist, not an engineer or a tactician."

"Actually," Carl Edlund said, looking up from a screen where he had been going over the layout of defenses on the Upper Sphere, "I think there's two major points. Right, Simon?"

"Three, if you count the fact that technically we have no real government in the old sense, and thus no organized way of supporting any large-scale actions—no drafts, no taxes in the classic sense, only SFGs and self-supporting oversight groups that generally report to the SSC. Leaving that aside, there are two others. First . . . we have to assume that there may be an assault force—and an extremely large one—launched at any time from the nearby Molothos colony in normal space. While the Arena apparently prevents Nicoll-Dyson laser or c-fractional assaults, it does not prevent the Molothos from sending an invasion force through our Sky Gates, and such a force could be . . . incalculably huge. We could be looking at a normal-space invasion force numbering in the *millions*."

Laila nodded. "All right. So our shipbuilding capabilities must be focused on making an immensely powerful home defense—something that at least can benefit from our AI resources. What is the second point?"

"Crewing the vessels. It is one thing to play simgames as part of the crew of a vessel in an interstellar war, quite another to actually be willing and able to *be* a member of such a crew. While many skills can be transferred to a person by skill download, you cannot simply turn an ordinary person into a capable warrior. Or rather, one *could*, but that would—"

"—be the equivalent of mindwipe and reprogramming to someone who wasn't such a person to begin with. Yes, I see. We are having trouble fully crewing even the vessels we have; selecting and training enough people for ten times that many vessels is simply not feasible." Laila sighed. "I *should* have deduced that one on my own, I suppose, but it isn't my speciality. So we are limited to our current forces, at least for the reasonable future—which includes our upcoming battle."

He nodded, seeing Laila's face suddenly mirroring the same strain he had seen on Ariane's more than once. *The position of Leader of the Faction . . . that is a weight I hope I never have to carry.* "I am afraid so."

"Then how are we planning to deal with this?"

"We have had multiple SFGs working on the problem. Overall, we have to exploit our advantages in a way that minimizes their own."

"The primaries."

"That is certainly one large advantage. The other is, of course, that we know that they are coming, how many of them there are, and have an excellent understanding of their capabilities. Thus, while they have every reason to believe their assault will come as a surprise, and are already slowly deploying their forces based on that assumption, we will actually be able to select the time and manner of engagement. They will also know nothing, as you say, of the primaries, so their target engagement distances will be based on false assumptions of how close they can get and still be reasonably safe."

Carl pointed to his own display. "Basically, the idea is to let them come in and think they've got the drop on us. Make it look like most of our ships are out on patrol, let the Molothos come in to try and take out the gateway picket boats in preparation for destroying the defensive stations. Based on the information from the battle against the Blessed and the *Zounin-Ginjou*, we're figuring on letting them get within about a thousand kilometers and then *wham!* All our ships start taking them out from ranges they can't match."

"Why are the ranges so *short*?" Laila asked. "I know that was the range for the battle you were in, Simon—in fact, you closed to around two hundred—but back home any battles in space are fought at ranges of hundreds of thousands of kilometers or more. Is it the fact that AIs do not work? I presume radar still does, yes?"

"The short answer is, 'the Arena,'" Simon said, feeling a rather cynical grin on his own face. "In more detail, because things like radar do not penetrate thousands of miles of relatively humid air, let alone such air with particulates of all sizes floating in it, flocks of creatures of many types, and so on to provide additional confusion and interference. The Arena allows us to see—variably—farther with visible light, but without automation of great capability, targeting and navigation tends to still rely on individual people's sight with modest, relatively wide-angle magnification."

The brown-haired biologist pursed her lips, then nodded. "I see. The Arena controls the nature of engagements in both spaces, and here they are much more . . . up-close and personal."

"Exactly," Simon said. Turning to Carl, he went on, "Once hostilities begin, we will target Dajzail's ship first, I presume?" Simon said.

"No," Laila said instantly. At his raised eyebrow, she went on, "Unless his ship is obviously in the forefront and exposed, anyway. Ambushing them is believable, though surprising. Unexpected weapons are believable, though surprising. Instantly knowing which vessel the Leader of the Faction is on? Much less believable, and your special capability is something we simply do not want anyone to even *suspect*. More importantly, we do not want to set a precedent that killing Leaders of Factions is the acceptable first move."

"Also, much as I hate to say it, we don't want them thrown into both chaos from losing their top dogs, *and* a worse vengeance mode," Carl said reluctantly. "Because right now? Our best projections show that we'll be able to *hurt the hell* out of them, but primaries and all, we'll *still* end up losing this battle. So we'll need to hope we can hurt them *so bad* right off that we can convince them to back off, at least long enough."

Simon heard his breath whistle in through his teeth. "That bad?"

"Simon, you gave us the count. They've got *four hundred times* as many ships as we do—maybe two hundred, if we count the Sky Gate defense stations. Hell, even if they lose *ninety-nine percent* of their forces and we take *zero* losses, they'll *still* have four times our forces. Aside from the primaries, their ships will be just as good as ours, crewed by people *used* to fighting interstellar wars in the Arena for God only knows how long." He shook his head. "And the movements you reported on your last glance? The SFGs say that means they're already alert for possible mines and other traps along their route. They're being careful. We'll sucker them *once*. But after that . . ."

The room was quiet for a moment, and Simon felt the coming assault weighing down on them all like an invisible mass of lead. Finally, he sighed, bent down, and picked up the case. "Well, all I can do then is try to improve the odds. I'd better get back to work."

He had to force his steps to their usual quick, precise motion. The thought that they would soon lose the Upper Sphere that DuQuesne and Carl had risked their lives to take back was almost intolerable. *Even worse . . . if they are right, should we even* try *to fight back? We'll be losing lives, ships, and the secret of the primaries for no purpose then. I may have to advise Laila and Carl to . . . abandon the Upper Sphere entirely. And the* thought *of that . . . well, as Marc might say, really sticks in my craw.*

A green comm-ball appeared. "Simon, my friend, are you possibly free to speak for a few moments?" asked a familiar rough-edged voice.

"Relgof?" He paused for a moment, but a request from a Faction Leader was not one to be brushed off lightly. "Certainly, Doctor. Go ahead."

"I would like to speak in person, if it is not too much of an imposition. Would you come to the Faction House?"

Simon felt his curiosity rising. "I am on my way, in that case. Give me ten minutes, five if I am fortunate."

"I will be awaiting you here."

It was seven and a half minutes before one of the floating taxi-platforms deposited Simon in front of the Faction House of the Analytic. He passed through the doors to see Dr. Relgof rise from a chair in the anteroom and come immediately forward. "Simon, my friend, thank you! I did not want to say, but it was *extremely* important that you come immediately."

"I am . . . intrigued by the urgency, Relgof. What—"

"Come, come," he said, beckoning Simon to follow, white feathery crest nodding with the quickness of Relgof's steps. "Our usual room awaits!"

In a few moments they reached the room with the chair tailored for Simon's comfort and the eating trough opposite for Relgof, and were seated. "All right, Dr. Rel, enough of the mystery; tell me what is going on?"

"Ahh, Simon, allow me my few moments of dramatics! Is it not true that the way of a Researcher is many hours of dull routine for the moment of understanding, insight, revelation, or, perhaps, of presentation?" The semi-humanoid face had expressions Simon had learned to read, and right now Rel was, in effect, smiling roguishly at him.

Simon laughed and smiled back, allowing himself to relax a bit. Whatever Relgof had in mind, it was clearly something he thought would at the least amuse his human friend. "True enough, Rel. So on with the show!"

"Show? Ahh, yes, the performance! Well, you may recall—certainly *must* recall—the *terribly* startling revelation of one of our most recent conversations?"

"That we had made a discovery of some importance about the Faith and Shadeweavers . . . a discovery you did not remember at the time?"

"*Precisely*. Oh, now, *that* was a shock, I must say, for to forget anything is a scientist's bane. To forget something so important? I think we both realized that this meant that the Shadeweavers or the Faith—or, perhaps, in this case, a rare union of *both*—had acted directly and deliberately to remove such knowledge."

"Yes, it certainly made no sense otherwise."

"But then, I asked myself . . . why was it that *you* were unaffected? For a short time I was at a loss . . . but then I remembered the ending of your Captain's duel against Amas-Garao, and the price she demanded—a price the Arena accepted and forced upon the Shadeweavers entire."

"Quite right," Simon said with a nod. Replaying that event in his mind, he quoted, ". . . From this point on, no Shadeweaver will *ever* read, sense, influence, brainwash, mentally assault, or in any other way outside of the mundane methods available to all other Arena species have any effect upon the minds of the Faction of Humanity or our direct and close allies."

"So! The Shadeweavers could not remove that memory from your mind. Yet I had kept that memory for at least some short time—you had not noticed I had forgotten before. So my suspicion was that I would not lose this knowledge until I left our Faction House; the Faction Houses are secure and protected, and without invitation even a Shadeweaver cannot enter, and presumably that meant that their powers could not reach within unbidden.

"This did leave me with a terrible dilemma, however. I did not dare *confront* the Shadeweavers about this issue, for many reasons, and I did not wish to lose knowledge. So I came to what seemed the only reasonable conclusion." He stood and did the wide-spread bow he had made upon their first meeting. "I, Relgof Nov'Ne Knarph of the Analytic, pledge myself personally to be a 'direct and close ally' of Humanity. My interests I shall align with yours. We have, of course, been friends, but it is clear that my prior actions have still taken the Analytic as my primary allegiance—and for purposes of the Arena, it is also clear that that was insufficient to extend the protection to me."

Simon felt a huge grin spreading over his face; he stood and grasped one of Rel's double-thumbed hands. "This is wonderful news, Rel; we couldn't ask for a better ally. But does that mean . . . you want to join the Faction of Humanity?"

Relgof straightened and his filter-beard flip-flopped in a laughing smile. "If necessary I would indeed have done so, because to make my mind fully my own? Nothing is more valuable."

Simon felt a tingle of awe and hope starting across him. *Could it be . . . ?* He remembered something he had seen in passing, when testing his omniscience . . .

"But I *am* the Leader of the Analytic, and I knew, too, that the sanctity of our minds—of our *knowledge*—was of paramount importance to the Faction as a whole. And so I have spoken—and lectured—and even argued with all the passion of my *life* with the Convocation." The alien smile was now even broader than Simon's. "And I am pleased to say that despite much reluctance, they finally acquiesced. As the Leader of the Faction of the Analytic, I am announcing to you—and will convey to your Leader in a moment—

that the Faction of the Analytic is now a full ally of the Faction of Humanity, and we would like to know if there is any service we can provide you to prove that this alliance is true and worthy."

For a moment, Simon could not believe his ears; and then he heard his own laughter echoing through the room. "Is there any service you can provide?" he repeated, and then his expression became serious. "Dr. Relgof, the Analytic may just be able to save Humanity."

Chapter 34

Ariane? Try not to react.

She *had* given a start and dropped the shirt she had been putting on when the silent voice spoke inside her head, but then sat back down on her bed and grabbed her foot as though massaging out a sudden cramp. *What is it, Marc?* she thought, cutting out her internal transmitter but otherwise concentrating as though she were trying to transmit the words.

Marc's instant response showed he heard her. *Sorry about the surprise, but there's things I want to tell you that I'd rather not have Vindatri know about.*

She lowered her foot and continued getting dressed. *Are you sure he can't pick this up?*

Sure? No way to be one-hundred-percent sure, but even back in my home universe, listening in on a two-way telepathic link was hard. Usually you had to know it was going on. Plus I'm shielding my mind, and I'm trying to keep yours shielded too. So . . . I'm pretty sure he can't pick this up.

Okay, then. What's up?

A rush of images and sensations followed; it took a *lot* of control to keep from getting dizzy, but the *real* challenge was keeping her face from showing shock and bewilderment. *What . . . the . . . HELL . . . is that?*

Damned if I know, Ariane. Looked like the universe's biggest waxworks display, and I'll be totally jiggered if I can figure out what that half-finished human shape was about.

275

Were there any *duplicates in that room? Two Molothos, anything?*

Mark's mindvoice was silent for a few moments. *I . . . don't think so. I can't* swear *to it—there were thousands and thousands of the things there, and we were running through the place* fast, *so my headware didn't record all of them, but I sure can't remember seeing any duplicates. You thinking what I am?*

Collection of all the species in the Arena, right? Or maybe all the ones Vindatri's ever encountered personally?

Maybe. Hard to say. We don't have a clue as to how old he is, or what *he is, for that matter. Question is why he'd bother locking the place up. Sure, it's impressive, but what's your take on why it'd be worth hiding?*

She could tell that Marc had an idea, but he wasn't saying it yet. He wanted her opinion without any of his input prejudicing it. *Only two things I can think of. First, that humanoid figure stands out. It means something, and it's different than all the others the way it's designed. Second, you said you thought that figure might be the very first one in the whole collection; why?*

Another pause, as she finished tightening her boots and checking the seals on her clothing. *It was just a feeling, but from a couple of things I noticed. First, the lines were all perfect, spaced evenly in both directions, except that the one nearest the door—the first one—wasn't complete. It was about three-quarters of the way from completion, so it was like that was where the last entry had been put in order. Second, we know that the Blessed to Serve were pretty recent in their arrival in the Arena, while from some of the other things we've heard the Rodeskri have been around a lot longer, and we* know *the Molothos had to be damn early in the order of things or a whole bunch of other Factions would've wiped them out right away. So the order of the species seemed to fit the order of their entry.*

She nodded. *Which, if we follow that logic, makes that humanoid figure . . . ?*

Something older than the Molothos. The oldest thing on his list. But why *is it indistinct? None of the others were like that; they're all so real I'm not sure they* aren't *real, which also gives me the willies.* A mental sigh. *What about you? Anything you want to tell me?*

Well, Wu will tell you about my being released. Telling Vindatri how I was Awakened was enough to pay him, or so he said. But one thing he doesn't know—I think—is that I'm pretty sure I can *answer your question about what* he *is.*

She opened the door and turned down the corridor towards the dining room Vindatri had provided; there was a flash of surprise from DuQuesne. *You're not having me on there? No, you aren't; can't lie in telepathic contact, unlike with a radio comm. Okay, don't leave me hanging, what is Vindatri?*

Remember the conversation I told you about that I had with Amas-Garao, a little before I got kidnapped? He talked about the obligations of the power his people wield . . . and how they keep it under control. Namely, they've got strict rules about how long you get to keep the power, and you're required to hang up your cloak and hand the power over to someone else. So my guess? Vindatri is a Shadeweaver who refused to give up his power when the time came, and managed to escape his fellows when they came to take it.

It was no surprise that DuQuesne instantly grasped the implications. *Klono's tungsten teeth, that's bad. That means he's the kind of guy who decided he had the* right *to keep power even when he'd sworn not to, he's been extending his lifespan in direct contradiction to his oaths, he was probably willing to fight or even kill to keep power and managed to get away with it against the wishes of the other Shadeweavers, which meant that he was one Big* Time *Operator even then . . . and if the power keeps getting stronger as Shadeweavers get older, his real power* now *would make Amas-Garao look like a sideshow magician. I thought his little knee-jerk anger about our mistaking his rituals indicated that, but this makes it about ten times worse. How'd you figure this out?*

Thought-conversations were a lot faster than verbal ones, so she was still barely ten meters down the corridor from her room. *I admit it was something of a guess, but it was a combination of knowing from what Amas-Garao said that it must be* possible *for someone to basically change their mind, and something Vindatri said. He started quoting the beginning of the Ascendance ritual, but the rhythm and word separation didn't sound anything like the way the Faith pronounced the words; it sounded a lot more like the Shadeweaver ritual fragment you let me hear from your headware.*

Good thinking, and you're probably right. A pause. *Other important thing—during our little trip, Orphan slipped me a little gadget; it's an encrypted transmitter and memory chip—with a message on it.*

Suddenly she was hearing another voice, through DuQuesne's memories: "Dr. DuQuesne, it is my *strong* feeling that we need a method to communicate that my friend Vindatri cannot monitor. While he has been my ally, I am sure you have noted his . . . capricious temperament, and the expedition on which I intend to give you this message is one that reveals something I find unsettling, to say the least.

"Now, you and your people have previously managed some *most* surprising innovations that I cannot fathom. If you could create a communications device that is more secure than this example transmitter, I think this would serve us very well. Contrive to respond whenever you find most convenient and secure."

Wow. He's as nervous as we are.

Explains the other reason he wanted us along. He's afraid of Vindatri, and he's got damn good reason from what I can see. But Vindatri's also his ace in the hole against things like Shadeweavers. He wants to cover all bases, and I can't blame him.

Can *you make something like what he asks?*

An inaudible chuckle. *Ariane, now that I know what the Arena will let me get away with? I'll bet I can make an ultra-wave communicator, or one operating on whatever the Arena will use to imitate fourth or fifth-order forces, maybe even sixth order, that Vindatri won't be able to read unless he knows what's going on. The real challenge will be building it under his nose, but I'll figure out an angle, trust me.*

As she approached the dining room, she could hear Marc in conversation with Wu Kung and Orphan. *You're managing to talk with them while we're having* this *discussion?*

There was a momentary bleak flash of awareness of being *different*, alien, *manufactured*, and she began an apology. *Don't apologize, Ariane. I have to deal with my own issues, and they're sort of stupid issues. That* difference *can save our asses, just like whatever's happened to you, and I shouldn't get all angsty about it. But yeah, I am. I can compartmentalize my brain into at least two different parallel and completely functional trains of thought. Mentor taught me that, back when. Seems it works just fine here.*

The name sparked a recollection. *Marc . . . do you think . . . well, my grandfather and Dr. Bryson, your . . . designer, were the same person. Is it possible that* Mentor *was . . .*

. . . my Mentor? *So that was the thought you suddenly had after the revelation of the connection.* A pause, as her regular yet molasses-slow

footsteps brought her in sight of the dining-room entrance. *Could be. He sure* sounds *the same, talks the same, but then if Bryson designed both they* would. *He's never* said *anything about it to me, yet . . .*

She saw a flash of memory: DuQuesne, mind filled with grief and fury, turning towards a doorway that might hide his enemy, taking a step—

"STOP, YOUTH!"

Yeah. The way he said that, the way it froze me in my tracks—the way it had *to, or I'd have been dead, dead, dead—that* sure *sounded and felt like my Mentor. Still, it's perfectly in character for any version of the old Arisian. I just don't know, and we can't ask him. Let's talk later about whether it actually matters.*

We will. I'll think about it. But now I have to concentrate on regular talking, because I *can't split my brain in two.*

An invisible grin. *Yet.*

She smiled as she entered the room. "Good evening, everyone!"

Wu Kung bounced up and took his place nearby. "I am sorry I wasn't waiting at your—"

"I would have been annoyed if you were standing outside my door all that time, and you know it."

He rolled his eyes. "I know, and that's why I wasn't. I still *should* have been."

Ariane patted his arm. "I know, Wu. You'll just have to deal with your unreasonable Captain as she is."

"As do we all," Orphan agreed, pausing in his draining liquid from some sort of red-brown fruit. "But I think there is little to fear in her walk from our quarters to this room."

"There should be nothing to fear at all," said Vindatri, stepping from a shadowed area across the room. "I, and the few other residents of Halintratha, pose you no threat, and I assure you there are no other threats within a hundred thousand kilometers of this place."

"Nothing to fear except *you*," Wu Kung said bluntly.

The half-seen eyes blinked. Then a low laugh emanated from under the hood. "Yes, I suppose, I could be a threat. But you would guard her from *me*, Wu Kung?"

The Hyperion Monkey King shrugged. "I would *try*. That is the job of a bodyguard, right?"

"Very true, and I should not laugh, though such an attempt—were

I truly hostile—would be futile on your part. To more cheerful subjects, do you find the meal to your liking?"

"Top-notch," DuQuesne said, giving a thumbs-up before taking another bite of steak. "Amas-Garao pulled this trick off when he was trying to recruit me, and you're going a couple better, by doing it for all of us at once."

Ariane saw that at her place was what appeared to be an assortment of classic Indian foods—*palak paneer*, tandoori chicken, a vindaloo hot enough that her nose tingled as she sat down, a plate of *nan* and other dishes—of exactly the type that were her favorites back home. "This sure *looks* good." She reached out, took a piece of the flatbread, and scooped out some of the palak paneer. "Wow. That's some of the best I've ever had."

"I am glad. As you might guess, replicating tastes by themselves is not difficult, but actually replicating the *food* in all of its aspects is a challenge, especially when one has had no experience of it." Vindatri took a seat at the far end of the table, and food materialized in front of him; it appeared to include a cut of some sort of meat, thinly sliced and fried or baked to have a crust, and several other dishes that might have been vegetables, starches, or even some type of bread with odd colors and shapes.

"You mentioned other residents," DuQuesne said. "Haven't seen any of those yet; where are they?"

"Most of them keep to specific sections of Halintratha," Vindatri answered. "They are . . . relatively primitive, I suppose one could say, and I do not wish to confuse them overly much by encountering other species."

"If they're so primitive, what are they doing here—if we can ask?"

"I am trying to . . . guide their development, would be the best way to put it. I do not wish to *force* them on any path, but I do want to assist them past various difficulties they encounter, and I do so, partly on my own but more commonly through representatives I select and educate."

"That's nice of you!" Wu Kung said. "Helping without forcing, I like that."

Ariane nodded, but inside she wasn't so sure. If there was *anything* she'd learned in the Arena, it was that you had to pay *close* attention to the way people talked, and that they'd often try to hide one truth within another. Vindatri talked something like Orphan, and something like Amas-Garao, and both of those were people who used words like mazes. *The not-good interpretation of that would be that Vindatri's playing God, in a pretty literal sense.* "So would these people be natives of the Sphere a short ways off?"

"Correct. That is one reason I remain here; observing the development of a civilization within the Arena itself is a rare opportunity. Perhaps I will be able to introduce you to one of these natives later." Vindatri took a bite of the meat; Ariane thought she saw a flash of teeth, but they didn't look as viciously sharp as those of Amas-Garao or other real carnivores. *Omnivore like us, with differentiated teeth, maybe.*

Vindatri's tone also indicated that the subject of the mysterious other beings was closed, at least for now. *Just as well; time to change the subject.* "Earlier you said you knew the meaning of the words of that chant that I used during my Awakening. What *do* they mean?"

Vindatri's quick glance at the others needed no translation. "Vindatri, I'm going to tell them anyway, so there's no point in hiding. And I'm sure they're interested."

"Damn straight I'm interested. Heard a bunch of fragments of that language, or whatever it is, but no one ever translated it," DuQuesne said. Orphan simply tapped his assent, and Wu Kung looked up from his food with interest.

"As you desire, then," Vindatri said after a moment. "But you will also recall that I said that I understood them 'in a sense.' There are multiple interpretations of the words—among both the Shadeweavers and the Faith, as far as I know, and I have my own various interpretations. All of them, understand, convey the same very basic meaning, but the *nuances* of that meaning carry extremely variant implications."

"How so?"

Vindatri gave his shadowy smile again. "'Oh, Masters of All, grant to this one ascendance to the Brotherhood, that I might see and shape the world as one of the Blood of Creation,'" he said. "That is one translation of the first portion of the ritual. However, so is 'Arena System, grant me access privileges to both read and edit Arena operations as one of the Shadeweavers'—or 'as one of the Faith,' I would presume. There are . . . many other variations."

"So even the *invocations* don't really tell us whether the Faith or the Shadeweavers are right about the Arena."

"Amusing, is it not? I have no doubt that the Arena itself *could* tell us the precisely correct translation, but it refuses to. There is, unfortunately, too little of that language actually known to allow for accurate translations. And I should correct you—not all of the Shadeweavers are the cynical materialists that it appears your acquaintance Amas-Garao is. Some believe fervently that they are accessing secret magics from the dawn of time, just as certainly as those who believe the Arena and these powers nothing more than the actions of a complex, but ultimately controllable, machine."

Another flash of that half-visible smile. "Such an attitude is much rarer in the Initiate Guides, and would not likely ever be verbalized, but there are a few Guides whose private thoughts would likely reveal a much more mundane attitude towards their powers than the First Guide would like."

"I guess we'll just have to keep looking until we hunt down one of these Voidbuilders and get to ask *them*, then," DuQuesne said.

Vindatri studied DuQuesne intensely for a moment, then nodded very slowly. "Yes. That may well be the only way to resolve the issue."

"Well," Ariane said, "at least that relieves me of the worry of whether I really need to join some cult in order to wield the power. How will this instruction go?"

"We will have to work together for some time," Vidnatri answered, "although as I mentioned, your surprising ability to begin to control the power already may reduce that time. I must teach you the basic symbols and words, and evaluate your ability to keep them focused and visualized in your mind during other activities. Whether performed by supernatural forces or by a machine with immense capabilities, the powers rely on a clear, focused mind which is not only verbally, but *mentally*, articulating their focus and desire."

"So will she be able to do stuff like you, or like Amas-Garao, or more like Nyanthus of the Faith?" asked Wu Kung.

"Yes and no would be the most appropriate answer," Vindatri said, and his voice held a smile as well. "Each of us is unique in our own way. Whether Shadeweaver or Faith, those known to us each have developed their own skills, their own spells, if you like, their own unique signature and approach. There are, of course, techniques and particular . . . spells, rituals, call them what you will—that I will be teaching your Captain. But which ones she can best master, and how she will ultimately express them? That even I can only guess."

A personal magic . . . or power, anyway. Ariane briefly wondered what hers would be like, then dismissed the thought. *I'll find out soon enough, I guess.* "How long did it take *you* to master these powers when you first got them?"

Vindatri did not answer at first, sitting utterly immobile at the head of the table, and the silence became tense. She saw Orphan's wingcases contracting, and Wu Kung subtly shifting in his chair in a way that would make it much easier for him to leap into action. *Did I cross a line? It is something that'll touch on his origin, but still it's a natural question . . .*

Before the tension became completely unbearable, Vindatri shifted the slightest bit and spoke; his tone was tense at first, but slowly returned to the easy delivery characteristic of his usual conversation. "A . . . reasonable question, I must concede. Understand that I do not often answer questions pertaining to myself, but in this case, perhaps I should be more forthcoming.

"I had, as you might suspect, my own teachers. With their help, I completed my training and became a master in a matter of a few years—quite swift, by their reckoning."

"*Years?*" Ariane heard the half-whining tone in her voice and winced. *Oh, that really sounds like a Leader of a Faction, doesn't it?* "My apologies, I shouldn't have allowed that to come out as it did. But . . ."

A low chuckle, and she thought she saw a twinkle in an eye that had a hint of violet in the darkness. ". . . but you *are* the Leader of your Faction, and you already begin to worry about what transpires in your absence. I cannot blame you for your concern. Yet where else will you have this opportunity?"

"Well," Wu Kung said, "you *could* just come back with us for a while and teach her there!"

Orphan froze and dropped the food bulb he had been draining; DuQuesne just grinned.

Vindatri's answer was more serious. "I am afraid that would be unwise for both of us. I have my reasons—very good reasons—to remain where I am, and you would most certainly not want to involve yourself in my affairs any further."

"It was worth asking, though! I remember how hard I *kicked* myself when I realized that the way through the Portal of Peace was to just *ask* the guardian to let me through, and so I reminded myself to always *ask* when there was something I wanted!"

"Not that you always remember that advice, Wu," DuQuesne said. "Especially about food."

Everyone, even Vindatri, got a chuckle at that remark, and Wu laughed in an embarrassed way, hand behind his head. "Sometimes my stomach does the thinking!"

"Still," Vindatri continued, "I can understand your concern, Captain, and with the most peculiar and positive indications I sensed during the Sealing, it may be that we can move forward more quickly. But to accomplish the most in the least time, we shall have to make your training regimen . . . much more *intense* than I had originally intended."

Ariane winced. *I have an idea of what he means by "intense." Been through some of those in simgames. Old masters drilling their students with impossible tasks, magicians testing their apprentices' endurance as well as talent. All pretty awesome when you can just shut off the game and come back later.*

But now . . . now I'm going to have to go through it for real. And there's no pause button this time.

"All right," she said, drawing a deep breath. "When do we start?"

"Tomorrow, Captain Austin," Vindatri said. "In either of our schedules, a few hours will make no difference. And I think you will want to be rested indeed before we begin, because," and now the smile was *clearly* unsettling, "you will have little chance for rest after!"

Chapter 35

"What other choice do I *have*, Marc?" Ariane asked, pulling her training suit's top on. "We *came* here so I could get answers about these powers locked away inside me. If I don't let him train me, I blew off my responsibilities as Leader of the Faction for *nothing*."

"Not *quite* nothing," DuQuesne corrected. "We'd committed to help Orphan in exchange for the ships, so we were paying off the debt." Seeing her mouth opening, he continued, "And still, yes, you're right because you could've sent someone other than you, and the only reason you could justify going was to get that information."

"So—"

"So it's still something we have to think about. This guy's a real Big-Time Operator; in some ways he's the biggest we've ever met. Doesn't belong to any faction, has the powers that ought to be limited just to two specific groups, and he's been around for a long, long time. He's got his own motives—that we don't know, and probably can't really guess—and if we don't know *that*, do we want to risk being *part* of his long-range plans?"

"I . . ." She sank into a nearby chair, shaking her head. "I don't know. Let me think a moment, all right?"

He saw the slightly exaggerated wrinkling of her brow and her momentarily intense expression. For a moment he couldn't figure it out, but then it was clear. He concentrated. *Okay, Ariane, you wanted to talk in private?*

A mental smile. *Knew you'd catch on. Marc, I know we're playing with fire here. And yes, I know Vindatri's got his own goals and I don't*

285

trust him much at all. And since he's not a member of the Shadeweavers, I know he might change my perceptions, my emotions, or even my thoughts.

Then maybe we shouldn't take chances with—

But also, *Marc,* and there was another mental smile, and an impression of a wink, *I know that* you *are here. And if he does mess with my mind, I* absolutely *trust Marc C. DuQuesne, Doc Smithian Hero, to put me back together when the time comes. In fact, I* order *you to do that—if it becomes necessary—and give you full permission to access my mind to check if you need to.*

DuQuesne projected his own grin. *Understood, Captain.*

I also order you to be sneaky *about it. By which I mean that we might have to let* me get affected by him in order to get through the training. If *he's got his own goals, that's obviously the best way for him to achieve it: make sure that I go along with him. So let's try not to force the issue if it looks like there's still more to gain.*

He kept his face from showing how very much he didn't like that plan. Outwardly, anyone (namely, Vindatri) watching would see him sitting quietly while Ariane thought. Telepathic conversation was quick. *That's not playing with fire, Ariane, that's juggling jars of nitro-glycerine while tapdancing on landmines.*

Yes, I knew you would hate this idea. But this is the way we're going to play it. Understood?

He gave an inward sigh. *Yes, Captain. Understood.*

Good. Now back to the outward show.

Ariane finally looked up. "Do we *want* to be part of his plans? I don't know, Marc. But I *do* know that we *absolutely* need to understand these abilities I have and that the other two groups that *do* understand them will not teach me—unless I desert Humanity for them. That would be even worse, I think. So my decision—as your Captain, and as Leader of the Faction—is that I have to risk it."

This time he sighed audibly. "If that's the way it has to be . . . yes, Captain. I've raised the questions, you get to make the decision."

"And I appreciate your input, Marc. You know that."

"Yeah. I know. I just hope this doesn't come back to bite us on the nethers." He gave her a quick kiss. "Better go, then. You do *not* want to keep that guy waiting."

"I'd guess not."

The door opened in front of her; Wu Kung was standing just outside. "Ready?"

"Ready, Wu."

"Keep an eye on her, Wu," he said.

"Trust me, DuQuesne! It is my job!"

The door slid shut, and DuQuesne looked pensively around the guest quarters. Vindatri had tweaked their appearance after their first night, based on their comments, and the result was a huge improvement. None of the disquietingly alien proportions remained in the design, and the lighting was much more Earthlike, as were the chairs and other furniture.

However, what he needed wasn't here; it was on board *Zounin-Ginjou*. He hadn't expected to be doing engineering on the sly, and to pull anything off under the nose of a being that was, at a conservative estimate, fifty to a hundred times his own age was going to be a hell of a trick.

On the other hand, he didn't think Vindatri was any *smarter* than a smart human being. *And that means, my friend, that you will not have much of your brain available to spy on me while you're trying to teach Ariane Stephanie Austin.* Vindatri had neither confronted him or Orphan on their prior adventure, nor made any oblique references to it, so he felt he had some good grounds for this assumption. Either Vindatri couldn't observe them when he was focusing on something else, or else he felt very heavily bound to *pretend* he couldn't.

If it was the latter, well . . . DuQuesne smiled to himself. If Orphan's reaction to the "primary" modifications was any guide, Vindatri would just end up confused. Unless the enigmatic creature suspected that DuQuesne had his own version of Arena-based superpowers, he'd never make sense of anything DuQuesne did with them.

DuQuesne ambled out, taking his time as he headed for the common room. The point was to look like he was being patient, and somewhat bored, until it was likely that Vindatri was fully wrapped up in training Ariane.

Orphan was there, sitting in one of the split-backed chairs appropriate for a tailed species, apparently absorbed in reading or viewing something presented by his own headware; DuQuesne could recognize the semi-glazed look of the eyes staring at things that weren't there. As DuQuesne sat down, however, Orphan became aware of him and straightened. "Dr. DuQuesne! A good morning to you."

"And you, Orphan."

"And Captain Austin? She has departed for her training already?"

"Left a few minutes ago. I guess she'll be gone all day. Since Wu isn't leaving her alone, that means it's just you and me. Probably for a few weeks, anyway."

"Could I possibly interest you in a game of *anghas*? I did bring the pieces with me."

He remembered the resource-strategy game well; they'd played a lot of it on *Zounin-Ginjou* during the time they were shuttling the Liberated vessels to Earth's Sphere, and on this trip they'd taught it to both Ariane and Wu. "Maybe later; it's not so exciting with only two players. If I can convince Wu to unstick himself from Ariane, maybe we could do a three-way game later. Right now, I've actually got some things I'd like to work on, but the stuff I need's back on the ship. Vindatri's preference for us staying here doesn't stop me from getting equipment out of our ship, right?"

"I do not think he would object. If you do not mind, I will accompany you."

"Sure, if you want. You looked like you were enjoying yourself alone, though."

"Dr. DuQuesne, I have become an absolute *master* at entertaining myself in isolation; it was, you understand, a necessity." DuQuesne nodded; Orphan had been the *only* member of the Liberated for a period of something well over a thousand years. "But also because of that, I must confess that I *vastly* prefer the company of other, living beings. I can endure solitude, yes . . . but I have come to detest it, too."

"I can't blame you. Sure, come along."

As they walked through the more-alien vastness of the docking area, Orphan said, "is this project one of interest to me?"

DuQuesne gave him the slightest wink—a gesture he knew Orphan had researched and learned—as he answered, "Probably not much. Mostly design and circuit work for stuff back home. I'm a power engineer, you know, but I dabble in a lot of the other areas, and the Arena's demands kinda change your design perspectives."

"I confess that while intellectually I understand, I fear that I will never truly grasp what it must have been like for you as First Emergents," Orphan said; his hands gave a tiny, quick version of the handtap, showing that he understood what DuQuesne was implying. "I, of course, was born and raised with the understanding of the Arena and its limitations, to the point that they are second nature to me. You, on the other hand, were confronted by its rules . . . rather rudely."

DuQuesne's sharp laugh echoed around the cavernous bay. "You can say *that* again. Whole ship powered down, AIs dead, and the only thing that saved our collective asses was that we had a racing pilot in the seat when it all happened."

"Really? I do not believe I have been told this part of your saga, Doctor."

"Huh. You know, you're right. Technically I probably shouldn't say any more. I mean, the tale of a First Emergence told by one of the people who was *there*, that's got to be worth something."

"Now, Doctor, you are beginning to be positively *predatory*. As a proper resident of the Arena should be, I confess."

"Still, what the hell. I'll leave out the parts I think are really valuable but I can give you some of it."

Telling *that* part of the tale took quite a bit of time. Based on things DuQuesne had heard from other people, he suspected there were a few things about their Sphere that were different—specifically, the huge dark, semi-ruined area immediately inside from the Docks—so he left those parts out. Still, by the time he had reached the point where they had confronted the Blessed To Serve and rescued Orphan, the two had reached *Zounin-Ginjou*, located all the tools and materials DuQuesne wanted, and gotten most of the way back to their assigned quarters on *Halintratha*.

"That is a *fascinating* story, Doctor. Absolutely *riveting*, and I do not say that lightly. Such a carefully prepared expedition, nearly destroyed because of factors you simply could not have imagined." He gave a buzzing laugh as they entered the common room. "But the most amazing part of it is your Captain, I think."

"She sure is something else, that's for sure."

"An almost completely supernumerary member of your crew, turning out to be the most vital and important person in the venture. If *that* does not demonstrate your good fortune . . ."

DuQuesne nodded soberly. "Yeah, thought of that. And there's other parts I left out—and will keep leaving out—that pretty much confirm your theory. We had pretty much the absolute best possible people to handle exactly what the Arena threw at us—and a lot of that was pure damn luck."

He turned towards the corridor that led to their own rooms. "Sorry to leave you alone, but—"

"—think nothing of it, Doctor. I have much enjoyed our little talk today, and I know you have something you want to accomplish; we will talk later." Orphan returned to his seat and began to gaze into nothingness again.

DuQuesne nodded, then headed back to his cabin. *Time to start violating the very laws of physics!*

Chapter 36

Boy, do I ache everywhere *now.* She had suspected Vindatri's training regimen would be both mentally and physically demanding, but he seemed to be trying to exceed any of her expectations.

"You are not *focused*," Vindatri's voice came from behind her, as she continued to struggle up the gravelly hillside that kept sliding away beneath her feet, forging slowly, grimly towards a glittering golden pole that marked the finish of this course. This was at least the fourth simulated—or, possibly, real—environment the training had covered, and on the positive side it was neither freezing nor baking her, but the now-hundred-plus-meter fall waiting for her would be no fun at all.

Without so much as a *blink* she found herself halfway back down the hill. "Captain Austin, you keep drifting into thoughts of the training *as a thing.* You must clear your mind of concerns of the future or the weights of the past. Recite the phrases as I have taught them, *dwell* on those phrases and *only* on them."

Great, and all my progress of the last half-hour is wiped out just like that. With an effort she tried to clear her mind, but there were too many questions. "Vindatri, why—"

"I will answer your questions when you reach your goal, Captain Austin, and not the slightest fraction of a moment sooner. Neither ask nor think questions, only the words you have been taught."

Wu Kung, of course, was *already* at the goal post, sitting cross-legged and watching with obvious amusement. *Damned show-off. Of course, he's not being tested here either.*

291

She sighed, then stood still, digging her boots into the gravel until the movement stabilized—for the moment. Gray clouds drifted far above, threatening rain, as they had since they first came here. *Concentrate. Just the words as they were given me. Wirthshem, vanens, zofron, araga, kuten . . .*

She began the trek up the mountain again, the hissing rattle of stone and sand providing a monotonous yet ever-shifting background to the words echoing in her mind. *Mindogo, seipodon, geunate . . .*

Her thighs ached with the effort of forcing her feet, ankle-deep and more in the shifting, clutching detritus, but she forced any consideration of pain or exhaustion away. *Just the words, again; wirthshem, vanens . . .*

The rhythm of word and legs became unified, indistinguishable; even when she stumbled and slid, the nonsensical, mysterious words circled through her head; when the words threatened to blur together, the slow, steady rhythm of her legs forced them apart . . . *araga, kuten, mindogo, seipodon, geunate . . .*

Her head was bowed, focused only before her, watching the sand stream by, both dizzying and steadying, an eternal motion, backwards as she walked forwards, a treadmill of flowing earth. *Seipodon, geunate, wirthshem . . .*

Her boots struck something solid, so shockingly *still* that she stumbled, fell forward, threw out her hands to catch herself, and felt one close around something cold and smooth; she looked up and saw herself gripping a shaft of glittering golden metal.

She had reached the goal.

"Satisfactory for now, Captain," Vindatri said.

She was tempted to just collapse in a heap, but she knew her muscles would just stiffen up on her. She settled for leaning against the pole for a moment, then doing a slow, steady, *not* impeded walk on the grass that surrounded the pole. Wu Kung watched her with a faint smile. "So . . . you'll answer questions now?"

"Some, yes. How many depends on what they are."

"What was the point of this exercise? Most of the others I get, but this one—"

"Endurance and focus are vitally important in the use of the powers of Shadeweaver or Faith, or whatever it is you shall become," Vindatri said. "If you would use your powers in anything other than the comfort of your quarters, you must be able to speak the words in exhaustion, in fear, while under assault, and speak them, think them, *precisely.*"

"But I don't even know what they *mean.*"

Vindatri nodded. "The Arena will not translate them for you, no. You must learn their meaning by example—and then their meaning shall be what *you* put into them. True, your meaning and mine will likely be very close . . . but not identical. The same is inevitably true of the words themselves."

"You mean . . . I will not pronounce the names exactly the same as you do."

"Precisely correct, Captain. The Arena is, in some ways, startlingly tolerant of variation. While you could recognize, with the correct context, that the ritual of Shadeweaver and Faith were the same, you must admit that in many ways they sound not at all alike. If you believe the Arena is a great machine and these powers are merely its technology responding to commands, then this makes some sense; some sounds cannot even be *replicated* by all species, yet all species can be members of Shadeweaver or Faith; the Arena in this case is adjusting its control vocabulary to account for personal and species variation in pronunciation.

"If, on the other hand, you see something more supernatural in the powers, why then it depends more on how you and your spirit resonate with the powers, and in that case how you say it is not so important as whether you can accurately and reliably imagine and direct the shaping of the power into the results you desire.

"In either case, each . . . magician, priest, or operator, whatever you might call them . . . develops their own unique articulation of the magic or power—both in the words, and in the precise nature and capabilities of that power's expression. My attack utilizing the power of electricity, for example, would be clearly related to that of your earlier acquaintance Amas-Garao, but would at the same time be clearly distinct from the precise details of that attack."

That made a certain amount of sense, and explained why it wasn't something that could just be taught by reading a book or something similar. "Not all that different from other training I've gone through, I guess." Simgame training might not be, technically, *real*, but if you played at high "realism" settings, it sure *felt* real, and the experience was very, very convincing. Astrella's old Master had certainly put her through similarly arbitrary yet effective training to get her to master control of her inner talents. "So, could you show me your electrical attack? I'd like to see an example of these differences."

"Certainly." Vindatri rose to his full height, then looked across the valley. His arm came up and the finger pointed, and he spoke a word that she heard, simultaneously, as "thunder" and as "wirthshem."

Corona-violet motes formed in the air about the tree he had gestured towards, and seemed to be *drawn* into the tree as though they were iron filings and the tree a magnet. Blue-white sparks instantly writhed across the surface of the tree and it *exploded* in a blast of lightning and fire.

Wu Kung leapt to his feet. "That is impressive!"

"A trivial example, no more. Did you recognize the word spoken?"

"It was 'wirthshem,' yes?"

"Yes. Very well done."

"And Amas-Garao would have been using that word as well, I just couldn't hear it because I hadn't yet been told it."

"Precisely. Now . . ." He studied her intensely. ". . . you seemed almost on the verge of controlling the powers before, when I was still attempting to place a seal upon you. Shaping and controlling the energies on such an essential level is a *much* stronger power, one that many Shadeweavers or Initiate Guides do not learn for a long time indeed. Can you recall what you were doing? Do you have an inkling of *how* you were gaining control?"

She considered briefly whether she should answer, but again, the practicality of the situation was obvious. "It was Astrella. A character I played in a simgame. Your people have or had simgames, right?"

"A simulated environment entertainment? One in which you . . . assumed a role not your own?" Vindatri's half-visible face frowned. "Some such entertainments were used by children that I have known, but it was not a major pursuit."

"Well, it's a very common thing in our civilization." Arguing whether it was something for children or not would be pointless.

Vindatri stared at her silently for a few moments, then gave a fluttering motion she guessed was equivalent to a shrug. "Perhaps I should come to understand your people better, in order to better instruct you. Wu Kung, do you play these simgames?"

Wu blinked. "I have not had much need to do so! My life has been too busy."

Dangerous ground there. Wu lived his life . . . not in what we'd call our universe. She wasn't sure how to divert from the subject, though; any action could draw attention to the fact that there was something she wanted hidden or forgotten.

Fortunately, it seemed Vindatri was more interested in a general survey. "What of your other companions? The ones who traveled here in your initial venture?"

"Well . . . I know DuQuesne's played some, he mentioned it. Carl definitely played a lot, we even teamed in a couple adventures. Same with Steve, though he was really into more high adventure with less realistic sims. Simon . . . yes, he played some, he had a sword he replicated based on some he played, so I know he did. Gabrielle played when we were younger, but she got pretty busy with her work for the CSF. I don't *know* for sure, but I'd bet that Tom did all sorts of complex adventure games—he was a transcender before we ended up in the Arena. Laila . . . didn't know her well enough before to say."

"Still, that does seem to agree with your thesis. Most of your companions, of—I would presume—diverse interests and responsibilities on your mission—participated in these not-real adventure entertainments. Very interesting. Might I inquire as to *why* it is so?"

Ariane found herself momentarily at a loss. *I was never really introspective until I got stuck with this job. Simgames were just stuff* everyone *did.*

But thinking now in a more historical perspective—and with the examples of other species . . . "I can't say for sure, but I guess it's that until we ran into the Arena, we thought we were pretty much at the peak of possible development. Oh, there was still basic science research going on—being done by people who thought that kind of stuff was fun—but no one *had* to work any more. So if you wanted risk, effort, reward—but not to actually get yourself potentially killed for real—simgames were the best way to go."

"I see. Yes, that type of . . . decadence, complacence, comfort, whatever one might call it, is not unknown among other species. Perhaps I have not paid sufficient attention to these things." Vindatri made a sound translated as a chuckle. "The mysteries of my fellow creatures are as vast as the Arena itself, after all."

"People are *always* a mystery," Wu Kung agreed. "At least until you see them in the Two Mirrors."

Vindatri glanced towards Wu, and Ariane raised her eyebrow. "Two Mirrors, Wu?"

"It is said that one can distinguish a person's true self clearly only when that person is seen in two circumstances; the first when he has all that he desires, and power over all he surveys, and the second when he has nothing, and a desperate need for all things. The Mirror of Power and the Mirror of Weakness reflect our true selves for all to see."

"That's . . . pretty deep, actually, Wu," Ariane said, and saw Vindatri make an approving gesture. "Instead of 'power corrupts,' you're saying 'power reveals' . . ."

". . . and so does desperation. What you're willing to do, or not do, when desperate, and what you will do when you're free to do anything without consequence. What will you excuse in the name of expedience, as Sha Wujing once said, and what will you forget in the face of complete freedom?"

"There is some wisdom in this," Vindatri said. "However, rarely will one have the chance to, as you put it, see a person reflected in both mirrors." He surveyed Ariane with a speculative air. "But we have work to do. I will meditate upon what else I might have to learn about you in order to properly instruct you. But now I would see how far your . . . game has taught you in your proper course.

"Return yourself to the state of mind you were in at the end of your Release, when I was trying to build the Training Seal about your power, when you nearly controlled it. Find that state of mind, that focus, and then see if you can use it along with the knowledge of the meaning of *wirthshem.*"

"My state of mind was mostly desperation right there," Ariane said wryly. "But no, I understand."

She closed her eyes as she had during that burning, ecstatic, terrified moment. *Astrella. Astrella with her mentor.*

She could *feel* that moment again, and realized—for a moment disrupting her meditation—that her surroundings were near-perfect for recalling it. For Astrella had been seated on the grass, high in the mountains, lowering clouds above, her teacher speaking . . .

Reach within, heed the rhythm of your heart, the flow of air inward and outward, Master Macha had said. *The water in the clouds falls to the stream, the cup is dipped into the stream, the water passes through us and is returned to the world. The winds of the world pass through the storm and the day and the night and we breathe them in, and return them, too, to the world. Hear the flow of water, know the world's heart is beating. Feel the caress of the wind, know the Earth is breathing. Your strength comes from the Earth, from its air and water . . . and its spirit. Reach out. Think of the world. Think of its place within the vastness of the universe. You are a part of that universe.*

She could picture Astrella's world as Astrella had, first envisioning the hillside on which she sat, then rising above, to see vast mountains, rivers, sensing somehow their flow, *seeing* the winds and storms gathering as her spirit touched them.

You are part of the universe, and it is a part of you. Your soul is as infinite as Creation, and you encompass each other. Feel your soul as the cosmos, the cosmos as your soul, and if you can but sense it, make that spark of Creation live within you, then you will know that you can do anything. Then, and only then, will you be able to raise your hand and spirit and change the very shape of the world to your will.

Ariane saw Astrella's entire world, a blue-green-brown-white globe, below, and felt herself trembling on the edge of understanding.

But . . . she thought. *But . . . I am Ariane, not Astrella, and I am not seated on her world. I am in the Arena.*

With that thought she suddenly remembered, recalled that moment of Awakening—the transcendent, terrifying instant when she *SAW* the universes, both of them, and something perhaps even *beyond* both the normal continuum and the Arena. She *looked* at that moment, looked at it fully, for the first time since it had happened, and knew it was utterly beyond her ability to understand.

And yet . . .

And yet . . .

She thought a part of her *did* understand, because she found herself seeing Earth's Sphere, as though she were rising above it, past the blazing Luminaire, seeing vague, distant dots that might have been ships or creatures, storms the size of the Solar System, other Spheres, a vision expanding at frightening, *exhilarating* speed to encompass more, an entire *Spherepool*, an artificial galaxy turning with infinite majesty within a space greater than a human mind should even contemplate, and yet she now grasped the vision, forced herself to view it, to rise farther, higher, seeing a dozen, a hundred, a thousand, millions, *billions* of Spherepools in the dream-cloud lit expanses of the Arena.

For one instant she even thought she passed *beyond* the Arena, and there was a light and a *presence* that watched her with apprehension and hope . . . and other Presences, far, far beyond, filled with malice and hunger.

But at the same time she suddenly *felt* herself, her heart, her breath, and somehow within also the motions and power of the Arena, as though the awful grandeur of the construct dwelt within her very soul, and she opened her eyes, raising her hand, pointing across the valley. "*Wirthshem*," she said.

Blue-white electricity spat crackling from her hand, tingling like the electric-eel implants she was already familiar with, and with a peal of earshattering thunder a bolt of lightning split a massive tree like an axe wielded by a giant.

Wu and Vindatri leapt back, and she vaguely heard a disbelieving, alien curse from beneath the hood. The echoes resounded through the mountains and Ariane lowered her hand, feeling a grin spreading across her face.

Vindatri turned slowly to look at her. "A . . . *spectacular* success, Captain Austin." His translated voice was filled with surprise. "I had expected—at most—a flicker of power."

"*I* expected more," Wu Kung said. "You said she was already starting to control the power before you sealed it. Ariane is *special*."

"So it would seem," Vindatri said, speculation replacing startlement in his voice. "Perhaps you *will* learn enough in time, Captain. Certainly it seems you already know—or sense—a great deal that I had not expected."

His half-seen eyes glinted, and Ariane was suddenly seized with the conviction that he had seen far more than just a lightning bolt. "Tell me, Captain Austin, as much as you can, exactly what you thought, what you saw, in your meditations. I am curious as to how you called this forth."

She hesitated. *Not sure I want to tell him* everything. *There's possible hints there of other things that—*

"Come, Captain. Understanding how you reached this point will be invaluable in knowing how quickly and well I can bring you along the rest of the path to the knowledge you seek." His voice was warm, reasonable, echoing in her head with a strange urgency. "Surely you want to make progress as quickly as possible. Come, tell me everything."

She blinked. *Of course I should tell him. How else will he know what it is that* works. *Why was I hesitating?* She didn't dwell on the last question; it wasn't important any more. "You're right. If I don't work with you, this will never get done. I was remembering what I had done before, and . . ."

She was vaguely aware of Sun Wu Kung's narrow gaze, but as she spoke and Vindatri continued his gentle yet insistent questioning, he, too, seemed to relax . . .

Chapter 37

"Only three hundred?" Simon found he could not keep dismay from his voice, and heard it echoed by the others in the conference room.

Relgof spread his hands wide in apology. "Simon, Laila, Carl . . . my friends, I truly wish it was more. But you understand, the Arena does not allow us to move military personnel and materiel through Nexus Arena, and it is, of course, *quite* cognizant of the fact that as your allies we are now involved in your war, and our ship movements will not be innocent. Thus we have had to very rapidly research connections between your *other* Sky Gates and those of our various Spheres."

He spread his hands again. "Unfortunately, given the time constraints before the confrontation, three hundred warships— perhaps three hundred and fifty—are as many as we will be able to move to your Sphere in that time. None of our other resources will be able to reach appropriate Sky Gate connections on such short notice. Had we even a month or two longer, it would be vastly different, but as it is . . . this is what we offer."

Simon closed his eyes and forced disappointment away. "Never mind, Rel. Three hundred is still more than ten times as many as we have currently." He wondered how many they might be able to "upgun" with primaries.

"Perhaps—*perhaps*, I say—this may not be as small a force as you believe," Oscar Naraj said.

"What do you mean, Oscar?" Oasis asked.

"I mean that what is *important* about this confrontation is that we

301

convince the Molothos that this war is one they *cannot* afford, yes? And while three hundred vessels is, undoubtedly, paltry opposition to their forces of four thousand and more, it is the *nature* of those three hundred, I believe, which can give our adversaries pause. If they see that these are *Analytic* vessels, and not merely vessels *of* the Analytic but crewed and operated *by* the Analytic, then they will know that in pressing the attack they will be irrevocably declaring war upon another Great Faction—and, if I understand the relations between Factions aright, yours is one of the Great Factions they have actually been at some pains to *not* offend, yes?"

Relgof flip-flopped his filter-beard in assent. "I see your point, Oscar! Indeed, the Analytic has generally been less ill-used by the Molothos—or other hostile factions—as we are seekers, and suppliers, of knowledge, and thus both less directly dangerous and more useful than others. The Molothos are closest to conflict with the Blessed To Serve, for rather obvious reasons, and the Vengeance, for other reasons. Yes, they will certainly want to weigh carefully the potential cost of initiating war with the Analytic!"

"If that is the case," Laila said, with hope animating her features, "perhaps we can avoid this entire conflict by notifying the Molothos of our alliance."

A sudden flare of elation and optimism was crushed when Simon saw Relgof gesture a negation. "I am afraid not, my friends. There will be no communication between the Molothos Embassy and the fleet now en route; no means of communication exists that can reach a vessel in the Deeps, unless it be something of the powers of the Shadeweavers or Faith. They will not learn of this until they face our combined fleets—and we will not arrive at your system until very, very nearly the time the conflict begins."

Carl sighed. "That sucks. Okay, I guess it's time we asked your opinion: should we just drop it? Back our ships out, hide 'em elsewhere, evacuate the surface, let 'em take the Upper Sphere?"

"Absolutely not," Relgof said without hesitation. "Even if you have additional Spheres I am not aware of, and thus would not be entirely cut off from Arenaspace itself, you cannot afford to in essence yield your upper Home Sphere to the Molothos. If they establish and secure that area—even for a matter of a few days or weeks—they will first be able to assemble a much larger force to *hold* your Upper Sphere.

Moreover, they will then be able to assemble a truly immense force to transition a relatively short distance from your home system."

"When you say 'truly immense,'" Laila said, "just how 'immense' are you talking?"

"In truth, I would have to make a guess," Relgof admitted, "since there are no *surviving* witnesses to a Molothos full-scale assault on a normal-space solar system, and their full resources are naturally a matter of great secrecy; in honesty, there are very few survivors of far smaller Molothos assaults. But as they have done this many times in their history, and have the resources of many, many thousands of Spheres, plus an uncounted number of colonized Upper Spheres . . . millions of vessels, at the least, and those carefully tailored for normal-space assault."

Millions of vessels. At least *millions.* Used as he was to cosmic numbers, Simon still could not quite get his head around the idea of that many military vessels. "Could we not—with the help of the Analytic—take our Sphere back before that becomes an issue?"

"It would be a *tremendously* difficult proposition," Relgof said bleakly. "They will control, and have completely fortified, the Sky Gates. Sending anything through without the proper codes would result in utter destruction, and we have no way of knowing proper Molothos security codes. Even if we *did,* that would only give us a moment in which to act, and I cannot imagine winning such a battle easily. It would require us to have a huge numeric advantage over our adversaries, and while I have convinced the Analytic to provide ships for this first battle, committing tens of thousands of ships—and their crews—for a battle to *re-take* a Sphere—"

"—will be a *much* harder sell," Oasis finished. "We understand, Doc."

"Then," Laila said, with a glance at Carl to confirm her decision, "we have no real choice. We may be outnumbered and outgunned, but we will make the Molothos pay *heavily* for this attack, and—perhaps—they will decide to stop the attack when they realize we are truly in full alliance with the Analytic."

"I believe you do not have a choice, no," Relgof agreed. "And in personal honesty, I do not think that the Faction of Humanity is the sort that tends to retreat when confronted."

"Nope," Oasis said. "We'd rather go down fighting."

"You said it will be a near thing to get your ships there, Rel," Simon said. "How near?"

Relgof looked at them, moving his filter-beard in an inquisitive manner. "I confess I do not understand how it is *possible* that any of you could even *know of* this attack force, let alone its composition and course, but given the value of this intelligence I will not press you for its source." His gaze halted and lingered penetratingly on Simon for an instant, and Simon suspected that Relgof was remembering his "luck" in finding the materials he needed in the Analytic's vast archives.

"Returning to the question . . . Well, partly that depends on whether our friends the Molothos decide to change their speed in the remaining time or not. If they were to suddenly accelerate to full speed, we would arrive too late. However, your information on current conditions indicates that the clouds around your Sphere are unusually dense right now, which should preclude any high speed approaches until they reach approximately fifteen thousand kilometers from your Sphere—perhaps even somewhat closer, if they do not detect any scouts."

His voice became softer, abstracted. "They will assume they have surprise and will not want to jeopardize that surprise by demonstrating high-energy signatures that might be detected. Now . . ." He paused, looking around, and a low laugh came from Relgof. "I apologize; I am analyzing the problem out loud. In short, if things proceed as you and I would expect . . . our few hundred vessels will be ready to transition a day or so before the battle begins."

Blast. Not nearly long enough to equip more than one or two of them with primaries. "Well . . . just make sure they are ready as soon as possible."

"I will attend to it *personally*, Simon."

Simon found himself staring at his alien friend. "Dr. Rel, you aren't—"

"Certainly I am. There will be no better way to *prove* our alliance to you than for me, myself, to transmit the Analytic's demands for the Molothos to stand down." He laughed anew. "Ahh, Simon, if only you could see your faces! I have learned much about reading your body and face-language, and I see I have managed to surprise you all!"

Laila gave her own short laugh. "You have. After what you told us about basic risk aversion—"

"*Most* precisely true, my friends, yet I will not risk much. I will remain on the rearmost vessel, and if and when the battle appears to be becoming too threatening, I will retreat. Not that I am unwilling to fight when necessary, understand," he gave another flip-flop smile, "but I think the Faction of Humanity would like me to remain at the head of the Analytic for as long as possible."

"That we do, and yes, please retreat as soon as you feel you need to," Simon said.

"Then it is agreed. I am sorry it comes to this, my friends, but at the same time, what an *opportunity*!"

"Excuse me?"

"As I said, there are vanishingly few survivors of military conflict with the Molothos. As with most of us, they prefer—"

"—curb-stomping to a fair fight," Oasis said bluntly. "So usually they totally wipe out their opposition."

"That translated phrase was rather vivid. Yes, exactly. So to be in a position to actually *witness* such a military action, with virtual assurance of safety? This is a wonderful chance to expand knowledge of a topic which is usually terribly perilous to pursue."

Simon sighed, but felt an involuntary smile on his face. "I suppose so, but I confess I will not be nearly as impartial an observer as you."

"Perhaps not, but—rest assured, Simon—I will be far from impartial! The Molothos are no one's friends, and you are most assuredly ours." He rose from his seat. "I must be off. If I am to lead our forces, I must depart soon to join them."

Everyone else rose. "Dr. Relgo." Laila said, "Thank you again, and convey the most heartfelt thanks of Humanity to the Analytic once more. If we have any chance of stopping this assault, it will be through your aid."

"Say nothing more of it," Relgof said. "Alas, our hopes all depend on one, rather fragile, frond of hope."

"No kidding," Oasis said, and her voice was grim. "Our whole plan depends on the Molothos deciding to be *reasonable*."

"You make a grave mistake, Oasis Abrams," Relgof said to Oasis.

"What?"

"The Molothos are nearly *always* reasonable . . . from *their* point of view. And as I noted, they always prefer to deal from a position of overwhelming power—as do essentially all of us in the Arena.

"No, it is not their *reasonableness* we depend on. It is their *empathy.*"

Simon stared at Relgof. "But they *have* no empathy."

"A pretty conundrum then, yes? But no, they have empathy. A minuscule amount, true, but they *can* translate their feelings and compare them to others."

"Why do we depend on that, though?" Carl asked in a puzzled tone. "I'd think it's just a rational—"

"*Rational*, my friend, is often very much dependent on the perspective of the one doing the evaluation. To the Molothos, the thought that the Analytic would truly put its full force behind Humanity? That one of the Great Factions would risk war with the *most* vicious and almost eternally victorious Molothos for the sake of First Emergents barely a year present in the Arena? This is not *rational* in any sense."

Relgof made an elaborate shrug with shoulders and arms. "And in truth? It is *not* rational, especially without the information as to *why* we have chosen to ally with Humanity at this time. Even *with* that, this is at least as much a choice of *emotion*, of doing what is *right*, of standing with the weak against the strong, as it is a rational choice to defend our interests.

"So in the end, my friends, we depend on the ability of the Molothos to understand that even the Analytic can choose to take a stand on *principle*—because we *feel* it is right. If they do not . . . then they will press the attack, sure that we will retreat as soon as their dominance becomes clear, and only realize *after* our ships are engaged with theirs—*after* the moment has passed—that we were, in fact, utterly serious."

"*Kuso*," Simon muttered.

Chapter 38

Wu Kung had a problem. He had a *big* problem, and he found himself pacing the dark hallway outside of their living quarters, trying to work it out.

He was *pretty* sure that this Vindatri, whatever he was, had been . . . influencing Ariane. Her scent had changed more than once in ways that basically didn't make sense otherwise. Caution and suspicion had faded away without anything being *said* that should have caused that. At least he didn't *think* so.

The problem was that even people like Ariane sometimes had kind of complicated motivations and made their decisions in ways that were . . . well, not the way that made *sense* to him. *Diplomacy, doublethinking, whatever, it makes my head ache.*

Normally, of course, that wouldn't be a problem. Someone tampering with his mistress, his *responsibility*? He would break their heads! Simple as that!

This Vindatri, though . . . he had a lot of fancy magician's tricks, that much was clear. Wu hadn't forgotten the humiliation of being separated from Ariane, the way in which Vindatri's power had caused him to change direction and position without so much as an instant's pause. Attack someone like that, you could find that you had just leaped out a random window, or even swing your staff to find your friend's head in front of it!

If only I was . . . really *Sun Wu Kung, and not just the best imitation some crazy people created.* Then *things would be different.* There were demons back home that had similar powers, and he knew how to deal with them. But here? No. No, much as he *hated* the idea, he had to try to be subtle, control his impulses, *think*.

He had the feeling Vindatri had been trying to influence *him* too, but, like DuQuesne, he had the same Hyperion protections. The . . . shifts had been subtle, enough to make him uncomfortable, and then they'd stopped, so he guessed Vindatri had decided not to push it unless Sun Wu Kung caused a problem.

The obvious thing to do was to talk to DuQuesne. If there was *anyone* he trusted to make tough decisions in the middle of dangerous territory, it was DuQuesne; Marc reminded him of Sha Wujing, and that was a high compliment.

Unfortunately, Vindatri was a problem there, too. Wizards like him could scry everywhere, maybe hear anything their name was mentioned in. DuQuesne called it 'bugging' and 'security monitors' and whatever, but no matter the name it amounted to a wizard seeing and hearing things inside locked rooms.

Wu Kung suddenly smiled; a spectator might not have found the expression comforting, for it revealed his fangs fully and his green eyes glinted dangerously. Why, this was *familiar!* This was a problem they'd *all* faced before. *Hyperion* had used dozens of those AI-familiar-spirit things to watch everything going on. Orphan and Ariane, they didn't know about that—even Ariane just knew the *story*, she hadn't *been* there.

But DuQuesne *had*. And that meant . . .

DuQuesne opened the door almost instantly on Wu's soft knock; Wu could sense that the big man had just awakened, but his eyes were clear and alert. "Wu? What's wrong? It's two in the morning, or whatever the equivalent is here."

"I just needed to talk to someone who would understand, DuQuesne, and you're the only one who will," he said. He tilted his head at *just* the right angle, moved a finger *exactly* this way.

DuQuesne gave a loud sigh, but Wu Kung saw his eyes narrow the tiniest bit. His body posture shifted the tiniest bit, and Wu could read the signal as well as though DuQuesne had spoken. *That bad, huh? Okay, come on.* "All right, Wu, come in, sit down."

"It's about Ariane," he began.

What followed was something that gave Wu a headache. He could only *do* this by following the teachings of some of his hardest masters, the ones that taught how to separate actions of mind and body and then bring them together, to make the flow of combat something that could be observed, dispassionately, at the same time as the observer was involved *in* the combat. He and DuQuesne carried on a conversation with *two* levels, often cueing the silent conversation from words or hints in the audible one, but with very different meaning.

The surface conversation was about Wu's—very real—frustration with being a "bodyguard" who knew his charge was constantly in the presence of a being that even Sun Wu Kung didn't think he could beat; this was *such* a by-the-Heavens *foreign* thought to him that his distress with it was completely real and honest. That was what made Wu pretty sure he could get away with this late-night deception; the surface was still real and a problem.

The other, hidden, conversation used a code and method of conversation that he hadn't used for over fifty years, but that came back with need and memory. Technically it wasn't words, and it was possible to misinterpret, but to Wu Kung it was a code of battle, the language of tactics and strategy, and for him it might as well have been a conversation.

"Okay, Wu," DuQuesne said. "That was damn good thinking on your part, treating this like Hyperion. Probably the best thing you could've done. So what's the real problem?"

"I think Vindatri is playing with Ariane's mind, DuQuesne. She is changing her attitudes towards him without a reason I can see."

A pause, during which the surface conversation continued. "Yeah, not surprising. Even if he had connections to the Shadeweavers some time back, he's definitely not one of them now, so he's not restricted."

"You *expected* this? And did not warn me?"

"Unless you're thinking hard about it—like now—you're not subtle, Wu. We didn't want you suspicious any more than you are naturally. The more Vindatri underestimates us, the better. Is Vindatri actually teaching her stuff? She *says* so but she's also claiming she's not far enough along to be safe demonstrating it, so I've only got her word on it."

"Oh, he is! He is a hard old master, and I have seen his like before. But yes, she is learning, and faster than he expects. Why? We should still not let him—"

"Damp it down, Wu, you're getting excited and your surface conversation's getting disjointed."

Wu paused, focused on continuing the discussion of how to deal with a seemingly invincible foe, or at least how to deal with having to trust said possible enemy around Ariane. *DuQuesne is right. I have to keep this flowing perfectly. Maybe Vindatri isn't listening . . . but if he is, he must be as completely fooled as the Hyperion designers were.* "Sorry, DuQuesne. But you are *letting* him affect Ariane's *mind*?"

A gesture that conveyed an apologetic sigh. "Wu . . . yes. And aside from saying that Ariane knew this and we had a way to keep Vindatri from guessing, I'm not telling you any more right now. Will you trust me on this? We *have* to let Vindatri teach her, even if he's trying to mindtwist her for now. Trust me that I know it's happening, and that I know a way to *fix* it afterwards. I swear it, Wu, I can and I will fix it. Will you trust me?"

That question lodged a sliver of ice in Wu Kung's heart. Ariane Austin was *his* charge. He had ridden the sound-breaking back of *Thilomon* and fallen through the endless skies of the Arena, and then summoned an army of sky-monsters to come to her aid.

An army I still owe a debt to, and I must find a way to pay it, he reminded himself.

But the truth remained that *he* was responsible for Ariane, she was *his* to protect . . . *and she is so very like Sanzo was*, his innermost voice whispered. How could he trust her protection to *anyone*, trust her very mind's safety to someone who thought it was worth risking that mind being *changed*?

Yet . . .

. . . this was Marc C. DuQuesne. This was the man who had entered their world and torn the veil away, and with K and Maria-Susanna and Tarell and Erision had led the way to freeing all those caught in the illusions of the Hyperion Designers.

This was Marc, who had understood and let him retreat, go back to the illusion and the family within that illusion. The same man who had apologized for coming to him even when Wu Kung had hidden for *fifty years, five decades*, from the truth that had cost him so much . . . and that yet had saved him, too.

And this was the man who had shown him the Arena . . . and told him to protect Ariane in the first place. The man who, he knew, loved Ariane as deeply as anyone could; Wu Kung could smell his devotion and focus towards the Captain and her well-being . . . and his anger at having to allow anyone to tamper with her in even the smallest way.

I owe him. Sha Wujin said so. Sanzo would be furious *at me for doubting him.*

As he thanked DuQuesne for listening, in the surface conversation, he answered the deeper question. "Yes, DuQuesne . . . Marc. I will trust you, even though . . . though it is very hard."

"Thank you, Wu. I know how hard it is for you to take this kind of risk, and believe you me, I *hate* doing it. But if it helps . . . it's also on her direct orders I'm doing this."

That *did* help; if Ariane knew the risks and had *ordered* it . . . well, he didn't *like* it, but she had already made clear that *she* was the Captain and even her bodyguard would, by the *Gods,* follow orders! He smiled and rose. "Thanks again, DuQuesne," he said aloud.

"No problem, Wu. I'm just as worried, but we're stuck, so we have to just accept the situation. Honestly, he's way out of our league, and we knew that coming here. But if you have to talk it out, I'm always here." Marc grinned. "But next time, could you wait until morning?"

"Ha! My brooding knows no hours, DuQuesne!" He waved and left, heading back towards his own cabin next to Ariane's.

All right, Vindatri. We all know what you are doing, and DuQuesne has a plan. I will wait.

But one day, I will *break your head for what you are doing to my* Captain!

Chapter 39

Reflexively Ariane dove aside as the swarm of violet-blue electric motes formed about her, barely evading as the electrical attack coalesced where she had been standing.

"Your ability to *dodge* is not being tested here, Captain Austin," Vindatri said with a condescending edge to his voice. "You were supposed to *defend* yourself."

"Sorry, Vindatri. I'm not used to just standing in one spot to take what people throw at me."

"I would be surprised if anyone *was* used to it. Possibly excepting your bodyguard, who seems positively amused by your difficulty in performing this apparently simple task."

She glanced over to see Wu Kung laughing from his spot atop a high boulder, overlooking the meadow she and Vindatri were practicing in. "Aren't you supposed to be ready to dive in and protect me?"

"Not when you are training! Then it is important you get hit many times, until you know how to *stop* someone from hitting you!"

She grinned and sighed. "All right, let's try this again."

She braced herself, tried to focus on not moving but defending. "Ready!"

Vindatri clenched his fist and slammed it outward, as though hammering the side of an invisible wall. "*Geunate!*"

Transparent ripples in the air, the shockwaves streaked for her, hammering the grasses flat as they came. She repressed the instinctive urge to dodge, but realized too late that she had failed to focus on the word of defense—

The impact tumbled her over and over across the meadow, skidding her through grasses, sending insectoid creatures flying or scuttling away; she finally fetched up against and partly inside a large and prickly bush.

"Ugh," she said, spitting out grass that had somehow ended up in her mouth, and peeling away the thorny branches. *At least my uniform's pretty good at protecting me from the minor annoyances.* She suspected that if she summoned that strange robe-like uniform she'd gained upon her Ascendance, it would protect her even more, but the point of the training was, again, not to demonstrate that there was armor that could protect her. "Well, I stayed in one place!"

"Until the concussion blast hit, yes," Vindatri conceded. Wu Kung was busy laughing again.

"When I *succeed* at this I'm going to have some more questions."

"By all means. I expect many questions and answers in our training. I am, myself, learning much. To salve what I suspect is a somewhat bruised pride, I can tell you that most Arena inhabitants, from almost all other species, would have a far harder time than you of standing deliberately before one such as myself and accepting the attacks directed at them."

Ariane didn't doubt it; the risk-aversion that was normal in the Arena would probably make this kind of training seem even crazier than it did to the average human. "All right, let's try this one again."

In succession she found herself hammered by fire (*vanens*), and a screaming sandstorm torn from the earth itself (*araga*), and struck by a blast of bitter cold that left her momentarily coated with ice (*zofron*). The first one she had braced herself for but still found she couldn't focus her mind and speak the word fast enough. For the second, the memory of the prior two blasts were enough to make her dodge, and the last one she managed to half-speak the word before the ice hammered her down.

"Okay, that is *it*," she said, gritting her teeth to keep them from chattering. "I know you've cut these things way down so they're not killing me, but it's really starting to piss me off."

"Anger is a weapon that cuts both ways," Vindatri observed. "But there is no reason for you to be weakened during the practice." His hands gestured outward as though welcoming a friend, and she heard an unknown word wrapped within the concept that translated as "Healing."

Sparkling white light enveloped her and she felt warmth spread across her skin, a tingle across her face and hands and rippling across her body. As it cleared, she realized she no longer felt cold, nor the tightness of burns across her hands and face, or the raw scrapes from the sandstorm, nor did she feel the enervation of multiple trials with apparent life-threatening powers. She felt as strong and alert as she had when she began.

"That . . . is really impressive. I have to admit it is hard *not* to think of this as magic."

"Especially as there are those of us who wield the power and believe that it *is*, in fact, magic," agreed Vindatri. "I do not . . . but I admit that I might well be wrong. Are you prepared?"

She took a few breaths, then focused once more on her experiences training as Astrella. *She could do this. So can I. I played her. I was her, in a lot of ways.*

Without warning, Vindatri's arm slashed outward. "*Kuten!*"

Ariane stood firm as the miniature tornado screamed towards her, and brought up her own arms, crossed in an "X" configuration. "*Sonderan!*"

The whirlwind ran headlong into an invisible barrier, a wall of absolute force that barred its passage, disrupted its swirling currents, and turned it to a breath of harmless wind. In the same moment, Ariane felt that same momentary sensation of elevation, of observing not just this event from this one perspective, but the Arena and beyond, from within and without herself at the same time.

"*Magnificent!*" Vindatri shouted. "*That* was what we sought, Captain! Well it is to be able to send forth destruction, but one must needs also be able to ward *against* such attacks."

She felt herself smiling like an idiot, both with triumph and relief. "Well, *thank* you. I'm glad I was able to pull it off!"

"I had no doubt that you *would*, in time. My question was whether you would surprise me again, as Orphan promised you would."

"And did I?"

A hint of a smile under the hood. "You did indeed, despite the fact that I have been revising my estimates of your capability upward. I was certain that you would not succeed in an effective block until tomorrow, at the earliest. So a rest, now, and ask questions. You will of course need more practice—I expect you will take many more hard lessons before such a shield becomes swift and instinctive, as it must be to be truly useful—but you have had quite a triumph."

"Great." She sat down and pulled out a jerky stick and bit into it. "So tell me . . . where do these words *come* from? I mean, is everyone limited to the . . . well, effects that are known to their masters, or do people invent their own?"

"A most penetrating question. Many of them are, as you say, handed down through the generations, from master to pupil and thence to theirs. But the repertoire of an individual can be quite different from that of others of their discipline. The Faith claim to discover more of the powers, the 'blessings of the Voidbuilders,' through meditation and inspiration. If you have the cynical interpretation of things, then the Arena favors the existence of the Faith and thus plays the part of their deities, imparting occasional tidbits of control code to them as needed.

"Shadeweavers research ancient records, especially searching for hints of words that may be Voidbuilder in origin (for those with the same material and realistic perceptions), or that may be remnants of other powerful wizards' work (for those who believe in the magic).

"And all of us sometimes attempt to combine the words we know, or test the variation of pronunciation or even the changing of words while focusing upon desired effects. The latter is rarely effective, but when it *does* work the individual is rewarded with knowledge of a capability that others do not have."

"So it *is* possible to just invent one on your own. The system isn't locked down and inflexible."

"If it is a mere—pardon me for the term—mechanism, it is quite flexible and tolerant. Presumably the . . . clearance, so to speak, granted by the ritual is something very advanced, permitting the user to do many things forbidden to the ordinary inhabitants of the Arena."

She considered. "So tell me something: if someone like you *wanted* to, could you do something like make a nuclear power plant or an AI work in the Arena?"

Vindatri considered. "I *believe* that would be possible. I have never attempted to do so, nor do I know of any who have, but I think that it would be within the power of an Initiate Guide or Shadeweaver of sufficient skill and knowledge."

So the Minds were probably right, she thought. Their all-or-nothing attempt to abduct her and learn about the powers locked within her *had* been likely to give them just the advantage they had wanted.

Vindatri had been studying her with a speculative air. "I sense something more than mere intellectual interest. Is this a subject that actually has come up in some way?"

Vaguely she thought she should consider not answering, but she heard her voice replying, "Well . . . yes. A while ago the Blessed To Serve basically abducted me, and it seemed their plan was to bring me to the Minds, who would try to release and then study the power locked inside me by the Shadeweavers and the Faith. If it hadn't been for Orphan, DuQuesne, and Simon—and Wu—they'd have gotten away with it, too."

"A fortunate thing that they did not! I do not care at all for the thought of the Minds of the Blessed able to function within the Arena."

"Gives me the cold chills, actually. It worked out okay, but that was a close call."

She noticed Sun Wu Kung was oddly quiet, but Vindatri spoke before she could think about what that might mean.

"I of course know Orphan, and have begun to know your friends DuQuesne and Wu Kung, but I know little of this 'Simon.' You have mentioned him before, and the way you speak of him seems to indicate he is someone of importance."

She shook her head, laughing. "Importance? If it weren't for Simon, none of us would be here."

"Indeed? How so?"

"He *invented* the Sandrisson Drive," she said, hearing again that strange babel of other names that echoed around the stardrive concept. "Invented it, tested it, and then assembled the crew of the *Holy Grail*—including me—to do a full-scale test."

"One of the *inventors* came with his invention? Rare indeed! And here, in the Arena? Does he remain a figure of importance for your Faction?"

"He and DuQuesne are my main advisors," she answered. *And maybe more. This will be confusing when DuQuesne and I get back, but I'm sure we'll work it out somehow.*

A very faint twinge of caution sounded from some deep, vague depths within her, warning her that there might be things about

Simon she should avoid. *Oh, yeah. Don't talk about his special new talent. But other than that, I don't think there's anything terribly unusual to hide . . .*

Once more, Wu Kung was strangely silent, as she and Vindatri continued talking about Simon and the rest of her crew.

Chapter 40

So, does it work?

An image appeared in his mind of a surprised and gratified Orphan. *Dr. DuQuesne, it works magnificently. You have designed this to integrate well with my built-in headware—which is, I would think, rather different from your own.*

DuQuesne smiled to himself, apparently absorbed in examining structural and electronic components in a far corridor of Halintratha. *I got a pretty good look at your interfaces and protocols when we were traveling together on Zounin-Ginjou the first time. Glad to know I got it right.*

And you are certain that Vindatri cannot detect this communication?

Nothing's certain, Orphan. But if we don't get a real rude shock in the next few minutes, I'm willing to bet a hell of a lot that he can't detect it unless he gets real suspicious and starts looking for something off-kilter.

And what is the range for these communicators? At the moment, of course, we are scarcely a few meters apart.

DuQuesne frowned absently as he noticed a particular type of structure. It struck him that there was, impossibly, something *familiar* about parts of Halintratha, and he couldn't quite place it. *Range? Can't be sure in this crazy place, but I'd expect at least a thousand kilometers. Back where . . . well, where they originated from, they'd have gotten a lot more than that, but I'd put money down on a thousand kilometers as a minimum.*

The corridor opened up into a vast space, dark, with faint echoes diminishing into unknowable distances. Vague, hulking forms of immobile machinery and walls of armor were just visible at the edges of their lights.

"Truly, the size of Halintratha impresses me anew with each visit," Orphan said aloud. "I have never seen this region of it before."

"Not surprising. The thing's the size of a small planet, and hollow, with decks mostly on a generally humanish size. You could spend a dozen lifetimes exploring it and never have seen a thousandth of the things it holds."

That conversation suddenly made him flash back to his earliest days in the Arena, stuck in the vast silent emptiness of their Sphere. *My GOD*, he thought, making sure the transceiver was off. *My God, that's it. Halintratha, at least this part of it . . . it feels like the deserted, abandoned layer of our Sphere. A huge maze of ancient machines and walls and parks and Klono-knows-what-all, hidden between the inner wall of our Harbor and the lit, "alive" layers of the Sphere that connect to the Inner and Outer Gateways.*

He looked back at the walls and their dead, enigmatic panels. *Looks like the stuff we found down there, too. What does it mean, I wonder? Is Vindatri connected somehow to our system? Did he build it? Did he build this, or is this something he found?*

Once more, the Arena's key characteristic was asserting itself: replacing every answer with about a dozen questions.

Orphan's transmitted voice was in his head again. *How, might I ask, do these devices work?*

You can ask, *but I don't see you offering anything* nearly *big enough to make that question one I want to answer.* Not that he *could* answer it, in detail. Oh, he could explain how it worked in the same terms he and Rich would've described it back in their Hyperion world, but here in the Arena, that description would sound like first-class bafflegab, nothing more. He just knew he *could* pull off those tricks here, somehow, and the communicator proved he was right.

Absolutely correct, Dr. DuQuesne; I suspect I do not possess anything valuable enough to actually pay for that secret. A subliminal impression of Orphan's wing-snap shrug. *Well, thus far we have seen no indication Vindatri has detected us.*

Yeah. He could be playing the deep, deep game and letting us pull off all these tricks while actually perfectly aware of it, but my gut says otherwise. And I've learned to trust that feeling.

Dr. DuQuesne, Orphan transmitted with another, very grim, symbolic smile, *there we are very much in agreement. Your instincts have been excellent, and mine have stood me in good stead. And, in this case, mine agree with you. Vindatri is volatile, as you have seen. To suddenly discover some new form of communication would surely trigger some form of reaction in him.*

"What gets me about this," DuQuesne said, his voice echoing through the gloom, "is that it's *deserted.* It looks like nothing's working in here—maybe hasn't been working in a thousand years. Why would you build something this size and have parts of it just gathering dust?"

"Perhaps," Orphan observed, gazing around and flicking his light from one towering, distant shape to another, "there were once more people living here. Though he is a lone—and I admit somewhat intimidating—figure today, perhaps there were many of his people here once." His voice took on a melancholy note. "It does have something of the air of parts of the Liberated's Sphere. Where once were hundreds, now only two walk—and until but a short time ago, only one, myself, had walked those halls for over a thousand years."

I feel the same about Vindatri. No reaction probably means we're in the clear, at least for now. So are you going to enlighten me as to why you wanted this gizmo? Not that it's not going to be useful, but you were the one who asked me to whip it up.

Indeed. I have . . . call it a premonition, call it simply foreboding . . . that we may eventually find ourselves at odds with our host. I desperately hope that this will not be the case. But if it must be, I very much desire a way to discuss plans for that eventuality without doing so in front of him. An impression of an ironic raised eyebrow. *Plans are usually so much more effective when your adversary is not present at the conference table.*

DuQuesne reflected that this was one of the times he didn't like Orphan's instincts coinciding with his own. On the other hand, Orphan's approach was exactly correct. *Hate to agree, but you're right, sooner or later we're gonna butt heads with Vindatri, and I'm betting on sooner.*

"Or maybe like buying a real big house because one day you'll have a family, and maybe you want a workshop, and for years you never get around to it," he said, continuing their audible conversation.

A genuine-sounding laugh from Orphan, with the higher-pitched buzzing overlay of the real sound clearly audible. "Why, Dr. DuQuesne, I had not yet grasped how *many* things our species *does* have in common! The Blessed—and Liberated—would recognize that sad tale of prudence becoming waste all too well."

Orphan's transmitted voice was less cheerful. *Your words make me most suspicious that you have a material and cogent reason to expect this conflict, not merely the native caution of your "gut," Doctor.*

He sent the impression of a deadly smile. *Nailed it in one, Orphan. I guess I'd better put you at least partly in the picture, though there's key stuff I still ain't planning to tell you.*

And when have I ever told you everything? I would be pleased to be given, shall we say, whatever elements of the "picture" that you feel are important at this time.

One thing you could say for Orphan: he'd been playing the game for a long, long time, and didn't hold it against you when *you* were playing the game around *him*. DuQuesne nodded internally. "Still," he said out loud, "this place sure looks like it was meant for something big. Really big. What in the name of everything sensible *are* those machines?"

The machines in question towered over the two like skyscrapers, enigmatic masses of contoured metal . . . or maybe, from the sheen, the nigh-invincible material the Arena used for construction, that Simon called CQC—coherent quark composite. DuQuesne had seen machines that big or bigger, both in his Hyperion past and in his work in the real world; the turbine generators providing power for a large part of the colony on Humanity's Upper Sphere were easily this size. But nothing about the shape of the brooding titan structures was familiar, and their dead panels gave no hints; even the vaguely-visible symbology on the panels was unfamiliar. *Bet that* Simon *could read it, though,* he thought.

"I cannot even venture a guess," Orphan said after a moment. "They are great and impressive creations, but not a clue remains as to their purpose. Perhaps we might cautiously broach the subject with our host and see if he can enlighten us?"

"Worth a shot," DuQuesne conceded. Beneath, the communication on the ultrawave frequencies continued. *Okay, here's the situation, Orphan. Ariane absolutely* had *to get this instruction, and we came with you not just because we owed it to you, but because you as much as stated that she'd have that chance where you were going.*

Indeed, I comprehend this perfectly.

Well, the thing is that we've also got good reason to believe he's got his own agenda—

Impression of a cynical smile. *And who, in the Arena, does not?*

Point. Maybe Sun Wu Kung?

Even he. Or do you forget his fascination with the prize he won?

DuQuesne paused at that. Orphan was right; Wu Kung had his own dream, and in some ways it might be one of the most desperate and tragic dreams . . . or the most frighteningly brilliant. *Okay, you win. Anyway, we have damn good reason to think that while Vindatri's teaching Ariane, he's also messing with her head.*

"*Messing with her . . .*" Ah. *You mean he is using his powers to mentally affect her?*

Yeah. I'm close to certain of that. And he sure ain't doing that just for the hell of it. He has a reason, *and I don't have warm and fuzzy vibes about that reason.*

The ultrawave was silent for a moment, as the two of them continued walking. *Alas, Doctor, no more do I. But . . .* Another pause, but this one filled with impressions of trepidation. . . . *But . . . Dr. DuQuesne . . . you do not intend to actually* confront *him on this matter, do you? For his powers are—*

Can't blame him for being scared, DuQuesne thought. Vindatri's plenty dangerous, and worth being scared of. Hell, *I* am scared of him, even with what I think I can do. Problem being that even with that, I don't know what *he* can do. *Best-case scenario, we finish up the training and I can address what was done to her* after *we leave. But that's way out on the optimistic side. Honestly, we've got secrets I don't want to hand over to Mr. Dark-and-Spooky there, no matter what he's teaching her. So yeah, at some point we probably* will *have words with him on this. And it might go way beyond words.*

Orphan did not immediately respond. When he did, his nervousness was palpable in the transmission. *Dr. DuQuesne, you must realize that Vindatri is—in any reasonable probability—almost incalculably more powerful than even Amas-Garao or First Guide Nyanthus, yes?*

Yeah, I'm assuming he's way up there on the scale of "things not to mess with."

Flash of surprise. *And yet you expect, and intend, to precipitate a confrontation with him—in the not-too-distant future?*

Not something I'm really looking forward to, but yeah.

When Orphan resumed transmission, a hint of his accustomed humor and confidence reappeared. *Dr. DuQuesne, if I have learned anything in my considerable association with Humanity, it is that you have infinite capacity for surprises. I know you have secrets and will not reveal them to me without cause; but tell me this, then; do you have reason to believe—knowing and guessing what we do about Vindatri— that you have a chance to survive and even prevail in such a confrontation?*

DuQuesne simply sent an image of his nastiest grin.

I . . . see. Then I ask you only this: if I will side with you against him, when that time comes—for I, too, do not approve of anything that tampers with minds, for reasons you must well understand—will this secret of yours give me a reasonable chance of survival as well?

If you trust us and work with us? We'll risk ourselves to make sure you *get out of it, if it comes to that. Yes.*

Then, came the resolute answer, *rest assured that the Liberated will be committed to your cause as well.*

Thanks, Orphan. That means a lot to me. And will to Ariane, too.

Think nothing of it. I trust, you see, that even my patron Vindatri has failed to fully grasp the implications *of carrying the "Blessing of the Arena" . . . perhaps because one must have been* present *at its more stunning manifestations to truly accept it.*

They had walked some distance past the first rank of machinery, and the air also had the same strange, *ancient* odor that DuQuesne remembered from that first venture into the interior of their Sphere. He looked down and then knelt. "I'll be damned. This is *dirt*, I think." *Just like in our Sphere. There's a connection, I'm damned sure of it.*

"How very odd. Was there, then, an intention to *light* this area? To grow plants of some kind? A garden, perhaps?"

"Sure doesn't look like how I'd design a garden, but then, I'm not Vindatri."

Might I ask if you have discussed our prior exploration with anyone?

You mean the room of statues? Yeah, me and Ariane discussed it . . . privately.

Have you any . . . thoughts?

DuQuesne hesitated, weighing his options. Any deductions or thoughts were obviously worth something . . . but on the other hand, it *had* been Orphan who had practically dragged him to see it. *Some. Based on my headware recording, looks to me like each of those statues is unique. Same for you?*

Indeed. I did not record any duplicates; a few that seemed similar, but close examination showed they were spurious resemblances.

Also looked to us like it might *be in a sort of chronological order—stuff nearest the door being more recent arrivals to the Arena, the farther stuff being older.*

I concur. This was also my conclusion, years before. Now, that most intriguing anomalous statue . . . ?

Yeah. That. Stands out in so many ways. Outline's a lot like us. But it's before *the Molothos, who have gotta be one of the oldest species around. Which means that shape . . .*

A sensation of a laugh. *You hesitate. You think the shape could represent the Voidbuilders?*

Well . . . what else would come before the Molothos?

He saw an image of Orphan's dismissive "no" gesture, accompanied by an ironic smile. *Ahh, Dr. DuQuesne, you still do not grasp the immensity of the Arena's history. The Molothos may well be the oldest remaining species in the Arena, but it is known the Arena's history goes back much farther than a few tens of millions of years. Cycles of life and extinctions of species through age, if nothing else, take their toll. The Molothos are astounding in their species' stability and longevity . . . but that only means that few if any of their contemporaries lived even to within a few million years of today.*

I have myself a far different theory of that statue.

DuQuesne grinned inwardly. *All right, Orphan, let me have it. You've obviously got a better handle on some things than the rest of us.*

Impression of a deep bow. *Then consider, Doctor, that our surmises are true, and that collection is a visual record of all the species of the Arena, in order of their appearance in the Arena. They are all extraordinarily detailed, a record in three dimensions of every unique feature and curious shape of each newcomer.*

There is, as of yet, none of your *people. I believe that, were we to return to that room just prior to our departure, we would find one. He studies you now, and will create that sculpture for you when you have left. But why would this supernal collector and sculptor choose to create such a well-executed, yet* abstract, *image as the first in the series?*

DuQuesne suddenly saw what he was driving at. *You mean, if it was a species he didn't really* need *a record of.*

Precisely, Doctor. A handtap of approval. *And of all the species of the universe, that species you would least need a special record of . . . would be your own.*

Chapter 41

I'm FLYING!

The thought echoed through her mind, bounced back and forth with a manic energy, repeating itself as she swooped and dove and spun through the air in the way her dreams had always *told* her she could, but the way that the world had never allowed. "I'm *flying!*" she shouted, and laughed aloud as she passed not a meter above Vindatri and a grinning Wu Kung.

"You are indeed, Captain Austin," Vindatri said, and his voice, too, held a hint of sympathetic amusement within. "And I can see that this dream is, perhaps, the one that resonates with you more than any other. You have mastered this word of transport completely, in a manner few ever do; clearly, this is part of your truest avocation."

She paused, still feeling wonder sparkling through her, like the silverlight sheen that surrounded her as she hovered. "It is. This is why I chose space racing and air racing. As close as I could get to . . . to *this.*" He nodded understanding, and she felt her smile widen. "Do you understand, really?"

There was no mistaking the smile even beneath the hood. "The dream of flight? Yes, Captain, I understand it well. In truth? It was the first word I asked for, when I was beginning my own lessons, very, very long ago. I am not a pilot, as are you, but the dream of flying had been mine since I was a child. I understand, and your joy echoes the joy I felt then. I am glad."

Not without regret, she finally forced herself to land. "Not really the most *practical* power."

He laughed. Oddly, she realized that *that* sound did not carry any hint of a double sound, as most Arena translations did. *Does he really laugh so much like us?* "In many settings . . . no. Still, it is not to be set aside lightly; any of us could find ourselves accidentally falling from a height, or cast out into the Arena, and with this power, such things are not to be feared. Still, there are other powers of transport vastly more . . . interesting, in a practical sense."

"Such as?"

Vindatri suddenly vanished in shadow. His voice spoke from behind her, "Such as this, perhaps?"

Even though she had half-expected it, *that* made her jump. "That's *spooky* but I don't know if it's practical. Amas-Garao used that trick a lot but . . ." She trailed off, remembering how *hard* it had been to even strike the Shadeweaver in combat.

"Oh, undoubtedly it has powerful psychological use, Captain; but from your sudden halt I believe you realize its more practical applications as well."

She nodded. "Yeah, I remembered them while I was talking. If you can get to be *good* enough with it to respond that fast while in combat, yes, it must be incredibly useful. As the old masters used to say, 'best defense against attack is to not be there.'"

Vindatri regarded her narrowly, hands folded together with the index fingers pointed up and touching where she thought his lips must be—a thoughtful pose that was unusual yet terribly *human* in appearance. "It does indeed have that advantage. But you underestimate its usefulness."

He disappeared again. After a moment, he reappeared and handed her something—a polished comb with a backing of mother-of-pearl.

"This . . . this was on *Zounin-Ginjou*!" she said, startled. The implications became clear. "This . . . it can be *long-range* teleportation!"

"Precisely so. Not *unlimited* in range, no, but ranges of tens of thousands of kilometers are quite practical, even longer with sufficient practice."

"And I can learn this as well?"

"I intend to teach it to you, yes. And a few other words, before your . . . abbreviated training must end. Your time is, after all, limited."

He's right. The longer we're away, the bigger the chance some disaster happens that really does *need me—or DuQuesne, or Wu, or maybe even Orphan—to handle.*

That reminded her of their first arrival at Halintratha, and of something else. "Vindatri, can I ask you something?"

"You have mastered a new word; as before, you now have the right to a few questions."

"You sent Orphan out to, basically, find people 'blessed by the Arena,' and that seems to connect to the Canajara . . . myth of the Faith. Why? What's your interest? And what else do these Canajara do, in the myths?"

The tall cloaked figure regarded her silently for a moment. Finally, he said, "I am neither Faith nor Shadeweaver, as you know, yet one might say I am close to, and interested in, both. Shadeweavers, as well as the Faith, have . . . visions of the future, prophecies, predictions. I am, and have always been, fascinated by them, especially the ones that deal with something beyond the immediate, the trivial. Those are of course far more rare, but what is of interest to *me* is that there is a form of the Canajara prophecy/myth in the *Shadeweaver* archives as well."

Ariane was sure he was telling the truth about himself. She was also equally sure that Vindatri was leaving out some other reason, maybe even a *more* important reason, for his interest. *But maybe he'll get to that?*

"Unlike the Faith, of course, the Shadeweavers have few coherent rituals and traditions, so it is not a . . . legend of veneration and a major mystery, as it is to the Faith, but it has many points of similarity with much of the Canajara prophecies. This led me to study both in detail."

He turned and looked around the deserted, moss-covered stone ruins that their current practice was taking place in. "As to what else the Canajara do? Many things. Many *contradictory* things, in fact. My studies have shown that it is implied that in essence the Canajara represent the two-sided coin of salvation and destruction, even in the Shadeweaver interpretations. They are predicted to do great works, to bring together the Arena as it has never been, to reveal the truth of the Creators . . . or to divide the Arena, set Faction against Faction, and shatter civilization to nothingness."

A flash of a smile, this one narrow and ironic. "You can understand, then, that I regard even a possible fulfillment of the Canajara with far more trepidation than the rather . . . optimistic Faith would."

Ariane nodded. She remembered that Mandallon had said some similar things. "How did that go? '. . . And for good or evil none shall say, for the Sevenfold Path they tread in both directions, and they shall be exalted in light and terror,' that was what Mandallon said."

"Succinctly stated, yes. So if you are, or are in any way connected to, the Canajara . . . I think I will say no more." She *definitely* did not feel comfortable with that smile.

Wu Kung snorted. "It sounds to *me* just like any prophecy; vague maunderings that will sound oh-so-wise *after* you've blundered your way through the mission, but that Buddha *and* all the prophets couldn't manage to make sense of *before*. Besides, all people are like that: light and dark, destroyers or creators. You make a choice, and if you can choose, you can choose either direction."

"Perhaps. I suppose you may even be right, and I have spent years pondering the texture of moonlight and the solidity of air." Vindatri sat on a nearby piece of stone. "Are you ready to begin again? While I know you would enjoy practicing flight, I think you need far less practice with *that* than with other words. Your mastery of shielding, for instance."

"I guess. I'll be actually kind of sad to see this end, though. There's so much more to learn."

Vindatri sighed. "*Vastly* more. I have been teaching you . . . the more simple and obvious tricks. The ways to *use* them, the subtle methods of power? That takes far more time. But perhaps you can leave and return. I can give you a route that will bring you here somewhat more easily than the one Orphan uses."

"Really?" She found herself even more excited by the prospect than she had expected.

"Certainly. You are now my student, and a unique student indeed. My only request is that you would bring others of your people here. I would especially like to meet your Dr. Sandrisson; he sounds like a most fascinating individual."

"I certainly think so!" she said with a grin. *That's a perfect solution. Get a quicker route here, and then I can just shuttle back and forth for training. And I'm sure Simon would love to see everything Vindatri has here!* "Sounds like a plan!"

"Excellent," Vindatri said. She thought Wu Kung started to say something, but when she checked, he wasn't even looking in her direction, but instead apparently watching a butterfly-like insect nearby. "Then let us begin again."

As she prepared herself to learn another of the key words and its application, she felt her decision firming up. *DuQuesne and Orphan don't need to keep hanging around here either. If I leave them back there, things can be kept under control much better, and I can keep studying this power with Vindatri.*

I can't wait to tell them!

Chapter 42

"Well . . . it's time," Simon said, hearing his own voice heavy with reluctance and, to be honest, fear.

Carl and Laila nodded slowly, almost in unison. "The Molothos will be at our Sphere very soon," Laila said, agreeing obliquely. "How long before they choose to engage?"

A flick of meditation and focus that had become all too familiar; he saw the position of ships, the movement of those aboard. "A day? Two or three? Or even within a few hours. I *must* be there."

"We know," Carl said. "Your ability to direct and coordinate the defense . . . it will be our only chance, honestly, if the Molothos don't just back off when they realize the Analytic is on our side. But," and Carl's usual easygoing tone and posture were suddenly gone, "you take *no* risks while you are there."

Simon felt his lips turn up in an ironic smile. "I am deliberately going to put myself into a battle against the most unforgiving species in the Arena. I think it's a little late to caution me against—"

"I *mean* it, Simon!" Carl's hazel eyes locked on his, and he saw Laila give a nod, backing up the other current Leader Pro Tem of Humanity. "Our *people* will have to take risks. You will—God help us—have to do what a general does and send people in to be killed, if that's what it takes." He looked to Laila. "But . . ."

". . . but," she picked up smoothly, "you will *not* unnecessarily risk *yourself*. Regardless of our defeat or victory at our Sphere, you are one of our most valuable—and utterly irreplaceable, as I understand it— resources. I understand, and agree, that you *must* be at the battle to direct it, but—just as with our friend Relgof—you *will* retreat if you, personally, are in any significant danger. That is our *direct order* to you as Leaders of the Faction of Humanity, and, I am *absolutely* sure, this is *exactly* what Ariane would order if she was here."

Simon sighed, but nodded. "Understood, Carl, Laila. And . . . you are right, that *is* what she would say."

"I notice you did not say, 'Yes, Laila and Carl, I will not place myself in any significant danger that I can possibly avoid,'" Laila said.

Kuso.

"Give it up, Simon. They've noticed you have a tendency to play hero when given the chance," Oasis said with a smile. "But they're right."

"Yes. I know. Very well, Laila, Carl, I accept your conditions and I will not place myself in any significant danger that I can *reasonably* avoid. I will not say *possibly* because there are many things that are *possible* that are not *reasonable*."

The two looked at him for a long moment, then looked at each other and shrugged. "All right, Simon. Good enough."

"I also intend—if you still approve—to conduct the briefing we discussed."

"Definitely," Carl said promptly, and Laila added her own nod. "We need all the edge we can get, and while the results will be ones that the Molothos would notice, they shouldn't have the faintest clue as to what the explanation is, which is really the important part, right?"

"I would say so, yes. The same applies of course to my talent; they will see the primaries, and note that we seem, well, impossibly well-coordinated, but they should have no way of even guessing *why* this is so . . . which will mean the advantage remains ours."

"Is that all?" Laila asked. At his own nod, she took a breath, let it out. "Get moving, then. And, Simon . . ."

He saw and understood the glance of concern and comradeship that went back to the time he had gone to her, rather than anyone else in the crew, for advice, and he smiled as she finished, ". . . good luck to us all."

"Thank you, Laila," he said, picking up his pack. "On my way."

Oasis matched his longer strides easily—not surprising, given what she was. "And," she said as they exited the Embassy of Humanity, "I'll make sure you stick to your promise."

He smiled down at her, and gave the practiced flip of his head that sent his white hair up and cascading in a silver waterfall back into place. "I expected you would. That's why I agreed; I wasn't going to get a choice. But . . . I also know that you understand when the other choice might *be* necessary."

"Always. It's my job, I guess you could say."

They flagged down one of the cruising hover-taxis and in moments were at the massive elevators that took them to the same level as Transition. It was busy, and the elevator up was moderately crowded; he and the flame-haired Hyperion stood towards the back and near each other. He noticed her eyes scanning the surrounding people ceaselessly. *Is this the way it is for all Hyperions,* he wondered. *Unending vigilance, or paranoia, along with the isolation of their nature?*

The doors opened and they slowly emerged onto the Transition level. Like all of Nexus Arena, this level was built on a titanic scale, ranks of elevators large enough to carry an entire mansion serving what amounted to a spaceport for ten thousand destinations. Crowds of hundreds of species moved, ebbed, and flowed like waves in a tide, ebbing and flowing with an unending yet ever-changing rhythm.

Oasis led the way, confidently cutting a path through the crowd with a more subtle yet no-less-strong force of personality than DuQuesne's. Simon glanced around, surveying the immensity as they moved forward. He was more nervous than he had wanted to show anyone, even—or perhaps especially, Oasis. *No matter what they say, or I promise, I am going into a war zone, a battle that I know little about, and I will be in grave danger from the very instant the battle starts.*

He suddenly caught a flash of white in the distance. For an instant he considered being silent, but realized that even at a moment like this, Oasis would never forgive him if he did not speak. "Oasis—to your left, about . . . ten o'clock."

There was the barest hint of a hitch in her stride, then she continued moving forward. "I see it. We can't afford the time or risk of pursuit, if it is him. Laila," she continued, and a green comm-ball materialized instantly, "Simon and I believe we have spotted Fairchild near Transition, heading for the observation area to the left as you are approaching Transition. Send whoever you can, but I doubt you'll catch him."

Simon looked at her face, so fixed with angry focus that it looked like a white-carven statue of determination. As the comm-ball vanished, he said, quietly, "I'm sorry."

"Don't be. Not your fault." She forced a smile, then managed a laugh that was a tiny bit more natural. "Hey, it's not the first time I've let a villain get away because the world needed saving more than they needed their beating."

"The scenario wasn't uncommon for you?"

She rolled her eyes. "Simon, we were based on *heroes* of fiction, and mostly really *heroic* fiction at that. A lot of us from long-runner shows, sims, whatever. So yeah, common. If the Big Bad gets caught on his first outing, well, what do you do for the rest of the series?"

"I didn't mean to touch a nerve."

They were approaching one of the gigantic circular Inner Gateways that were the center of Transition. "Oh, don't worry about it, Simon." She took his hand and squeezed it for a moment before letting go. "It's not you, it's *me*. I'm terrified of him, and I'm going to *have* to face him to get over it. And I'm not *used* to being scared of things, really. Oh, I got a lot of jump-scares at times, but existential fear? Not really my thing. So this gives me the total creeps sometimes."

"I can't blame you, Oasis. With what he did, and tried to do? I would be terrified of him myself."

A moment of freezing heat and flashing darkness, and they stepped out into the foyer of the Sphere of Humanity, now fully equipped as a secure checkpoint for personnel and cargo both. The guards recognized Simon immediately—although Simon still felt the ID ping query on his headware—and let them both through. "You know the way, sir," said one he recognized, saluting.

"Thank you, Sergeant Byrne. I do know the way."

The atmosphere here was different, tense, hurried and grim. The bustle of work parties, of casual merchants as they passed through the larger rooms along their path, were almost gone, and what remained was subdued. *Anyone non-essential has been evacuated. We believe that there is no way for the Molothos to force their way into the Sphere . . . but if anyone* does *know how to do it, the Molothos do, and they* will *use that—or perhaps try to force someone they capture to do it for them.*

The Upper Gateway's chamber was vastly larger than he recalled, and filled with more military hardware than Simon had ever *seen* outside of a simgame. Soldiers, armed drones waiting in arrays, fixed emplacements aimed at the actual Gateway itself, every possible internal defense was set and ready. *I wonder how they enlarged the room? The exterior and interior walls are of CQC, which is beyond our capability to work or even destroy without nuclear weapons or something on that scale. Perhaps Ariane simply directed it to be so; the Arena seems quite accommodating to Leaders of Factions in their home areas.*

"Whoa, check it *out*," Oasis said, staring as they exited the Upper Gateway.

"*Subarashi*," Simon said in agreement.

Massive fortifications had been erected surrounding the Upper Gateway, with batteries of anti-aircraft cannon, rocket launchers, gargantuan energy weapons, and—visible below—multiple airstrips. "I had seen this in progress previously, but it truly is impressive now that it is complete."

"Nowhere near complete," said a familiar voice; Simon turned and saw a tall woman with green and blue hair in a military cut, wearing the uniform of a General in the CSF.

"General *Esterhauer?* What are you doing here?"

General Jill Esterhauer shook his hand and returned Oasis' salute. "I will be directing the ground-based defenses for our Sphere. Follow me, please—I'll escort you to your fleet transfer shuttle personally."

After a few moments, she glanced at him. "I am given to understand that *you* will be providing overall intelligence to the entire fleet and ground forces during the battle. May I ask how?"

Simon hesitated. "General . . . that is, I am afraid, need-to-know information, and you do not need to know it. Yet. All you need to know is that Captain Austin is aware of how, and that my . . . source is absolutely reliable both in general and in fine detail. If I tell you about a coming assault and its direction and composition, that information *will* be precisely correct."

He could see her studying the small amount of baggage he and Oasis carried. *Probably trying to figure out what kind of super-gadget I could be carrying that would do all that. She's certainly aware of the primary beams—several of the energy cannon up there are gigantic primaries, which took me* days *to set up—but even there, she doesn't know how it works.*

The General sighed. "I suppose you're right. If the intelligence is reliable, I don't really care if you're getting it by spies, remote sensors, or tarot cards. If I understand all my briefings, though . . . we are, basically, screwed."

"I will admit that it does not look good for us, General," Simon answered, as they made their way up to the overlooking plateau. "But we do have our allies waiting for the signal torpedo to be sent, and they will be on high alert once I arrive. While they will not even the odds, we have a few other advantages which you are already aware of."

Esterhauer nodded. "Your primary beams, for one. Although I am still utterly at sea as to why you are the only one allowed to install the systems."

"I wish it could be otherwise. But there is that advantage, and of course the advantage of the intelligence I will be providing."

Oasis was surveying the area now with the practiced air of someone used to watching for danger. *She's taken her role as my protector seriously. And . . . that* does *make me feel safer.*

Esterhauer was studying him with the eye of a hawk sizing up a competitor. "You seem the crux of things in multiple ways, Doctor. In a sense, you even started this whole thing."

He blinked, then laughed. "Yes, I suppose I did." He looked up. "Ah, there's the *Yeager.*"

The blunt, stubby shuttle waited on the magnetic launch rail; unlike the long, sleek forms common in low-mach vehicles, high-hypersonic vehicles—even ones using modern materials—tended to stolid and simple forms dictated by the hideous pressures and temperatures experienced by surfaces traveling at Mach numbers in the double digits. *Yeager* would take them the ten thousand kilometers or so to the waiting fleet in less than an hour.

In itself, that told him how close the battle was. *If the Molothos had a clear line of sight to our Sphere, they could be here, even limited by lower ultrasonic speeds, in mere hours. They could* get *that line of sight . . . any time now.*

"She's prepped and ready to launch immediately," Esterhauer said. "Anything you need to do beforehand?"

"No, no. Get us up there as fast as possible."

"Will do. Your destination is *Andraste*, yes?"

"*Andraste?*" Simon paused a moment before he recalled that the fleet had been renamed to a consistent pattern of Earthly war gods— Joani Cleary's *Paksenarrion* had become *Hachiman*, and *Andraste* had originally been called *Orion*, if he remembered aright. "The flagship, yes."

The boarding ramp to *Yeager* was already open, and he and Oasis jogged up and took their seats; he heard the General in the cockpit: "Get them up to *Andraste* as fast as you possibly can. I want them to think a meteor's on its way."

A low chuckle. "I'll do my best," came a slightly rough voice that Simon thought he recognized.

"Hawke? Is that you?"

The former racing pilot—Ariane's biggest rival on the racing circuit—turned in his seat enough so that he could nod to Simon. "Been a while, hasn't it, Doc? Since you stole Ariane from her own victory party, that is?"

"It has."

General Esterhauer gave both Oasis and Simon a quick salute. "Good luck, both of you." She disappeared out the hatch.

Simon raised an eyebrow at Hawke. "I thought you were going to be a combat pilot."

"Sure am," he said, turning back to the controls; the hatch door was sliding closed. "*Yeager's* gonna stay onboard *Andraste*. I'll be flying your flagship."

"Then I know we'll be in good hands."

"Fast ones, anyway. Though those big-ass ships are sure a change and a half from racers; regardless, turns out people like me are still the best at flying them, leastwise so far. Probably get better pilots once we finish training people from the start to run these big boats." He raised his voice. "Sphere Control, this is *Yeager*, requesting priority launch clearance for least-time flight to *Andraste*, currently at Sky Gate Control."

"*Yeager*, you are cleared to launch at any time. All other traffic is well away from your flight path and you have top priority."

"Understood, Control. Launching momentarily."

With a roar audible through the soundproofing, *Yeager's* rockets kicked her skyward, pressing Simon into the cushioned seat with twice his own weight. The stubby vehicle bulled its way through the atmosphere, adjusting shape slightly to provide more lift at the lower airspeeds, but mostly using brute force to thunder its way up and through the sound barrier. A cough and sudden growl announced the ignition of the ramjets, which propelled *Yeager* ever faster, Mach 3, Mach 4, and then the sound shifted again, a distant howl as the engine reconfigured to a scramjet, supersonic air rammed through and then set aflame to send *Yeager* hurtling forward at meteoric speeds. Simon's headware connected to the shuttles showed how the Sphere was dropping away below them with almost ludicrous alacrity.

Where is Andraste? he thought, and the local systems fed him the coordinates and relative location. Noting their current speed—which seemed to be nearly stable—Simon nodded in appreciation. He turned his head towards Oasis. "We'll be there in well under one hour. Thirty-nine minutes, now."

"Fast ship. I like it!" Her face became serious. "What about the Molothos?"

He closed his eyes. The god-like sight came far more easily now, and that was one of the things that worried him. But at the moment, that was something he needed.

The immense fleet of ships was easy to find, even without the instinctive knowledge that took his vision there; he knew the course they had been following. "They are starting to spread out, assuming some kind of attack formation. They have not yet cleared the heavy clouds that have blocked their path, but they will soon. I would presume that they will accelerate to attack at that time."

"How long?"

He gauged their speed and distance within the cloud, looked along their heading; he could make out the luminaire, and now a faint dark hint of the Sphere. "Not days. Seven, eight hours, perhaps."

"Damn."

"Yes."

Andraste soon became visible, first as a dot in a cloud of dots, then as one of a fleet of ten warships—the core of Humanity's fleet, all of them adapted from the ships Orphan had gifted to Humanity. Orphan's other ships hadn't been suited to being front-line warships, but would be serving as tender and other support roles; unfortunately, the Tantimorcan vessels that Naraj had helped negotiate for were not yet complete. Smaller combat vessels—fighters, small missile-focused frigates, and so on—had been manufactured by human facilities, but the ultimate limit on numbers had been how many *people* were available to fly them.

With the memory of the Molothos fleet clear in his mind, Simon could see how terribly fragile and minute Humanity's forces were, and he swallowed a lump of fear. *I must not allow fear to override my thinking. Nor, alas, my compassion. Laila and Carl are right: I will have to send people to their deaths today, and the* best *I can hope for is that only a few thousand will die today. The worst . . .*

The worst would be that he would see the entirety of Humanity's forces, and those from the Analytic, wiped from the sky, and be forced to flee alive while all the rest of the defenders died.

We must not let it come to that.

Yeager docked without incident, and Captain Fitzhugh met them as they debarked. "Dr. Sandrisson, Colonel Abrams, welcome aboard. The briefing room is ready as you requested. When do you expect we will deploy?"

"To get into proper position . . . I think we will have to begin soon. Captain, you will be in charge of overall fleet action as well as that of this vessel, yes?"

"Subject to your intelligence on enemy movements, yes."

Simon nodded. "We have only a few hours, I believe, before the Molothos come into full view of our fleet and fortifications. Should we send the message torpedo now? Give our allies from the Analytic time to come through and integrate with our fleet?"

To his surprise, Captain Fitzhugh shook his head, slate blue-gray hair echoing the movement. "No."

"No? Might I know—"

"Certainly. The other captains—and General Esterhauer, among others—have debated the overall strategy for this battle several times. I've personally spent a *lot* of time studying everything we have on the Molothos and trying to get inside their heads, if you know what I mean."

"Perfectly, yes, Captain. Go on."

Captain Fitzhugh led them through the corridors—although Simon, having been on all of these ships at least once, already knew the way. "Well, our conclusion was that these people absolutely won't stop with just words. We have *got* to bloody their noses *hard* before there's a chance they'll pull up and listen." His lips set tight for a moment, grim and worried. "And even then, none of us are giving high odds. But we're as sure as we can be that unless we treat them like the proverbial mule, there's no chance to cut this short."

"Like the mule . . . ?" Simon repeated. For a moment he didn't get it, then he remembered the old joke. "Ah. 'First you have to get his attention,' yes. And I suppose the primaries *will* do that."

"Not *just* those. Trust me, we have other plans, based on your intelligence." He looked at Simon narrowly. "You *are* certain of your information, right? Especially including their maneuver preparations?"

"Absolutely certain, Captain. They have been practicing and coordinating that four-pincer assault en route for *months*. Their orientation appears reasonably stable, as well. My projections as to their likely assault remain exactly as they were."

Fitzhugh grinned fiercely. "Then we *definitely* have at least one more surprise for our genocidal friends; we'll go over that and our other plans at the briefing."

Simon felt a—very small—trickle of hope. *This will be the first real war humanity has fought in . . . two centuries? But it sounds like these people know what they're doing.* "Very good, Captain. Tell the other captains to be ready for their briefing and tactical information in . . . one hour."

"Understood." Captain Fitzhugh saluted and turned away, presumably for the command deck.

Simon and Oasis reached the briefing room, and its lone other occupant stood up quickly. "K! I mean, Oasis! It's great to see you!"

"And you, Vel!" The red-headed woman hugged the black-haired young man.

Slightly below average height, Velocity Celes had a boyish, cheerful smile, with brown eyes below glossy black hair; his face, like Simon's, had more than a hint of Japanese ancestry. He turned to Simon. "Dr. Sandrisson, it's an honor to really get to meet you! I know we saw each other at that one party, but . . ."

"But we hardly had time to talk. And unfortunately we have little time to spare now. Ariane does send her love, as does DuQuesne." He gestured for the young man (*young? Something of a misnomer; he is as old as DuQuesne, despite his behavior and appearance*) to sit again.

"Well, likewise, if I don't get a chance to see them before you do." He looked at the two curiously. "So . . . why this hush-hush meeting with me, alone? The Fleet's got tons more questions than I do, really, and I've gotta get over to *Hachiman* as soon as I can."

"Because," Simon said, and this time with a smile that had more real cheer in it than others of late, "there is something you need to know—something absolutely *vital*—about yourself, and what you can do, before we begin this war . . ."

Chapter 43

"I appreciate you shifting our temporary quarters to something with a view," DuQuesne told Vindatri. "I don't do that well in what feels like a sealed box."

"Think nothing of it, Dr. DuQuesne," Vindatri replied. "Once you mentioned it, I understood completely. And while I am somewhat inured to it, the view is, indeed, quite spectacular."

"Can't argue that." The huge picture-window that covered one whole wall of their common room showed the colossal, multihued cloudbanks that surrounded Halintratha, flowing with ponderous majesty, boiling up on a timescale of months or years, lit from within by occasional bolts of lightning that might span an Earthly continent. Flocks of creatures—*zikki* and others—flew past the windows periodically, and once Ariane had pointed out the monstrous, streamlined shadow of something that had to be a *morfalzeen*, one of the largest predators in the Arena; the titanic thing had cruised onward, slowly fading into nothingness in red-shadowed cloud.

"So, Vindatri, you know we've been exploring Halintratha while you and Ariane have been training, right?"

"Of course. I had given you permission to do so, and it is thus scarcely surprising you would take me up on that offer."

"Well, we came to this one area that looked like no one had been there in centuries, filled with huge, unused machines. Why's that place so deserted, if we could ask? Did you build it and stop using it, or did you find Halintratha and this is just a part of it you've never had a use for?"

Vindatri tilted his head, and there was a faint flash of a smile. "Something of both, in truth. You are correct that I have not constructed all of Halintratha myself, and some of the parts of this structure I have not had a tremendous use for. However, if you are speaking of this location," an image shone out above the table, and DuQuesne nodded, "then it is a place where the . . . mechanisms, so to speak, were needed for various purposes a very long time ago, but they served their purpose and I have had no need of them for many centuries indeed."

He saw Ariane and Wu staring at the image; Ariane opened her mouth, but then closed it once DuQuesne caught her eye. *They recognize the similarity with our Sphere. Which, as Rich used to say, "gives one furiously to think."*

"Thanks," he said to Vindatri. "Gives me the idea you think a lot differently than we do; building something like that—or like this station—and living in it mostly alone, and not using most of it?"

"When you move into a new home, do you always instantly fill each room? Especially if nothing has constrained you as to the size and nature of the rooms?"

"Well, no, but eventually . . ." He saw what Vindatri was driving at.

"I see you understand. *Eventually* means something rather different for you or Captain Austin than it does for your friend Orphan, and different still than it does to me."

By implication, he's saying the difference between him and Orphan is about the same as that between Orphan and us. Which is about two orders of magnitude. Is Vindatri really that old? That'd make him maybe older than homo sapiens.

Then again, if that room of statues maintained its implied order to the end, Vindatri might be older than the *Molothos*, which would make him . . . what, *millions* of years? Older than the entire *genus* Homo.

"Indeed, perspective changes many things," Orphan said. "I am, however, curious to know how much longer the training must continue. I have many things to attend to in Nexus Arena—as you know—so it is somewhat urgent for me to know when I can expect to return. And, of course, I suspect the Leader of Humanity cannot long abandon her duties."

Ariane smiled. "Well, actually, I have good news on that front. Vindatri and I have been talking, and we think that it's best we head back home very soon."

That's a relief. Once we get out in the Deeps, I can find out what he's been up to in her head and none the wiser. Hopefully. He was still tense; a part of him was sure it wasn't going to be that easy. "So you're done?"

"Oh, not even *close*," she said with a laugh. "But we'll go back and drop you and Orphan off. I'll get one of our own ships and come back."

"What?" Orphan said in surprise. "Not to discourage you from returning me to Nexus Arena, Captain, but I am quite sure that you have not memorized the route, and—if I understand Dr. DuQuesne's position, he does not want you traveling solely with your bodyguard."

"I," said Vindatri, "shall provide Captain Austin with her own route to Halintratha. Yours shall remain yours, Orphan."

"And I won't be alone. Marc needs some time to do his own stuff back home. I'll bring Simon." She glanced at Vindatri. "Vindatri *really* wants to meet him."

Oh, Klono, Noshabkeming, and every other blasted curse I can think of. SIMON. *I didn't cover* that *up, and of course he wants to meet Simon. There's no damned way he didn't get some hint from Ariane that there's something special about Simon. You stupid, incompetent, half-baked excuse for a superman, you've gone and blown it this time. Mentor would be* roasting *me over this, and he'd have every right to do it.*

Although—to give himself the very tiniest smidgen of an excuse—the more of Ariane's memories and thoughts he had to wall off, the more obvious it would've been that someone had been doing some kind of work on her head. Walling off the very specific information about the Hyperion advantage hadn't been a big chore. But *Simon* was another huge part of Ariane's life, and the Human entry into the Arena itself, and trying to keep all that surface stuff available while preventing any possible detection that Simon himself now had unusual powers? That would've at least doubled the difficulty, and maybe more than doubled the chance that Vindatri would catch on.

Aloud, he said, "If you've learned the basics, we can probably just go on our own from there. Simon and the rest of us are still gonna be busy as hell for a while."

She looked at him in surprise. "Marc, with a chance like *this*? For me to learn from someone outside the two main groups, and for Simon to learn things about the Arena that even the Analytic probably doesn't know? It's well worth the risk."

On the surface, of course, Ariane was one hundred percent right. But the problem was he had no idea how much Vindatri knew or guessed about Simon. Even a little was too much; no telling what Vindatri would do with that information.

And then he felt it: cold, subtle, insinuating itself into his surface mind as though the Hyperion-engineered defenses weren't even there. *He's figured that trick out—not that I'm surprised.* He could feel the surface DuQuesne becoming more receptive, ready to accept whatever directions Vindatri gave next. Beneath, he considered the situation. *Still . . . maybe the best course is to just go along with it. He'll just be making sure we go along with his plan. Once we're well away, I can counteract that. He'll wonder what went wrong, but I don't think even he can guess the truth.*

The one part of that he *really* didn't like was that he still would have no idea what Vindatri knew about Simon . . . and Vindatri certainly wasn't *restricted* to this area of the Arena. If he was sufficiently intrigued, he might just come straight to Nexus Arena for his answers, and DuQuesne had a very bad feeling that none of the normal Arena protections would work against Vindatri.

There was a growling noise.

Sun Wu Kung half-rose, shaking his head. "You . . . you are . . . in my head! Get out! *GET OUT!*"

Like lightning, Wu Kung leapt across the table straight for Vindatri. *That's torn it. This is it, the blow-off!*

So unexpected was Wu's assault that he actually *caught* the tall, cloaked figure with one blow, sending Vindatri tumbling across the floor. But even as Wu charged after him, Vindatri gestured.

Ropes of black light lashed out of nowhere, caught Wu in midair, dragged him back to the wall. As DuQuesne started to his feet, he found the same ebony tendrils yanking him back; they dematerialized, to reveal shackles integrated with the wall itself.

Ariane was frozen, eyes blank, unmoving, unseeing; flicking his gaze in that direction, DuQuesne saw the same was true of Orphan.

"How inconvenient," Vindatri said. Wu swore at him in half a dozen languages, and yanked futilely at the chains. "Do not waste your effort, Sun Wu Kung. Those chains are made of the very foundation of the Arena, what your people have called CQC, matter woven of the most fundamental particles in a single self-supporting mesh."

Vindatri studied them dispassionately. "There are . . . anomalies about the two of you. I wished to be more subtle about this, but your reaction makes that the less desirable and useful approach. While these others wait, their minds frozen in a single instant, I shall finally perform the *very* detailed examination I have had in mind all along." His hand rose, and green-yellow light played along it.

"Now I will learn *all* of your secrets."

Chapter 44

Wu struggled against the chains despite Vindatri's warning, but in his heart he knew the Shadeweaver-like being was right. *I don't think I could break ring-carbon composite chains half this thick, even on my best day. This CQC, it will be like the Heaven Chain wrapped around my rock. Only the power of a god will break it . . . and the only god here is Vindatri.*

The thought itself was a crushing weight. He could *see* Ariane, her eyes staring into nothingness, a scant few meters away but beyond his reach . . . beyond his protection. He was going to fail *again*, and the tearing *shame* of that fact threatened to tear him apart. "Ariane! *ARIANE, wake up! Ariane!*"

But she did not blink, did not shift; whatever spell Vindatri had on her mind was absolute. Glancing to his side, he saw to his utter horror that DuQuesne's eyes also looked blank, gazing only inward, completely unseeing.

As always, rage was his only antidote to despair. "Sorcerer, I will *kill* you! I will—" he shifted into the native, mangled tongue that had been his, and filled the air with invective, threatening Vindatri's body and soul with every injury and torment he had ever seen.

"Fascinating. I could understand the first part, but the latter is incomprehensible; yet I am sure you are speaking coherently, if rather predictably." Vindatri shook his head. "But it is your companion I am more interested in."

Wu Kung found himself so furious, yet so filled with a complete knowledge of his failure and dishonor, that he fell silent as the alien turned away from him, dismissing Wu Kung as unworthy even to

351

speak with. *And . . . he may be right. Even the time I fell from* Thilomon, *I was still free, I could still* act. *Here . . . here I will merely stand in chains as this monster rips my friends' minds apart.*

Vindatri paced the short distance to stand in front of the massive Hyperion. "Dr. DuQuesne, you and Sun Wu Kung had some *intriguing* defenses around your minds. It required some thought to devise a means of circumventing it; and I now see that Wu Kung's was somewhat different than your own, thus allowing him more latitude to act than I had expected. I will certainly investigate him in depth later. But for now, I think I would like to know what you know about Simon Sandrisson, and most especially what unique capability he has that I have sensed in Captain Austin's mind. I could of course ask it of her—and I shall—but I will have your view first. It . . ."

Vindatri trailed off as both he and Wu Kung became aware of a tremendously incongruous fact: a smile was spreading across DuQuesne's face, a broad, savage grin, and the black eyes were glittering with a keen awareness. "Like I told Maizas of the Molothos, Vindatri—your problem is that you think that you have the *faintest* idea of what you're dealing with!"

DuQuesne's head snapped around, and he looked straight at Wu. "Wu, I'm sorry, but I've kept a couple secrets from you. And it's time you knew one."

"Secrets? What . . . ? "

Vindatri gestured at DuQuesne again, but though the black brows furrowed and tension rose in the big man's body, his voice did not change. "That you're not as limited as you think. That the Arena *is* like Hyperion in one way. It *accepts* us, Wu. Accepts us for *what we truly are in our hearts.*"

Accepts . . . ?

And suddenly Wu Kung remembered DuQuesne's startled glance when he talked to the animals on Humanity's Upper Sphere; the astounded, disbelieving stares of Sethrik and Ariane as he made his return aboard *Thilomon*; the insistence of the Vengeance that what he had done was *impossible*, that it *could not happen.*

Accepts us for what we truly are.

For what I truly am . . . ?

A tremulous wonder and hope began to rise in him. *For what we truly are in our hearts.*

In my heart? In my soul?

He lifted his arms, scarcely daring to believe, but even as he did, he realized he barely *felt* the chains, they felt light as cobwebs, not even as heavy as the Hyperion-designed body would have sensed them.

In my soul? What I truly am?

"What are you saying, Doctor? How are you *speaking*? How can you resist me?" Vindatri's voice was rising in annoyance and confusion.

"He is saying," Wu said, hearing awe and gratitude echoing in his voice, "that I have been playing a part even to myself all along, and that the chains that bound me this time were those of my own making, of my certainty that I was only what I seemed to be."

"What you *seemed* . . . ?"

"What they *told* me I was. And I believed them, and so was chained." He looked up, and knew his green eyes were dancing with emerald flame. "But the chains are gone.

"*The Monkey King lives again!*"

He threw his strength against the shackles, and the concussive force threw Vindatri, Ariane, and Orphan to the ground. He heard a groaning noise from the chains, chains they thought could bind the one who once took the Pillar of the Ocean and made it his staff! HA! This Vindatri would be taught the error of his ways!

DuQuesne's laugh boomed out. "And as for me, Vindatri? Let me find out how strong *your* mind is!"

Wu could *see* the bolt of psychic power that screamed from DuQuesne and hammered Vindatri like an avalanche, see it with the senses that had been dark for decades. *I'd* forgotten *what it is like to see the realm of spirit, the fire of life.*

Forgotten myself.

Vindatri was on his feet somehow, and a shield surrounded him, protecting him from DuQuesne's assault for the moment. "My . . . mind is . . . strong enough. What mysteries! What *surprises!* Yet you are still restrained, and—"

"*NOTHING* restrains *me* except the Gods assembled, and even their armies shudder to face the Great Sage Equal of Heaven!" Wu shouted, and threw all his strength into a single great pull. Muscles bulged on his chest, on his arms, and the veins and tendons stood out on his neck. His breath came quicker, and he let his anger kindle to full flame, caught it, shaped it, *channeled* it into himself, into his spirit. He could *feel* the power around him now, the world of the Arena, so different . . . yet so very much the same . . . and it *answered* his call.

"Even the gods of a thousand worlds could not break those chains, Sun Wu Kung," Vindatri said, and his voice was stronger, his shields seemed to be reinforcing themselves. "Even the power of nuclear fire could only wear them away slowly, not tear them asunder like crude matter. What hope have you of . . . *Segatha's Mercy!*"

The Soul-fire ignited around Sun Wu Kung, and Halintratha vibrated with a deep, bass thunder like the string of a colossal cello. "I . . . ," he ground out, and strained against the quivering chains, claws digging into the deck below him, ". . . will never . . . ," and drew the Soul-fire *inward*, catapulting his strength to that which he had needed when tested against the Three Stone Brothers, strength to lift the Brothers *and* the mountains they stood upon, ". . . be chained . . .", and he heard the whining, stretching sound of something strained beyond its limits, threw the last ounce of self and soul into one final lunge, "AGAIN!"

And those chains—chains forged of the elemental essence of matter, beyond even the strength of legend—shattered with a detonation like the essence of triumph.

Chapter 45

Where . . . am I?

It's okay, Ariane. It's time you woke up. The voice was DuQuesne's, in her mind, the strong, deep voice that spoke without sound. *Vindatri was playing us like we figured, and locked you and Orphan down. And now . . .*

Ariane's vision and mind suddenly *cleared*, and she found herself thinking like *herself*—really, truly like herself—for the first time in weeks. *He did! That son of a—*

Wu Kung's *chi* detonated in white-gold flame around him, and Ariane felt Halintratha itself rock beneath that manifestation of sheer power. Vindatri had staggered back, thrown up his arm, as Wu ground out, "I . . . will never . . . be chained . . . *AGAIN!*"

The chains—glittering with the sheen of CQC, chains whose strength made the ring-carbon Ariane knew so well seem less than cobwebs—parted before the absolute, unstoppable strength of the Monkey King. But she didn't allow herself to contemplate the incredible. "Take this, Vindatri—*vanens!*"

Fire.

A mote of pure incandescence streaked from her pointed finger towards the cloaked figure, who whirled and gestured barely in time; flame erupted across a hemisphere of shield, even as DuQuesne straightened to his full two-meter height and grinned savagely. "You wanted our secrets, you triply-unprintable bastard? Here, *have a sample!*"

She thought she saw a polychromatic sparkle emanating from

DuQuesne's wrist, the ghost of a concept that was, here, as real as herself. Vindatri staggered as though struck, but seemed to recover—

As Sun Wu Kung *tore* through his shield as though it wasn't even there and kicked Vindatri so hard the enigmatic being was flung arrow-straight across the hundred-meter width of the room, to impact with groundshaking force against the wall, leaving an imprint of his body in the polished metal. "Ha! We have *many* samples for you! This is an all-you-can-eat *buffet* of samples! Get up, Vindatri!" He advanced, twirling his staff as though it were a weightless baton. "This would be *boring* if you're down already from a little hit like *that!*"

The crumpled figure stirred, and then a sound emanated from the cowl that sent creeping chills skittering down Ariane's spine.

Vindatri was *laughing.*

"Oh, Sun Wu Kung," he said, rising with careful deliberation, "I would certainly never wish to *bore* my guests!"

Crap. She had really believed that *that* impact had killed Vindatri, or at least knocked him out. But from his voice, he was barely stung. *Wu called it a tap, anyway. That means Wu wasn't really serious yet, but—*

Even as Wu Kung started forward, Vindatri cast both arms outward and shouted an invocation she could only partially understand. But even the beginning was enough to get her to shout out, "*Sonderan!*"

Only a bare fraction of a second saved her, for the instant her shield materialized, the room became a *sea* of seething, crackling lightning. Wu Kung was driven back and she was afraid to see what it did to DuQuesne, and then she heard a buzzing scream behind her.

Orphan! My God, he's going to get killed!

The lightning field subsided, leaving Vindatri standing, tall and forbidding, on a clean and polished spot in the center of blackened chaos. Wu was rising slowly to his feet, and—to her astonishment—DuQuesne looked relatively unharmed. She risked a glance behind her.

Orphan, too, was rising, but with the sluggish motion of one barely a step ahead of unconsciousness. "Orphan!" she shouted, and saw the eyes blink, focus after a moment on her. "Orphan, run! You'll *die!*"

"He will not be alone, Captain Ariane Austin," Vindatri's voice said, echoing throughout Halintratha and shaking the deck beneath her feet. "I will discover your secrets better when you *all* lie dead or dying at my feet!"

Wu Kung gave a grinning snarl and leveled a tremendous blow at Vindatri—only to start in surprise as his staff rebounded from empty air. DuQuesne, too, blinked in wary surprise. "What the . . . that's a mind-screen. Top-drawer, too. How the hell—"

"Do you *children* believe that you have power?" Vindatri said contemptuously, and though he seemed to be almost whispering, Ariane's very bones vibrated with every word, even through her shield. "You know so little, you have seen scarcely the interval of a *illita's* wingbeat in all your lives together, and because you have a surprise or two you believe that makes you the equal of one who has seen civilizations . . . seen *species* rise and fall? I am *Vindatri*, and those who know that name speak it in fear, or revere it as the name of a god!"

"Big talk," DuQuesne said. "Oh, you're a Big-Time Operator, I'll give you that, but all the power you have comes from the Arena, and so do all our little 'surprises.'"

"I have heard that talk a time or two myself!" Wu Kung was grinning broadly, showing his fangs with cheerful savagery. "Demons and gods, dragons and sorcerers, they all say the same things—and I have beaten them all!"

"You're nothing but a renegade Shadeweaver," Ariane said, straightening and stepping to the side, to make sure Orphan had cover behind her. "Older than they let their brethren get, maybe older than we can imagine. But you're still doing the same thing I am . . . and you've been surprised by me a *lot* of times." She raised her hand and let a glow gather around it, as her clothes transformed to the strange uniform she had worn after her Awakening. "I am the Leader of the Faction of Humanity, and you are about to learn the same lesson Amas-Garao learned—and by *God*, it's going to *cost* you!"

She braced one hand with the other. *Time to see if luck's still with us.* "*THIS* is for screwing around with my mind, you son of a bitch!" Focusing all her will on envisioning the result she wanted, she combined *wirthshem* and *geunate*. "*THUNDERQUAKE!*"

The floor *heaved* upward, shattering and splitting like the ground in a quake, and as it did so a concentrated mass of lightning played around and through the rising blocks—rising around Vindatri, and his insubstantial shield quivered under the assault.

Behind her, she heard hesitant footsteps, staggering, then regaining strength. *Orphan's running.* She was relieved, and couldn't blame him; a part of her thought *running* sounded like a real good idea against this being, and Orphan . . . for all his cleverness and secrets and age, he wasn't anything *like* ready to play in this league.

And as Vindatri's shield *surged* outward, blasting the shards of floor to dust, she wondered if *she* was really ready.

He's got a lot on the ball, this guy, came DuQuesne's mental voice. *I'm hitting him hard and his mindshield's still holding. Ariane, you and Wu have to keep him distracted for at least a few seconds, give me a little time to work in.* She could sense a similar message being sent to Wu Kung.

I'll do what I can, Marc . . . but I don't know how long that will be. That chill down her spine was stronger.

Vindatri towered up before them, now surrounded by a sphere of flame and electricity that made his form waver threateningly behind the veil of power. "Surprises, yes, you have shown me many; combining two powers so swiftly, so instinctively, this is yet another. And mysteries, as to why the Arena permits *you* such powers when I have never seen such before, not in all my ages of watching and learning."

A gesture fast as a blink, and brilliant green energy parried another blow of Sun Wu Kung, with a concussion that pushed Ariane back and drove DuQuesne to one knee. "But a mere renegade Shadeweaver? You think far, far too small, too petty, to grasp the truth. I am the *First*, Captain Austin. I am the *reason* the Blood of the Skies fear to let any of their people continue down the path beyond a single lifetime, and I am the nightmare the Faith have in their darkest dreams."

Vindatri's hooded gaze swept the three of them, Wu Kung gathering his own golden power inward, DuQuesne bracing himself with his right arm raised across his chest and a multicolored glow beginning to shine, and Ariane, preparing another strike, wondering how she could draw on the power that she'd felt on her Awakening and release, and behind Vindatri she saw a streaming of ebony and smoke, heard the building howl of a wind from beyond any sky. "But you wish to try these powers against *me*? Come, then—if you are prepared for what awaits!"

"HA! Are *you* prepared?" Wu Kung streaked forward, and his strike could have leveled a skyscraper; instead, it touched nothing, for Vindatri was gone. Instantly, Wu disappeared, reappearing behind the rematerialized alien, who disappeared again in turn. Ariane found herself staring open-mouthed as the two figures blinked in and out of existence, flickering around the room and exchanging blows that shook Halintratha like a shanty near a battlefield. *Dammit! I can't get a bead on—*

Let me help you on that, DuQuesne thought. *He can move all he wants—but he can't move faster than thought.*

Suddenly Vindatri was still, figure tense, fighting off an unseen assault. *DuQuesne—tell Wu to hit the deck, and you too!*

He didn't question her; she felt the order go out, and let her own savage grin show as she flung her arm up over her head. "*Wrath of God!*"

Astrella's weapon, that she had worn on her wrist for so long she didn't even think about it—detonated, firing a starburst of ring-carbon needles trailing superconducting cable. As she had hoped, with DuQuesne hammering his mind, Vindatri's physical defense had dropped for just a few moments, and one of the needles struck home; instantly the others curved about, swung in, and drove inward.

Through those cables surged not just Ariane's natural electric-eel derived shock, but all the power of lightning she could throw from the powers Vindatri himself had taught her. The superconducting wires suddenly flared and exploded, but not before delivering what amounted to a full-on bolt of lightning directly to the alien would-be god.

Vindatri was hurled backwards, convulsing with the shock, and Wu Kung was up in that moment; his staff swung like a baseball bat and caught the staggered Vindatri perfectly in his midriff, folding him up and pitching him straight into the far wall to create another dent in the alien alloy. She could sense DuQuesne hammering against Vindatri's mind with all the iron, unbreakable will that his Hyperion design had implied. *We still haven't been able to give Marc his few seconds.*

But Vindatri was *rising*, holding off the assault, and with a gesture stopped Wu Kung in midair, sent him flying in the opposite direction. "Mundane and empowered together, a wise and innovative choice, Captain Ariane Austin," Vindatri said in a voice whose pain was rapidly fading. "You are beginning to coordinate, to recognize your *only* chance is in a union I cannot begin to match. But it takes thousands of *nytill*, an entire hive, to pull down one person. There are but three of you, and all you achieve so far is to *show* me how very important it is that I learn *everything* about you!"

Dammit. This guy makes Amas-Garao look like a pushover. But . . . But . . .

She could *feel* the power, that same strength that had been unleashed twice beyond her control, waiting within, a roiling inchoate mass of energy that was vastly beyond anything she had yet reached.

If I can figure out how to tap that . . .

We all have that somewhere, DuQuesne's voice agreed, tensely. *Wu's getting stronger every minute. I think I am, too. We've got a chance.*

But as the dark energy she had sensed rampaged through the room and sent her and her friends flying, made her twitch and scream as in a seizure of acid and ice, she knew the real question was whether any of them would *live* long enough to *take* that chance.

Chapter 46

"Lead elements are about to clear obscuration. If the enemy is not blind throughout their eye, they will spot us in the next several minutes," Alztanza said.

"Once all four forward elements of the formation are clear enough to guide, I want the whole formation to go to charging speed," Dajzail said. "Give our enemies as little chance to prepare as possible."

"What distance should we begin engagement?" Alztanza asked.

"You're the Fleet Master; I leave that to you."

"Understood." He studied the display, which was now showing with increasing detail and precision the layout of the enemy forces. "Currently we have located . . . six major enemy vessels, plus the fortresses around the Sky Gates. They have *many* Sky Gates—eight, to be exact."

He heard his own buzz of surprise. "That will require a bit more to secure than we had originally calculated. And also makes this Sphere even more valuable. But they *must* have more than six major vessels."

"Closer to ten, perhaps as many as fifteen, though I incline to the smaller number based on both our prior intelligence and the preliminary data our scouts transmitted. While this makes little difference on the scale at which our fleet is operating, I am still not comfortable not knowing the location of perhaps half my opponents' fleet."

"The six seem grouped fairly closely near the Sky Gates."

"Hm. Yes, that actually makes sense. They have some outer patrols. But with only four ships in the patrol—"

"—yes. Their chance of detecting us was always very low, and now it is too late." Alztanza gave an amused chuckle. "Not that it would make much difference."

Dajzail watched as Alztanza opened up an encrypted Fleet channel. "Ship Masters, this is Fleet Master Alztanza speaking for Leader Dajzail. Upon all four elements—Claws and Mouths—reporting clear forward, the entire formation is to go to charging speed. Maintain radio buoy relay deployment to assure communications.

"Engage the enemy at five hundred kilometers, or when first they mount an effective attack."

Dajzail nodded after a moment of consideration. Major warship-class missiles could strike at ranges of up to two thousand kilometers, and *very* powerful energy weapons could engage at about half that range—but to penetrate the defenses of large warships even such cannon required either good fortune, or much closer range. Hypersonic cannon were even more limited with a range no greater than approximately three hundred kilometers. *A shame that the limitations of the Arena effectively mean that most species have already reached, or at least approached, the peak of reasonable weapons development even before they enter.* The basic rules of weapons engagement had not changed for millennia, at least.

Alztanza was taking a slight risk—the enemy could easily wait until they were within, say, a thousand kilometers and then unleash many missiles and hope for fortunate shots with energy cannon—but the Fleet Master was obviously hoping that the human undercreatures would *also* want to wait for closest approach so as to be able to strike with maximum effective firepower.

Dajzail actually doubted that would happen—the sight of a force so huge approaching would undoubtedly panic almost anyone, and they would want to do their best to destroy as many ships as they could as soon as possible. But Alztanza probably knew that, which is why he allowed engagement as soon as the enemy really began to fight back.

The attacking force (measured from the forward points) was nine thousand, two hundred and seventy kilometers distant from the Sky Gates when the lower Mouth finally broke cloud cover. Moving as smoothly and steadily as though welded into a single unit, the Claws and Mouth formation accelerated to full charging speed.

"Beautiful maneuvering, Alztanza. You really have them well-drilled."

"Credit to the Ship Masters; they've drilled a *lot* along the way."

"How long before we reach engagement distance?"

Alztanza checked instruments. "We are limited of course by the slowest elements of the assault force, so can barely reach the lower limits of the hypersonic range; engagement will be in . . . one hour and twenty-six minutes."

"And the battle?"

The big Molothos gave a wry chuckle. "The event we have come all this way for? Even with eight Sky Gate fortresses, I would be surprised if it lasts for a third of that. In less than two hours, the Faction of Humanity will be broken and crippled before the power of the Molothos."

Dajzail very much liked the sound of that. "And enough time to have a few bites before coming back to the main engagement. Care to join me, 'Tanza?"

"I'd be honored."

Despite his rapidly-rising optimism, Dajzail did not break out the celebratory *ithyan* and *amakka* yet. Long experience had taught him that premature celebration of victory was exceedingly unwise, and tempting the unknown chance of the Arena? He refused to be that foolish, though others might call his thoughts superstition.

He could not, he found, *quite* shake a niggling feeling of worry as his mind kept coming back to two facts:

Blessing of Fire had been a powerful, modern exploration warship, just like *Claws of Vengeance*. It had been commanded by a well-trained crew, veterans of many ventures into the Deeps.

And yet *two* human beings had somehow defeated that ship and her entire crew.

Ahead of them were *thousands* of those unpredictable undercreatures.

But he shoved that concern to the back of his mind. This was a fully-prepared assault force, ludicrously larger than any that would have been reasonably expected. Everything had been taken into account.

Finally, as they were clearing the platters, Alztanza looked up. "Past two thousand kilometers. No fire so far."

"Shorter-range missiles won't be able to reach until our people are almost half that distance in."

"True. They will probably initiate their first assault then, at about twelve hundred kilometers from the Gates."

The speaker went live. "Fleet Master, the six vessels are moving."

"Course and likely destination?"

"Acceleration is slow; judging by their maneuvers, concensus is that they are going to form an interception force ahead of the Sky Gates along our vector."

"Sensible, if futile. Begin closing Claws and Mouths."

"As you direct, Fleet Master."

Dajzail stood. "Let us go to the command deck. I wish to watch this directly."

By the time the two of them had reached the command deck, all four elements of the attack fleet were less than fifteen hundred kilometers out. "No attacks yet. The six ships have formed into a tight group at the calculated junction point of the four elements when Claws and Mouth close."

"Understood. All weapons are prepared?"

"All weapons prepared, all defenses active. We—"

A signal from the fleet broke in. "Detecting an anomaly on our bearing—"

A second ship. "—metallic echo from debris—"

Alztanza went rigid. "*Shear off! Shear—*"

Detonations erupted from the speakers, explosions whose sound would quickly cut off. On the display, the multiplicity of images from the fleet showed explosions throughout all four of the assaulting forces.

"What—"

"Mines!" Alztanza said, his voice wavering in disbelief. "Mines distributed and concealed *long* before our arrival in a pattern that *saturated* our formation!"

"How many—"

"Reports are still coming in. But Daj . . . Daj, this means they *knew we were coming!*"

"A scout we missed—"

"If so, it was a scout *tens of thousands* of kilometers out, that returned and left no trace! This minefield wasn't put up in a day and a half!"

"Three hundred ninety-seven ships destroyed," reported Fleet Operations, in the dispassionate tone required of such reporters. "Fifty-three additional vessels significantly damaged."

Four hundred fifty vessels—nearly one-tenth of the assault force— destroyed or damaged before we could fire a shot?

"Open fire and advance!" Alztanza ordered. "Observers watch for additional mines—although that was likely a timed detonation of all mines they had laid. Concentrate fire first on the mobile forces, and— *Homeworld's NAME!*"

Dajzail felt himself sag to the deck in disbelieving horror.

From every one of the human vessels, from the huge Sky Gate fortresses, from emplacements on the distant Sphere's *ground*, and from four distant locations in the sky itself—intolerable spears of brilliance lanced out, and where any of them struck, one of the Molothos vessels *vanished* in a blaze of light.

For an instant he and Alztanza were frozen, unable to comprehend what they had seen. *Some of those attacks were from* thousands *of kilometers away. Beyond any distance of any weapon ever fired in the Arena!*

The impossible fires streaked out a second time; one of the ships *not thirty kilometers away* went up in an explosion whose echo shook *Claws of Vengeance* seconds later.

That broke his paralysis. "This is Leader Dajzail. Fleet, free to operate in Seventh-Seventh forces. Reserves, we are already in range of this new weapon, so retreat may be impossible. We will not desert our forward comrades. Seventh-Forces Nine through Thirteen, close and support." He glanced at Alztanza for confirmation as he continued, "Evasion and countermeasures as Ship Masters deem necessary. Primary targets are ten ships, the six already at the Sky Gates and the four which have revealed their presence with this new weapon. All ships, free to fire at will."

He observed a third salvo of the new weapon, but now what he saw gave him new heart, especially as one of the six defending vessels shuddered under a fortunate strike by a Molothos missile. "This super-weapon of theirs is powerful, yes—but it still has to be aimed and fired, and it can—and *does* miss. They have limited emplacements of this weapon. We still have overwhelming force on our side, and they are not invincible."

Dajzail leaned forward and let his furious war-screech echo through the fleet. "We *will* destroy their pathetic fleet, and when we are done we will sift the ashes of their fortresses and arm *our* fleets with their own weapon!"

Chapter 47

We underestimated him.

DuQuesne had rarely felt such an overwhelming aura of danger and power as was radiating from Vindatri, and never before outside of Hyperion. *The First. First Shadeweaver? Damnation, how old does that make* him?

Another wave of that dark power surged towards him, and he barely shattered it with one of the strongest mental bolts he could muster. *It's like fighting Fairchild when Mentor's opposite numbers were backing him! Except Fairchild didn't have blasted* magic tricks *in addition to his mind!*

Wu Kung somehow tore his way through shields of gloom and deception and caught Vindatri, clawed hands grasping, the cloaked adversary weaving, blocking, but unable to evade the greatest warrior of Hyperion, the two of them disappearing, chasing each other in another duel of flashing steps that made a mockery of distance.

Ariane was rising once more from where Vindatri's last hurricane-storm attack had sent her, and her blue hair rose in the blazing aura of energy she called forth from the Arena's secret heart.

Ariane, we need a strategy!

A mental grin. *I know, but while we're working it out, we need to keep hitting Vindatri. And I've got a few new tricks, I think.*

How? He didn't finish—

Luck, Marc. I've got to trust to luck that my guesses, my inspirations, are going to be mostly on the money. If we've got the Blessing of the Arena . . . well, we sure as hell need it now! As Vindatri crashed to the floor so violently it bent under him, Ariane raised both hands. *"Twin Sevenfold Path!"*

A cone of rainbows, rippling colors in succession almost too fast for even DuQuesne's eyes to register, enveloped Vindatri and he convulsed, let loose a cry that echoed with pain and joy and hatred and love. Ariane kept the spectral energy flowing, teeth gritted and eyes wide, stopping only as Wu Kung plummeted from above, driving his staff hard into Vindatri's back.

DuQuesne half-expected, and hoped, to see that blunt shaft drive straight through the Arena's archmage, pinning him to Halintratha's deck like a bug to a collection; instead Vindatri merely gave a grunt of agony and splayed out his arms in a halfhearted gesture of defiance.

Halfhearted or not, the wave of freezing, flaming shards of steel that exploded from the deck was almost enough to finish DuQuesne instantly; the mental power of someone *designed* to be the ultimate product of humanity—both within and without Hyperion—barely blunted the impact; he flung up his arm barely in time and felt ice and fire impaling him across half his body.

Get up, *get up, dammit, you sorry excuse for a superman!* He heaved himself back up, yanking out the remaining splinters, just in time to see Vindatri roar out an incomprehensible phrase that sent Wu Kung *streaking* across the room like a meteor, to strike the huge picture-window dead-center; the crystal-clear window cracked and then *detonated* into flying glassy fragments as Wu Kung hurtled out and into the dark Deeps beyond.

"Wu!" Ariane shouted, half-turning in that direction.

No! He'll be fine. Focus, Ariane. I need you to work with me, channel your strength through me, a mental bolt with both *our wills driving it!*

He suddenly felt her mind, angry but clear, certain and stubborn, filled with a fascination for this world that was still alive, still *there*, even in the midst of this battle, and he found himself laughing for a moment. *She is everything I thought she was.*

And you, Marc, are everything I hoped you would be. Let's take this guy.

We'll sure give him something to remember, by every one of those rows of apple trees!

Their combined wills hammered like falling asteroids against

Vindatri's mindshield, and the alien would-be god staggered backwards.

But . . .

But he's getting stronger, Ariane's mindvoice said grimly. *We're cranking up the power and he's running right along with us!*

DuQuesne felt icy fingers trailing down his spine. *Is he . . . still just testing us?*

"A . . . most substantial . . . effort, DuQuesne, Captain Austin." He glanced sideways. "And Wu Kung."

Wu had reappeared at the window, literally riding on clouds beneath his feet. "I am not so easy to get rid of!"

"So it would appear. Yet there are so many more ways to try!"

His outflung arms sent a circle of pure white energy expanding outwards, and DuQuesne braced himself against the tremendous impact; it half-stunned him, like a boxer being struck a blow that *could* have knocked him out but missed by the merest fraction of a centimeter. But even as he registered the fact that the others, too, had somehow stayed standing, he smelled a hint of something sweetish.

He stopped his breathing reflexively, his air-passages sealing themselves as a ghostly memory of someone shouting, "Vee-two gas! Get tight!" echoed back from the past that had never been. "*Gas! Ariane, Wu—*"

Sun Wu Kung had lost his battle in Hyperion when his adversaries had chosen gas as the final weapon, and DuQuesne felt the remembered horror and shame reverberating through Wu as he tried to fight off the effects. Ariane had thrown up one of her spherical shells of protection, but it had merely sealed her in with the gas that was already around her. DuQuesne saw her starting to sag, and Wu's charge towards Vindatri was sluggish, uncertain.

DuQuesne felt his own body starting to slow down. *Dammit; it's a contact poison, through the skin, not just an inhalant!* But even as his body was shutting down, he realized that his *mind* was as strong and active as ever.

Well, I will be damned. Even that *part of Second-Stage training works here; no drug or intoxicant, howsoever powerful, can affect the workings of a mind at that level. Thanks, Mentor—wherever you are.*

He allowed himself to collapse slowly to the deck, slightly ahead of

Wu Kung, without showing any sign of the fully-active mind still within the inert frame. *My best chance yet.*

"Well fought, all of you," Vindatri said quietly, as even Wu's tail finally slid into complete limpness. "Yet even within combat there can be subtleties, and you forgot that for one who can control the various aspects of reality, even the very *air* can be a weapon. Against one sufficiently prepared, of course, this is of less use, but with the right . . . enhancement from the power, it can overcome the defenses of your medical nanotechnology."

He glided forward, moving now with the same unnerving smoothness that Amas-Garao liked to affect, and lifted Wu Kung, studying him. "Unique. As with all of you. I will learn more from the three of you, I think, than I have learned in *millennia.*"

Then, DuQuesne spoke into Vindatri's mind, *learn THIS.*

The mental bolt he threw then would have staggered Mentor himself; though the vast majority of its power was in pure telepathic fury, there was enough physical mindpower to catapult Vindatri thirty meters and more across the floor. He tumbled limply to rest, a doll cast aside by a child.

DuQuesne focused, both on his nanos and on the imitation of Hyperion's power the Arena granted him. *Come on, come* on, *burn this crap out, I don't think even* that *is enough to finish him.* He'd felt resistance, a hard core as obdurate as adamant, at the center of Vindatri's mind, and it had not cracked under that assault.

As he felt the gases' effect fade, he switched his focus. *Still shackled. That's almost killed me more than once in this battle; my psionic defenses wouldn't have been* crap *in this fight if Telzey and Locke hadn't taught me how to channel the physical power too. But for this I can't use brute strength . . .*

He remembered, and for once allowed the memory its full force. *Here it's just as though it was real. It is real. I have to believe it, accept it . . .*

A wise old face before his, pale green skin with a huge white square-cut beard and flowing white hair framing it. "As you know, matter and energy are but two sides of a single coin. Manufacturing the ultimate form of matter is merely a process of structuring energy. But the mind, too, can control energy . . ."

He focused on the shackles. *Believe. What that old Norlaminian said, what Mentor taught me,* believe *it. Sense of perception, focused down to the level of the fifth order* . . .

And suddenly he could *see* it—the structure of the Coherent Quark Composite itself, a glorious, interconnected, almost infinite net-like matrix, a webwork of energy that somehow held itself frozen in crystalline perfection. It would take incredible energy to shatter those bonds, and doing so would probably shatter even ring-carbon enhanced bones.

But if you could *unravel* it . . . just along the narrowest of lines . . .

Wu's fingers twitched, and then he rolled slowly to his feet. "I . . . am not . . . so easily finished," he grated out.

"And," Ariane said shakily, "I'd *almost* cleaned it out when I fell down."

DuQuesne felt a broad grin on his face as he rose—the last, instead of the first, of his friends to do so.

Vindatri wobbled, but he, too, was rising.

DuQuesne flexed his arms—and the CQC shackles fell away, cut in razor-fine perfection on both sides. The others stared, but Vindatri froze in utter consternation. *Wu, Ariane, are you ready?*

What's the plan? Wu asked, as Ariane muttered a word he heard as "heal" and he suddenly felt stronger.

In a single mental image he showed them, the actions, the thoughts, the motions. And the three of them moved as one.

Ariane ran forward, summoning and then reinforcing her shield, enclosing all three of them. Vindatri's defensive ward, too, was up, but his eyes were narrow and his stance less certain and arrogant. DuQuesne shielded his friends' minds from sparkling lashes of deception and ensnarement, and Wu sent a veritable *cannon* of spirit energy forward, striking like the hammer of the gods.

The three of them separated to take Vindatri from three directions at once, but somehow Ariane's shield split *with* them, and DuQuesne felt his grin widen viciously as he saw disbelief in the hooded eyes of their enemy. Now all three were protected in their own shields, and DuQuesne kept up a ceaseless barrage of mental attacks, preventing Vindatri from making any but the most cursory attempts to control or mentally assault his other friends. *We're just about evenly matched there, looks like. But that means he can't afford to focus on anyone but me with his mind-powers.*

Wu Kung kicked, punched, and slammed his staff against Vindatri's defenses, and each blow carried the force of a falling redwood. Ariane sent storm and fire and ice and wind and lightning and the power of earth like an avalanche of the elements, piling up ruination and devastation against the First Shadeweaver's shuddering defenses. *They're still getting stronger! Maybe he is too, but there's three of us, and together I think—I really think—we're starting to outpace him!*

With what terrific mental effort DuQuesne could only guess, Vindatri managed to focus long enough to disappear. *Is he running? I don't know if we can afford him escaping!*

But it appeared Vindatri felt *he* could not afford to lose this battle—and, DuQuesne thought, he was probably right. They'd learned an awful lot about Vindatri, and if they managed to *beat* him and escape, that mystique he talked about would come apart if word ever got out. The dark-cloaked figure sent a rain of red firebolts screaming through the entire volume of the room, causing their shields to waver on the edge of dissolution.

Ariane shouted out something new, an invocation with words like *galzeldis* and *ottilra*, and a column of blue-white fire ripped through Vindatri's shield as though it wasn't even there, struck him so hard and with such clawing, savage fury that part of his robe was shredded, and sea-emerald blood trailed behind.

"Ruyi Jingu *Bang!*"

From halfway across the room the Monkey King's staff extended, a spear a bowshot long, and sent Vindatri spinning, the so-called god having barely evaded a direct strike. DuQuesne found himself staring. *That staff can't . . .*

And then he realized that by telling Wu he was what he believed, Wu Kung had simply *believed* that this was really his real staff . . . and it had become so.

Spheres of black metal formed around the three, and DuQuesne found himself in blackness. But he could sense the interior of the sphere was filled with vicious spikes, and it was contracting . . .

Still, it couldn't block his *mind*, and so he went for Vindatri's thoughts, directing bolts and beams and needles of mental force to slow and weaken Vindatri's will. The sphere fell apart; as he emerged, he saw that Ariane had somehow burst hers apart from within, while Wu—unsurprisingly—had simply punched his way out.

The room was a complete shambles now, and the combatants were now ducking and leaping and taking shelter around and behind sheared and ripped deck-plating that rose a dozen meters into the air, leaping over holes that dropped away to other decks below, sending debris of all types at each other. DuQuesne felt even his muscles starting to give the first warnings of fatigue. *Dammit. We're slowly pulling ahead, but if he can manage to outlast even one of us, he'll get the upper hand, sure as water's wet.*

And then a voice spoke in his head—but not a telepathic voice at all.

Dr. DuQuesne, can you hear me?

Orphan? Yeah, I read you, but we're still in this little discussion with Vindatri.

A mental buzzing laugh. *Indeed, and I am convinced that the noise of your "conversation" can be heard on Nexus Arena itself! Halintratha shakes impossibly beneath your feet.*

DuQuesne parried another mental assault, then visualized a focused, flaming needle of psychic energy stabbing, piercing, ripping through shields; Vindatri withdrew his attacks, threw up multiple courses of defense, even as Ariane and Wu hit him from both sides at once.

So if I might, please, could you take the conflict outside?

DuQuesne felt an eyebrow raise, then he grinned. *Gotcha. I think. Hold on!*

He switched back to the mental links he had forged with his friends. *New plan, people—hit Vindatri hard in that direction!*

Ariane's puzzlement was clear on the sideband, but she showed no hesitation, and Wu Kung simply laughed. *It doesn't matter to me which direction I hit him from!*

DuQuesne sprinted forward with all the speed his Hyperion body could muster, just as Vindatri was recovering from yet another blow from Wu. Focusing all his mental force on his fist, he penetrated the First Shadeweaver's wavering shields and then swung, a massive uppercut driven by every muscle from the tips of his toes to the clenched fingers as they drove straight up into Vindatri's chin.

The combined psionic and physical concussion lifted Vindatri from his feet and hurled him forty meters up, impacting with earthquake force on the ceiling; Vindatri floundered, trying to regain his bearings and control, as he began to drop back down, and that was when both Ariane and Wu Kung *hammered* Vindatri with blasts of energy that struck simultaneously at his center of mass.

The cloaked figure streaked like a meteor through the air, his robes now alight, and hurtled through the shattered picture window. Ariane rose from the ground and Wu Kung called the clouds, but even as they began to move DuQuesne could see that Vindatri had slowed, was recovering with hideous speed.

And then a voice spoke, not in his head, but from outside, a voice with the echoing power of a god . . . and the ironic, deep tones of Orphan:

"Goodbye, Vindatri."

Four spears of intolerable coruscating brilliance eradicated the gloom with eye-searing intensity, all focused on Vindatri. The combined beams continued on, and DuQuesne felt Halintratha quake as four primary beams ripped a hole completely through the brooding, massive structure.

The inconceivable radiance faded . . . leaving nothing in its wake. For a moment all was silent, and then Orphan spoke—at considerably reduced volume—as *Zounin-Ginjou* slowly drifted into view.

"Consider this . . . my resignation from your service," Orphan said.

Chapter 48

"Has the message torpedo been sent?" Simon demanded.

"Sent three minutes ago, Doctor," Captain Fitzhugh said. "Remember that they have to absorb the intelligence we sent; they want to come out of the gates in the right positions, at the right speeds, and with a good idea of what they're going to see, or it could be a disaster for them and us instead of the Molothos." His back was tense. "But I sure as hell hope they get a move on."

Even as he said that, three Molothos missiles evaded *Freyja*'s defenses and the warship detonated. "Dear God," Simon heard himself say.

"Dammit! *Menhit*, *'Oro*, and *Ogun*, concentrate fire on their force designated M-17! They're getting too close to Gate Six!"

"We'll do our best," came the deceptively smooth and calm voice of Captain Takei on the Polynesian-named *'Oro*, "but there *are* just a few more of them than there are of us. The minefield and the primaries have shaken them up, but I think they're starting to recover."

"Where the hell is *Hachiman*?"

Oasis gave a laugh, a heart-lifting sound on the desperate command bridge. "Driving the enemy *nuts* out there, ten o'clock high!"

Seven Molothos warships were chasing *Hachiman*, but even with superior numbers and a squadron of deployed fighter-craft, they were losing ground. The massive, kilometer-long *Hachiman* suddenly spun about—a maneuver that should have torn her apart, even if it were physically possible—and drove straight into the teeth of her pursuers, who scattered in desperate and uncoordinated directions to evade as she unleashed her primary beams in all directions. Suddenly there were *three* warships in pursuit, and *Hachiman* was driving through a cloud of expanding vapor.

Even knowing *about the "Hyperion Advantage," I can scarcely grasp what I'm seeing. Simply because Velocity Celes is at the controls,* Hachiman *is able to achieve speed and maneuverability completely beyond anything such a vessel should be able to survive.*

But even that did not grant *Hachiman* invulnerability; the Liberated-gifted warship shuddered visibly as one missile detonated at the tip of one of the control vanes. *We've lost one of our ten ships already; now* Hachiman, Ogun, *and* Nayanazgeni *are damaged, and three of the Molothos' forty-nine-ship task forces are almost close enough to start bombarding the surface.*

As he thought that, chimes rang through the air. "Gate Four activated. Multiple transits detected."

A *torrent* of warships exploded from Sky Gate Four, moving at full speed and fanning out in a coordinated movement to englobe the Gate. Some of the ships were *immense*, five-kilometer-long wedge-shaped monsters, which were disgorging *clouds* of one-person fighters, while others were sleek, dagger-like vessels that reminded Simon of the aesthetics of the Vengeance, not the Analytic.

Whoever was directing the Molothos' fleet action was not asleep at the switch; almost instantly the Molothos' vessels sheared off from their attack vectors, adjusting course and deployment to prepare for assaults from this new entry into the combat.

"Broad-band signal detected from the Analytic fleet, Captain," said Lieutenant Reynolds from the comm station.

"Put it on, Lieutenant; I want to hear this. And if the Molothos answer, make sure that gets cut in."

"Aye, Captain."

The main viewport suddenly lit up to show Relgof standing before a command chair in the center of a huge operations center. "This is First Researcher Relgof Nov'ne Knarph of the Analytic, broadcasting to the Molothos force now assaulting the Sphere of Humanity and specifically to Dajzail, Leader of the Molothos. Break off your attack *immediately* or face the consequences of war—not merely with humanity, but with the Great Faction of the Analytic!"

It was, Simon thought, a credit to the ability of a Molothos to deal with sudden shocks that it only took twenty seconds for a second transmission to light up the other side of the viewport. "This is Dajzail, Leader of the Great Faction of the Molothos. We reject your empty threat. Retreat! This battle does not concern you, and you will not risk the war and inevitable defeat that comes with opposing the True People. I give you five minutes to comply and begin your retreat."

Rel drew himself up taller, and his rough tenor voice was suddenly sinister and grim. "You misjudge the power and resolution of the Analytic at your peril, Dajzail of the Molothos. The Analytic has entered into a full and unfettered partnership with Humanity—attested to before the Arena itself—and injury done to them is now done to us. I repeat myself—*break off immediately*, or the Analytic and the Molothos are at war, and we shall place the full resources of the Analytic at the disposal of Humanity! You have *two* minutes to comply!"

Simon found himself holding his breath. Oasis whispered, "Do you think Dajzail's going to blink?"

The transmission from the Molothos had not yet resumed. *They are thinking; perhaps debating, arguing.* "I hope so. I *desperately* hope so. A war between Great Factions will be terrifying, and cost the lives of so many on both sides. But . . . we cannot surrender, and I do not know if Dajzail and the Molothos—"

The massive red and black armored creature appeared again, and the razor-edged fighting claws gestured, a gutting slash of negation. "The Great Faction of the Molothos will not be intimidated or threatened, Analytic. You have three hundred sixty-three vessels added to their feeble forces. Even with their surprising weapons and an ambush, our forces utterly outmatch yours and theirs combined. Stay or flee as you will; Humanity must pay for their insults to the honor and power of the Molothos, and if the Analytic chooses to step between us and our rightful due—then war it shall be. Dajzail of the Molothos—ending communcation!"

Relgof was suddenly alone on the screen. His image flickered for a moment. "Transmission is now narrow-beam and encrypted."

"It was worth a try, my friends. And I truly believe that they considered retreat; but their pride . . ." he spread his hands. "So now war it will be."

"I'm sorry, Relgof," Simon said.

"As am I. But not sorry for our choice." He looked in the direction of his own viewscreen. "Only for the people—yours, ours, and even theirs—who are about to pay the price for that pride."

Captain Fitzhugh nodded. "So am I." As Relgof vanished from the screen, he turned to Reynolds. "Lieutenant, open a fleetwide secure channel."

"Open, sir."

"Combined Human-Analytic fleet, this is Captain Fitzhugh. Our attempt at a peaceful resolution has failed. Speaking honestly, we have virtually no chance to win, even with superior weaponry and the advantage of home ground and the various surprises we have prepared. The Molothos are going to take this one. Our only choices are either to retreat . . . or to make them pay for our Sphere, pay in their ships and blood for every single one of our ships, every one of our people, that they're going to kill today, tomorrow, and every day after that until they're beaten.

"Because they *will* be beaten, I promise. The Analytic is on our side, and I think—I *know*—that we will find other allies. But today, we are—without a miracle—going to lose."

He straightened and looked directly into the screen. "Retreat *is* an option. But we do not choose to *take* that option. The Molothos think they can destroy us, they think they can terrify us, with such numbers that even now they can send ten ships against our every one.

"I say they are wrong. We will make them pay for every millimeter of space they take. And we will not be terrified of them."

He smiled coldly, and Simon was glad of Oasis' presence nearby, even though Fitzhugh was his ally. "Ladies, gentlemen, allies—we will teach *them* to fear. All ships, all emplacements, free to target and fire. *Hachiman, Triglav, Athena*, draw fire and try to bring a force through minefield seven-two. Analytic forces, you've been given the secondary minefield deployments and IFF signals, all fields are active; make use of them."

The captain then turned to Simon. "Dr. Sandrisson, your knowledge of ship movements is now no longer needed; we can see what they are doing. I want you in the courier shuttle *immediately*. If it looks like we're going to get hit, you're going back."

A part of him wanted to protest, but he felt Oasis' hand clamp on his arm and knew he had no options. "Understood, Captain. But . . . wait as long as you can."

"You want to see it all?" Captain Fitzhugh asked in surprise.

"In a sense . . . I *did* start all this. And if all these people are dying for what I began, and what I have seen . . . yes, I owe it to them to see it all."

"All right. But go *straight* to the shuttle."

As Oasis half-dragged him out, he heard the Captain command, "Helm, get us up to Gate Four. When we launch the shuttle I want Dr. Sandrisson to be able to go out and straight to transition . . ."

"It isn't your fault, Simon," Oasis said from next to him as they ran.

"I know. Yet I feel as though it is. Foolish, but true." He looked at her grim but certain face as they ran. "You do know that *Andraste* is likely to be destroyed. We probably will never launch that shuttle, let alone escape." The thought of Oasis dying—after everything she'd *already* gone through in her life—was at least as painful as the thought of losing Ariane. He found he was much less concerned with his own death; he had, after all, achieved so much.

"I know that's what the *odds* say," she answered, and there was a fleeting smile on her face, a momentary twinkle in the green eyes. "but whose rules do *I* play by?"

Simon suddenly laughed. "Of course. You play by *yours*, because this *is* your Hyperion kind of thing, isn't it?"

"Hopeless situations, snappy one-liners, an escape from impossible odds, and saving my companion along with me? You bet!"

She laughed and dragged him forward, and he let a tiny smile lift the corners of his mouth. A war was nothing to celebrate.

But the thought that she would live *was*.

Chapter 49

Ariane stood staring, half-blinded by the afterimages of the four titanic beams. Then she turned around, feeling a smile of incredible relief spreading wider and wider across her face, and found both DuQuesne and Wu Kung there, hugging her so tight she almost couldn't breathe. "We did it. We *beat* him!"

"All *four* of us, yes," DuQuesne said, laughing.

Subtle shadow fell over them, and Ariane looked around to see *Zounin-Ginjou*'s forward lock open and extend a ramp into the broken picture window. To her surprise, Orphan literally *flew* down the ramp and lifted all *three* of them in a momentary embrace before stepping back. "My friends, I am *very* glad to see you all intact!"

"Thanks to you!" she said. "My *God*, I never imagined he'd be that powerful. I mean, I knew he'd be strong, but . . ."

"I had somewhat more time to contemplate his potential power . . . but yes, he was even more than I had expected," Orphan said.

"That was a *heck* of a brainstorm there, using the primaries on him. I hadn't even thought of that," said DuQuesne. "Not that it's usually a practical approach, firing large-scale naval ordnance at one person."

"Indeed—rather fortunately not practical, I would agree. And in truth, I confess I did *not* think of it at first."

Wu Kung nodded. "I could smell it. You were running away, back there."

"I confess it most completely. When Vindatri revealed his powers and you were *matching* him, I . . . fled. Quite abjectly terrified. You understand, of course, the usual attitude of an Arena resident such as myself towards risk, and how . . . one-sided the risks would be for someone without your . . . extraordinary gifts . . . in the middle."

She remembered well how the average citizen of the Arena seemed to react to odds that a human being might risk without blinking . . . and this situation was one that would've made even a seasoned human warrior blanch and run. "Orphan, if I hadn't had pretty much no choice, *plus* everything he'd taught me, believe me, I'd have been running right next to you."

A buzz-chuckle and a deprecating flutter of the wings. "Ahh, Captain Austin, you must pardon me for doubting your kind imagery. Having see you dare such odds before, I suspect you would have still attempted to best Vindatri were you armed with naught but a spoon."

DuQuesne's laugh was a startled explosion of mirth. "I think you know Ariane too well for her own good."

"Ha! That he does!" Wu Kung agreed, his fanged smile wide and cheerful. "But he does not add that the captain would have *won* using that spoon!"

"Oh, stop it, all of you." She felt a touch of heat on her cheeks. "Luck and balls only go so far. Well, okay, this time the luck was that we all had something he didn't expect."

"As it has been . . . rather dramatically . . . revealed to me, might I at least be given some *explanation* for the impossible?" Orphan asked. "You successfully hid these . . . *unbelievably* formidable capabilities from me for all the time of our association. And—I agree—completely justifiably. The fact they were unknown to me assured us that Vindatri, too, would be little if any less surprised than I, a rather crucial factor in this battle. But now that the secret is out . . . ?"

She glanced to DuQuesne. The towering Hyperion shrugged. "Maybe. Tell the rest of *your* little adventure first."

Orphan gave his customary handtap of agreement. "Mine is, undoubtedly, the less difficult tale to tell. So, I fled in utter terror for my life, and great fear that Vindatri would still win—for he was not only powerful but ancient beyond our knowledge. I confess freely that when first I arrived in *Zounin-Ginjou*, my only thought was to launch and travel at all speed away from this place, never to return."

Ariane really couldn't blame him for the thought. "But you didn't. Why?"

"At first . . . because I had made a *promise*, Captain. To DuQuesne, when he had provided me with a means of secure communication that, I believe, even you did not know of, that the Liberated would remain committed to your cause."

"You are a being of your word! Good; that is something to build trust upon!" Wu Kung said.

"It is, in many ways, the foundation of the Arena," Orphan agreed. "But even that . . . I was committed to your *cause*, but really, your *cause* was Humanity, not your individual survival—something all of you had shown, or told me, more than once. So even in fleeing I could do that—bring what I knew to Humanity, though I knew that talking freely about what I knew might well bring Vindatri against me as well."

Orphan leaned back, supported by his tail. "Yet . . . I found that I did not *want* to leave you behind. You have, truly, become my friends. You have trusted and supported me, at times when it might well have been wiser to do otherwise. And . . . just perhaps . . . I feel a touch of *responsibility* to you because you are—does this sound foolish?—*my* First Emergents."

Ariane found herself laughing. "It sounds . . . *human* to me, Orphan. I mean, completely understandable. You found us. You brought us into the Arena. You helped introduce us to its wonders. In a way, we're like your adopted children."

The flickering buzz was translated as an embarrassed cough. "Your imagery . . . is even more apt than I had expected. Yes. Foolish, perhaps, but very real. As are your friendships.

"Yet even then I found myself frozen with indecision. I *wanted* to help you, but I knew that I had not a hundredth the power necessary. I saw Halintratha brooding about me, and thought that I had a better chance of striking at *it* than at Vindatri . . . and then, suddenly, I wondered if I could use the same weapons. After that I contacted you and, well, you all saw the results."

"*Spectacular* results," Ariane said with a grin.

"Spectacular . . . indeed," agreed a faint, deep voice.

A fist of ice seemed to close around her heart as she whirled; DuQuesne cursed and spun; Wu Kung came on guard, and Orphan staggered back, his black and green coloration fading.

The towering figure stood not fifty meters distant, although—Ariane belatedly realized—"stood" was perhaps not the right term. Vindatri leaned heavily against one of the shards of debris scattered about the room, and his voice had lacked the majestic thunder usually characteristic of him. "Calm . . . yourselves," he said, his voice now no longer that of a would-be god but of something ordinary, mortal, in pain. "You have won the battle. I am not your enemy . . . and in truth, I never have been."

Wu Kung slammed Ruyi Jingu Bang so hard on the deck that Halintratha shuddered. "What makes you think *you* get to decide whether you're our adversary or not? I—"

Wu Kung broke off as Vindatri slowly reached up and pulled back the hood that had obscured his face for so long.

Ariane heard herself gasp.

Vindatri's appearance was not *human* . . . but it was so *close* to human that it passed ordinary belief. Long, pure-white hair framed a face whose features were too sharp and delicate for an ordinary human; his eyes were a brilliant red, and his skin grayish in tint; his ears were long, large, and pointed. Yet for all that it was a face easily imagined among the various body-modded natives of Earth system.

"Holy moley," DuQuesne said finally. "Is the rest of you that human?"

"Or the rest of *you* that Halinthi? Yes."

"A most peculiar conundrum," Orphan said after a moment. "Such a close parallel seems exceedingly unlikely."

"Even more unlikely than it appears," said Vindatri. "For my scrutiny of this 'human' species shows that we share not merely exterior, but interior, and even chemical, similarities beyond easy belief."

"I'll be damned," Ariane said. "So where's the rest of your people?"

Vindatri's eyes narrowed, then he looked down. "Gone. We share other similarities, humans and Halinthi, you see. We also appeared in the Arena amidst tumultuous times, and made great strides in so short a period that other factions stood amazed, some perhaps afraid; and it was whispered that, perhaps, *we* might be the Canajara.

"And then—in a time almost as short as our rise—we were cast down. The hands of others were raised against us, and our fortunes began to turn, even though we had . . . unique and powerful secrets of our own. Enemies of our own making, of our own people, arranged much of our downfall.

"But there were other . . . events, forces, that spoke to me of something darker, frightening and powerful. Whispers of *things* seen that could not be easily described, of Spheres left bare and dead, of madness stalking unchecked through the crew of entire fleets. Things that even I, Vindatri, could not trace."

He gestured around them. "I found Halintratha in my youth, a secret, a conundrum, a refuge and a mystery that I kept for myself. And perhaps that is the only thing that saved me, for when death—a death I shall not describe, not even here—came for me, I fled, my strength barely adequate even for escape, and came here; and the shadows of the void did not pursue me here."

Ariane stared at him. "But . . . if this force was so powerful that it could pursue people across the Arena, why stop here? What does it mean?"

"I cannot say for sure; but I spent millennia piecing together fragments of knowledge, and I learned one other thing. Those who first built Halintratha—and a few other ruins hidden across the Arena—also stood on two legs, as did we, with a head and eyes and mouth and hands much like our own.

"And they, too, disappeared without a trace in what must have been a cosmic blink of an eye."

She felt a cold prickle of gooseflesh across her body. "Holy crap. You mean that the other species are basically left alone, but humanoids—people like you and me . . ."

". . . seem to draw some sort of unwanted attention, yes," Vindatri said, with a bitter smile at the understatement. "But if the prophecy is true . . . perhaps that is no great surprise. The Canajara is a tale of hope and terror; those who fear might wish to prevent it, and those who hope may have enemies indeed."

Ariane nodded. "Still . . . That doesn't explain everything *you* did here. If you don't want to be our enemy, I think you owe us one *hell* of an apology."

"For tampering with your mind? For arranging the battle itself? Perhaps. But I did what I did to *know* you, as best I could, for I had much to fear—even I, Vindatri, had much to fear, and not just for myself."

DuQuesne frowned, then nodded. "Go on."

"I had *hints* of your . . . uniqueness, of capabilities that Orphan had glimpsed yet did not understand, and under those other capacities that even he did not dream existed. I had, too, the prophecies of the Canajara, and—from Orphan's testimony—I suspected that your people might well be the Canajara incarnate."

Vindatri gazed around the group. "Perhaps you do not understand—cannot grasp—the significance of the Canajara to someone like myself. The prophecies of the Canajara are *ancient*—there were such prophecies long, long before the Halinthi became First Emergents, and though the way and detail of expression has changed from era to era, the *nature* of the Canajara's people has not: they have *twin* aspects of creation and destruction, of saviors or destroyers, and it is implied—throughout all versions of the Canajara—that *individuals of that species* will be the ones who precipitate the event called the Canajara; if for good, possibly an apotheosis of all, an ascension to something so great and wonderful that even all the words I have learned in my lifetime could not describe the smallest aspect of it, but if for evil, the opposite—a torment and destruction beyond any imagination.

"Thus, I *had to know* if you might indeed *be* the ones destined to bring the Canajara—and if you proved to be the *dark* aspect of the Canajara prophecy, to do what I could to restrain or destroy you. Understand well, Captain Austin, Dr. DuQuesne, Sun Wu Kung—the darker aspect of the Canajara, fully contemplated, is enough to send fear through even the heart of one such as myself."

"I wasn't sure if you could read our minds directly or not," Ariane said.

"I could read surface thoughts and some deeper emotional impressions, and in *guiding* your thoughts I also learned much—though I had to proceed with considerable caution. I knew that even these actions would undoubtedly be met with . . . no great joy. And I did not wish to damage you in any way, if you proved to be no threat. As soon as I *saw* you I knew there was a kinship between us, and I feared that, whether you *might* be the Canajara, that the same forces might seek your end that sought that of my people."

Ariane looked at him skeptically. "What exactly could you learn from 'guiding' my thoughts, as you put it?"

Vindatri's smile was a flash—there and gone. "I could not—dared not—probe deeply. But what I could do was attempt to change your attitudes and guide your behavior, and observe *what you resisted most.*"

DuQuesne's eyebrow rose. "Huh. All right, yeah, that's clever. It's easy to get her to be reasonable and from that to be trusting, but making her unreasoningly hostile or murderous would be almost impossible. And you don't have to probe deep to feel the resistance."

"And that was, indeed, what I discovered. Captain Austin had little indeed of malice in her, and a vital humility—one I could even sense in you, although from our battle I now assume that all I could do to you was what you permitted. Sun Wu Kung was certainly capable of immense violence, but he also seemed to harbor no malevolence as such, while he did incorporate a tremendous loyalty and code of honor. I saw you, Dr. DuQuesne, reflected in the responses both had towards you, and by this I knew who you appeared to be. I also had Orphan's detailed reports on your behavior in his presence to draw upon.

"Ultimately, therefore, I decided that, if you *were* the Canajara species, the three of you represented the best of your people."

"Well, of course the Captain is!" Wu Kung said emphatically. "But if you figured *that* out, why the battle at all?"

"Because," Vindatri said, settling himself gingerly on a large, flat block of tumbled deckplating, "*benevolence* is not sufficient. Besides the more obvious uncertainties in your future, there was the enigma of my unknown enemies. I knew I could trust you *morally*. But I did not know if you were truly sufficiently formidable that I could trust you *practically*. I need allies, and—I believe—so will you.

"But I do not need allies that *I* would have to spend my life protecting." His face was suddenly overspread with a grim sadness. "I failed to protect my own people, in great part because I was but one being. I . . . my *spirit* would not dare take such a responsibility again unless my allies had their own strengths, abilities that might give our shadowy adversaries at least as much pause as my own."

"So you had to find out whether we had enough of what it takes to run in your league," DuQuesne said. "I guess that makes sense. So, *do* we?"

Now Vindatri threw back his head and laughed—a laugh that also showed no little pain in the way he winced. "Judge for yourselves," he said finally, and gestured.

For an instant the figure before them shimmered, and the cloak faded—to show a body that must be on the edge of death, legs gone,

one arm missing, blackened for most of its extent. The vision faded, returing to show Vindatri as they had always known him, but Ariane knew that what they had seen was the truth. "Jesus, Vindatri! If that's what you're like now, how are you even *talking* to us?"

"The power supports me, makes up for the loss, suppresses most of the pain, substitutes for those parts of the body currently missing. It will be regrown in time." A sharper smile. "Even had my body been utterly destroyed, I myself would not have died; I have bound my self—my soul if you believe in such things, my data backup if you do not—to Halintratha, so unless you had utterly destroyed this station, I would, eventually, have been reborn."

Vindatri glanced in Orphan's direction. "In the end, it was also Orphan's actions that decided me. You had gained the loyalty and trust of one who had, literally, thousands of years of reasons to avoid extending either very far. Yet Orphan, after only a few moments of terror, chose to return, to confront me alongside you, no matter the risk to himself—and he knew well that it might be a fatal risk.

"I have known Orphan for many centuries—and studied him in far more detail than he knew. Perhaps there are monsters within your ranks, Captain Austin—given the prophecy, I would say certainly there are. But if the Canajara truly refers to you—and I believe it does—you and your friends represent its species at its brightest and best."

He bowed. "I apologize for the methods and the offense. But I do not apologize for the ultimate test of your power and character."

"Huh," DuQuesne said, a pensive look on his face. "Then some of your prior rants were pure posturing, I think."

"Chosen for a specific effect, yes."

"We needed to think *we* were up against someone dangerously unstable, so that if any of us had a likelihood of bailing on the others, we'd do it," Ariane said slowly.

"That was certainly part of the test, yes. And sheer power was another part, one which," he gestured to his lower half, "you passed with startling facility. It is true that I *survived* the assault . . . but far from unscathed, and I am, after all, vastly older than all of you combined. I am *much* encouraged by such might in ones so young and unfamiliar . . . and still mystified by how it is possible."

DuQuesne nodded. "You're still not getting all of *that* explanation yet. Okay, Vindatri—so what's your angle now?"

"My . . . angle? You mean my intent?" Vindatri suddenly smiled, and it, like Wu Kung's, was a smile punctuated by very sharp canines. "These forces destroyed my people. They left me alone in the universe. No matter their motives or justifications, they are *my* enemies. And, I believe, they are or will be *yours*.

"So my intent is to give you assistance—from Halintratha—when no other aid will serve. I dare not tip my hand often, for I suspect these forces will be *extremely* displeased at my survival—but perhaps—just perhaps—it will be enough to prevent your people from suffering the same fate as my own."

At Ariane's astonished look, he smiled; it was not, entirely, a comforting expression. "And I am afraid that you require that assistance *now*."

Chapter 50

Captain Fitzhugh turned to glare at him in surprise. "Dr. Sandrisson? What the *hell* are you doing back here?"

"The better to watch things from, Captain. I will return to the shuttle if our ship is damaged at any point."

Fitzhugh rolled his eyes. "Colonel Abrams, I thought your *job* was to keep him from risking himself."

Oasis smiled sympathetically. "It is, sir. But . . ."

"Do you realize that the first time we are 'damaged' may also be the *last*?" the Captain demanded. "This is an all-out *war* and—Oh, Jesus."

Simon's eyes flicked to the display just in time to see *Nayanazgeni* split apart and vanish into vapor and fragments as her super-conducting storage coils were severed, releasing all their energy in a single instant.

"*Antonia!* Dammit, *no!*" Hawke said. His hands twitched on the controls.

"Nothing we can do, Hawke," Fitzhugh said, a brittle tone in his voice. "If anyone survived, all we can hope is they stay out of the way."

"Someone you know was on board *Nayanazgeni*?" Simon asked quietly.

"I know *all* the pilot-navigators on these ships," Hawke said, a dark intensity in his tone. "And a lot of the ones in the fighters we've got. Where do you think me and Ariane and Vel recruited them *from*? Unlimited Space, Air, and Ground Racing, that's where."

"I'm sorry, Hawke," Fitzhugh said. "But we're all like that. Only ten warships . . . eight, now . . . in the whole Human fleet. I know all their captains, most of their officers, a lot of the men and women at all levels." He glanced around the bridge, obviously looking at the ones he knew best, his own crew, and Simon could see the worry in the creases of the man's long face. "We'll lose a lot of good people. We've already lost them. So, please, Simon," he turned back to Sandrisson, "get back to the shuttle."

Simon smiled sympathetically. "I know it will sound . . . well, crazy, but it actually is safer for me to stay here for now."

It had taken a few moments of arguing, but it had been Oasis'— K's—own words that had crystallized the realization. He and Oasis wouldn't *really* have the protection of her Hyperion nature unless they were in the right *position*. In other words, last-minute, impossible escapes from death. Sitting in a shuttle, waiting to push a button? That didn't fit, and might well end up with a lucky shot from the Molothos blowing *Andraste* to kingdom come, and them along with it.

But standing on the bridge and seeing death come for them? A desperate run through a ship coming apart in battle? That would fit her Hyperion past to perfection. So—paradoxically—he was almost certainly safer here, more than three hundred fifty meters through multiple corridors from the nearest shuttle, than he was if he stayed inside the shuttle.

Fitzhugh's expression showed he didn't believe a word of it, so Simon added, "Captain . . . let's just say this also comes from the same source as my . . . unique intelligence on the combat situation." He closed his eyes, rose to transcendence, looked a moment. "And warn everyone on our Sphere; there is a force of Molothos who have broken off under cover of that distant cloudbank and are heading for an attack on the ground-based forces."

"What? How many? What's their vector?"

"About . . . one hundred fifty vessels. Location and direction . . ." Simon used his headware to send the data directly to Marie Leingod, *Andraste*'s tactical specialist.

A dozen Molothos warships exploded almost simultaneously, but at the same time one—no, two—Analytic vessels broke up and detonated. *The Analytic is fighting well, but they will be bearing the brunt of the fight. And they are falling fast.*

"*Hachiman*, you're somehow ridiculously faster than everyone else, and *Athena*, you're nearest, get the hell down there and try to keep those bugs off our boys! Relgof, can you—"

"We see the situation. *Otrebla Evaw'Kohs*, join your battle force with theirs!"

Fifteen Analytic warships, with attendant fighters, broke off from the main battle and streaked towards the Sphere of Humanity.

Simon felt Oasis' hand gripping his and tightening as the battle raged on. So far *Andraste* was unscathed, but the sky was *filled* with Molothos warships and fighters and dotted with desperate defenders. With a morbid curiosity and a feeling of irrational responsibility, Simon let his perceptions rise, looking, watching that desperation, the heroism and hopelessness of the defenders, *Triglav, Ogun, Menhit*...

Menhit spiraled and twisted and dove, primary beams stabbing left and right, up and down, and the dark, angular ships of the enemy were cut and punctured, twirling out of control or disappearing in blasts whose concussions could be heard hundreds of miles away through the atmosphere of the Arena. Three ships, five, seven, and fighters of the Molothos too, evaporating before *Menhit*'s energy cannon and hypervelocity point defense like insects alighting on a wire, but suddenly *Menhit* wobbled, an engine gone, half the control surfaces eradicated by a too-close superconductor loop warhead, and three more Molothos warships caught it, heaped fire upon it.

Simon gasped and tore his vision away, shaking, feeling Oasis catch him. "Simon, what ...?"

"Saw ... watching the battle, I saw it. Saw the fire *race* through the corridors, tearing steel and men and women apart, vaporizing them, or sending them spinning away into the void," he whispered. "And the Molothos, too, shattering, withering like ants under a magnifying glass."

Belatedly he realized what he was saying and looked up, but Oasis was the only one paying attention to him; Captain Fitzhugh and the rest of the crew were focused entirely on survival.

"Crap, Simon, don't *do* that," Oasis said. "War and fighting's bad enough as it is when you see it normally. Watching everyone, *seeing* everyone who suffers in it all at once? *I* couldn't handle that." She shivered and shook her head. "It's bad enough as it is," she repeated. "Don't punish yourself like this."

"But—"

"It's not your fault. It's the Molothos' fault. Yeah, these people wouldn't be up here fighting now if it wasn't for you; instead the Molothos would've just have come here, wiped out all our ships and stations without warning, and they'd *own* our Sphere. At least now they have to *work* for it."

"And they are," Simon said. "But so are we."

Dajzail braced his legs, feeling the ship tilt and shudder as a superconducting warhead detonated a scant hundred meters from *Claws of Vengeance.* Alarms screamed briefly before being silenced. *It is at least a satisfaction that the source of that missile has been obliterated.*

"Damage report!" Ship-Master Fathinalak demanded.

Titanivig responded from her Tech-Master station. "No major systems affected, Ship-Master. Minor breach in armor at Segment Five Starboard." The little, blue-tinted youth's accustomed cheerfulness was subdued, and Dajzail could see the fear in the way her legs vibrated subtly against the deck. *But not giving into her fear; Fathinalak's a good commander, his people trust him.*

He heard Alztanza at his Command Oversight station talking to other forces: ". . . work, and our sympathies and condolences. They will be remembered, Vashatanil." His old friend's head pivoted, and his eye glowed somberly.

"What news?"

"The bad and the good, Daj. Those obscene monster cannons on the surface are dealt with, but we lost one hundred twenty-seven of the one hundred fifty-four ships in the task force. Vashatanil's mediant pair was commanding one of them."

"Homeworld's *Blessing.* How many of the enemy did they finish?"

"However many were operating those cannon, plus one of the Human ships, designation *Athena,* and six Analytic vessels, plus associated fighter craft."

"'Tanza, I don't know if we can *afford* an eighteen-to-one ratio of losses!"

Alztanza's head rotated as he buzzed a tired amusement. "No, we can't; they'd take this battle if that was the ratio. But it isn't; we lost a large chunk there because we were flying straight into the rippers of those monster guns. Overall ratio is running about eight to one, and I expect that to become more in our favor as the battle continues; they've also lost one Gate Fortress, so their external support is severely reduced." Another buzz, but this had less amusement and more grimness. "Of course, I wish to rip off my *claws* for being in any way pleased at a loss ratio of seven or eight to one."

Seahive, one of the largest carrier vessels, chose that moment to erupt in fierce flame and shatter to dust. Dajzail felt his mouth and body spasm in sympathetic reaction, heard himself say "Dyara!"

"Dyara? Dyaratamzin? *She* was on *Seahive*?"

"Hive audit observer, should have stayed behind, but insisted on staying on to see a real military operation," Dajzail answered numbly. "Mother and Homeworld, 'Tanza, what can I tell her nest family?"

"The same thing we will be telling them all," Alztanza said bleakly. "That they died well."

A faint cheer went up around the bridge of *Andraste* as a mass of Molothos vessels shattered in one of the secondary minefields, led there with a skillful bait and chase trap by Analytic high-speed duelship *Aynegi* and her combat group. Simon managed a smile, but he was too busy calling out advice. "Relgof, another Molothos force is trying a pincer attack on Gate Two."

"Understood, Simon."

"Captain Fitzhugh, *Indra*'s just been badly damaged. They destroyed the last of their attackers, but more are—"

"*Indra*? Dammit, that's Caine's ship! He was doing better than . . . never mind. *Hachiman*, are you—"

"On our way, *Andraste*," came Captain Cleary's voice, "but we can't keep them off for long."

"Tell *Indra* to dive for the surface. They took out the big cannon but we've still got enough ack-ack to keep pursuit off her tail. If she can manage to ditch in Big Pond—"

"I got it, Fitz," came the calm soprano of Sakat Caine. "Hate to run on you now—"

"You've done more than your part, twenty-two of the enemy aren't going home because of you. Now get going!"

"We're on our way—"

Simon saw a flicker of motion in his god-like sight. "Look out, *Indra*! Port quarter, elevation thirty seven—oh, *no!*"

One of the Molothos fighters *screamed* past *Hachiman* at

hypersonic speeds and rammed directly into *Indra*, plowing through the already-damaged armor and detonating into the stricken warship. A split-second later, *Indra* vanished in a ball of fire.

"God*dammit!*" Fitzhugh exploded, then instantly got under control. "*Hachiman,* coordinate with *Emasa Rum'ij Ken* and get back here to defend our Gate; we'll need it at the end!"

"Understood, *Andraste*," responded *Hachiman*, the cheer of the earlier response completely gone.

"Are we really managing a twenty-to-one ratio?" Simon asked. *If we are, we might even* win *this.*

Fitzhugh shook his head. "Average? Dropping close to seven to one overall. *Indra . . . Indra* was just really good."

His face seemed set in stone now. "And with *Indra* gone, there's just five of us left . . . and it doesn't look like our Analytic friends are doing much better.

"It won't be long now."

Blessed Unifier, Dajzail thought with a touch of unwilling respect, *these undercreatures know how to* fight. He had lost track of how many losses they had already sustained. *I cannot afford that, as the one ultimately responsible.* "Report on our forces?" he asked.

"One thousand, four hundred, and twenty-two of our primary warships have been destroyed or crippled," came the reply from Alztanza. "Twenty percent of our independent fighters are also destroyed."

"Enemy forces?"

"Of the original vessels of Humanity, there are four . . . no, three remaining vessels operational, designations *Andraste, Hachiman,* and *'Oro,*" responded Kanjstall, his Salutant and constant third claw. "In addition to our destruction of their Sphere-based monster-cannon, three of the eight Gate Stations have been crippled or destroyed. Of the Analytic forces, less than fifty percent remain."

"We are winning," Alztanza said to Dajzail. "But the victory will be costly."

Dajzail did not reply for a moment. *Fourteen hundred warships. Hundreds or thousands of our people on each.* His eye dimmed. *Perhaps a million of the People have already died for this battle.* And some of those were people he, or Alztanza, knew well.

But anger rose again and he shook the mood off, slashing outward in a gesture of defiance. "Costly indeed, beyond anyone's guess of how much that price would be. Yet we are committed. Will they let us turn and flee, escape back into the mists of the Deeps? Surely not. Leaving aside that they seem to have a warrior's savagery, if nothing else, we have seen their secret weapons—that beam that strikes across incredible distance, and whatever they have done to the one ship to allow it to maneuver and accelerate as no such vessel could ever manage. Those secrets they will ensure belong only to themselves and the dead."

He snapped his claws across his chest, a penitent gesture. "And even were we to do so, the honor of our dead would scream at us in sleep evermore; their lives would have been wasted, thrown away."

Alztanza vibrated his feet on the deck, then was still. "You are right, Daj; you usually are. And," he said, with returning energy, "all we need do is *win*. As things stand, we will still have more than sufficient forces to picket the Gates and secure the surface, at least long enough to bring through more forces once we scout the destinations and find a link. With eight, it is virtually certain we will find *some* route we can use, and we can be almost certain that there is one that leads to Nexus Arena. That will allow us to, at the worst, call for forces to assemble at the nearest colony again."

"Still . . ." Dajzail hesitated, then took a breath that expanded his carapace four centimeters, let it out with a whistle of resolve-to-do-the-distasteful. "I would save our people, if I may. Open a channel to our enemies."

Almost instantly, the gray-maned human officer named Fitzhugh appeared; a parallel screen showed Relgof Nov'ne Knarph. "What is it, Leader Dajzail?" Captain Fitzhugh said.

Though Dajzail had studied humans little, he was fairly certain the man was neither as calm nor as in control as he appeared. Relgof he knew better, and could see the stiffness of the other's stance. "Captain and First Researcher, you see the progress of the battle. There is—quite literally—no possibility you will be victorious. You have destroyed fourteen hundred of our major vessels, while we have destroyed nearly two hundred of yours; seven of ours to one of yours. A ruinous exchange, were all things equal, but I can *afford* that exchange. You have also lost supporting fire, which worsens your position. At *best* you can maintain that ratio, in which case the battle will end with the Molothos having two thousand vessels and you having none at all.

"But I do not like throwing away my peoples' lives. If you will surrender, I will permit your people to retreat through the same gate from which the Analytic vessels came. Yield the battle, and neither you creatures nor the True People will suffer more this day. Fail to yield and we will kill every single one of you, including survivors on derelict ships. The choice is entirely yours; I give you one minute to consider. But consider *wisely*. The Molothos do not often show such mercy; it will not be offered a second time." He gestured to cut off the transmission.

"Thoughts, 'Tanza?"

The older warrior rocked claws from side to side. "In honesty, I believe they will reject the offer. If they wished to flee, they could have begun the process earlier. And for the humans, at least, this is their *only* Sphere, their *Homeworld*."

Dajzail found himself drawing inward in a vanishingly rare moment of empathy for the undercreatures. He had not, truly, allowed himself to think of what that aspect really *meant*. For a Molothos, the Homeworld was everything. It was the source of all true people and civilization, it was the birthplace of knowledge, it was the very seat of the *life* of their people. A threat to the Homeworld would justify any sacrifice, any promise, any effort to address. *And we are threatening them with that.*

The screens lit again; Captain Fitzhugh spoke first. "You want our home Sphere?" He made a beckoning gesture with his hand. "Come and take it."

"As for us, the Analytic has declared its allegiance," said Relgof.

Dajzail spread his arms. "Then today the Analytic will need a new Leader." He turned to Alztanza as the screens went dark. "Target his vessel and that of the captain specifically. I want them destroyed first, as a signal. This is no longer a battle. It will be *extermination*."

He banished the clinging, alien feelings of empathy to undercreatures. *A waste of my energy and destructive to my mind.*

The remaining ships of the defending fleet were drawn together, gathered near the still-active Gates. It was, really, their only practical option, unless they chose a *vryzztiz* or suicide approach, dispersing to destroy as many as possible without regard for their survival. He glanced at Alztanza.

"No," 'Tanza said, as though reading his mind. "I don't think they'll try that, not yet. I think they'll try to send some of their more valuable personnel through the Gates while the rest provide cover. And if they maintain formation and defensive fire, they have a chance of surviving longer, and doing more damage to us. But if we *do* take out their commanding vessels they may become more disorganized."

Another of the humans' warships split apart in a flare of fire and shattered steel. *Two remaining, their command vessel* Andraste *and that impossible flying anomaly* Hachiman. *I see the Captain's ship near the Gate. Would he actually* leave *his forces? No. He has another reason.*

Now Dajzail's forces moved in relentlessly. Those incredible beams of energy from the remaining human vessels and Gate fortresses continued to punch effortlessly through the heaviest vessels, and missiles and beams and even hypersonic cannon *fountained* from the Analytic warships with frenetic abandon, shattering armor, penetrating to armories or drive coils, vaporizing thousands of his people . . . but they, too, losing another vessel here, seeing another hull cleaved and broken.

The humans and Analytic fought with the vicious, hopeless savagery of a *kantha* in a trap, taking six, seven, even eight or nine of Dajzail's forces for every one of their own lost, but it was hopeless.

Mere minutes now, and the battle will be over—and our vengeance will have truly begun. He allowed himself to contemplate a celebration before having to begin the grim task of tallying the dead.

At that moment, *Will of Ice*, on the far edge of the fleet, exploded.

"My *God*, Marc . . ." Ariane heard herself say.

The enhanced display of *Zounin-Ginjou*'s main viewport showed a horrific battle. Fragments of uncountable ships drifted, sharp-edged shrouds of fatality, throughout the volume surrounding Humanity's Sphere. For a terrible moment she couldn't find any human ships at all and thought that despite Vindatri's assurances they were, truly, too late. But then a twisting motion utterly at odds with the more stately, deliberate movements of the other vessels caught her eye, and she recognized *Hachiman* and, near it, *Andraste*.

"Only two left," she said. Then more of the flow of battle became clear. "But . . . wait, there's *other* ships fighting on our side!"

"Who the hell is that?" DuQuesne murmured. "I don't know those ships at all."

"I, however, do," Orphan said, his voice carrying an impression of somehow expected surprise. "I have no idea *why*, but it appears that your people have, in some manner, convinced the Analytic to risk themselves in battle!"

"They will not be risking *anything* for long," Wu Kung observed, "because the Molothos are about to wipe them all out!"

"All right, Orphan. It's time."

One of the elaborate wing-shrugs. "A single vessel to challenge hundreds, if not thousands, of Molothos warships! Ahh, Captain, part of me is *screaming* at this very thought, let alone the fact that I am about to *act* upon the thought. But I trust in you and your impossible friends. Let us hope that what you have planned can *work*."

"Vindatri thinks it can," DuQuesne said, "and if he wanted to just off us he probably could've managed it a lot easier than trying to drop us into a battle. You ready, Ariane?"

Ariane looked at the immense array of warships ahead and felt her own gut quail at the very thought of taking them on.

But she was Leader of the Faction of Humanity, and this was a battle for Humanity's survival. She—literally—had no choice at all. "Ready, Marc."

Link achieved, she heard in her head. *Wu, you here?*

Wow! It has been so long since I was inside another's head. For an instant, Wu Kung's cheery voice was quieter, almost shy. *You have . . . a very beautiful mind, Captain.*

She felt a touch of heat on her cheeks. *Focus, Wu.* A sense of amusement from DuQuesne. *You too, Marc C. Hyperion DuQuesne!*

I'm focused, Ariane. But it's really all on you. I'll be the channel, Wu's the source, but you're the one doing the real work.

"All right, Orphan—pick a target and *go!*"

"As you wish." Orphan made a grand show of seeming to pick a ship at random. "There. We are on our way, weapons are on line. Once we fire—or get too close—we *will* be noticed, so I hope you are ready."

Ariane felt it now, a shimmering well of potential, hovering somewhere at the very edge of her mind. She reached out for it and spoke a single word:

"*SONDERAN!*"

"*Gokalavik!*" Dajzail screeched in horror, and saw Alztanza's color flicker. Gokal had been in their same training-nest, a comrade and friend in arms since childhood . . . and now he and his ship were gone, from an attack where no enemy should have been. "How? What attacked—" Dajzail's words trailed off, and he felt himself sagging down in disbelief for the *second* time in this battle.

An immense warship emerged from the wreckage and smoke, and from it multiple lances of ravening, eye-searing brilliance struck out, carving their way through another four Molothos ships as though they were nothing but paper, ships that detonated with a fury that sent visible shockwaves through the Arena's sky. The newcomer turned, and Dajzail *recognized* it.

"*Zounin-Ginjou!*" Alztanza buzzed in disbelief. "How . . . why . . . and those *weapons*—"

The Liberated? The Survivor *has come* here, *and joined a hopeless battle?*

The communication screen lit up (*What? How? I did not give the order!*). The Survivor looked out at them, and gave a mocking seated salute. "Ah, Dajzail! I must confess, I had not entirely expected you would lead the assault yourself."

"This is not your battle, Survivor!"

"Alas, I must differ with you, Leader of the Molothos. I have, you see, allied myself wholly with Humanity, and as one who honors his commitments, I had little choice but to come to their aid." As Dajzail was about to speak, Orphan held up one hand. "But really, I am not the one you should concern yourself with; I am merely a pilot and a ferryman for my passengers, who wish to speak with you directly."

The display flickered, and Dajzail heard himself give a low screech of incredulous fury. Instead of the sardonic green-and-black Leader of the Liberated, he saw the most hated faces of all looking out at him.

"This is Captain Ariane Austin, Leader of the Faction of Humanity," the blue-maned woman said, and just behind her stood the monster DuQuesne, along with the enigma Wu Kung. There was something in her gaze, transcendent and strange, as though even as she spoke with him, she gazed upon something else. "Dajzail of the Molothos, you are hereby ordered to surrender."

He tilted his head and looked at Alztanza. "Fleet Master, even with *Zounin-Ginjou* being so armed, that will not tilt the balance, yes?"

The other shook himself out of shock. "No . . . no, certainly not, Leader."

"A preposterous demand," Dajzail said, feeling a sudden surge of eagerness. *Why, this will be perfect! Destroy the Leaders of three Factions here, along with the being credited with our first defeat, and this will be the ideal resolution!* "Powerful or no, a single vessel makes no difference whatsoever. The Molothos reject your pathetic attempt at a bluff." He gestured, and the screen went blank once more. "All vessels in range, fire at *Zounin-Ginjou*. Wipe the Leader of Humanity, the criminal DuQuesne, and the Survivor himself from the sky, in front of their defeated forces, before exterminating the rest!"

There was an answering scream of war and triumph from the command circuits, and a hundred warships seemed to lunge forward eagerly, spewing energy beams and missiles and armor-piercing shells in so intense and focused a barrage that *Zounin-Ginjou* disappeared in actinic brilliance.

But as the screens adjusted, Dajzail heard a whistling buzz of shock from all about, including his own breathing tubes. "Mother of *Worlds*," vibrated Orishikat from his Sailguide's station, horror and disbelief echoing in his words.

The flagship of the Liberated soared from the apocalyptic fire, untouched, unmarred, and the next tremendous salvo spattered harmlessly from some immaterial, invisible barrier more than fifty meters away from *Zounin-Ginjou*'s hull. The mighty flagship of the Liberated turned, a motion majestic and slow, and those terrible, destroying lances of coruscating luminance pierced through and through, eradicating six more of Dajzail's warships like toys thrown into a blast furnace. Now *Zounin-Ginjou* was headed directly for *Claws of Vengeance*.

Once more the screen lit without his direction. "Dajzail of the Molothos," Ariane Austin said, and her translated voice was colder than the darkest Deeps, "I say again, *surrender*. You have seen that all of your weapons are useless against *Zounin-Ginjou*. If you persist in your attack, it will be my duty to hunt down, and destroy, each and every one of your vessels. *And I will do this.*"

Her small glittering eyes met his wraparound gaze, but he recognized the icy glare as one no less chilling than that of a Molothos. "Do not doubt that. Our remaining vessels can flee, and we can destroy yours one by one if we must. It will not be easy and it will not be quick, but we can do it, and we will, and I do not think you can stop me. Your people will then *all* die for no purpose."

He glared at her, vibrating with such anger and fear that he could not speak.

She folded her arms. "Don't be stupid, Dajzail! No one likes the Molothos, for plenty of reasons, and you don't like anyone else. But one of your people, Maizas, once said to DuQuesne: '*You care for your fellow creatures, one would hope; you may be animals and less than animals, but even such creatures care, even if with less delicacy and sympathy than we for our own.*' If you care *at all* about your people, then *surrender.*"

Dajzail found himself frozen with furious, terrified indecision. *Nearly two million of us left in this force. Two million with this monster's fighting-claws at their eyes.* Such numbers cried out that she was bluffing, she *had* to be bluffing.

But *Zounin-Ginjou* had appeared from nowhere, without warning, and the fire of a hundred warships had made less than no impression upon her.

Alztanza suddenly leaned forward, bellowing into the Fleet Command panel. "No! *Fireswarm*, sheer *off!*"

Dajzail realized that *Fireswarm*—one of the largest Hiveships, carriers for fighters, ever constructed—was charging into a position between *Zounin-Ginjou* and *Claws of Vengeance*. But the desperation in Alztanza's voice was even stronger than Dajzail would have expected—a desperation suddenly all too clear when Alztanza shouted again, "Ship-Master—Zintavalin, Zinta, stop, *don't do it—*"

Even as he spoke, the immense Liberated warship rammed completely through *Fireswarm*, that invisible yet utterly impervious barrier plowing a hole six hundred meters wide in a formerly untouchable warship of the Molothos, a warship that then tore its remaining fragments to flinders as storage coils detonated. *Zinta. Alztanza's first matebond. Gone, in the flicker of a single strike.*

With an effort so extreme that he felt his sight fading towards darkness, Dajzail finally forced himself to lower his claws. "What . . . What are your terms?"

He had not *said* he surrendered, yet, but all on the command deck gave a hissing whistle of pain and humiliation; Alztanza's choked scream of anger and denial was like a claw to his heart.

Captain Austin straightened. "All of your ships of course cease combat immediately. Your vessels power down everything but life support and minimal stationkeeping. You will stay that way until all of our ships are gone, except *Zounin-Ginjou.*

"After that, you will return to the base from which you came. We know where it is, and what star that equates to in the normal universe. You will then return your ships and people to whatever of your colonies they would be at were they not currently on this mission."

He could read enough expression on her face to know that her "smile" was not one of happiness, but more of a threat. "And then, Dajzail of the Molothos, you will cede that Sphere and system to Humanity."

"What insane demand is this? I will not, you . . . *undercreature!*"

"On second thought, you're right, you won't do that. You will cede that Sphere to us *right this instant*, although I allow you to retain control of it *just* long enough to go home."

"This is no Challenge—"

"How do *you* know that?" she said, cutting him off again. "Seems to me that this could be a just *dandy* Type-Two Challenge. Of course, we won't *know* for sure unless and until the Arena pipes up, but it sure could be—and *one* Sphere would be a damn cheap payoff for winning it."

Suddenly she sighed and her translated voice was that of weary resignation. "Dajzail, from our point of view, your people are monsters, and I wouldn't get much push-back from anyone else if I just wiped you all out. Hell, I don't think there is a *single species in the Arena* that would care. I don't know if it's *possible* to actually reach any sensible accord with your people.

"But I do know that I am not going to commit my own genocide when I have any other choice. So I am giving you this one—and *last*—chance to surrender, under my terms. If you do not accept them, then *Zounin-Ginjou* will erase your entire task force from existence."

It was almost impossible to resist the urge to shriek an obscenity that the Arena couldn't even translate at the screen and cut off all communication. But . . .

. . . but Maizas had been *right*, if Austin had quoted him correctly. His peoples' lives *mattered*, all of them, and though the honor of the dead would wail in the Deeps forever, there was no honor in throwing away the lives of the living against an impossible, invincible ship. He had lost people; 'Tanza had. With almost fifteen hundred ships in the fleet gone, almost everyone left had lost *someone*.

It was of course possible . . . even *probable* . . . that there was a limit to that invulnerability. Perhaps one or two or three more powerful salvos would find that limit. But there had already been *three* incomprehensible surprises in this battle; how many more of his people would die for the next of the Arena's twisted jests—for he was sure, somehow, that the Arena itself had to be involved.

And there was *Orphan's* inexplicable presence. He had not become The Survivor by being rash and taking chances he could avoid. If he had chosen to come here, to a battle of thousands against a handful, he knew something that tipped the balance of power in the entirely opposite direction.

Suddenly Dajzail remembered Ariane Austin's victory over Amas-Garao, and felt his body contract inward with horrific realization. *A Shadeweaver. That is the only sane explanation. Somehow she has mastered that power* on her own *and become a Shadeweaver.*

He had no proof—and doubted that he would get any, unless in a very final fashion—but Dajzail was suddenly completely and utterly certain that *that* was the source of the inexplicable power and Captain Austin's completely unshakeable confidence. *Somehow she has unlocked the power sealed by both Faith and Shadeweaver, done so without pledging allegiance to either—or surely she would no longer be the Leader of her Faction—and now she is showing us the* extent *of that power.*

And it was, in the end, too much. *The odds have shifted. I have still vast numbers of ships . . . but I cannot weigh the chances against a Shadeweaver armed with such weapons.*

A rattling sigh vented from him, and once more he felt his vision dimming with the effort. "All ships—break off combat and return to Sphere formation around *Claws of Vengeance*. Cease all attacks. Defensive action *only.*"

Alztanza stared at him, as did the rest of the bridge crew. He looked back at his old friend. "'Tanza . . ."

With a tremendous, buzzing cough, Alztanza roused himself. "Of course, Daj. We . . . have no choice." He relayed the orders.

There was reluctance and incredulity, of course, but the forces had been well-drilled; grumbling or not, they returned to formation.

Ariane Austin was still on screen. "And . . . ?"

His mouth irised shut so tightly it took a few moments to force it to open again. So repelled was he by the thought of what he must do that his body thought he was trying to swallow poison.

But I am still the Leader of the Molothos. Humiliated or not, I must stop this . . . behaving like an undercreature!

He straightened, raising himself up high on all seven legs, and heard his voice suddenly stronger. "And as the Leader of the Molothos I cede to Humanity the System corresponding to the Sphere from which this assault force was launched, their control to begin once our forces have returned and used that system's Sky Gates to transit to other locations."

She tilted her head. "And—"

She is no fool. I will not waste our time further. ". . . and these forces will begin the trip immediately after concluding any additional discussion needed, and we will travel directly to said Sphere, and transition all forces to other locations as quickly as practically possible. Is that satisfactory, human?"

"Satisfactory, yes."

"Are there further conditions you wish to impose?"

She again gave the teeth-baring expression that they called a smile, though he did not gain a pleasant impression of it. "Ones I *wish* to impose . . . yes. But only one more that I *will* impose.

"As you have surrendered, that you agree—and announce, upon your return to Nexus Arena—that there is now currently a state of peace between the Molothos and Humanity and our allies the Liberated and the Analytic, and that you *mean* it. Unless we do something to provoke you, you will not send any more forces against us or attempt to contest with us in any ways outside of the regular Challenges."

And this, too, I must suffer. One day . . . but no, for the sake of my people, I must not even think that. "I . . . agree."

Captain Austin nodded her head. "Then I will let it go at that, if you do not attempt to find some way around the spirit of these agreements."

"But *I've* got one more piece of advice for you," said a far deeper human voice.

DuQuesne stepped forward, and *his* smile was definitely not pleasant. "Before you *ever* think about attacking us again, Dajzail— and I know you people well enough to know you will, no matter what promises Ariane's wrung out of you—I recommend you do one thing."

"What is that?"

"Consider—very carefully—an iceberg. Its every aspect and feature." The black-maned human smiled again, and the image was suddenly cut off.

Dajzail felt his legs trembling from reaction—from restraining himself, from anger, from fear, from elation, all through different phases of this now-futile battle. But he did not allow it to affect him yet. "Signal the fleet: return to base. Do not permit any questions of this order. We move as swiftly as we may."

With all the control he could manage, Dajzail turned and left the command deck. Behind him was nothing but silence and defeat.

Chapter 51

Simon stood in awe and amazement as he watched the confrontation and Dajzail's capitulation, capped by DuQuesne's darkly enigmatic warning. *My God. It's over.*

The screen flickered again and this time it was Ariane. "Captain Fitzhugh, Dr. Relgof, are you both still there?"

"We are," Fitzhugh said, and Relgof echoed him. "I don't know how the *hell* you pulled that off—*any* of it—but from the bottom of my heart, thanks."

"No," she said, and Simon *knew* that tone, the tone that was Ariane punishing herself for not doing *enough*. "Thank *you*. All of you, for somehow keeping this going long enough for us to get here." She looked away from them; from the suppressed horror on her face, he was sure she was surveying the scans of the space around them. "How many did we lose?"

"Captain Austin," Relgof said gently, "we would have lost *everyone* had you—"

"I am *aware* of that, Doctor," she said. "And I am glad we did get here. And I thank you especially, the Analytic, for coming to our aid. But I still have to accept that a hell of a lot of people just died because we couldn't get here a few hours sooner." The smile she managed then made Simon wince; it was heartbreaking. "I'm not saying there's nothing to celebrate, just . . . just that before I celebrate anything, I have to salute the people who will never make the celebration."

"Of course," Fitzhugh said. "You can . . . well, you can see what we have left. Just *Andraste* and *Hachiman*, plus forty-seven fighter craft—

most of them will take a bit to get back to base—and four of our Gate fortresses. The ground batteries were taken out fairly early on, although most of the other ground forces are intact; they never got to the point of landings."

"And of our vessels," Relgof said slowly, "only seventy, plus a proportionate number of fighter craft, will return to their homes."

Eighty percent losses, thought Simon, and saw DuQuesne bowing his head in the background, Wu Kung obviously offering a prayer, and Orphan in a pose that must be a salute to the dead. Ariane merely nodded, though he could see her rigid pose betraying the control she required. "My condolences to the Analytic for your losses; is there any preferred way to salute such a sacrifice for our people?"

Relgof tried a casual gesture, but it was clear he was also affected by the losses. "We . . . will discuss such things later. The important thing, Captain Austin of Humanity, is that they fought for something they believed in, for a future we hope to make, and their hope is still alive, for we saw victory when we thought we had no possibility of anything but utter defeat." A spark of his usual ebullience resurfaced. "And I fear that the Analytic will have to wait long for the explanation of *how* you achieved that victory!"

Simon *did* chuckle at that.

"So," Oasis said from next to him, "Captain, I guess you must've succeeded at your little side trip?"

"You could say that," she said, and this smile was just a *tiny* bit less strained. "I'll do a full debrief back at our Embassy. But we have a more pressing problem first."

DuQuesne nodded. "Search and Rescue. There's *got* to be survivors—people who bailed during the battle, left in the few ships that didn't get mostly vaporized, what have you. And unlike regular space battles, they don't need spacesuits to live, so they could still be okay, even if all they did was dive out an airlock at the last second."

Orphan nodded. "I have been in that position. As has your friend Wu Kung."

"But also not like your black empty space," Wu said, "there will be things looking for easy meals. The jackals scent easy pickings, the sharks begin to circle, the vultures watch from high above."

Kuso. Of course, in a place like the Arena, there will be just such scavengers, like the zikki, waiting for a battle to conclude. "I will assist in the search-and-rescue effort, Ariane. I can apply the same information source to locating stranded people."

"What do we do about Molothos survivors?" Captain Fitzhugh asked.

"The same we do for human or Analytic ones, Captain. We are at peace now."

Simon could see DuQuesne's darkly-cynical grin at that, and his gut agreed with the big Hyperion. "Peace" with the Molothos was going to be, at best, a fragile thing.

"The problem is we need more *searchers*," Ariane said. "There are hardly enough—"

"If you pardon me for interrupting," Relgof said, "that depends on how much you will trust the Analytic."

Ariane raised an eyebrow. "How so, Doctor?"

"If you allow us to traverse the Sky Gate that leads to Nexus Arena directly, we can call upon *immense* numbers of Analytic vessels to assist. The war is over, these will not be warships, so the Arena's restrictions on movement for war-like purposes will no longer apply."

Simon saw a burst of relieved revelation on Ariane's face. "Of *course*! Yes, Dr. Relgof, you've proven your right to be trusted—proven it at great cost. We would be greatly indebted to you if you could call in these forces as swiftly as possible."

Relgof's filter-beard flip-flopped and they heard a translated laugh. "As Simon will tell you, this was a payment for a service. As there are far more of my people waiting to be rescued—and even more Molothos—this will not be a debt for you. But as you say, swiftness is called for. Which of your Sky Gates should we use?"

"The one designated as Gate Station Two during our battle," Simon answered. "That emerges considerably to the azimuth of Nexus Arena. I know that it will be extremely difficult, but—"

Relgof gave an expansive gesture. "—but endeavor to keep the precise location of your particular Sky Gate as obscure as possible, yes. We shall do all in our power to confuse the issue. And," he added, with a roguish tone to his voice, "the Analytic's power in this area is considerable indeed."

"Then go as quickly as you can," Ariane said. "I have no idea how many people are stranded out there, but it must be many hundred, maybe many thousand."

"Counting the Molothos?" Simon said. "*Many* thousands. At a rough guess, the destroyed ships had on the close order of a million crew in total; if even one percent of those survived, that will be ten thousand of their people in need of rescue. I confess . . . I am rather surprised Dajzail did not insist on staying for search and rescue."

"I'm not," DuQuesne said bluntly. "He knew the answer would have to be 'not a chance in Hell.' No way we would allow a former belligerent, and still not trusted, force still outnumbering us by more than ten to one in the space surrounding our home Sphere. It's a sucker bet that *they* wouldn't allow it."

"Which gives us a chance to live up to our word," Ariane continued. "I've said we value even the lives of people like the Molothos; if we rescue their lost and deliver them home, safe and as sound as we can, this at least shows we *mean* what we say in both directions. I don't know if it's actually possible to get any *good*will from the Molothos, but it sure won't hurt."

DuQuesne grunted. "No, not now that we've established that we're no pushovers, anyway. They've seen us fight, so they'll know it has nothing to do with trying to pacify the scary Molothos."

"We can continue the discussion later," Ariane said. "Right now, we start S&R; it will take a while for Relgof to get back with a fleet to help search, so for now, every ship in condition to do so, begin rescue operations!"

"Begin near our Sphere and work outwards towards the direction of battle," Simon said, even as he allowed his perceptions to rise past the level of mere mortality. "Objects approaching closer than a certain distance to our Sphere, as you know, will be affected by its gravity. Some survivors have already entered that zone; many have parachutes or similar survival gear, but some do not; I am transmitting vectors and locations now." He was vaguely conscious of a grimace. "Some survivors are already down on the Sphere—and some are Molothos. We will need to be cautious on rounding those up, as it is not at all certain they will be aware that their fleet suffered an unexpected reversal."

"We'll take those," DuQuesne said. "Feed us the data, Simon; the other ships concentrate on the people still in the air."

"If there are *thousands* of Molothos survivors," Fitzhugh said, even as he directed *Andraste* to begin a near-Sphere search pattern, "where are we going to *put* them? I'd rather they were all in one place so we can have comprehensive security."

"We just need to house them until we can jump over to Nexus Arena, right?" Oasis asked.

"I would think so," Ariane replied.

"Then get *Nodwick* to do it; I think she's in the Harbor right now."

"That's an *excellent* idea," Simon exclaimed, remembering the giant transport that had been designed to ship large amounts of materials of all kinds from the realspace solar system to the Arenaspace Sphere. "*Nodwick* will have plenty of room to hold them for a short time and the cargo areas are separated from the crew and control areas."

"For transport, that's a fine idea," came General Esterhauer's voice, "but not possible right now."

"Why not?" asked Ariane.

"Because that assault on the ground-based cannons didn't just destroy them, it brought wreckage—thousands and thousands of tons of it—down atop the Outer Gateway. It's sealed and so are the Straits. There's no way to get any word into our Sphere until we either clear all that wreckage off and someone gets the Gateway open, or someone goes back to Nexus Arena and Transitions back to our Sphere to break the news."

"Then we'll just have to set up a camp until we can get *Nodwick* out for transport," DuQuesne said. "Esterhauer, can we clear out the area around the old crash site for *Blessing of Fire* and drop 'em there?"

There was a pause. "You like ironic taunts, don't you, DuQuesne? Yes, we can put them there. We can set up temporary security perimeters and such—good enough for a little while, anyway."

"Then do it," Ariane decided. "Easy enough to keep an eye on the camp from above, too. They're not stupid, they'll know we can take them out if we have to."

Simon found the next hours blurring into each other, as he located survivors—human, Molothos, and two dozen other species that had been on board the Analytic's vessels—directed ships to their locations, warned of any potentially dangerous situations, and then moved to the next group. Spread across so huge a volume of living air, there were almost limitless opportunities for potential disaster: fragments of Molothos vessels with still-active armaments and survivors who did not realize they had lost the battle, a group of Analytic castaways drifting helplessly directly towards the Luminaire, a school of *zikki* circling the remnants of *Nayanazgeni*'s crew, hundreds of survivors of all types caught in the fringes of the Sphere's gravity and plummeting straight down, past the Sphere, to be ejected into the immeasurable void if not found.

And Simon knew he was almost the *only* hope for these people, for in the environment of the Arena, radar, sonar, and radio beacons were terribly limited. The ships could find some few stranded, but they would miss many, even most, of those who needed rescue. So despite Oasis' increasingly worried entreaties, he stayed at his post on *Andraste*, searching the skies and relaying what he saw with a throat going raw from constant narration.

One other event stood out from the fog of envisioned desperation and relayed horrors; at some point, Ariane had asked him if they were *sure* the Molothos had followed through on the surrender and departed, or merely moved a short distance, to observe and perhaps strike again. Her tone showed she didn't think it was a terrible concern . . . but it *was* a question a wise leader had to ask.

"I will look," he said, and brought up the Arena-sight again. Suddenly he was like a cosmic giant, standing and gazing down at all the space surrounding Humanity's Sphere as though it were spread out on a table before him, tiny, trivially easy to visualize and understand.

Immediately, he focused his attention on the Molothos fleet, and directly into the command deck of *Claws of Vengeance*.

To his surprise, Dajzail was no longer on the command deck; his second, who had been visible during the brief parley (the name *Alztanza* came instantly to mind, without so much as the smallest of efforts) was clearly in command. Alztanza raised his insectoid head and gazed at the screen, and Simon realized he could even read the Molothos' gaze and posture. *He has taken them far already, very far; they move swiftly.*

Another omniscient glance and he understood the vastly greater speed at which the fleet was traveling. *A trail of radio beacons, buoys leading them home, likely telling them the conditions near each buoy so that they know if any obstacles lie ahead. As they pass, one of their number slows, retrieves the beacon, then rejoins the fleet.* He smiled faintly. *Of course. There is no requirement they make it easy for us to travel to our new Sphere, even if we do know roughly where it lies. More importantly, they continue on their course. He is angry, yet relieved. But what of their true Leader?*

Instantly he found himself gazing down upon Dajzail, in his private quarters . . . and saw the powerful alien squatting on the deck, legs pulled in so far that they were curled completely beneath him, and the two great bladed fighting claws were arched above and around the head, a gesture that Simon did not need the god-sight to interpret; it was no different than a man in despair covering his head with his arms.

Despite all that he knew about the Molothos—and this pitiless and genocidal monster in particular—Simon felt a sudden flash of pity. *What must it be like to be the leader of a species that believes itself superior, that has lost no significant engagement in untold centuries, and then find oneself defeated, driven off, and forced to a peace by events you cannot even* understand?

The sensation did not linger long; Simon was all too aware that the Molothos were unchanged. *But it is an important reminder to me that even the worst of our adversaries are not purely evil, do not lie beyond our ability to understand . . . or even emulate. Similar monsters have worn human faces.*

He allowed his sight to make a quick survey of the rest of the fleet. All were following and showed no sign of hesitating or changing course. There were no trailing scouts, no remaining monitors.

"They have left for certain, Ariane," he said. "And at a speed that will bring them home in weeks, not months."

She nodded. "Then it *is* over. Thanks, Simon. Let's get back to the important part—"

"—saving lives. Yes."

The grinding, desperate near-routine took over again, and even in his half-deific vision he found himself appalled by the immensity of the task. Thousands of survivors scattered throughout *trillions* of cubic kilometers of space, and all of them in danger . . . all in need of rescue . . . and he, Simon Sakuraba Sandrisson, the only person who could find them all in time.

At one point he became aware of a new fleet of ships materializing from Gate Two, the Analytic come to the rescue—new ships to be directed, but also vast new resources to rescue the lost faster.

Even with all he could do, it was not enough; he saw crewmen plunge screaming into the sea or forest of the Sphere, having fallen too far, too fast, for anyone to catch, watched helpless as *zikki* and other scavengers ripped Molothos and Analytic survivors to pieces, even witnessed the tragedy of small, fierce battles when stranded Molothos refused to believe they had been beaten and rejected surrender or rescue. But he forced himself to look away, to search for the living rather than let the dead haunt him.

At last he cast his vision out . . . and found no survivors waiting, no lonesome castaways adrift in the endless sky of the Arena. "That . . . that's all," he grated out, and found himself collapsing.

Oasis caught him. "Simon!"

"I'm . . . fine . . ." he tried to say. It came out more as a croak, a voice he could barely recognize as his own.

"The hell you are." She picked him up as though he were a child, despite the fact that he was fifteen centimeters taller than he was. "You need something to drink, something to eat, and *sleep*."

He wanted to protest that he could at least *walk* on his own, but he was suddenly aware of the utter exhaustion permeating every millimeter of his body—bone-dryness in his mouth, despite vaguely-recalled cups of coffee drunk in distraction, strained muscles from tension, the whiff of old sweat and a phantasmal yet very *real* feeling of being . . . *stretched*, having pushed himself to limits he did not even understand.

So instead of protesting, Simon let himself relax against the smaller yet incredibly strong figure. "As you wish," he said, and smiled.

Chapter 52

"Is Simon all right?" Ariane asked, trying to keep any excess concern from her voice.

"He'll be fine," Oasis assured her from a secured channel. "I know *you* were running about as long as he was, but you could take breaks, at least; he couldn't, and he was doing that . . . see-everything trick for most of it. He's *wiped*. Probably won't be up and at 'em for at least a few more hours; I got enough food and water into him and then stuck him in bed, then caught some Zs myself when the whole S&R thing was finished."

"We *all* got some rest then, finally. Thanks for looking after him." She shook her head. "Simon *will* drive himself, I've already seen that."

The red-headed Hyperion gave a brilliantly-sunny smile. "Hey, I'll look after *him* anytime! But you're welcome. And yeah, he's got that 'with great power comes great responsibility' schtick going for him now, so he'll be pushing himself even harder. *Someone* has to keep an eye on him."

"We'll be heading back to Nexus Arena shortly. Can you take one of the Sandrisson-capable shuttles and meet us back there?"

"Well, sure, but why can't we just drop down to the surface and use the Outer Gateway, then just pop straight to Nexus Arena? Oh, wait," Oasis bopped herself on her forehead, "that's right, we can't; the Outer Gateway's buried."

"And won't be un-buried for a while, either," DuQuesne confirmed from behind Ariane's shoulder, making her jump. "We still need a bunch of manpower dedicated to watching our not-very-friendly prisoners of war, and we don't have equipment left intact for clearing the stuff anyway."

"Gotcha. Okay, then we'll bring *Yeager* over once Simon's ready to leave." She looked at DuQuesne. "And Marc . . . I don't want to speak over a channel that's not secure, but we have a . . . real problem back home to talk about."

She saw DuQuesne stiffen. *He can probably read more from her posture than I can.* "Is the problem . . . immediate?"

"I don't *think* so. But watch your back, Marc, until we can debrief you." She turned back to Ariane. "We'll make the best time we can. Get to the Embassy and *stay there* until we get there to debrief you, okay, Captain?"

"Understood, Oasis." She was not stupid enough to ignore obvious Hyperion advice. "See you there. Austin out."

She broke contact. "What was that about?"

"Don't know for sure, honestly. Obviously *something* Hyperion-related, and it's got her spooked. But no point in chasing our tails over it, we'll find out soon enough."

Ariane nodded and stretched. "God, even after a night's sleep, a shower, and getting dressed before that call, I *still* feel like I've been, how'd you put it, dragged through a knothole?"

"I know the feeling," DuQuesne said. "Probably Wu does, too. That shield trick was *no* picnic."

"You can say that again." She gave DuQuesne a quick kiss, still amused by the fact that she had to stretch *up* to kiss him; very few men ever managed that. "Well, back to the bridge; we've got to get ready to head back."

Wu was waiting outside their cabin as the two stepped out. "Wu, did you *get* any sleep?"

He grinned, showing his fangs. "Of *course* I did, Captain! I just sensed your *ki* strengthen when you awakened, so I prepared myself and came to guard you."

Now that he's . . . himself, I suppose I'd better get used to him acting on senses that don't exist *for the rest of us.* "That's fine, Wu, but just a reminder—you and the rest having your special abilities is still a secret for most people, so don't show off. Got it?"

"Yes, Ma'am!"

Arriving on the bridge, they saw Orphan already in his seat. "Ahh,

Captain Austin, I was wondering if I should awaken you. Most of the Analytic vessels have already departed, and your ground-based people would very, *very* much like you to get *Nodwick* released to pick up the Molothos refugees as soon as possible." His voice was filled with his usual dry humor. "Based on the comments from Dyaratamzin, the apparent spokesbeing for the Molothos, they are equally eager to depart this place and, perhaps, never speak of it again."

"Understood," she said with an involuntary grin. "We'll do the best we can to accommodate that wish. Is *Andraste* still here?"

"It is. Do you wish to speak with Captain Fitzhugh?"

"To him and General Esterhauer, if she's awake. I know both of them were up as long as we were."

A few short inquiries later, both Fitzhugh and Esterhauer appeared on the main viewport. "Captain Austin, Dr. DuQuesne, you both still look a bit tired," Fitzhugh said.

"No more than both of you," Ariane said, and it was true; Fitzhugh had noticeable circles under his eyes, visible even against his dark tan skin, as did Esterhauer. *They both lost people they knew in this battle; I just had to put up with a hell of a physical strain, not watch people I knew personally die in front of me.* "You both did an *extraordinary* job defending our Sphere, and as Leader of the Faction of Humanity I will make sure your efforts are remembered by those at home. I do have one more . . . difficult request to make of both of you."

"Go ahead, Faction Leader," General Esterhauer said, as did Fitzhugh.

"I need you to go over the battle carefully and in addition to producing a complete list of our losses, determine who among the fallen . . . and the survivors . . . should receive particular recognition."

"Understood, Faction Leader Austin. For the survivors, am I to presume you wish to perform presentations yourself?"

"You should, yes. And I will personally read the commendations for all those lost."

"Yes, Ma'am. We will do our best to get that to you quickly."

"Thank you, General, Captain."

Not looking forward to that litany of losses, she thought as the viewport returned to simple clarity. "All right, Orphan—take us home!"

Orphan gestured to the pilot's position. "Captain Austin, with all due respect, this *is* my vessel, so I do not believe you can give me orders so blithely. But I *do* give you permission to take us home yourself!"

She heard her own laugh echo around the command deck of *Zounin-Ginjou* as she slid into the seat—which Orphan had thoughtfully modified to accommodate human *and* Liberated. "Aye-aye, Leader Orphan!"

The massive flagship of the Liberated turned easily and headed towards the center of the Gate Station. In a relatively few minutes, *Zounin-Ginjou* reached the Sky Gate and, in a flash of light, found itself far above the titanic cylindrical bulk of Nexus Arena. "All security protocols active," DuQuesne said from one side. "No immediate sign of detection. Here, Ariane, I'm feeding you the course to follow. You in a hurry?"

"Sort of," she said. "I want to get back and let everyone know the outcome of the battle, debrief Laila, Carl, and the others, and send a runner to get the Sphere and the home system updated—as well as get *Nodwick* released to do refugee shuttle duty. And from her remarks, I think we need to have a talk with Oasis and Simon in a more secure location."

"You're right about reporting the outcome," DuQuesne said. "Relgof wouldn't have let anyone know what was up when he came back, given the circumstances, and with the Outer Gateway down no one inside will know; they're sure as hell not going to open the Straits without knowing it's safe outside, and that's the only other way they'd be able to find out."

"Which is why I'm in a hurry. Can you *imagine* how they must feel, wondering if the battle is finished or not, and *how* it was finished?"

Wu Kung grunted. "I would be running in *circles*."

"You do that all the time anyway," said DuQuesne.

Ariane restrained a snort of laughter as she continued to guide *Zounin-Ginjou* towards its ultimate destination.

It took several more hours before they finally docked. *I'm exhausted already,* Ariane realized, but there *was* something of a strain to carefully adhering to a given course and wondering if you were successfully fooling any watchers. *Someone will eventually locate our Nexus Arena gateway; I can't imagine that secret will hold much longer. But we're already a lot stronger and more secure than we were. It's not going to matter that much pretty soon.*

"Orphan, are you—"

"I have my own Faction—small though it is—to attend to, so I will bid you farewell for now," Orphan said, already shutting the flagship down. "Go, ease your people's minds. They have waited long enough."

With a smile, Ariane dropped to the deck and did a pushup-bow; she saw that DuQuesne and Wu Kung followed suit. "Many thanks, Orphan," she said as she rose.

"Captain, there is no need—"

"Of course there is," DuQuesne cut him off. "Sure, we started this partly as a favor for you, but the way things turned out? You had every chance to cut out on us, and sure as I'm standing here you had damn good *reason* to do it—and you decided you were on our side, after all. You've proven the Liberated are just as much our allies as the Analytic, maybe more, because the Analytic sure weren't risking half their members for us. So it's for sure that we owe you at least a few real bows."

Orphan was silent a moment, and then he, too, dropped and delivered a pushup-bow. "Then to you I return the honor; I have learned secrets and seen wonders that no other has ever seen, and you do not know all the honors you have done me." His voice held no trace of his usual irony—though it returned in the next moment. "Now, go; I fear we tremble on the brink of being maudlin."

The Docks were a welcome, familiar sight after their long time in Halintratha and the devastating passage at arms over their home Sphere. "Home again, I guess," she said.

"And people are noticing," Wu Kung said from ahead of her. "I've seen two comm-balls summoned already. If we do not move quickly, our friends will get the news from someone else!"

But it didn't take long to get inside and find one of the floating taxi-platforms to whisk them to the Embassy of Humanity. As Ariane stepped through the door, she called out, "Laila! Carl! We're back!"

The comm-ball materialized even as she spoke, flickered red momentarily before going green. "*Captain! My God*, Captain, we *must* meet immediately!" Laila Canning's voice was uncharacteristically worried, her usual analytically-calm manner entirely absent.

"Conference Room One, Laila. I only want you and Carl right now."

"Of course, Captain," came Carl's voice. "But there's something you—"

"If you mean the Molothos assault, yes, I know, and that's part of what I'm here about."

A pause, and Laila emerged from the central elevator with a raised eyebrow and some of her accustomed equanimity reappearing. "Indeed? *This* should be interesting."

"That'll be one word for it," agreed DuQuesne, as they entered the conference room. Carl popped in the doorway, slightly out of breath; he'd obviously run from wherever he was. "How the *hell* could you—"

"Sit down and we'll tell you. First, so we don't keep you in suspense—we've won. The Molothos have been beaten, it's over."

The two stared at her in such total shock she found herself giggling. "I'm sorry, but . . . your *eyes*."

"I . . . admit, I have no idea what to say." Laila said after a moment. "I had so completely accepted the fact that we were going to *lose* . . ."

"Oh, you *would* have lost," Wu Kung said, "if *we* hadn't shown up right at the end! Oh, it was a *glorious* battle, but the Molothos had ships enough to darken the sky!"

"Slow down, Wu. Let 'em absorb it."

"When you say 'it's over,'" Laila began again, "do you mean the *battle*, or the *war*?"

"Both," Ariane said. "We'll get into details later, but for now, the important thing is that we got a surrender out of Dajzail himself. Yes, he was leading the assault. Probably a major stroke of good luck for us there."

It struck her then. *Stroke of good luck.* In a sense, if Vindatri and Orphan were right, it wasn't a random event; the Arena had made *sure* that the Leader of the Molothos chose to lead the assault. *That's . . . creepy as hell.*

"So," Carl said, looking at her with a suddenly-growing smile, "you got what you were looking for, huh?"

"In *spades*, as Marc might say. Yes."

"Can we *announce* this victory?" Laila asked. "We have a lot of people waiting to hear what happened."

Ariane hesitated. "I want to keep it quiet for a little while; there's some, well, *diplomatic* aspects to this. But we do need to notify people back home; the Outer Gateway's buried under debris and so no one inside knows that it's safe to let the Straits open. Last they knew, the

Molothos were strafing the surface." She glanced over to DuQuesne. "Marc, can you carry a message to our Sphere? Just jog over to Transition, drop it off, and come back?"

"Sure thing. What's the message?"

"Umm . . . Tell them 'we have suffered heavy casualties, but the Molothos forces have been driven off and will not return. Open the Straits and help clean up the Upper Sphere, and especially deploy and assign *Nodwick* to be a transport for Molothos survivors back to Nexus Arena. This information may be transmitted to the home system, but do not allow *anyone* through Transition until I give the all clear; the political situation is still very delicate.' How's that?"

"Good enough. It'll relieve the immediate concern. I'm guessing you're waiting on the lists of the lost and the honors?"

"And on *Nodwick*, yes."

"I'm off. Just wait about ten minutes, I'll be back by then."

"We'll wait, Marc; I won't spoil the fun for you."

Laila raised an eyebrow as Marc departed. "Fun?"

"Telling *this* story?" Wu said with a grin. "Oh, *fun* will definitely be involved!"

Ariane busied herself with getting some snacks sent in; this was going to be a long debriefing, but she wasn't going to put it off. Laila and Carl had been Leaders of the Faction, and she knew what a burden that had been.

True to his word, DuQuesne was back in nine minutes, thirteen seconds, and not apparently breathing hard. *Showoff Hyperion,* she thought.

You think loosely and muddily, youth, came DuQuesne's mind-voice, filled with humor as he imitated Mentor. *Had I intended to show off, I'd have done it in* five *minutes.*

Okay, touché. You're right. She looked up. "Now that we're all here . . . Embassy, full security on this room. No intrusions." The doors locked themselves. DuQuesne, she saw, also gave the room a quick once-over. *He isn't trusting that no one's bugged our rooms. Good.*

"Now . . . before we tell our story, I *do* have one question. How the *hell* did we end up with the Analytic sending a *fleet* to our aid?"

Laila laughed. "So it seems we will have a few stories to tell *you.* But that one . . . that should be for Simon to tell."

"Then I guess we'll wait on that for now. You want to know what happened on *our* trip, and about what we learned." She gestured at her cup and whispered *"zofron"*; instantly frost formed, spreading across the shiny ceramic surface and crackling softly into the liquid within. At their stares, she smiled. "That," she said, "is a hint."

Leaning back, she began.

Chapter 53

"All right, Simon," Ariane said. "Time for you to tell us the big secret as to how and why you managed to pull a battlefleet out of nowhere to save our Sphere."

DuQuesne saw Simon give a deprecating wave of his hand. "Oh, it was hardly all *my* doing. More yours, really, if we trace it back." He straightened. "The short of it is—you recall, of course, the condition that you wrung out of Amas-Garao after your unexpected victory?"

"Hard for me to forget, given what I went through."

"Well, the key is that you—with commendable foresight—made sure to include our 'direct and close allies' in that protection."

"That certainly makes a fine potential benefit for becoming one of our close allies," DuQuesne said, "but that's quite a jump to get someone to throw hundreds of their ships and thousands of lives into the fray on our side. There must've been something more than the abstract protection involved."

"Quite right, Marc. You will also recall how Relgof and I managed to uncover proof that, indeed, the powers of Shadeweaver and Faith extend beyond the Arena?" DuQuesne nodded, saw Ariane do the same, and saw Simon's smile take on an edge. "So you may imagine that I was rather taken aback to discover that Dr. Relgof *had no recollection of that fact, nor even of the research we did to uncover it.*"

"Sweet spirits of niter," DuQuesne heard himself murmur. "Of course. The Shadeweavers *wipe out* that evidence. Maybe the Faith do, too, but I'll bet they just count on the Shadeweavers to do it; either side's evidence would be enough to blow the secret, so the

Shadeweavers get stuck with the dirty work. Somehow they guessed Relgof knew, or sensed it from him, and made sure to wipe that data. Couldn't do it to *you* because you're part of Humanity."

"*That* was an immediate motive," Ariane said, picking up the thread. "The Analytic *runs* on knowledge—and on having secrets others don't. The idea that someone *else* was deciding what secrets they could have, what knowledge they could keep—that must have made them frothing mad!"

"Right, Captain. Relgof argued to their Conclave that the integrity of their *knowledge*—and of their minds, since obviously the Shadeweavers had affected his—overrode even considerations of ordinary safety. We had shown our general positive qualities to them and the Arena previously, and so Relgof convinced the Conclave that it was in their interest to ally with us. But they also knew that it was likely not enough to just *say* they were our allies; they would have to *prove* it, in a fashion that would leave no one in doubt as to whether they were aligned with us."

Ariane's smile was like a flash of the sun. "Amazing, Simon. You managed to get them to commit a fleet to our support *as a payment for the proof of their allegiance*—and thus the protection of Humanity against the Shadeweavers' mental tampering. So we aren't indebted to the Analytic—not in the Arena sense, anyway," she added. "In a moral and personal sense, we certainly are, but as a *Faction* they consider this their payment for a service only we can provide."

"Yes, and Dr. Relgof confirmed this to me. I agree that we owe them as *friends*, naturally."

DuQuesne looked across the table to Oasis. "No argument there, and I know Ariane's already working on how we can properly recognize their help. But right now I need to know what it was you were hinting at, Oasis."

Both his old Hyperion friend and Simon went suddenly grim. "Marc," Oasis said slowly. "Marc . . . *he's* here."

"*He?*" For an instant he didn't understand . . . and then he *did*, in a horrid flash of revelation. "*Fairchild* is here? *Here* in the *Arena?*"

"I saw him. Twice, I think."

It wasn't often that his brain tried to ignore truth, but it was sure doing a lot of fancy gymnastics of evasion now. "Oasis . . . K, look, did you *talk* to him? How sure are you—"

"*Dead* sure, Marc," she said, and the coldness in her voice brought him up short. *She's terrified. And I can't blame her one little bit.* "No, from just what I *saw* I can't be sure, but we used Simon's talent. He couldn't quite *localize* Fairchild, but we got enough evidence to be sure he's here, somewhere, on Nexus Arena."

Fairchild. Holy Hells of Niffleheim, I'd rather it was almost anyone else, Moriarty, Loki, Monolith even. "How the *hell* is that possible? He's an *AI*, and the Arena doesn't let them play up here. Even the Minds haven't figured out how to game that, and they've had *millennia* to work on that problem."

"It was Wu Kung's racing challenge results—and your theory, that you rather extensively proved in your own adventures against Vindatri—that explained it," Simon answered.

"If the Arena was willing to change its limitations rules based on the fact that we Hyperions were raised utterly ignorant of the fact that we were in any world other than the one we saw," Oasis continued, "then it didn't seem ridiculous that it would do the same for an AI if the AI cloned or manufactured a living body to match the one it had been created to believe it *had*."

"Damnation. Makes sense."

"Marc, who is this Fairchild? I know the name—he was the one who almost killed Oasis, forced K to rescue her—but even *you* seem worried, and that worries *me*," Ariane said.

DuQuesne took in a deep breath, held it, let it out. "I *am* worried, Ariane. Who was Fairchild? Well . . . he was *me*, I guess you could say. When Bryson and his assistant AIs on Hyperion decided to make me into a good guy, with Seaton my best friend, that kinda left a big hole in the plot, a big hole in the shape of the *real* Marc C. DuQuesne, a cold-hearted gold-plated bastard with a yen for total world control and a brain like a computer.

"So they took this really pretty dangerous guy from another of Smith's books, and then loaded him up with my kind of skills plus a big chunk of the villain Gray Roger, and, poof, Dr. Alexander Fairchild, me and Rich's nemesis for years—*decades*, actually. Almost got us both killed more than once, damn near brought down the Patrol right when we thought things were starting to go well . . . believe you me, Fairchild was the biggest of Big Time Operators."

He saw her shiver. *Yeah. She's the only one here who read the old books, so she's the only one other than me, Oasis, and Wu that can really get it.*

"And he's *here.*"

"If Oasis and Simon say so, yeah."

She nodded slowly. "And *now* we know who that escaped AI was, the one pulling Esterhauer's strings, killing off the Hyperions that Maria-Susanna wasn't after."

"I'll bet anything you like on that, yeah. Fits Fairchild's MO perfectly."

"What's he like?" Ariane asked after a pause. "I understand he's *dangerous*, but what kind of a person is he?"

DuQuesne paused, trying to figure out how to answer that question.

Oasis spoke first. "*Refined* is the first word that comes to mind, really. He's a monster, but he's an unfailingly *polite* monster. Dresses in almost completely white suits—a white fedora with a black band, white coat, pants, vest, gloves, shoes, with just a few touches of other colors. Chessmaster, of course—not literally, figuratively. Though I guess he probably is one literally, too. He manipulates people to do what he wants, and back in . . . well, the world of Hyperion, 'people' included species of beings that *should* have crushed him like a bug."

Unexpectedly, Wu Kung entered the conversation. "He *likes* frightening and hurting people. Maria-Susanna . . . she is *broken* and she does dangerous and crazy things." He looked very sad for a moment. "I have . . . looked up what she has done. She is very scary and I am very sad for her. But she is like . . . like a volcano, or a storm; she may do something very destructive but she really doesn't *mean* to hurt people; she really thinks she's *helping*. And sometimes she does. Not like Fairchild."

"What does he want? What will he be after here?"

"Power," DuQuesne answered, without even having to think. "He wants control—of as much of everything as he can. Part of it is that he is absolutely certain he knows, better than anyone else, how to run things. And to an extent, he's right. But that's really more an excuse than anything else. He likes power for its own sake, and he likes to have the ability to use that power whenever and however he likes."

"And he's your equal?"

"At least," DuQuesne ceded reluctantly. "Like many other villains in stories we've all read, the thing that really gave us a chance against him was that there were more of us than there were of him, and we were willing to work together and trust each other. He may work with other people . . . but he doesn't trust them, and he intends to dispose of them as soon as they have fulfilled their purposes. He's *damned* convincing, though, to anyone who doesn't know him; he's gotten people loyal enough to him to lay down their lives for him, even people from other species."

Laila was looking at them all with an exasperated expression; she was particularly staring at Oasis.

DuQuesne met her gaze. "What is it, Laila?"

"I understand the potential danger, DuQuesne—but unless I have misunderstood things for a considerable time now, this Fairchild *does not know* he has his powers. Correct?"

That stopped DuQuesne, and he suddenly felt a grin spreading across his face. "No . . . no, he probably doesn't."

"I'm particularly confused by *you*, Oasis. We had this conversation, and I had thought you were no longer—"

Oasis' smile was a shadow of its usual sunny self. "Sorry, Laila. Mainly I took it as a reason I could expect to handle him for a little while—long enough for Marc to get back. But even *without* his powers, I had to think . . . there's *no* chance he wouldn't have built himself the best body science could buy."

Laila blinked at that, and DuQuesne picked up the thread, liking the idea not even one little bit. "No, not one chance this side of Hades. And since his 'real'—as in, what he *seemed* to have inside of Hyperion—body would be a lot more formidable than anything he could build . . . well, we'd have to assume he'd get everything he built."

"Which means that he might kick my ass even *with* my Hyperion badassery-switch set to ON. Remember, *my* Hyperion background wasn't a superhuman psionic Smithian space opera. I ran with James Bond, not people like you."

"Don't sell yourself short, K," he said. "But you're right, that would make him a lot worse than we were thinking."

Oasis/K looked up at him bleakly. "And after the last time . . . Marc, I just have to be honest and say I'm too freaked out by him to be sure I'd do my best. Maybe I need a shrink or something."

"I don't think any of us would fault you for that," Ariane said. "If you need help, well, we can find you some."

"I have more faith in you than that, Oasis," DuQuesne assured her. "When it comes down to it, you'll do your best, and that'll be one hell of a lot." She gave a slightly brighter smile and nodded.

"Still," DuQuesne went on, thinking out loud, "Laila's right; he almost certainly doesn't know he's got access to his Hyperion-world powers. Like the rest of us, he'll *know* those were phonies from the word *go* and he'll need to run into something really strange to tell him otherwise."

"So is there a way we can use that?" Ariane asked. "A way we can track him down and catch him before he really gets ahead of us?"

"There just might be." The more he thought about it, the more he felt certainty spreading through him. "You know, there *has* to be. Sure, he'll figure it out sooner or later, but if we catch him before he realizes it, we'll have the advantage, enhanced bod or not."

Ariane smiled, buoying his feelings, and he saw Oasis' tension starting to melt as well. "Then I want you, Oasis, and Wu—and if you have to, Velocity and any other Hyperions you can recruit to get on this. The Arena doesn't seem to *care* what happens . . . but it's not going to stop us, either. So you figure out how to find this guy, and catch him, before he catches on to the fact that he's got the same mind-powers you do, Marc."

"Right, Captain. We'll figure out how, as soon as we can." He caught Oasis' eye, and that of Wu Kung, and saw both of them with the same expression on their faces. In turn, they read *his* expression. *Leave it. We'll talk later.*

Hiding anything from Ariane wasn't easy, but he was pretty sure she hadn't caught that one.

That was confirmed when Ariane smiled, then gave a jaw-cracking yawn and stretched. "*Whoof.* It's actually been a long day—leaving our Sphere, taking the long way around to the Docks, and then all the time we've spent on the review." She had an apologetic look on her face as she turned to Laila and Carl. "But I'm afraid I'll have to make it a little longer for you two. Besides the big battle, I'm sure that there's a lot of Leader of the Faction of Humanity stuff I need to at least get a summary of. The rest of you don't have to stick around."

Laila grimaced. "I am afraid you are correct." Carl's expression echoed hers, but the two settled back into their seats as Marc rose, the others following him. As they left, he heard Laila continue, "First, there was the matter of a lynching . . ."

A *lynching?* He was half-tempted to go back in, but heck, if it had anything of real interest in it, Ariane would no doubt tell him later. Instead, he continued on, aware of the others behind him.

Sure enough, Oasis convinced Simon to go off by himself—a convincing that included a quick kiss. *Well, I'll be damned. So that's the way it's gone.* He wasn't quite sure how to feel about that, but—being honest with himself—Simon probably would have a similar reaction to him and Ariane. Though—again being honest—Ariane hadn't actually ruled out her interest in the white-haired scientist.

The important thing was that he, Oasis, and Wu were now alone. He gestured and all three of them went into one of the other conference rooms. "Embassy, full security on this room, no intrusions." He looked at the others. "You've both got the same thoughts I have, right?"

Wu looked as dead-serious as he ever had. "*Catching* Fairchild— that I can do! Or we can, if I can't do it by myself. But *holding* him? That is something your Patrol couldn't do, could they?"

"No, they couldn't."

"Ariane will never give us orders to go out and kill someone," Oasis said bluntly. "And I'm glad of that. But *Fairchild* . . ."

"Yeah. Fairchild. If anyone was an argument for the death penalty, he's the guy. I don't like the idea either, but . . ."

He didn't have to finish. *But this guy tried to rip Oasis' brain out just to use it for an escape pod. He almost killed me and Rich more than once. And he's got the same powers I do. There's a reason the Patrol did have the death penalty, and was damn reluctant to give any quarter to most of our top enemies.*

They were silent for a moment, and then DuQuesne heard himself give a frustrated snort. "Dammit."

"Ha!" Wu said with a touch of his usual humor. "We again have the same thoughts."

"Yeah."

"We *have* to play it the way the Leader of Humanity wants us to, or we're not people she can trust," Oasis managed, grudgingly, to say. "So we have to *capture* Fairchild."

"I'll talk to Ariane. I know, I know, dollars to doughnuts she's not gonna go for it, but I'll make sure she understands what kind of a monster we're going to be catching, and just how hard it's going to be to lock him down once he understands that he really *is* that monster for real. And you can bet anything you like that once we *catch* him he'll figure that out."

Wu Kung and Oasis nodded agreement.

Then as they turned to leave, Wu broke out in a smile, and laughed.

"What's so funny, Wu?"

"We are! DuQuesne, you are his equal, yes? You have beaten him before. And you have me, and you have Oasis, and there are others, yes?"

"Yeah," he admitted, "but he's one hell of—"

"So are *we*," Wu said, and the indomitable spirit of the Monkey King was back. "But even if he equals *us*, he will still have to deal with the *Captain*."

And remembering everything Ariane had done so far, DuQuesne had to admit that Wu Kung had a very, very good point.

Chapter 54

"You're *sure* he's at the Embassy, Simon?"

She wanted to kick herself almost before the question was out of her mouth, and it didn't help that Sun Wu Kung broke into a huge grin even as Simon—commendably—restrained a sigh. "Captain, I *followed* Dajzail there, so to speak, once I had discovered he had taken one of their fastest ships and gone ahead of the fleet."

"Sorry to ask the question, Simon. It's just perfect timing, and I wanted to be sure. Do we know *why* he went on ahead of his fleet?"

"I don't," Simon admitted. "I missed whatever discussion or event it was that caused him to do so, and I still feel . . . *stretched* when I use that ability, so I dare not watch him for hours at a time." He shrugged. "I feel a bit guilty doing so at all, to be honest."

"Can't say I blame you," DuQuesne said. "Anyway, I've got a pretty good guess as to why, Captain. He's trying to light a firebreak, if you get my meaning."

"I guess. You mean preparing people for the news, giving it to them in small groups and so on, rather than having the whole fleet's return be the first anyone knows of it."

"Exactly. See, the way I figure it, he's lost a whole *hell* of a lot of face with this. Sure, the Molothos as a Faction have too, but as the Faction Leader who decided on this expedition, that's *got* to come back to him somehow. So he's got to do all the spin control he can manage before the story gets too big to keep quiet—or he just might be out of a job."

"You mean killed?" Ariane envisioned a council of Molothos executing Dajzail for complete failure.

"I doubt that," Simon said instantly. "What I saw of them . . . Your Maizas, DuQuesne, was probably a good representative of his people. As far as I could tell, they act around each other the way we do around our own people. They're just so emphatically hostile to all other species that we never see their softer sides."

"Wonderful," Ariane said, and got to smile herself at their startled expressions. *Hey, as long as we have this "Blessing of the Arena" I figure we'd better milk it for all it's worth.* "Marc, *Nodwick* will be docking any minute. I want you down there to coordinate the unloading, and the *timing* needs to be right."

Are you . . . yes, you are, came Marc's quick thought. *I can see what you're up to.* Aloud, he just nodded. "I'll get right on that, Captain. Simon, Oasis, I'd like you along—if that's all right?"

"Take anyone you need, Marc."

She watched them go, then stood. "All right, Wu, I've got to make a stop by my cabin to change, and then we're going out."

"Whatever you say, Captain."

When she emerged, Wu nodded. "You are wearing *your* uniform!"

"Yes, I am." The dark-blue outfit, reminiscent of formalwear and monkish robes and even, somehow, military uniforms, with its starship-and-cup motif, had materialized from the light of her Awakening, not consciously chosen or designed by her. Yet it *fit* her, and its symbolism fit her position, her crew, the symbol of the Holy Grail—the ship and the endless quest object combined.

And maybe signifies the quixotic nature of that quest, that it's a goal that recedes away as fast as you pursue it. Given what I'm about to do, that's probably the best interpretation yet. "Come on, Wu, we've got a meeting to attend."

"A meeting? You did not tell me we had anything scheduled. Oscar *hates* it when you do that!" Wu's grin showed that he didn't mind annoying Oscar at all; he was unlikely to forgive the diplomat for his earlier behavior.

"Oh, Oscar would probably want to spend a week discussing it from every angle. No time, and if it works out, he'll love it, so best not to even mention it to him."

"What if it *doesn't* work—whatever 'it' is?"

"Eh, I don't think it'll be a disaster," she answered. Maybe she wasn't *quite* as blasé about that as she sounded, and Wu's sideways glance told her he could smell it. "Okay, only a *minor* disaster, especially with you around. But I think it'll be okay."

"Like DuQuesne once said to me, mine not to reason why, just to kick them to the sky." Wu bounced along, sometimes in front of her, sometimes behind, as they moved through Nexus Arena. By now she was used to Wu's irrepressible motions, and could see the tiny glances and moves that allowed her Hyperion bodyguard to see everything around her, while appearing to be a distractible fool. *And he plays the part well.*

It didn't take long to reach the outskirts of the Grand Arcade, and from there walk across the intervening park and walkways to her destination. *I'm here, Marc,* she thought.

Got it, he responded instantly. *On my way.*

Before them were five immense buildings, so huge that even within the immensity of Nexus Arena they loomed like brooding titans. One a rising whirlpool of spheres that came together and spiraled into the sky, reaching towards the simulated heavens in a symbol of unity; the second a collection of smooth, shimmering towers that arced upward, a behemoth pipe organ of crystal, gold, and light; the third an assemblage of clean, sharp edges that rose like a blade to challenge the sky; the fourth a stepped pyramid of steel and glass, symmetrical, practical, functional; and the last nearly a cube, dark and massive and threatening, decorated with curved points and edges.

The Five Great Faction Houses.

Without slackening her pace she strode past the galaxy-symbolizing tower of the Faith, the challenging blades of the Vengeance, the redoubts of Analytic and Blessed to Serve, and stopped before the black-and-red grimness of the Faction House of the Molothos. She sensed Wu Kung on close guard next to her, and his presence made her able to ignore the danger; she knew she was safe.

"Dajzail of the Molothos, I know you are here. As the Leader of the Faction of Humanity, I ask you to speak with me here and now." She was conscious now of other movement—the curious of the other Great Factions, stepping from their doorways to find out why any would *ask* the Molothos to pay attention to them.

The comm-ball shimmered red. She said nothing; patience was her only real lever. He would look, and see she was there, and was not moving.

Finally it turned pure green. "I come."

She waited.

The doors—great quarter-circles of metal—slowly parted, and Dajzail came forward, his seven legs carrying him in a rippling gait towards her. At least ten or fifteen other Molothos followed him; most were warriors, but two had exoskeletal ornaments and posture that told her they were something more important; these were only just behind Dajzail. He stopped less than four meters distant and crossed his claws before him. "What do you want of the Molothos, Captain Austin?"

Though sharp and rough, Dajzail's voice held just a *hair* less than its accustomed arrogance . . . and he had chosen to use her title. "We had reached an accord, Faction Leader Dajzail. I come for the condition of public announcement. Here, within the view of all four other Great Factions, is more than public enough."

Dajzail stood immobile, only the slightest vibration of his legs showing he was something other than a fearsome statue. One of the others—a huge Molothos, mostly brilliant crimson with black highlights—buzzed something that Ariane couldn't catch.

Wu's senses, however, were much better than hers. "He has just said that they do not need to acknowledge the demands of such an undercreature."

Dajzail turned slowly, his legs rotating his whole body, and without warning, one of his fighting-claws whipped out and caught the other about the head, gripping the base of the head like a pair of shears. His retort was so savage and high-pitched with fury that, even as softly as he spoke, Ariane felt as though a sharp spike had gone through one ear and out the other.

Dajzail shoved the other aside roughly, despite his greater size, and faced Ariane again. "The Faction of the Molothos will not deny an agreement made, even to . . . such beings as you." He rose up, a gesture of pride and resolve, and then spoke so loudly his words echoed about the plaza. "As of this day, a state of . . ." he hesitated, then continued, ". . . *peace* . . . exists between the Great Faction of the Molothos and the Faction of Humanity and that Faction's close allies, the Liberated and the Analytic. If you seek not to provoke us, this peace shall endure."

She could see the rippling of startled glances and hear murmurs in the small but noticeable crowd that had gathered from the other Great

Houses. "Your declaration of peace is heard and accepted, Dajzail of the Molothos. We are glad to no longer be at war."

Dajzail dropped back to his normal pose and gave a buzzing hiss. "There is no goodwill here, *Leader* Austin. I believe we are finished."

"There is one additional thing."

"*WHAT?*" he snapped, and his fighting-claws were half-raised to strike. "You have demanded much already. Do not think we are infinite of tolerance, regardless of power or threat—and *here* you have no threats to make!"

"Not an additional demand, Dajzail," she said, and saw his claws drop a few centimeters. In the distance, she heard a faint hubbub, far off, but drawing closer. "You left our Sphere immediately—as agreed—and made no attempt to argue, discuss, or otherwise test the limits of the bargain."

The Molothos Leader stared at her, his glowing yellow eye impassive, unreadable.

"That must have been the hardest demand of all, Dajzail; for whatever you feel for *us*, your words and actions showed that your own people mattered much to you." The noise was getting closer, and some of the people—including, she thought, Nyanthus himself—were now turning away from the tableau before the Molothos Great House and seeking the source of the new disruption.

"And so the Faction of Humanity, in recognition of this effort of honor and, as we would call it, good faith, have chosen to value your people as we would our own, regardless of how you might view us." She turned, and extended her arm. "It is a small thing, perhaps, but there were those who were not lost. I hope you will welcome them home."

Across the plaza of the Great Faction Houses came a vast, dark, rippling motion, rank after rank after rank of Molothos, led by a light-carapaced female with one fighting-claw bound up. To the sides she could see Simon, Oasis, and DuQuesne.

For the first time she saw a Molothos stunned, not with fear or anger, but astonishment; Dajzail's fighting-claws dropped almost to the ground, and he sagged, his entire eye focused forward. "Dyara . . . ?" he buzzed.

Then he rattled forward, Wu Kung yanking Ariane out of the way as Dajzail sped to greet the smaller, light-carapaced female. "Dyaratamzin?"

Dyaratamzin drew herself up. "Leader Dajzail, I apologize—"

"Enough. We will speak of nothing before these . . ." he began something that sounded like "undercreatures," but then paused and changed it to, ". . . others. Tell me only this—how many were saved?"

"Fourteen thousand, two hundred and twenty-seven," she answered.

Dajzail was silent for a moment; Ariane thought she saw a trembling of his manipulator tendrils, something she had never seen before. "And the . . . human creatures assisted you?"

Dyaratamzin's voice was uncertain—the tone of someone who is afraid their answer will get them in trouble, but who dares not lie. "Yes."

Dajzail turned slowly to face Ariane. He stared at her, immobile. Wu edged up, at the right angle to protect her if Dajzail were to act rashly.

But the Leader of the Molothos finally turned away. "Come, then. All of you are coming home. Come into the Embassy, for there is room enough, and we shall arrange for you to return. You have all done well." He scuttled aside, watching as the army of refugees streamed past.

Ariane began to move away, but then realized that Dajzail was still looking at her. He slowly approached, as most others' eyes were focused on the immense crowd of Molothos, and stopped only when Wu interposed himself.

"Why?" he buzzed finally.

"Because—regardless of your beliefs—I think of your people as *people*, and I'm not letting anyone die a castaway in the Arena's skies— no matter what species they are. No matter what they think of me and mine. Simple as that."

And Dajzail was still and silent as she turned and walked away, feeling a smile of satisfaction spreading across her face. "C'mon, Wu. Let's go home."

A great tone rang out across the Plaza.

"Type Two Challenge concluded. Winner: Ariane Austin and the Faction of Humanity against the Great Faction of the Molothos."

FIN.